SEPARATION OF FAITH

—————————— A Novel ——————————

CHERI LASER

iUniverse, Inc.
New York   Bloomington

Separation of Faith
A Novel

iUniverse books may be ordered through booksellers or by contacting:

iUniverse
1663 Liberty Drive
Bloomington, IN 47403
www.iuniverse.com
1-800-Authors (1-800-288-4677)

Because of the dynamic nature of the Internet, any Web addresses or links contained in this book
may have changed since publication and may no longer be valid. The views expressed in this work
are solely those of the author and do not necessarily reflect the views of the publisher, and the
publisher hereby disclaims any responsibility for them.

ISBN: 978-1-4502-3219-7 (pbk)
ISBN: 978-1-4502-3218-0 (cloth)
ISBN: 978-1-4502-3217-3 (ebook)

Library of Congress Control Number: 2010907557

Printed in the United States of America

iUniverse rev. date: 8/16/10

For Natalia—
because there will never be a goal too grand for you,
or a dream beyond your reach.
Always remember that!

I love you *so* much!
Grammie

Acknowledgments

There are so many! But let me begin with a huge thanks to my daughter Melissa Maritsch for leading me to my characters' names in *Separation of Faith*. I'd been having difficulty cutting the cord from the characters in my first novel, an issue that was preventing the characters in the new story from coming to life. Then, during a Saturday dinner where I explained the basics of the plot, Melissa suggested a biblical theme for the names. Her idea immediately removed whatever block I'd been facing, and both the story and the characters began taking off from there.

A very large thank you is extended as well to Sr. Mary Martin at the Monastery of Our Lady of the Rosary in Summit, New Jersey. She very kindly agreed to meet with me in the earliest stage of my research, answering my questions and imparting invaluable information regarding cloistered life. She also provided a reality check regarding some of my initial ideas and their plausibility in the 1940s. In concert with Sr. Mary Catherine, who was also at Our Lady of the Rosary, Sr. Mary Martin gave additional time to subsequent emails and a questionnaire offering further insight. But in the end, as the *Separation of Faith* story shifted away from many of my original thoughts, the most significant thing I held onto from those sisters was the depth of their commitment and the sanctity, humility, and power of their religious calling. I tried very hard to imbue those qualities in Abby Ryan. Without the grace and generosity of Sr. Mary Martin, however, and the collective contribution of the other sisters at Our Lady of the Rosary, I think I might have missed the very essence of the character I was trying to create.

My heartfelt appreciation also goes out to Carolyn Sapp-Daniels and to Beverly and Al Parent in Kettle Falls. They welcomed me with trust, and they gave me their valuable time, as well as access to historical information about the town, the valley, and the former convent. Memories of their warmth and hospitality never left me as I was writing *Separation of Faith*. The hours I spent with them enabled me to transport myself back to Kettle Falls so I could effectively insert the characters into that incredibly beautiful setting.

As *Separation of Faith* began coming together, I let four people read the first three chapters: Melissa, Elaine Horsley (my friend for forty years), Diane Menditto (my friend for ten years), and Lucy Stamilla (my son-in-law Matthew's aunt). All four women loved what they were reading and wanted more. So I proceeded to torture them by keeping any further peeks away from them for the next *four years*!

In 2009, prior to reaching the point where I was ready to engage the help of beta readers, I faced an issue with the title, which was not yet *Separation of Faith*. The title I'd been using was resoundingly vetoed by a number of agents and editors at a conference I attended in New York in March of that year. Subsequently, Diane Menditto and I exchanged a series of emails that went on *for days*, in which we dissected the original title, word by word, using our creativity and synonym references to come up with alternatives that would be applicable to the story. I lost count of the number of word combinations we presented to each other before we finally arrived at *Separation of Faith*, which bears not even the slightest resemblance to the original title. And I'm not sure how many people would have had the patience to hang in there with me through all of those emails that started with, "Hey! How about *this* one?"

At long last, I finally arrived at the beta reader stage by early fall of 2009. Six dear people, all of whom are voracious novel readers, happily agreed to give *Separation of Faith* a test run. Elaine Horsley, Diane Menditto, and Lucy Stamilla were the first three I approached (since they'd been waiting for four years already). Tony Marseglia, Annette Marseglia, and Lisa Moran rounded out the group.

When they'd finished their reading, I gave each of them a short questionnaire to fill out, and their input was so valuable that I'm not sure how to adequately thank them. Although they were hesitant at first to explain their issues, they finally realized that I wasn't going to dissolve in a heap no matter what they said. Then they proceeded to tell me *little* things, such as the fact that I'd apparently forgotten to write significant parts of the story! Yee gads!

In my blog (www.cherilaser.wordpress.com), I wrote several posts on that entire process, because the issues they raised were so important that I wanted to share them with other writers. The ensuing edits and rewrites ended up taking another two months.

The honesty and insights of those six people helped me fill in major holes and smooth out the rough edges of *Separation of Faith*. Of course, there have been six full edits since they read the manuscript, so I'm hopeful they'll enjoy the published book as a fresh experience. That would be the least I could do for them!

Bringing up the rear of those who helped me are the members of the editorial team at iUniverse. My goal was to earn for the manuscript the Editor's Choice designation, an honor awarded to iUniverse books that meet the highest of writing and publishing standards. Securing that award was essential, I believed, in order for this novel to compete on the same playing field with novels coming out of mainstream publishing houses.

The rigorous editorial reviews and copyediting performed by the professionals at iUniverse led to several more editing cycles for me—and when I resisted, they persisted. Throughout the iterations of resisting, complying, and revising, I can't begin to tell you how much I learned. And as I was learning, I watched the transformation of my manuscript into a high quality literary product. In the end, I was honored that *Separation of Faith* did receive the Editor's Choice designation—and believe me, iUniverse is uncompromising in the standards required for that award. I'm so grateful for their adherence to that rigid criteria.

Finally, I want to thank my entire circle of friends and family, all of whom have been unconditionally supportive since I began reinventing myself to seriously pursue my literary dream. I especially want to thank my father, Jim Keyes, who, at age eighty-nine, is my most loyal fan, and who never fails to go through a case of tissues while reading my books. (I have to temper my pride, though, because he'd probably respond the same way while reading a version of the phone book, if he thought I was the author.) I do love him so much, and I'm grateful beyond words that he's here to watch all of this happen.

Writing *Separation of Faith* has been a long but joyful experience, made even more fulfilling by the fact that I know more about what I'm doing now than I did with my first novel. And one of the reasons I've become a better writer and editor is that so many amazing people have selflessly offered me their time and knowledge. Thank God I finally learned how to listen.

Author's Note

There really was a Lady of the Valley Convent in Kettle Falls, Washington. All references to the historical chronology of the convent's existence, through the sale of the institution in 1971, are drawn from public records. The headstones in the old cemetery are real.

But beyond those points, *Separation of Faith* is a product of my imagination, originally inspired by the discovery of the old convent's history. Any characters or events set at the convent within the referenced historical time frame are completely fictional, and any resemblance to actual people or events in that setting, or in any other setting within any of the novel's historical time frames, are purely coincidental.

In addition, characters and events in the contemporary settings of the book are also fictional, with any resemblance to real people or events being coincidental as well.

Faith sees the invisible, believes the incredible, and receives the impossible.
—Anonymous

CHAPTER ONE

July 1945

A brutal act of violence is hard to imagine on the serene grounds of a convent. But that afternoon the idea had been hurriedly conceived and was just as quickly being set into motion. The moderate winds whipping through the narrow mountain valley were growing stronger and began blowing the white folds of the young postulant's veil up around her face, obscuring her view of what was going on around her.

Abby Ryan, formally referred to as Sister Mary Abigail, had been sitting in the gazebo, reading through a stack of pamphlets that one of the convent's retreat guests had collected in villages, churches, and other landmarks throughout Europe. He was an army officer and had been among the first waves of soldiers returning to the States after German forces surrendered to the Allies three months earlier. Like so many others who'd seen combat in that theater, he'd not only come home with physical injuries but also with the prickly inner demons that continued to wage battle against the soldiers, even though the war was now virtually over.

Consequently, Lady of the Valley Convent, along with various religious and secular institutions nationwide, had begun holding retreats catering to servicemen. The small additional revenues from registrations helped sustain the convent's operations, while the remote, idyllic valley setting offered a place where weary and troubled soldiers could tend to their fractured bodies and souls.

As a postulant—the only one currently in residence and thus going through this first stage of training by herself—Abby was still free to carry on conversations with outsiders until she took her interim vows in

September. So she had been engaged to help the husband and wife team that drove up from Spokane to run three five-day retreats each month. Her exposure to the soldiers and their war stories, overheard while she was serving their meals, had instilled in her a reverence for all they'd accomplished on those unmerciful battlefields. But more importantly, she had become acutely aware, for the first time in her nineteen years of life, of the overwhelming power and presence of evil in the world and the need for an even greater power and presence of good in order for peace to prevail.

This awareness offered some validation of her decision to join this community of sisters, although increasing doubts had been plaguing her of late. She longed for the opportunity to talk about her misgivings with her friend Tess, who would surely offer her the wisest of counsel. But as a novice and thus already in the cloistered part of the convent, Tess would largely remain off limits for at least another three months until Abby became cloistered as well.

She could tell that her hour of free time was nearly over just by the angle of light in the sky. The pamphlets, which had momentarily transported her across the world, had been gathered together again and refastened with a rubber band, just as the soldier had given them to her. But her tranquility was abruptly shattered as an overpowering force plowed into her from behind, viciously shoving her to the ground and propelling the pamphlets out of her hands. Somehow a scream managed to escape her lips just before her nose and face slammed into the gazebo's stone floor.

The weight of the attacker on her back was excruciating, and the acid burn of terror began choking her as she felt hands reaching beneath her skirt—grabbing, shoving, probing. The multiple layers of her habit's fabric were frustrating those movements and buying her precious seconds, although her prayers of thanks would have to come later. Struggling to catch her breath, she was shaken even further when she realized that more than one person was in the gazebo with her—somebody on her back and someone *else* with the hands.

Time was oddly compressing and expanding in the same instant, creeping in one element like slow motion while, in the other, the gazebo walls whirled around her from her vantage point on the cold ground. Then the scene appeared to freeze as she felt the weight on her spine lighten and shift while the hands hesitated, as if rethinking their next movement.

Mobilizing a strength wrenched from some unfamiliar place within her, she surged over from her stomach to her back, throwing both attackers briefly off balance. Without wasting a moment, she yanked her thighs against her chest and, with every ounce of fury she could muster, rammed the heels of her heavy black postulant shoes up and forward into one of the blurred faces staring down at her. He grabbed at his eyes and began shouting obscenities as the other man lunged at her, missing her as she rolled over on her knees and struggled to stand up.

Suddenly, a wild commotion erupted as other voices were being added to the mix. Staggering to her feet and raising her hands to catch the blood dripping from her nose and mouth, she turned and saw four figures in olive green fatigues drag the two attackers out of the gazebo and throw them face down on the grass. Once the pair had been subdued, with their wrists somehow tethered behind their backs, one of the olive green figures came into focus—the soldier who'd given her the pamphlets.

"Oh my God, Sister, are you all right?" he asked, his anxious voice and expression both blessings to behold.

"Yes," she stammered. "I … How …?"

He placed his hands on her shoulders and gently lowered her to the built-in bench encircling the inside of the gazebo. She felt his arm wrap around her and, as she realized she was going to pass out, she believed that God was speaking to her through this calamity and through this handsome warrior, who had just saved her from far more than a rape.

*****

The 1942 Chevrolet Woody station wagon—a gift from the Archdiocese so the convent could offer transportation for retreat guests—bumped south on Highway 395. They were driving away from Our Lady of the Valley's cloistered Garden-of-Eden setting, away from Tess, en route to Spokane and the train station, where Abby would begin her journey home.

Seated in the front passenger's seat, she looked to her left at the uniformed driver. Finding his familiar face comforting, she decided to let him know she was awake.

"After all of this," she said, shifting her body so she could lean her back against the car door and look right at him, "I can't believe that I don't even know your name—and I'm terrible at reading the markings on uniforms, so I'm not sure about your rank or how to address you."

He smiled and took his eyes off the road for a moment to glance at her. "My name is Sinclair Mellington," he replied, his voice still the most reassuring sound she'd heard in a long while, "and I'm an army captain—but just plain Sinclair will be fine."

"All right … Sinclair. I'm not sure that I'll ever be able to thank you sufficiently. Not only did you rescue me, but volunteering to drive me into Spokane was unbelievably kind of you, since this is taking almost a whole day out of your retreat time."

"Don't you worry, Sister," he began, the *joie de vivre* from his smile lifting her spirits without effort. "I'll still have three days left after I get back to the convent to catch up on whatever I'm missing, which couldn't possibly be better than this anyway."

"That's very nice of you to say."

"It's the truth. And besides, I don't deserve your thanks as much as my three buddies. *They're* the ones who saw what was happening to you through the window. I only ran along to help." She didn't respond right away, and an uncomfortable hush filled the car. "I'm sorry, Sister," he said, his contrite tone breaking the silence. "Did I just say the wrong thing?"

"Don't be silly," she answered, trying to find a way to make things feel less awkward. "And rather than referring to me as 'Sister,' I think that just plain Abby is more appropriate now. Abigail Ryan to be precise."

"What? I thought you were only going home for a short break." His concern sounded genuine and oddly endearing.

"No. I'm not coming back."

"But this wasn't *your* fault! Surely they can't suspend you, or fire you—or whatever they call it—for something like this, can they?"

"Certainly they could, I suppose. I haven't earned any rights up here yet. But this is my decision, not theirs—and yes, I do believe I'm the one responsible. I've been too friendly with those maintenance men, visiting with them when I wasn't supposed to during my free time. Somehow I must have led them to believe that—"

"Wait a minute!" Sinclair interrupted. "What maintenance men are you talking about?"

"The ones who live in the bunkhouses on the back side of the property—employees who take care of the grounds. I don't know how the sisters could get along without them, and even though their souls are a bit rough, they've always been very respectful, until now."

"But Sister Abby," he persisted, "the two men who attacked you were *not* maintenance men! They were from some town north of Kettle Falls, on the other side of the river. They'd been drinking, went for a drive, and ran out of gas. Apparently, they were walking outside the convent gate when they saw you in the gazebo and jumped the front fence. *You* had no fault in this whatsoever! I hope you didn't make a rushed decision based on wrong information. Are you sure you want to leave?"

She nodded and turned away from him, watching through the window as the station wagon hugged the two-lane road snaking through the rural landscape. Her absence of a response signaled the end of their conversation for the moment. *Yes, I do want to leave,* she thought, trying to reassure herself. *Whoever those men were, I think they're part of a message being sent to me—and this time I'd better pay attention.*

*****

Lady of the Valley Convent had been tucked away on forty acres of land just south of Kettle Falls, Washington—ninety miles north of Spokane—for eleven years. From the time the sisters had settled the property in 1934, there had been a great deal of controversy throughout the valley about the odd congregation. But the eventual discovery that they were not the least bit dangerous, and would be keeping completely to themselves, resulted in a gradual acceptance of the unconventional new residents by the valley's conservative farming community.

Abby had first been introduced to Lady of the Valley through her periodic cross-state train trips from Seattle to Kettle Falls to visit Tess—known now as Sister Veronica—following the girls' high school graduation in 1943. Initially, her goal had been to convince Tess to leave what Abby viewed at the time as a form of imprisonment. She couldn't understand how Tess had allowed herself to be coerced into joining, and she was increasingly fearful for her friend's safety.

But the more she visited, the greater sense of peace she began to experience while she was there, especially with the uncertainties of the war impacting every American, sparing few citizens at least part of the sacrifice, on one level or another. Over time, she came to understand the convent's mission and to admire and appreciate the nuns' commitment to their vocations and their obvious affection for one another, despite their quirky personality differences.

During a Thanksgiving trip to see Tess in 1944, when Abby was a sophomore at the University of Washington, she agreed to stay on for a thirty-day period of "exploration," which led after only a few weeks to her decision to give the lifestyle a more lengthy trial. Nothing else she'd experienced—neither her journalism classes at the university, nor her part-time job at a military administration facility in Seattle, and certainly none of the men she'd ever dated—had given her any meaningful sense

5

of direction. Lady of the Valley was where she seemed to have found her purpose, and that development had come as an even bigger surprise to Abby herself than to her family and friends, who were universally stunned at her decision.

Becoming a nun had always been the obsessive province of Tess—Therese Elizabeth McDowell—who'd been Abby's closest friend and next-door neighbor in Seattle since they were born, five months apart (Tess first) in 1925. They were both "only children," unusual in Irish Catholic families, but their parents spent so much time together that the girls viewed each other more as sisters than as friends and thus never felt the least bit deprived of a sibling.

Having a curiosity about religious vocations wasn't unusual for students attending St. Agnes School from kindergarten through high school in the 1930s and '40s. But despite their immersion in catechism and the scheduling power of church and school calendars, Abby knew that Tess was the only one in their circle of friends who actually took every detail seriously. By the time the girls were ten, Tess was speaking regularly about becoming a nun, setting herself openly apart as having been "called."

The saving grace for Abby, on the other hand, was the fact that St. Agnes was coeducational. Not that her interest in the opposite sex, or in sex at all, was ever licentious. She simply loved being in and around the company of boys, fascinated by the divergence of their interests, their preoccupation with playing in the dirt, their insatiable curiosity, their fearlessness, their contagious laughter. Even their conversations and vocabularies seemed to be of a different species, and Abby never tired of studying them. They didn't seem to mind her hanging around, either, finding both her admiration of them and her burgeoning dark-haired, emerald-eyed beauty easy to tolerate.

When the girls were fifteen, Tess began warning Abby about the potential of being misunderstood. "I've been overhearing things," Tess had admonished gently. "The boys think you're flirting with them and inviting their attention, if you know what I mean."

"That's absurd," Abby had countered. "They've known me since we were kids and couldn't possibly think I'm that sort of person."

"I'm sure that's true, but they're getting older now. So are *we*. Lots of things are changing about all of us, and I just wish you'd be more careful about what you say and do when you're around them."

"Thank you for being so protective, my dear Tess," Abby had replied, nudging her friend with her elbow and flashing the alluring smile that was part of what worried Tess so much. "But you have way too many sinful thoughts in that nun-to-be head of yours."

*****

How prophetic, Abby considered, remembering her friend's words as she continued to ride in silence while her savior soldier drove into Spokane. *And how embarrassing this whole thing has turned out to be.* In fact, the convent's prioress had been so mortified about the situation that she would most likely not have called the police at all if the army retreat guests hadn't been there. But the soldiers had insisted, making the fairly obvious point that the two men in makeshift handcuffs needed to be taken into custody by someone in local authority.

Anticipating that Abby would be asked questions, the prioress had moved her into the convent's public front parlor, where lay people and open conversations were permitted. There Abby waited for the emergency help to arrive, stretched out on the sofa in front of the stone fireplace and raised hearth, with blankets wrapped around her shoulders and legs.

Sipping hot tea through swollen lips while holding ice cubes in a towel over her eyes and nose, she was also beset with personal humiliation. But she'd been containing her emotions, not allowing herself to release a single tear—until her friend suddenly appeared in the room, sitting down on an upholstered wing chair that she'd pushed up alongside the sofa.

"My dear Abby," she asked anxiously as she placed her hand on Abby's arm. "How are you feeling?"

"Oh, Tess," Abby replied, her voice echoing in her ears through her battered and swollen nasal passages. "I mean ... *Sister Veronica.* I'm sorry. I'm just so happy to see you."

"Please try to relax. The police and medical assistance will be here shortly—and I won't tell anyone if you call me Tess," she added with a coy smile.

Abby did her best to smile back. "I can't believe they let you out of there to come visit me."

Tess withdrew her hand from Abby's arm and noticeably stiffened. "You say that as if you still believe I'm in some sort of detention. Remember, that's where you're planning to be too."

"Forgive me if that sounded disrespectful. I'm just a bit shaken at the moment, and I've been aching to talk with you for weeks. Seeing you under these circumstances caught me off guard, I guess."

The expression on Tess's face softened. "Of course. I can't imagine what you must have gone through out there. How terrifying! When I heard about it, I wrote a note to the prioress requesting a special dispensation to see you. She very graciously agreed, but I only have a few minutes. What happened, Abby?"

"I don't really know. I'd been reading in the gazebo in my free time, as I always do, when all of a sudden I was thrown to the ground. The rest is too horrible to …" The remaining words stuck in her throat as her body began shaking.

Tess responded instinctively with a nurturing embrace, and only then did Abby finally feel safe enough to cry. Several minutes later, with the crush of emotion spent, Abby wiped her face on one of the extra towels stacked on the floor beside her and repositioned the ice pack on her nose. "Do I look absolutely ghastly?" she asked.

"Frankly, yes," Tess answered, pressing the inside of her wrist against Abby's forehead as if checking for a fever. "But I've seen worse. Remember in the fourth grade when that boy was fooling around, sliding down the banister in school from the second floor? And then he tumbled over the railing, all the way to the first floor below?"

"Oh my God, yes! I can still see him falling, like it was happening in slow motion. I thought he was surely dead!"

"Well, thankfully he wasn't, but he certainly was a bloody pulp of a mess—my point being that you don't look nearly as bad as *he* did."

Abby surprised herself by laughing out loud. "Please don't take offense, but being a nun hasn't done much for your skills as a comedienne."

"Nor has that been a priority. But for you, Sister Mary Abigail, I will add that improvement to my prayer list."

Abby lowered the ice pack into her lap and turned to look at this woman who'd been in her life for as far back as her memories traveled. "Don't be mad at me, Tess, but I don't think I'm going to *be* Sister Mary Abigail anymore."

Tess stared at Abby in silence for several moments. "What in God's name are you talking about?"

"Somehow I feel as if I brought this on myself—that this is a sign telling me I've made the wrong choice. I've already talked with the prioress, and I called my mother. I'm going home tomorrow. One of the soldiers will drive me into Spokane."

"I see." She paused, and Abby watched those kind mahogany eyes as moisture welled up and then receded just as quickly through the power of her friend's enviable self-control. "You need to understand your own heart, that's true," Tess continued, "but I hope you've thought this through and that you're not overreacting. If you'll pardon the truth, my dear Abby, you've always been rather melodramatic."

"I know, but I'm not fooling around this time. Being here doesn't feel right to me now. Perhaps that will change one day. Hopefully, the path I'm supposed to follow will become clear to me. Sooner rather than later, I can only pray."

"Yes … sooner. But I must tell you that this is extremely disappointing. Even though you and I haven't seen much of each other for some time, I've taken great comfort in knowing that you were here, somewhere on the grounds, and that we were going to be cloistered together before long. I will truly miss your presence."

"Oh, please don't make me cry again, Tess. I can barely breathe through this nose as it is."

Tess stood up, pulled her chair back across the rug into its original position, and smoothed her hands over her long black skirt. "My few minutes with you are over, Abby, and I probably won't see you before you leave, if tomorrow is the day. Do write to me, though," she added, her eyes closed, her head erect, and her fingers laced tightly together against her chest, as if in urgent prayer.

Abby took a breath and started to speak, but the interruption was denied.

"And please let me know what you'll be doing," Tess said, her voice softening as her eyes opened and her focus returned to Abby's face. "I'd like to hear about where you go and what keeps you busy. I'd enjoy updates about my parents, too, and any of our old friends you might run into. But most importantly," she went on, her eyes connecting directly with Abby's, "I want you to remember that *we* are *here*. Never forget that *this* option still remains available to you, along with all the rest you'll be considering. First, though—and please listen to me, Abby—you will need to believe, from the very depths of your soul, that life behind those doors over there will not represent confinement or oppression. Instead, this life offers an unimaginable freedom, coupled with a purpose so powerful that our biggest challenge is to remain humble. Naturally, no life is without sacrifice, but this one delivers an unending and enviable inner peace as a reward. If the day comes when you are drawn here because you're convinced that what I've just said is true—and if you have no doubt that you've been *called* here—then our open arms will await you. Meanwhile, I will always love you and will carry you in my heart, on this earth and beyond."

Leaning down, she kissed Abby on top of her head before moving stoically across the room where she disappeared through the door in question. The effect of her departure was palpable, as if she had taken part of the air with her.

Something is missing in me, Abby thought, lowering herself farther into the sofa and pulling the blankets up around her neck when her friend was gone. Tess was so confident of her choices and priorities that Abby didn't think she'd ever be able to catch up or compete. *I could never be that saintly or that graceful*, she thought, *and I never should have come here in the first place. Dear God, please forgive me for asking this, but what was I thinking?*

As she was repositioning the ice pack on the upper half of her face, she heard the wavy sounds of a siren drawing closer to the convent grounds. Knowing that she was their destination, her heart raced as she began whispering a prayer for strength to get through the embarrassing moments just ahead.

"Why bother?" she muttered aloud, her prayer abruptly ceasing. "I need to find my own strength, which is what I'm sure God would say anyway, if He felt like answering my prayer—if He's even there at all."

*****

At the completion of their two-hour drive, Sinclair Mellington parked the Woody station wagon beside the curb in front of the Spokane train depot and unloaded Abby's small chestnut-colored suitcase from the backseat. Then he took her arm and guided her slowly inside to the ticket counter. She was wearing the same ankle-length black wool skirt and white pullover sweater that she'd worn on her arrival the previous fall, her white socks, saddle shoes, and short cropped black hair making her look like a college coed dressed for the wrong season. But despite feeling overheated in the warm July weather, she was thankful that the clothing covered the scratches and bruises on her legs and arms, although there wasn't any way to camouflage the damage to her face.

She'd been immensely grateful when the ambulance medical team told her that nothing appeared to be broken, especially her nose, which had worried her the most. They had urged her to let them transport her to the hospital, just to be certain, but she had declined their offer. Now she ignored the curious and seemingly judgmental stares of others in the train station, feeling a welcome tranquility as she looked forward to reentering the cocoon of her parents' home in Seattle, where she would have private time to heal.

"Here you go," Sinclair said, handing her the one-way ticket he'd purchased for her.

"I can't tell you how grateful I am for this, and for all you've done," she said, "and I will pay you back as soon as I get a job."

"There's no rush, and no obligation, Sister … I mean, *Abby*. I'm just glad we were there."

"Well, I don't care what you say. I *will* repay you."

"All right. If you wish. At least that means I'll get to see you again." Noting her obvious discomfort at this comment, he added, "I'm sorry. I didn't mean anything by that. Seems like my words always come out the wrong way around you. It's just that I think you're a very interesting person, and I've enjoyed talking with you."

"I understand—and meeting you again, under different circumstances, would be nice, I suppose."

He removed a small pad and pen from an inside jacket pocket and began writing. "My family and I also live in Seattle," he said, "on Queen Anne Hill. Here's our address and phone number, and I want you to feel free to call me there any time, for any reason. I'll be stationed at Fort Lewis until my active duty is over in six months, and then I'll be resuming my studies at UW, eventually going into law. At least that's the current plan. So, I'll be in the area, if you ever need anything."

"Thank you," she said, placing the small piece of paper he'd torn from the pad into her handbag. "I'll call you as soon as I get the ticket money together. Meanwhile, God bless you, Sinclair, and your friends too. Without you, I—"

He raised his index finger to his lips to gently quiet her and walked with her to one of the long, high-backed wooden benches in the waiting area. Without either of them speaking another word, he stayed there with her until her train was called for boarding. Then he carried her suitcase and escorted her to the car number on her ticket, where the porter allowed Sinclair to help her inside to her seat. Once she was settled, he briefly stroked the back of her head, said "Good-bye for now, Abby," and then returned to the platform outside. She watched him through the window while they smiled at each other as the train began pulling away.

Though she barely knew this man, her heart felt heavy when he waved to her, his image growing smaller and smaller with the locomotive's increasing speed. Leaning her head back, she sighed and did her best to think of something other than the crowd of emotions bearing down on her, all stemming from "the incident." She'd refused to press charges against those two men, believing at the time that her attackers were maintenance personnel and, more importantly, still blaming herself. But the police had taken the men anyway, promising to hold them for twenty-four hours. Perhaps this would be a wake-up call for them too, helping them straighten out and find a better path.

She placed the small pillow the porter had given her between the window and her face, gingerly avoiding all of the swollen and bruised places. Then she tried to relax her head and neck as she closed her eyes and let the rackety-rack motion of the train calm her. Still uneasy about trying to put a prayer together, she reached back in her mind for Tess, visualizing her saintly image and hearing those last words that gave rise to so many questions. Would any of the paths stretching out ahead of her ever lead to the freedom and joy Tess told her she'd need to believe in before she could return to Kettle Falls? Would she ever be able to enter into the commitment of those vows she'd been so looking forward to taking? Would she ever know the peace that Tess had been able to find, absent any self-reproach or second-guessing? All of that sure seemed like a long shot at the moment.

The war that had gripped her nation for four years, taking tens of thousands of soldiers to their graves, had finally, thankfully, ended, filling the summer of 1945 with jubilation across the country and the world. But that joy was somehow escaping Abigail Ryan, and she didn't know why. Worse, she felt guilty because her problems were so small by comparison. *What in God's name is wrong with me?* Breathing deeply, she was pulled into a sleep that temporarily released her from the questions and the struggle.

CHAPTER TWO

October 2008

His room's oppressive air hung thick with the smoky haze and sour odor that typically collect in places denied open windows and sunlight. Dressed in dark, threadbare clothing, his skeletal body remained seated in a frayed and faded upholstered rocking chair that squeaked back and forth with a numbing rhythm. Facing the doorway, his eyes were glassy and unfocused, appearing to have sunk even farther than yesterday into their shadowy sockets. The room offered no sound except a crackling static from the radio that had slipped out of tune, the red line on the dial hovering between stations that had once delivered music to his life.

When the doorway opened, a much younger man stepped in, one adorned in the finest of contemporary fashion and appearing to have been groomed by a lifetime of gracious example. His stance was tall and elegant, his skin taut and tan, his black hair full and enviable. Flickering with animation, his luminescent green eyes studied his surroundings at first, and then he saw the figure facing him from the rocker.

Stopping his forward motion, the man who'd just arrived struggled to catch his breath in the atmosphere drained of energy and oxygen. Yet some force kept urging him deeper into the room to get a closer look at the one who'd summoned him, the one who just kept staring and made no attempt to rise from the rocking chair.

"Who *are* you?" the newcomer asked the old man as he always did, feeling the bile of fear back up in his throat so predictably. "Why have you asked me to come here? What is it that you have to say?"

But the cadaverous stranger remained silent and seated, his vacant eyes fixed ahead at nothing. Then he took all the answers with him as he slowly began to disappear from the chair in sections, as if unseen hands were dismantling a human puzzle, piece by piece.

*****

Isaiah Mellington awoke with the same jolt he'd experienced several times over the last year since the dream began haunting him. As usual, his hair and body were damp and clammy in the aftermath, and his heartbeat continued to accelerate. Without delay, he switched on the bedside table lamp and reached for the pad and pen he kept in the table's drawer to capture any new details while the images were still fresh.

No one had advised him to do this, although he was periodically tempted to run the whole thing by a shrink. His personal circle didn't include anyone with those qualifications, however, and he wasn't about to ask his friends or his mother for references, as if they would ever admit to seeking assistance from their own versions of Dr. Phil. So he'd been doing his best to self-analyze the bizarre scene by jotting down notes as soon as his consciousness took over. Then he would go back to sleep and have little interest in the analysis or speculation by morning.

Nonetheless, he'd developed a couple of theories since he'd begun recording the flashes he strained to remember. One possibility was that the ghostly figure in the rocking chair was actually Isaiah as an old man, trying to scare the younger version of himself into ... but there was the rub. Into what? The most annoying answer he could come up with was *into getting a job*, and this aberrant dream seemed a bit heavy-handed just to make that particular and rather evident point.

Another inference was that the old man represented Isaiah's father attempting to reach out from the afterlife. But Sinclair Mellington had been a detached parent while alive, so his son had trouble believing that this much effort was being expended to make some sort of supernatural paternal contact four years after his father's death.

The part of the dream with the most palpable intrigue was, of course, the ending, where the eerie man came apart in puzzle pieces, and yet Isaiah no longer deliberated about any potential hidden meanings. He believed he would eventually arrive at a satisfactory explanation, as long as he could continue recalling a few new details after each occurrence.

Tonight he wrote a comment about the old man's eyes. When the dream had pulled Isaiah into the room for a closer look, he thought he'd noticed a spark of light not seen before, although he was still unable to discern any specifics. *Eye color would be helpful*, he thought. *At least that would offer a clue about whether the guy is supposed to be Dad or me.* Not wanting to awaken completely, he wrote only that one note. Then he dropped the pad and pen back into the drawer, turned off the light, and curled up inside the nest he'd made in his comforter.

*****

"Hello, Mother," Isaiah said, speaking to her voice mail two days later. "Sorry I missed you, and I wish I didn't have to put a kink in your weekend plans, but I received a fax from Dad's firm about an hour ago."

The letter was one that his late father, Sinclair, had written himself, which Isaiah found a bit creepy. He knew that leaving this message for his mother was cowardly. But today was Friday, and she was probably at her spa anyway. And frankly, he didn't feel like having a two-way conversation with anyone at the moment.

"The letter out of the blue tells me that I need to go to Kettle Falls as soon as Sister Abby dies," he continued, holding one edge of the faxed page between the tips of two fingers, as if he'd just picked up something unsavory off the floor. "Since I haven't really been keeping up with what's been going on out there, I called Tess and learned that Abby did, unfortunately, pass away, just last night. I didn't even know she was sick, and now I'm supposed to help tie up some loose ends for her. Did *you* know anything about this, Mother? It's a little after ten o'clock right now, so I should be at the lodge in Colville before dinner, and I'll head up to Kettle Falls after I get settled. Sorry I won't be able to take you to the gala tomorrow night. Why don't you give Doctor Edwards a call? He's in love with you, you know, and I'm sure he'd jump at the chance to be your escort. Meanwhile, I'll have my cell phone on while I'm driving, but reception gets pretty bad through the mountains. Love you, Mother. 'Bye."

As he reset the phone in the charger on the kitchen counter, he wasn't sure why he even bothered with the "cell reception" excuse. His mother knew him better than anyone else in their wide, opulent world, a fact both remarkable and pitiful at the same time for a man of fifty-eight. She would understand immediately that he had no intention of speaking with her for at least the next seven or eight hours.

Walking out of the kitchen, through the skylit foyer and down the curving Spanish-tiled hallway toward his bedroom, Isaiah remained puzzled by the Kettle Falls development. Had someone told him about this when he hadn't been paying attention? Maybe there was something to be said for having other people around all the time—to make sure he was listening. What else had he missed, he wondered, since he'd made the big move out on his own two years ago, about three decades later than most normal people?

Prior to becoming a homeowner, he'd either lived in the Mellington's family residence atop Seattle's Queen Anne Hill, or in a fraternity, or in a condo with at least one other buddy. Then, of course, there had also been his engagement to the fiancée from hell, which had proven to be his breaking point.

She'd seemed like such a blessing, at long last—a woman who finally appeared to be a match. She was almost forty, which sounded ever-so-much-better than twenty-something, now that he was fully embedded in middle age. And she had never been married. Not that there was anything wrong with her having a history, but the pairing was without complication since Isaiah had never succumbed to matrimony either. Furthermore, the woman was tethered to a premier Seattle family and came with a noteworthy set of pedigree papers—a somewhat irreverent phraseology that she actually found amusing.

Thus, in the beginning, even Isaiah had believed there might be hope for the relationship, not so much because of the screening process, but because she was purportedly a professional artist rather than a neurosurgeon or a perennial volunteer worker—the two ends of the spectrum usually foisted upon him. And her creative sensibilities looked as if they would blend nicely with his left-of-mainstream interests and points of view, not to mention that she was Grace Kelly–gorgeous, with a body straight from God that many women pay five figures to acquire. Nonetheless, there was something about her *mind* that had begun to trouble him. The one she'd apparently borrowed during their courtship had evidently been returned to the original owner by the time they'd launched their prenuptial cohabitation, leaving them with a range of conversational topics that began with shopping and ended with … well, shopping.

Six months after their lavish engagement party, Isaiah had felt himself teetering on the rim of a fissure, staring down into the murky molten hole of what promised to become his forever-after. From a corner inside his psyche that he seldom called upon, he produced the wherewithal to say no, without regard to what everyone else might think. His decision to terminate the relationship caused a tsunami of emotional reactions from the woman and her family, while most of the men in his health club were covertly supportive of his courage. Adding to his misery was his mother, Sarah, who claimed she was going to have apoplexy over the engagement's demise. But as far as he could tell, she never did—although he wasn't sure if he knew what apoplexy was supposed to look like—and within a few weeks, the crisis had passed.

Now, two years hence, Isaiah continued to hold all women in the deepest of regard, albeit at a reasonable arm's length that kept him in control while nowhere near celibacy. And even though he understood that his mother kept praying he'd settle down and give her at least one grandchild to worship, she had finally ceased her blatant and unremitting efforts to help him find a mate.

Shortly after the fiancée debacle, Isaiah had decided to relocate to the opposite side of Lake Washington, where he thought the fresh surroundings might unveil some sort of regenerated reason for getting up in the morning. Once he'd sold the preconjugal condo, his mother had initially pressured him to move back into the family home with her, and he was proud of her now for honoring her commitment not to complain about his planting a flag elsewhere. Yet he also understood that her power over him had only been marginally diminished. The knowledge that he'd still be spending an inordinate amount of time with her—at lunches, dinners, galas, and private mother-son hours in the house where he'd grown up—massaged any penitence he felt about moving a thirty-minute drive away.

In the town of Bellevue, he'd discovered a neighborhood called Somerset, where graceful luxury homes were constructed all around and on top of a mammoth foothill. Having been raised where there were breathtaking views from every window of the Mellington's Queen Anne Hill residence in the heart of Seattle, Isaiah was captivated by the array of sights from Somerset's upper streets, lanes, and courtyards. Unspoiled reflections of Lake Washington, the floating bridges, the city's skyline, and the Space Needle were only part of the scene. Puget Sound and an ice-capped Mount Rainier also merged into the montage whenever sunlight and cloudless horizons were perfectly aligned.

After only a couple of house-hunting excursions, he purchased an unassuming ranch-style home on a corner near Somerset's crest. The dwelling was unusually long from left to right, with a semicircular driveway that curved past the double entry doors on its way to and from the street. A small, well-manicured lawn bordered by hedges and bushes sculpted into topiaries completed the tidy picture. But the most captivating attribute was revealed by making a right-hand turn at the corner onto a side lane that sloped sharply downward. There the back of the house came into view—two stories of thick, floor-to-ceiling, wall-to-wall glass, supposedly tempered to survive earthquakes, looking out upon the incomparable panorama of lake and city.

The first time Isaiah stood on the plush carpeting in the second-floor living area, peering through the wall of windows that overlooked his textured backyard below and Seattle's skyline on the horizon, he felt as if he were watching a wide-screened sales pitch produced by the Chamber of Commerce. Since that moment, he'd never been able to pass through the room without stopping to look, nor had he ever failed to appreciate how fortunate he was to be living there. He had begun to wonder recently, however, if he might have isolated himself a bit too much, since phone calls and anything that could qualify as personal mail had dwindled to a trickle.

With his packed duffel bag on the floor at his feet, Isaiah stood facing the awesome scenery as he readied himself for the seven-hour drive to Kettle Falls. The October morning was a misty gray, with low-hanging clouds that spit out what locals referred to as a "dry rain," a familiar Seattle weather pattern and quite in line with his mood of late. In the distance, the Space Needle rose like the center of his emotional compass, with Queen Anne Hill just to the right. He suspected that, given the appropriate telescopic lens, he could probably locate the Mellington home place—perhaps even see his mother as she came and went from a full day of whatever she did. *But this is quite close enough*, he reminded himself.

Picking up his bag, he switched off the living room lights, double-checked the front locks, and headed down the stairs off the foyer. Once on the lower level, he walked past his pool table and bar in the recreation room, opened the door to the garage on the back of the house, entered his code to arm the security system and then pressed the garage door opener on the wall. Since he'd already loaded the car's front passenger seat with a cooler of fruit, bottled water, a six-pack of beer, and a couple of sandwiches, he walked around to the driver's side, leaned in, and lobbed his duffel bag through the console opening onto the backseat. Then he slid onto the creamy gray leather inside his silver Jaguar XJ8 / Vanden Plas.

After fastening his seat belt, he inserted six of his favorite CDs into the player, pushed open the inside cloth cover of the moon roof, adjusted the climate control, and backed out of the garage, watching as the automatic double door then closed in front of him. Slowly descending the curves of Somerset's main road, Isaiah set aside for the moment his curiosity about this weekend's expedition as a classic Eagles tune began playing. Then he leaned back into the bucket seat's aromatic leather and wondered if the rain was going to let up before he made the return trip home on Sunday night. Of course, the possibility that he might *not* be coming home on Sunday night never even crossed his mind.

*****

Sarah Mellington entered through the ornately carved front door after lifting her mail from the wrought iron mailbox at the edge of the stone walkway. First she had to pass through a small vestibule only six feet square and tiled with bronze ceramic flooring. On the walls to her left and right were brass coat and hat hooks of various sizes and shapes mounted above wooden boot benches upholstered with a needlepoint fabric. After deactivating the security control behind the front door, she slipped out of her raincoat, looped the fabric hanger inside the collar over one of the hooks, and transferred her feet from her high-heeled designer rain boots into the furry black mule slippers that had been parked beneath one of the benches. Then she opened the next doorway, which was made almost entirely of opaque beveled glass, and walked into the core of the Mellington family home.

Standing in the circular foyer, she closed her eyes and thought back to the fragrances that used to welcome her while Sinclair was still alive. Whenever he would leave the house for his office or a board meeting or a golf game, the scents from his ablutions would linger, delivering a comfort and sense of intimacy that she'd never fully appreciated before he was gone. Alone now for four years, she still had difficulty coming through these doors without pausing to remember.

When Isaiah was living with her, the loss of Sinclair had been mitigated slightly—for both of them, she'd hoped. But even though she'd finally grown to accept the fact that the special effects of those days would never be recaptured, she struggled each time she arrived at her beloved home, where no one waited to greet her anymore. She was thankful, however, that her son had only moved a short distance away, across the lake, rather than to New York, or Texas, or Florida, as so many of her friends' children had done.

Stepping forward to the mahogany drum table in the center of the foyer, she examined the face of each envelope in the mail. Deciding that none appeared important or interesting enough to open, she dropped the whole stack on the table and shuffled in her slippers across the hardwood

19

floor down a long hallway that led to the kitchen. There she flipped on the recessed ceiling lights, filled her percolator with water and freshly ground hazelnut coffee beans, and placed the pot on one of the six gas burners in the cooking island. While waiting for the coffee to perk, she circled around the first floor, through the family room and small computer niche off the kitchen, through the library and the formal living and dining rooms, turning on all the lights and igniting the see-through gas fireplace that opened into both the living room and library.

"One of the things I simply cannot bear," she'd told Isaiah shortly after he'd moved to Bellevue, "is coming home to a dark house. I really should hire someone to set up all of the lights on timers. Even on a brilliant day, this old place can feel quite gloomy, and when the weather is foggy or drizzly or rainy, I tell you, Isaiah, I feel as if I'm walking into a cave."

"Good idea," her son had said. "The lights could probably be worked into the security system. I also think you should consider hiring some full-time help. It's one thing to have a housekeeper and yard man come by once a week, Mother, but quite another to manage the rest by yourself—even though I'm not that far away and I try to be there as much as possible." She knew he'd added that last comment because he still felt guilty about moving out of Seattle, an emotion she admitted to nurturing on occasion.

Nonetheless, upgrading the house and bringing in extra help were sound suggestions, despite her being a remarkably fit and active woman of eighty-one. But with Isaiah in Bellevue, no one was around her consistently enough to push her into action. "Of course, I could always *sell*," Sarah would mention periodically when her son was visiting, knowing full-well, as did Isaiah, that she could never bring herself to let the house go. Too much history lingered in every room, where she'd lived with Sinclair since his parents passed away within a year of each other when Isaiah was a toddler. An unyielding sense of loyalty to her husband would not allow her to imagine any other family living there. Thus, she remained alone, while the lamp-and-fire-lighting routines replaced the sound of her two favorite voices in the closing spaces of each day.

Having illuminated the entire first floor, she poured herself a mug of coffee and went back out to the foyer, where she picked up her handbag and continued to ignore the mail. With her pocketbook strap over her right shoulder and the mug in her right hand, she clutched at the banister with her left and cautiously ascended the wide, curved staircase. Despite all the time she devoted to keeping her mind and body in strong working order, her legs and deteriorating knees made living in a Tudor house a daily challenge. And second only to her dislike of darkness was her fear of falling down the long flight of steps to the hardwood floor where she wouldn't be discovered until well after she'd joined Sinclair in the Great Beyond.

Safely upstairs, she leaned for a moment against the railing overlooking the open two-story entranceway. Suspended from the domed ceiling arching another twelve feet above her, a heavy silver chain extended all the way down past her to the tiered Austrian crystal chandelier attached at the end, which hovered over the drum table and mail in the foyer below. She still found herself mesmerized by the massive light fixture, measuring four feet in diameter, which Sinclair had shipped home during a European trip shortly after they were married in 1948. At full power, reflections from the hundreds of lights and crystal droplets flickered up and down the foyer walls, casting a soft hue on the second-floor landing where she stood.

Smiling at the soothing, incandescent effects, she turned and entered her bedroom. Not until after she had set her mug on the bedside table and turned on the lamp did she notice the red message light on her phone's cradle. *First things first*, she thought as she slipped out of her dress and hosiery and into her pink fleece robe. Then she moved with her coffee and cordless telephone over to the loveseat in front of the window. Placing the mug on the small end table, she dialed her voice mail number. There was just a single recording.

"Dear God," she said plaintively once she'd listened to Isaiah's voice explaining his revised itinerary. "Oh, no—not now," she whispered as the color began to fade from her fresh facial. "Not yet."

Brushing a surge of exasperating tears from her eyes, she rose, walked over to her desk, and opened the center drawer. After sifting through her collection of notebooks and newspaper clippings, she removed a small leather address book, closed the drawer, and returned to the loveseat. There she dialed Isaiah's cell phone, but she wasn't surprised when he failed to answer. *After all*, she thought, looking at her watch, *it's not even two o'clock yet*. Still, she had hoped.

Fingering the address book, she hesitated before turning the pages to the last part of the *A*'s, where her eyes came to rest on her husband's handwriting. "Abby—Sister Mary Abigail, Lady of the Valley Convent, Kettle Falls." Just below that notation was another listing that read "Sister Veronica," which had a single red line drawn through those printed letters. Written next to that was "Tess now—1971," followed by a phone number and the words "house, not convent."

Sarah picked up the telephone but then lowered the handset just as quickly into her lap and took another sip of coffee. When she raised the phone again, nearly an hour had evaporated before she'd summoned enough courage to make the call.

*****

As was his custom whenever he traveled the route, Isaiah had driven leisurely toward the horizontal spread of Cascade Mountains that popped up directly in front of him the minute he merged onto I-90 heading east out of Bellevue. A laid-back ride in the right-hand lane was something he'd learned from his father, who'd loved to savor the beauty in every detail of the massive range they needed to scale in order to navigate from the Seattle area across the state of Washington. The sweeping expanse of alpine peaks stretched out ahead of him like a brilliant oil painting in pastel blues, the solid line of mountains seeming to break open in the middle as Isaiah approached, swallowing and disgorging one by one every vehicle going and coming on the eight-lane highway.

After he drove into the belly of the blue mass, each fresh curve in the sharply ascending road was negotiated in tandem with caravans of eighteen-wheelers and an unending stream of passenger vehicles. Every turn led to something new—to giant rocks that seemed to cut the sky's edges, or to waterfalls that dropped from unseen origins and disappeared into pools or streams blocked from sight by I-90's bumper guards—all of this under the watchful majesty of soaring sapphire and purple summits with frosted white tops.

Isaiah felt the excitement of his youth resurface every time he made this drive. The only difference now was being alone in the car—and, of course, the fact that he was driving a Jaguar instead of a Buick. Sinclair Mellington would never have approved of his son's extravagance, which is why Isaiah was fifty-four years old before he felt free enough to indulge in the car he'd romanticized about all his life, making the purchase only a few months after his father's death.

En route slightly more than an hour, Isaiah reached Snoqualmie Pass, the highest elevation in this part of the Cascades at 3022 feet. When he was young, he and his father used to stop here to buy hot dogs and Cokes—delicacies rarely enjoyed at home—which they would eat while looking out over the unbounded view. So he pulled into the visitor center parking lot and went inside to indulge himself in a few moments of nostalgia, feeling a little self-conscious as he became aware of other people in the center watching him.

As much as he loved his Jag, he had not yet grown accustomed to the stares that he and the car inevitably drew. His mother had warned him, explaining that a Jaguar, with glistening silver paint and boot-shined chrome, might not be the best choice for someone uncomfortable with being the center of attention. She had also tried to help him understand the striking statement he made all by himself, even without a car, but he'd always assumed that she was just expressing her maternal partiality. He considered features like his abundant head of salt-and-pepper hair—much heavier on the salt than the pepper—to be more of a marquee that blazoned "I'm getting old" rather than an asset. And he couldn't imagine why faded jeans, brown scuffed loafers, and a dark leather bomber jacket on his six-foot-two-inch body would cause anyone to give him a second look.

He'd never thought of himself as handsome, believing that he was too tall and skinny to have any measurable sex appeal. What's more, despite his pedigree and availability, there had been a distinct absence of beautiful women—or *any* women, for that matter—in active pursuit of him. That fact only served to bolster his negative self-assessment and had forced his mother into her now historic matchmaking frenzy.

"You obviously view yourself through a different lens than everyone else does," she'd told him not too long ago. "And I suppose you might be better off if you have no idea how compelling you've become."

"Right," he'd said, dismissing her comment with a raise of his eyebrows.

After standing in line at one of Snoqualmie's food concessions for about ten minutes, he paid two dollars for a puny hot dog, which was about a dollar fifty more than he remembered paying as a kid for one twice as thick. Biting into the cylinder of meat through the squishy bun, he also noted that the taste differed from his memories, although he suspected that the ingredients were just as disgusting as they'd been back then. Taking another bite, despite the gastrointestinal danger of doing so, he wandered over to the windows, sliding his sunglasses up over his forehead for a clearer perspective.

He couldn't recall how old he'd been when he'd first confessed his sense of invincibility at the top of this pass, looking down on the world below and whispering to his dad that he wondered if this must be how Superman felt. But Isaiah had no trouble remembering his father's response.

"Yes, Son," Sinclair had said, with a tone that signaled the onset of a sermon. "It's easy to have a sense of power up here. But look at the *rest* of the mountain range over there. Each of those peaks—and more just like them that we can't even see—rise much higher than where we're standing. So don't ever get too comfortable with yourself at the top of any hill, because there are usually others out in front of you that will impose even greater challenges." Sinclair had then laughed and patted his son on the back, as if his foreboding caution about life's never-ending struggles had been a *good* thing.

Perhaps if there'd been some effort to give those mountains names—positive names that corresponded to dreams he could reach for—the long-term effect of those early lectures might have been more constructive. Instead, what he remembered was the threatening imagery of massive, lurking, inevitable impediments to *any* dream. Nonetheless, Isaiah had always envied his father for his wisdom and bravado, and for his bring-it-on attitude that almost taunted fate to throw obstacles in his path. Isaiah, on the other hand, had nightmares as a kid about nameless man-eating mountains lying in wait for him. As he matured, he found himself steering away from risk, preferring more predictable, comfortable choices that gave him a sense of security while promising less fruitful or fulfilling outcomes as a trade-off.

That pattern had brought him to this particular midlife juncture, where he had no passion for much of anything. And he had a particular aversion to ball-busting careers requiring twelve- or fourteen-hour days filled with one competitive gamble after another—careers that were actually coveted by most people in his family's circle. In order for someone to win, someone else had to be crushed, and Isaiah had never been able to stomach the battle.

He loved the study of English literature; he loved to tell stories; and he loved to write. But, again, he'd never been shown how to sculpt those passions into dreams that could be developed into a livelihood that might actually be meaningful as well as fulfilling. *Dreams are for vagabonds*, his father had groomed him to believe. *Serious* people secure a solid education and then go to work in a real job.

Consequently, Isaiah had been a good soldier, sticking with the blueprint all the way through law school, and then passing the bar, at last, on his third try. But despite his air of calm and confidence, and a respectable level of success, he considered himself a fraud. Furthermore, he was miserable, although he'd never expressed any open discontent; his healthy trust fund was supposed to be making him happy, and he didn't want to appear ungrateful.

At length, once Sinclair was no longer around to make the decision impossible, Isaiah had chosen to withdraw from the dragon-slaying lifestyle and pursue the slim chance that there might still be time for one or two of his own secret aspirations to materialize. He knew how lucky he was not to need a job while he figured out what he wanted to be when he grew up, and he went to great lengths to avoid becoming a poster boy for the rich and famous. Each year he spent hundreds of hours working with his mother on fundraisers and foundations for the homeless and for disadvantaged children in the Seattle metro area. He served dozens of meals at shelters, stuffed thousands of annual appeal envelopes, helped stock the shelves at the Food Bank, and dressed up as Santa at heart-wrenching holiday parties where starry-eyed kids were thrilled to receive one measly gift per child.

He also donned a tux every month or two, inevitably falling prey to his mother's insistence that his "Hollywood looks and sexy demeanor always bring top dollar" for charities that loved to put him and other available men "up for auction." Those "dream dates" usually included an evening with a specific bachelor who'd been packaged with a five-star restaurant for dinner followed by something like a ballet performance at Seattle's McCaw Hall or a professional sporting event at the appropriate venue. But lately he'd begun to feel sort of pimped, believing that the winning bidder was reaping more value than the poor men and women—especially the children—who he'd hoped to help by selling himself off for a night.

Since deciding almost a year earlier to take a "sabbatical" from the practice of law and the firm his father had founded, he'd become uncommonly self-disciplined. Five days a week were religiously dedicated to writing feature articles on political and social topics du jour—which he sent off to dozens of magazines and newspapers. Some of those articles had actually been published, for a nominal stipend, although he would have been happy to see his writing in print for free. He was also drafting a novel with autobiographical undertones. But as busy as he kept himself on his quest to refashion his goals, he still found that his most uncomfortable moments were those times when someone asked him, "Hey, Isaiah! What have *you* been up to lately?"

Everyone knew he wasn't "working." So, despite the patronizing words of encouragement and support from his friends, as well as from his mother, he was fully aware that absolutely *no one* took his comments about trying to become a published author seriously. They were simply waiting for him to "get over it" and come back into the fold.

Perhaps they were right. File folders of rejection letters from agents and from editors in publishing houses were collecting on his office bookshelves. Cases of printer paper and dozens of ink jet cartridges seemed to vaporize each week. And three different story lines for the novel had been discarded, despite relentless editing, after failing to excite anyone, including Isaiah. Nonetheless, the laptop currently inside his duffel bag contained the outline for a fourth version, which he thought might finally have some potential. "Might," of course, was the operative word that even he had begun to tire of repeating month after month. The gnawing truth was that, other than his charitable activities, nothing he'd done since his father's death had produced anything of value.

Yet the unexpected summons to Kettle Falls indicated that someone apparently needed him for *something*, although he couldn't imagine that the job was going to be all that challenging. *After all*, he thought, *this is Sister Abby we're talking about here.* He had a hard time believing that the little nun's so-called "loose ends" would require much tying up. What sort of complications could someone's life have after being in a convent for forty or fifty years, the first twenty or twenty-five of which had been in complete seclusion? *And besides, aren't nuns supposed to give up everything before they even go into the convent? What could she have left that requires my involvement?*

Sliding his sunglasses back over his nose in a symbolic attempt to block the dreaded, nameless mountain peaks from view, he sighed, tossed his half-eaten memorial hot dog into a garbage can, and returned to his car. He knew he had another six hours to go through the terrain of central Washington, which was markedly different from the lush trees and vegetation west of the Cascades. Sections of earth in the midportion of the state almost looked as if they'd been ripped away from each other, leaving dry, serrated plateaus on the horizons, with I-90 curving up and over them like a slithery gray band of steel. The sheer monotony of the drive had always resulted in at least one more turnoff along the way for another bite to eat. *But not today*, he thought. *Next stop, the lodge in Colville, and then Tess in Kettle Falls. Hope she has a pie.*

CHAPTER THREE

The yellow frame house was the only one not decorated for Halloween on Kettle Crest Drive in Kettle Falls. Tess believed there was something pagan about the holiday's rituals, although she conceded that the majority of her neighbors were only playing around with the scarecrows, witches, ghosts, and tombstones, applying not a whiff of sacrilege or heathenism to their traditions. Nonetheless, she couldn't help but feel a bit skittish every year at this time, and she said a few extra rosaries each day while staying indoors from the afternoon of October 30 until dawn on November 1. With almost two weeks remaining until she needed to take cover, the curtains in her four small rooms were drawn wide open.

She had just returned from running errands, her junket having taken her first to Hunter's Market a quarter mile away. She suspected that Isaiah would prefer to have dinner out by himself somewhere tonight, as was his custom, especially once he'd heard what she had to say. But she'd decided to pick up an array of fresh fruits, cheeses, and cold cuts at the market anyway, and a pie from the bakery, so she would at least appear hospitable.

Then she'd driven five miles south to Colville, the largest town in this part of the Stevens County Valley, where Isaiah stayed whenever he came to visit. She'd made the extra drive to purchase two bottles of quality wine, since there wasn't much of a selection anywhere in Kettle Falls. She generally kept some of the grape on hand, occasionally enjoying a sip on her own. Two nights ago, however, once Abby's death had become imminent, she'd finished off her supply, and now she was fairly certain that her first few hours with Isaiah would be made easier for both of them if they each had a bit of sauvignon blanc or pinot grigio close by. She picked up a bottle of merlot and one of shiraz as well, for good measure.

She also bought a box of dark orange chocolates in the candy shop three doors down from the liquor store. This was partially because they were among her favorites of God's creations, especially when paired with a perfectly brewed cup of coffee. But she also wanted to appear as if she were shopping for gifts, to moderate the vision of this eighty-three-year-old woman loading up on alcoholic beverages. Even so, she'd been a little paranoid that word about her shopping list would filter back up the road to Kettle Falls, although she had no idea why she cared. There'd been far worse stories circulating about her in the thirty-four years since she'd left the convent.

Our precious convent, she thought to herself as she unpacked her groceries. She'd evolved to the point where she didn't dwell on those times incessantly anymore, as she had for so long after leaving the order. Since Abby's illness had taken such a sudden turn for the worse, though, and especially in the hours after her death, the memories had been crushing in around Tess, carrying her back. But she had to force herself to stop daydreaming for the moment while she dealt with the immediate crisis at hand.

She was grateful that she didn't have much trouble with stamina at her age, but she wished for a return to the days when she could walk without so much discomfort. Of course, the extra fifty pounds she was carrying now on her short, round body didn't help much and kept her in dark baggy dresses and orthopedic shoes. But her hips and knees were the big problems; they felt as if they were almost locked in place. Without flexibility in all those joints, her legs were stiff as she walked, causing her body to sway from side to side as she moved around. She was thankful that she could still function in any capacity, though, and especially that she could still drive.

Always a low-maintenance woman, with her short hair now completely white and combed back over her ears in a boyish style, she didn't need much time to take care of herself. But she was a little vain about her skin, making certain to keep her face moisturized throughout the day and then again before bed at night. She thought that minor obsession might have originated with all the stories she'd heard and read about lepers throughout her long religious life.

Whatever the reason, she didn't feel guilty as she checked herself in the mirror mounted on the side of her kitchen cabinet. Unscrewing the cap on a jar of cream she kept on the counter—the same cream that she also kept in the bathroom and at her bedside—she dabbed a little under each of her greenish brown eyes and then a little more on her forehead and on her neck, gently massaging her skin until all the cream had disappeared. Then she pinched her cheeks to pull in some color, as she planned to do every thirty minutes until Isaiah arrived, hoping to look as presentable as possible for the dear boy.

Once the food was in the refrigerator, she put the white wine in the vegetable bins for a quick chill and began brewing a pot of tea. Then she snipped a diagonal cut across a dozen stems each of dahlias and Peruvian lilies, which she'd just brought in from her fall garden behind the house. After arranging the flowers in a clear, cut-glass vase, she placed the bouquet on top of the stubby drop-leaf table she'd discovered at a garage sale.

Having lived in the convent for so many years, she didn't require a collection of furniture or accessories to make her happy. But she did savor an occasional bargain purchase like this sweet table, tiny and perfect for the open end of her small galley kitchen. On the wall next to the table was a steam pipe radiator hidden behind the custom cover she'd had made, with the vented front grill in a cane design. Normally, she spent a couple of hours each morning sitting at the little table, enjoying her tea, fruit, the local paper, and the *Wall Street Journal*, which miraculously showed up on her front porch five days a week in this remote part of the country. In the winter, the popping and whooshing of the steam in the radiator had sort of a sedative effect on her in this, the toastiest spot in her house. And in warmer weather, the custom radiator cover gave her extra display space for her floral arrangements.

Glancing at both newspapers sidelined and unread on the small table today, she fluffed the flowers one more time and then moved through the arched doorway from her kitchen into the living area. As she did so, her eyes were drawn to the telephone stand centered under a pendulum clock hanging on the wall in the bedroom hall. The cordless phone in the stand was the only modern electronic device in her possession—a luxury she'd acquired when Abby's condition had begun to deteriorate—and the blue message light on the phone was flashing. The last few times she'd seen the light flashing, the signal had brought worsening news from the hospital, but that certainly wasn't the reason now that Abby was gone. *Perhaps Isaiah tried to contact me while I was out shopping*, she thought as she pressed the PLAY button.

"Good afternoon, Tess," the woman's voice said. "This is Sarah Mellington. First, let me tell you how very sorry I am for the loss of Sister Abby. I can only imagine how difficult this must be for you. As you might guess, the news has affected me as well. According to a message I received from Isaiah, he began the drive to Kettle Falls this morning after receiving some sort of communication from Sinclair's law firm and after speaking with you. If you would be so kind, I would deeply appreciate your calling me back before he arrives. I need to discuss a few things with you that I realize we should have probably covered some time ago. But I would very much like to do so in advance of your meeting with my son today. Thank you. I'll await your call."

Tess pressed the STOP button and looked at her watch, which showed 3:18 PM. Assuming Isaiah's drive was on schedule, and allowing time for him to settle into the lodge, he should be at her house by six o'clock.

"Yes, Mrs. Mellington," she whispered, directing her words toward the handset. "But I'm not so sure you really want to find out what you *think* you already know. So it's probably good that you'll have to wait your turn."

Still feeling pressed for time, Tess nonetheless paused from her Isaiah preparations in order to say her daily rosary and take her thirty-minute afternoon nap. She was convinced that her loyalty to this routine was one of the reasons she was still alive, *especially after all those years of living on the edge,* she thought, an impish smile spreading over her face.

After adding another log and stoking the flames in her small living room's wood-burning stove, she stretched out in her black leather recliner and tucked in a blue velvet throw around her feet and legs. Too wound up to actually fall asleep, she did a few deep breathing exercises to slow her pulse and then gave her mind permission to wander back to those days of innocence. *Just for a few minutes,* she thought, *since I was the one who really started the whole thing.*

*****

Childhood friends of Tess and Abby in Seattle had whispered their secret dreams of becoming famous movie stars, like Errol Flynn, or Greta Garbo—or maybe singers like Bing Crosby, or Mildred Bailey, whose voices they'd begun hearing on their household radios. In Abby's case, those dreams had involved having her own byline on the front page of a major newspaper after she'd researched and reported on some important story that would change the world. But for Tess, no matter how hard she'd tried to be like everyone else, she had never been able to suppress the desire to become a nun.

She'd studied the history and mission of the Sisters of the Holy Names, the order of nuns who taught, disciplined, counseled, and nourished Tess and her classmates throughout their twelve years of Catholic education at St. Agnes School. She also visited the convent across the street from the school every chance she got, running errands for the sisters or just stopping by to ask some question she'd created in her head, hoping she'd be invited into the house for the answer.

No aspect of the nuns' Spartan, regulated lifestyle in any way discouraged her. In fact, on a couple of occasions when she was asked to join the sisters for dinner, she found herself wishing she were already part of the order. And she fell in love with the ambience of the big convent house, so different from the bungalows on the street where she and Abby lived in Seattle's congested University District.

Tess first had dinner at the convent in 1938, when she was thirteen. What she'd anticipated as being a quiet, pious evening with teachers and saints had turned out, instead, to be an introduction to a world surprisingly rich in texture. Beneath the trappings of their habits and holy demeanors, the nuns were actually a group of women who mostly loved each other— with a few who apparently had to pray a bit harder than the others for strength to get along with some of their convent-mates.

Also, when they were in their own protected environment, they were uninhibited and nothing short of hilarious. They wore lighter-weight habits and shorter veils when "at home," making them look less formal, more comfortable, and oddly normal. Further, their personalities were noticeably unrestrained by the effects of garnet-colored wine poured liberally throughout the meal, a few sips of which were offered to their young guest in a magical crystal goblet ceremoniously retrieved from a small china cabinet.

But what caught Tess most unaware was their conversation. They were all extremely well-read and well-versed in current events, both on a local as well as a global level, and they spoke with great concern about the worsening situation in Europe. As Hitler's quest for Lebensraum— "living space"—expanded, Germany had just finished occupying Austria, expelling all Jews and political opponents. Despite warnings from the United States, Great Britain, and other Western allies, Czechoslovakia appeared to be next on Hitler's list. The sisters were very troubled about the possibility of a world-wide war, as well as the fate of the millions of

Jewish refugees who had been made homeless by the Third Reich. No one yet knew about the burgeoning concentration camps, whose malevolent legacies would one day horrify everyone on the planet.

As the sisters talked, they expressed differing points of view regarding how involved America should become in the situation, and a spirited debate broke out. Later, as if to relieve any built-up political pressure in the room, they slipped suddenly into a stream of almost irreverent, mildly off-color humor, which amazed Tess because she hadn't realized that nuns even *knew* about some of the anatomy or activities being referenced. Unbeknownst to her at the time, but confessed many years later, they had agreed in advance to let her in on their humanity, dropping their defenses a bit so she would have an inside view of their private lives, with the myth of sainthood being dispelled as much as possible.

But at the evening's conclusion, as Tess bid an affectionate farewell to each of the sisters, there was an eerie, unspoken understanding that what she had experienced was not to be shared with anyone outside the convent. They were entrusting her with their confidence, and she was beginning to realize that a nun's life necessarily involved a level of secrecy. In order to be truly effective at their jobs—and the Sisters of the Holy Names *lived* to be teachers—there had to be an air of mystery about them, a stiff persona that compelled students and their parents to take them seriously. Rather than being put off by this duality, Tess was only drawn further into the net, and by the time she and Abby entered high school, she was already gathering information from Mother Superior about the process for becoming a postulant.

Abby was quite vocal about what she called her best friend's obsession with such nonsense, and Tess was aware of Abby's conspiratorial efforts to make sure that Tess's dance card was always full at every high school social event. *Bless her heart.* Abby had tried to be as religious as the next person, which wasn't difficult in a coeducational Catholic school where everyone wore uniforms, attended Mass daily, and took mandatory religion classes three times a week.

"But high school graduation is supposed to *free* us from all of this," Abby would say, "not lead us into *more* confinement. How can you seriously want to close yourself away in a life that's basically an eternal penance! You need to think this through, Tess, before you make a horrible mistake."

"You really don't understand, do you?" Tess would counter. "Their lives are full and wonderful, with pure intentions that actually lead to something meaningful."

Abby's next move would be to arrange "chance" meetings at Garrety's Fountain & Pharmacy, the neighborhood soda counter, with one set of boys or another, who were sometimes from St. Agnes and occasionally from—*gasp!*—the public high school down the street from Garrety's. Tess, who was never fooled by Abby's shenanigans, appreciated her friend's good-natured motives and loved her so dearly that she inevitably played along. Usually the boys were decent fellows, full of fun and innocent pranks that made the girls laugh, and occasionally a few interesting words even came out of their mouths. So the soda fountain afternoons weren't a complete waste of time—and letting them happen without protest was a less stressful option than making Abby accept the fact that her friend's vocational choice had already been made.

What a study in irony, Tess mused sixty years later, *the way everything eventually ended up, with me on the outside and Abby still in.*

On December 7, 1941, life was turned upside down for Tess and Abby, all of America, and the world at large. Japan's bombing of Pearl Harbor not only drove the United States into war with Japan but also into the European conflict as well, just as the sisters had feared would happen. By the time Tess and Abby graduated from St. Agnes in June of 1943, World War II had been underway for eighteen months and had become entwined with the fabric of virtually every American family.

Most of the older boys from school and the soda fountain had become soldiers. Victory Gardens were sprouting up everywhere—in compact urban yards, apartment window boxes, and sprawling farm fields across the country. This nationwide phenomenon enabled every citizen to play a part in the war effort by planting vegetables, fruits, and herbs at private residences to reduce pressure on public food supplies. Additionally, war bond sales to finance the fighting were at a fever pitch, and unabashed patriotism and support for the offensive were universally shared throughout all of America. This unity persisted despite dead, injured, and maimed soldiers who'd begun to number in the tens of thousands. Some of the boys from the soda fountain had already come home in caskets. More had been buried in massive cemeteries on European shores, and a number remained missing in action, never to be found.

Over time, however, the discordance of war had somehow managed to strike a rhythm with normal life, and Abby and Tess were making plans, excited about their respective futures. Tess was scheduled to become part of a postulant class for the Sisters of the Holy Names, starting the week after Labor Day, and Abby was scheduled to attend the University of Washington in the fall, where she would major in journalism. She'd already secured a full-time summer secretarial job at the *Seattle Times* to help pay for her tuition and books, and she'd been promised part-time work there once she began her college courses. Because the campus was only a short bus ride from the small house where she lived with her parents, she wouldn't have to worry about room and board in a dormitory or sorority. Abby told Tess how pleased she was with herself and her orderly set of objectives.

"The only thing missing," she said to Tess as the two of them prepared a picnic lunch together in Abby's family kitchen one summer morning in 1943, "is that *you* won't be there. I know you're going to eventually change your mind about the convent, as soon as you find out what it's like to actually be *in* it. But in the meantime, how often will I get to talk to you once you start your training?"

"I don't think it's called 'training,' Abby. It's a 'course of study.' Your career will be as a journalist, and mine will be as a teacher. We will each have a curriculum to follow, tests to pass, grade levels to achieve. Very much the same."

"Oh, please, Tess. *Nothing* is going to be the same. I'll be going to school and work each day and then out to the movies and on dates during my free time. You, on the other hand, won't be going *anywhere*. You'll be in a completely different world, leaving all of this—and me—behind."

"Don't be silly. The sisters are very much a part of this world too, and they have a wonderful time together."

"Right. *Together*. That's the problem. What about *me*? When are *we* going to do things together? And you didn't answer my question. How often will I get to talk to you once you begin your training? Excuse me … your 'course of study.'"

"Honestly, Abby, I really don't know. But I'll try to find out just to keep you quiet. Oh, by the way, I've decided to go on a retreat at the end of this month—sort of a transitional step for my mind and soul that Sister Helen told me about, something to prepare me emotionally for my entry into the Holy Names postulant class. After thinking it over, I thought the retreat would be a good idea too."

"Really? What kind of retreat? And where?"

"It's a week of meditation, prayer, and discussions. There's limited space, but it's open to anyone who's interested. Apparently, there are lots of people drawn there, with the war and all, like soldiers who've come home, and men and women who've lost someone. Even *you* could go, believe it or not. Want to come with me?"

"Gosh, Tess. Thanks so much for the invitation, but I think I'd rather slam a brick down on my foot. Besides, I'm pretty sure I have a date—or maybe a dozen—during that week. Not all the handsome, fun boys are overseas, you know."

"So you tell me—constantly," Tess replied, smiling as always at her dear friend and embracing their differences, all of which made her love Abby even more.

"Where'd you say this retreat is going to happen?" Abby asked again.

"I didn't, but it's at a place called Lady of the Valley Convent in Kettle Falls, Washington, about ninety miles northwest of Spokane, so I'm told."

"You have to be *kidding*, Tess. That's clear up in the opposite corner of the state! Ninety miles north of Spokane must be practically in Canada! Don't tell me there isn't someplace closer where your soul and mind can undergo this transition and your *emotions* can get *prepared*." Tess just shook her head and started arranging their picnic fare in the basket. "Seriously," Abby persisted, "it'll take you a week just to get there."

"Not true, my friend. The train ride from Seattle to Spokane only takes about eight hours. Then the people who organize the retreats will have a bus or something meet us at the station for the ride to Kettle Falls. *Very simple—and quick*."

"I see. But what's so special about this place that you have to go so far away?" Abby asked.

"I believe the attraction is the setting," Tess said, sitting down at the kitchen table, her eyes drifting off in a strange way. "The convent is run by cloistered Dominican nuns in a valley surrounded by mountains. There are supposedly forty or fifty acres for visitors to explore on the convent grounds alone. And then there's the little town of Kettle Falls itself, plus a lake, the Columbia River, the new Coulee Dam—lots of places for people to peacefully reorder their lives. With so many going there who are troubled by the world's turmoil, or their *own*, Sister Helen said the exposure to such a wide range of stories would be good for me—help broaden my perspective so I'll be a better teacher."

Abandoning the basket for the moment, Abby sat down at the table beside her friend.

"Wait a minute, Tess. *Cloistered* nuns really *don't* go anywhere—ever! They're in a whole different setup than the Holy Names sisters we're used to being around. When nuns are cloistered, they stay locked up in their convent all their lives and aren't even allowed to visit their families. How can they be running a retreat?"

"I asked the same question. Sister Helen said there's a separate wing that's used for the retreats, which are run by priests and lay people from other parishes in the Spokane Archdiocese. The nuns have made the facility available because they need the money. I guess they have extra wartime expenses and projects, and the fees that people pay for the retreats help cover those costs. Sort of clever, actually."

"Maybe. But what sort of expenses and projects could they possibly have? I didn't think cloistered nuns *did* anything—except pray, of course. And how do they manage with all those people being around? I thought they weren't supposed to come into contact with *anyone*."

"Good *grief*, Abby! I don't *know*. But I'll find out in a few weeks, and I'll be sure to give you a full report when I get back."

"Terrific," Abby replied, with a touch more sarcasm evident than her standard measure. "So, how long did you say this retreat is going to last?"

"One week."

"And you *are* coming back as soon the retreat is over, right? I mean, your postulant class here will be starting in a little over a month."

"You know something, Abby? If there was a way to get paid for worrying, you'd already be a very rich girl!"

They both laughed as they gathered their picnic basket, a blanket, and one novel each that they'd checked out from the library. Then they caught the bus to the far side of the UW campus where they walked up their favorite hill, which offered an unfettered view of Lake Washington.

The low early morning fog and light drizzle had predictably given way to a sharp blue sky marked by poufs and swirls of clouds that looked as if they'd been bleached white. The sun, which had burned through the fog a couple of hours earlier, had begun to dry the grass where the girls spread out their blanket and sat down. Sailboats dotted the lake, and flashes of metal from their masts and sails reflected in the daylight as several motorboats buzzed across the water's surface, causing nearby crafts to tilt and roll in their wakes.

A few cooing couples and solitary loners, all of whom looked like they might be university students, had also found their way to this hill where they could take advantage of the view, along with the brief window of warmth and sunshine.

"You can hardly tell that a war is even going on when you look out on all of this," Abby said. "Makes me feel sort of guilty."

"Me too," Tess replied, arranging two lunch settings on paper plates, each containing a generous chicken salad sandwich, slices of apples and oranges, and three chocolate chip cookies. "But I'm glad we decided to come here anyway. A day like this inspires me and makes me excited about what lies ahead for us."

Abby opened the thermos and poured lemonade into two plastic cups. "We should do this again before the summer's over, before we both head off to our *courses of study*."

Tess smiled, taking the cup of lemonade from Abby's hand. "Okay," she said. "I'd like that."

"How about the weekend after you get home from your retreat?"

"Sounds good, assuming we're lucky enough to get another rain-free day like this one."

"Promise? Right after your retreat?"

"Geez, Abby. I *promise*. Now eat your sandwich."

The childhood friends talked and shared dreams and spent a little quiet time reading and watching the lazy activity on the lake. After two hours, they gathered up their trash and leftovers into the basket, folded the blanket, and headed back down to the bus stop.

Over the next couple of years, Abby would often refer in her letters to that unspoiled afternoon and mention that she'd been back to the same spot again. And whenever one of those letters arrived, Tess would feel another surge of regret over her broken promise about coming back to Seattle—a return trip she never made—as she pictured her friend sitting on that hillside alone.

*****

Shaking herself free from thoughts of the past, Tess refocused on the importance of today's upcoming meeting with Isaiah as she returned to the kitchen and poured more tea into her mug. Carrying the warm beverage between both hands, she went back into the living room where she surveyed her surroundings and conducted a quick mental review of her remaining to-dos.

Positioned on a raised brick platform that took up most of the front wall, her potbelly stove was the sole source of heat, other than the kitchen radiator, for the whole house and was centered between two single-pane sash windows covered with delicate white lace curtains. A metal pipe on the stove extended up from behind the flat heating surface and went all the way through the ceiling for ventilation. The two front windows opened onto a narrow, covered porch, as did the front door on the far left end of the wall.

After unlatching the stove's iron hinged opening, Tess added another log from the stack she kept a safe distance away on a low rack in the corner. She shoved the wood into the fire chamber and closed and latched the iron door. A regenerated heat would soon begin moving throughout the house, keeping at bay the valley's October chill and bringing the heavy metal pot of water on the stove's flat heating surface to a slow, constant simmer for tea.

In 1971, after she left Lady of the Valley and found this house, she'd purchased a rectangular cherrywood dining table, which she'd centered lengthwise in the small, narrow living room, directly in front of the potbelly. She'd acquired the table to use primarily as a desk for her teaching work. The set had included eight comfortable captain's chairs, one of which was placed on the side of the table opposite the stove, so she could look out the windows while she studied or corrected papers. A second chair was paired with the drop leaf table in the kitchen, and the remaining six were all lined up in a stiff row across the entire short end of the living room wall. Her black leather recliner was the room's only other seating and was positioned near the row of captain's chairs, angled toward the right-hand front window, again so she could look outside during her afternoon rest periods.

On top of the long table, on the end nearest the recliner, were the three black corrugated file folders she needed to review with Isaiah. She patted them gently each time she walked by, as if to embolden her resolve. In the table's center was a large antique oil lamp topped with a Tiffany-style shade. Scattered around the base were several spiral notebooks, a stapler, and an oversized chipped coffee mug filled with a half-dozen pens, a mixture of paper clips, and rubber bands.

A bookcase created with three layers of eight-feet-long two-by-fours resting on twelve-inch-square cinderblocks filled almost the entire wall separating the kitchen from the living room. On the top shelf were twin brass lamps surrounded by a collection of porcelain figurines and knickknacks. On the next shelf down, a small black television occupied one end, with a 1940s-era radio shaped like a cathedral on the other, and a dozen photographs in mismatched frames were in between. The remaining shelf contained old Bibles and missals from the convent, textbooks from her teaching years, and an extensive array of paperbacks, many of which had pictures of horses and cleavage on the covers. Tess had one indiscretion, other than her wine, and that was an insatiable affinity for racy romance novels.

She took about thirty minutes to tidy up, swiping every surface with a feather duster and pushing her cordless sweeper over the hardwood floors and the brown braided rug under the table. After turning on the bookcase lights, she ignited the oil lamp on the dining table and looked around with satisfaction. Despite the small, sparsely appointed room, she'd managed to revive the snug atmosphere where Isaiah had always been so comfortable. And considering what was about to be unloaded on him, she thought that making him feel comfortable was the least she could do.

CHAPTER FOUR

Isaiah arrived at the little yellow house in Kettle Falls shortly after six thirty, as the last cranberry-colored traces of daylight splayed across the sky and sank behind the mountains encircling the valley. Tess thought he was even more handsome now than he'd been as a young man. He'd put on a little weight since his last visit, a change she approved of since she'd always thought he was too skinny in the first place. And now he had a stronger, more rugged look about him. The sharp sculpted lines and angles on his face seemed to have softened in his fifties, making him look wiser somehow, although the deep green of his eyes still danced with the magical light of a boy. *One of the continuing mysteries*, she thought as she welcomed him with unabashed affection, *is how this fellow can still be single.*

Once she'd hugged him hello repeatedly and they'd exchanged light conversation for a few minutes, Tess brought out one of the chilled bottles of sauvignon blanc; the two crystal wine goblets she'd been keeping in the refrigerator; two small china plates; her prepared trays of cheeses, fruits, cold cuts, crackers; and the pie. She arranged everything on the dining table while Isaiah opened the wine. Once both of their glasses were filled, she placed the wine bottle in the antique copper wine chiller she'd found at another garage sale.

Soft low flames were rustling around in the stove's iron chamber, and just the right amount of heat was seeping out through the vents. She motioned for him to be seated in her recliner. Then she sat down in the dining chair at the table, turning herself slightly to face Isaiah and keeping the three black file folders within her easy reach. After biting down on a cube of Swiss cheese, she added a healthy sip of sauvignon blanc to her mouth, the combination of flavors provoking a hum of pleasure. Isaiah was nibbling on his own assembly of cheese and crackers—and emptying his wine a bit too quickly, she thought—as she began explaining to him why he'd been summoned.

"Abby's death has caused a ripple effect of things that need to be done," was her well-rehearsed opening line. He nodded, appearing attentive and curious. "Not everyone comes directly to the convent from their parents' home, as I did," she continued. "In fact, nowadays, with the shortage of women who are drawn to the vocation, I think the age limit is something like forty-five, which leaves plenty of room for lots of life to happen first. Back then, forty-five might have been a *little* old, but the church has always understood that God doesn't necessarily make His calling crystal clear when we're all young and unblemished. Sometimes we have to accumulate a big chunk of experience before we even hear Him. And that was certainly the case with our Sister Abby," she said, her face lighting up and a hint of a smile breaking through as some private memory touched her.

Isaiah nodded again, adding a fresh assortment of cheese, crackers, and fruit to his plate, and downing another large swig of wine.

"She thought she wanted to be a journalist," Tess continued, noting that his attention appeared to be more on his wine and cheese than on what she was saying. "And she had just finished her freshman year at the University of Washington when she came here for one of her periodic visits with me. *That time,*" she said, raising her voice and pausing until he looked up and focused on her again, "she ended up staying in the convent's postulant dormitory to explore the idea. Within a month, she'd signed on to begin serious study. She tried so hard to acquire my same level of certainty about our professional choice, but something awful happened to her that led her to believe she'd made a terrible mistake, and she ended up leaving us long before taking her final vows. That's when she went back to school, earned her degree, and embarked on that big chunk of life."

"What was so awful that caused her to change her mind?"

"Well, let's just say there was an incident … on the grounds at the convent. She made a number of notes about the whole thing, which you'll be able to read shortly. I don't mean to sound secretive, but that incident, although certainly significant, isn't really the major news here. The point is that she decided to leave the convent, and that decision started a sequence of events which, in the end, led us—you and me—here today." She observed him working to reconcile her words. Now that the moment was at hand, she realized that the task ahead of her might be a bit more challenging than she'd imagined. "Obviously," she said, "Abby eventually came back to us at Lady of the Valley. But by then several years had passed."

"I didn't know you could do that," Isaiah responded. "I mean, leave the convent and then come back. And I'm having a hard time visualizing Sister Abby dressed up in something other than her long dress and face-pinching veil."

"The veils didn't pinch our faces, Isaiah. And leaving before final vows is not that uncommon. Sometimes the commitment just doesn't feel right, and there's no sin in that, you know. God doesn't put people in convents and monasteries against their wills. He simply wants everyone to discover their own unique mission and then follow accordingly."

"By the way, Tess, why did *you* leave, if you don't mind my asking? And what was *your* mission?"

Worried at first about veering from her rehearsed approach, she decided that this detour might actually prove to be useful.

"*My* mission? Well, that's a good question. I suppose that, ultimately, my mission became *Abby*, if you want to know the truth. But before that, honestly, I was always searching for a precise answer, knowing I'd been called to do *something*, yet never feeling as if I'd opened the right door or chosen the right path."

"Boy, do I ever know *that* feeling! So what happened? Did the right door turn out to be leaving?"

"I wouldn't put it that way. But a change was forced on all of us, and I was quite disillusioned."

"About what?"

"The church."

"Oh. Is *that* all? Isn't that kind of a big 'what'? Are you talking about the *whole* church, as in *from Rome on down*?"

"Yes. I guess that's the way I was looking at it."

"But after wanting to be a nun your whole life, what happened all of a sudden to make you feel that way?"

"Hoo boy. I really hadn't planned on getting into this."

"I'm sorry, Tess. You don't need—"

"Actually," she said, holding up her hand to stop him, "I think I do." She bit down on another cube of cheese, let a sip of wine work more flavorful magic, and then began sharing with him the reason why she, of all people, had chosen to walk away.

In 1970, the sisters at Lady of the Valley were informed that the operation of their convent could no longer be sustained. The news had come as an enormous shock to all of them who'd worked so hard to hold the place together. At that point, most of the nuns had been there for twenty or thirty years, and many others had died there, buried in their own cemetery on the grounds. But despite all those years of dedication, the nuns had not been allowed to be a part of the decision-making process regarding the convent's fate. Instead, their beloved property was sold right out from under them to a group called the Circle Bar J Ministries that eventually used the facility as a home for boys. Once the deal was finalized, all of the sisters were uprooted and relocated.

"*Oh.* So *that's* why Abby moved to Colville," Isaiah said.

"Yes, that's why we *all* had to move. And Lady of the Valley was more than our home. It was also our place of work, our place of worship, our spiritual center, and our family. So the change was pretty shocking, to put it mildly."

She went on to say that the necessary relocation hadn't been the main problem, however. Despite their sadness and disappointment, the sisters understood that the church owned the convent, and those in authority had every right to dispose of the property as they wished. The issue at stake was the fact that they'd signed up for *cloistered* vocations, and their expectation was that they would be moved to other cloistered environments. Instead, they were given only three options. Each one was a hospital run by Dominican sisters, and each had a small convent attached. One was Mount Carmel in Colville, where Abby ended up going. One was Chewelah Hospital, about twenty-five miles away heading back out of the valley on 395. And the third was Holy Family in Spokane. And, unfortunately, *none* of those options was cloistered.

"That, in my opinion," Tess said, "was a breach of the contract we'd made with the church. Being asked to leave Lady of the Valley was hard enough, but finding ourselves ripped out of the monastic environment and shoved into the open, unsheltered world was an unbelievable shock."

She told him that some of the sisters had become so fearful that they'd requested work assignments in the kitchens or laundries of their new convents where they would never be obligated to go outdoors. No more mountains and open sky for them. No more brilliant gardens. Other than what little they could experience through a raised window, they would never venture outside again.

"But how could the church do that?"

"Don't even get me started, Isaiah. I eventually made my peace with everything—and with the church—a long time ago. But the truth was that we had no *power* at all. And forcing us to change some of the sacred vows we'd taken was, for me, an unconscionable violation of trust. Plus, I had a hard time visualizing the church imposing such cruel consequences on any group of *priests* who'd been living in a monastery. So there was a clear gender inequality involved, as well. But what else is new in religious life, or life in general? Most of the sisters obediently relocated in lockstep, without complaining—Abby being among them—but two of us left the convent life entirely. That other poor woman was devastated and returned to her family somewhere on the East Coast, never to be heard from again. As for me, well, here I am."

"Did you ever have any regrets about that decision?"

"Hmm. You know, in all these years, no one has ever asked me that question. And yes, I suppose I did have some regrets on occasion, especially when I saw how joyful and peaceful Abby was each week when I joined her for Mass and lunch—occasions we would never have had in the cloistered world, I might add. But I found my way back to doing God's work through my teaching, something else I would have missed if nothing had changed. So I eventually came to believe that the whole thing—the sale of the convent, the move to noncloistered institutions, and my decision to leave— were all part of God's plan for me. And once I began to see things that way, I started to recover my trust in our church hierarchy. But that took several years—and many trips to the confessional to clear my heart of the bitterness."

"Would it be rude of me to ask what made you want to sign up for that gig in the first place? I mean, how would the idea of becoming a nun, especially living all the way out here, ever even come into your mind? And no offense intended, but what did you guys *do* all day, especially since you never went anywhere?"

"Oh, Isaiah, our lives were *so* full! We prayed, around the clock, on behalf of humanity, often in response to specific requests from individuals who somehow found us—without any Internet, by the way—and wrote to us from all parts of the world. We worked in shifts, just like other businesses, except our shifts were twelve hours long, and our *product*, if you will, involved unbroken recitations of the rosary twenty-four hours a day, every day of the year. A variety of other prayers were going on simultaneously as well, in the chapel, and also in our choir room, where our appeals were offered up through song."

Isaiah's eyes were fixed intently on her. "I remember hearing that singing as a boy," he said softly, his focus shifting away from her, as if he were viewing the memories. "And I remember that there was a heavy wire grille wall that separated the choir room from the chapel where Dad and I used to sit for Mass. But I have to tell you—and again I mean no offense—that I always felt a little creepy watching the fuzzy images of all the nuns on the other side of that grille wall. You could sort of see them moving, and you could hear them singing, but you couldn't see their faces. Really weird, especially since I knew that Sister Abby was in there somewhere."

Tess tilted her head back and let out a laugh. "Remember that *I* was still in there too, at that point. And if you want to know a secret, dear, we thought all of you looked a little creepy too."

"Seriously?"

"Scout's honor."

"But didn't you ever feel like you were in prison?"

"Oh heavens no! Abby and I both came to that life of our own free will, because we believed in the power of what was happening behind those walls, for the good of the entire world. But I don't want you to think that *all* we did was pray."

"Well *that's* a relief!" he said, shaking his head with a slight smile. "What else was there to do?"

"We grew our own vegetables, baked our own breads, raised a bunch of chickens for our eggs, along with a separate group of birds so we'd have poultry to eat. And we had incredible flower and rose gardens, wove our own fabrics, and we had a huge room where we created pottery and woodworking crafts. We also had a little free time each day for games of basketball in the gym, or ice skating on the ravine at the back of the property when it froze in the winter, or conversations out in the gazebo."

"Wow! Sounds like that much fun should be illegal."

"We did have fun, and don't be so flip. But the most important thing, Isaiah, was that our lives were full of *meaning*—and I'm talking about full beyond anything you could measure. Hard as I tried after I left, I never quite got that feeling back."

Isaiah poured himself another glass of wine, emptying the bottle, and then sat back down and threw both of his legs over one arm of the recliner. "What did you do after you left? Where did you go?"

"Obviously, I stayed right here. I was given a small stipend to get me by for one year. And, unbeknownst to me, my parents had maintained a savings account for me, in case something went wrong with my decision, they told me later. That account had been earning interest since I first came here in 1943. So I was able to buy this little house, some regular clothes, a sewing machine, and a few other things to help me get started as a civilian. Then I took enough correspondence courses to secure a teaching position at the elementary school, where I worked until just a few years ago. I also bought a secondhand automobile from a rancher whose family owned the town's feed store. His brother taught me how to drive on his property and then performed general maintenance on my car in return for blankets that I made for his family and his horses. Life was certainly challenging for me during the first few years on my own. But I was still a nun at heart and fairly comfortable with hardship and sacrifice."

"Did those people who were helping you know you'd been part of the convent?"

"Yes, they did, and I could tell that they were curious in the beginning. But no one ever asked me any questions and, after awhile, they didn't seem to want to anymore. They were quite wonderful, frankly, and I eventually grew to feel very much like a part of the community."

"And Abby? You said you saw her regularly?"

"Yes, I did. After I got my car and learned how to drive, I went to Colville every Sunday to attend Mass with her, and then we'd have lunch together. She became very active in the hospital and managed to create a new mission for herself where she worked with the terminally ill and their families. She actually became something of a legend in the valley, and I was in awe of the way she put the convent upheaval behind her without any resentment. Of course, she had the advantage of already living through lots of changes and difficult times before she found her permanent way back to us—which sort of brings me to the point of our meeting today. You see, before any of what I've just told you happened—before Abby returned to us and spent fifty years here making such a huge difference in the lives of so many people—there was, well ... a *lot* more."

✳✳✳✳✳

Both letters that Tess had handed to Isaiah were identical and dated April 30, 1997. One was addressed to a Mr. Daniel Whitmore in San Francisco and the other to a Mr. Zeke Gerard in North Carolina:

> This communication is being sent to you on behalf of Sister Mary Abigail, formerly known to you as Miss Abigail Ryan, for whom I am providing legal assistance. Although I am the messenger, the message itself is clearly

hers, and she has reviewed and approved this letter in advance.

As of this writing, Sister Mary Abigail is celebrating her seventy-second birthday. She has asked me to inform you that her health is beginning to fail, and she wishes this communication to be mailed prior to any further decline. When the time of her passing does ultimately arrive, you will receive another communication from me or, in my absence, from another member of my law firm. Furthermore, your daughter will be contacted as well. All of the relevant information will then be released to *both* of you, along with a few of Sister Abigail's final requests. She hopes the arrival of this letter to you privately and personally, so far in advance, will give you ample opportunity to make whatever preparations might still await you.

In the interim, should you wish to speak with me, I would be happy to discuss the matter, or to answer any questions within my purview. Please feel free to contact me at my Seattle office, as noted below.

Sincerely,

Sinclair Mellington
Attorney-at-Law

Tess had pulled the letters from two of the three folders on the table in front of her, and Isaiah had read them obediently. But she could see him struggling to keep his eyes open, *Probably from the wine,* she thought, *not to mention his long drive and the heat from the fire.* And she was becoming increasingly concerned that he did not appear to have been briefed about any of this.

"How much of this did your father discuss with you?" she asked, daring to know.

"Zero. Zip. Nada," he said, abruptly sitting up in his chair. "Why? Was he supposed to?"

"Well, yes, as a matter of fact he was. I didn't expect him to tell you everything, but I thought for sure that he would have at least provided you with a little introduction, since arrangements have to be made rather quickly."

"What arrangements?" Isaiah asked, placing the two letters back down on the desk and peeling himself out of the recliner. "What *is* going on here?"

"Oh, my," she sighed. "I'm afraid I'm doing a dreadful job of this."

As he stretched his arms above his head in an apparent attempt to revive himself, Tess saw him spot the large carton seated on one of the six captain's chairs lined up in a row against the wall. The box was stacked full of paper rising several inches above the top opening, and the word "ABBY'S" was printed in large black lettering on the carton's side.

"What's all that stuff?" he asked.

"Oh. I almost forgot about those. That's Abby's collection of *Life* magazines. At least that's *part* of her collection. I pulled out the years that I thought would be most relevant for you."

"*Years?*" He wandered over to the carton and stuck his arm all the way down inside the box then fanned the magazines upward against their bound edges as he removed his hand. "Feels like there could be a hundred in here," he said, looking over at Tess.

"Which would be at least two years' worth."

He picked up a copy of the tabloid-sized periodical from the top of the pile. On the cover was a full-page head shot of an African American man wearing a baseball cap. In the lower left-hand corner was a headline that read: "Jackie Robinson, Star Ballplayer Stars in Movie." In the lower right-hand corner was the date—"May 8, 1950"—and the price of the magazine—"20 cents."

"This is fascinating, Tess." His voice was little more than a whisper as he began thumbing through the pages of the magazine printed three days after he was born.

"Abby wasn't alone in her obsession with that particular publication," Tess said. "The magazine captured the essence of whatever was going on in America and around the world every single week. She never missed an issue, except when she was cloistered, of course—although I think the extern sisters used to sneak one in now and then for her. She would never admit it when I confronted her, but sometimes, in our free conversation periods, she simply knew way too much about a current event or a famous person. After she moved to Colville, she was free to buy the magazines again, and she would pass them along to me once she'd poured over every word. There are more up in my attic. Maybe we can find a library that could use them. There's so much history in there."

Isaiah put the magazine back down and pulled one of the captain's chairs alongside of Tess. "I apologize," he said, sitting down, "if I snapped at you a minute ago. I'm guess I'm just tired and, frankly, I have no clue what all of this is about. *Why* am I here?"

"Of course, my dear boy. You have every right to be confused, and I suppose I should have expected that something like this might happen." She found herself sifting cautiously through the jumble of thoughts in her head, selectively choosing how much she should say and worrying that she might pick the wrong words. "As you know, Sister Abby and I were acquainted with your father for a very long time."

"How exactly *did* you guys get together?"

"He came here—came to the convent, I mean—for a retreat in the summer of 1945, after returning from Europe at the end of the war. That's when Abby met him, at least. I wasn't introduced to him until later, after she returned to the convent. We weren't allowed many visitors while cloistered, you know. But I wasn't receiving any at all because my parents didn't like to travel. So one time when you and your father were here, Abby convinced the prioress to let me share your time."

"I remember that. I didn't realize you'd never met him before, though. You all seemed so friendly, and since you were there many times over the years, I just assumed that the three of you went way back."

"That was thanks to Abby's gift of gab—and to her skill in persuading the prioress to let me join you periodically for those wonderful visits."

"I really can't believe I never knew any of that."

"You and me both, Isaiah," she said through a deep sigh. "But it is what it is."

"Apparently. Just for the record, though, I never asked Dad any questions about what was going on. So I guess I can't blame this whole surprise on him."

"I see," Tess replied, deciding that none of her rehearsed sentences would be useful or relevant any longer. "Well, there's a bigger surprise coming, my dear. By the time Abby returned to us at the convent, any struggle she'd had with her convictions about becoming a nun seemed to be completely behind her. At that juncture, I think she would have remained obedient to her vows no matter how she was tested or where she was sent, unlike me. I believe the difference between us was that Abby had experienced life in such depth that her faith was bulletproof, as they say."

"Why? What sort of trouble did she get herself into?"

"Yes. Finally, the point," she responded with a sigh. "Well, the two families referenced in those letters you just read played a significant part in her life while she was in between her convent commitments. I've never met Danny Whitmore or Zeke Gerard, and I don't know very much about either of them. But I do know that each of them has a daughter. Danny's is Salome, and Zeke's is Zoie. One of Sister Abby's final requests was that both girls be notified and given the opportunity to attend her wake and funeral, which are the arrangements we need to make as soon as possible. In fact, tomorrow morning we have to go to the mortuary."

She watched Isaiah's eyes narrow as he began processing what she guessed were unpleasant funeral home visions. She also suspected that his mind might be trying to take him in a certain direction, but he was having difficulty getting there on his own.

"According to the letters," he said, lifting them from the tabletop again and glancing back and forth between the two pages, "this Salome person lives in the San Francisco area, and the one named Zoie is way out in North Carolina."

"Yes. At least, that's the last information we have on record."

"Do they know that Sister Abby's passed away?"

"Not yet. But that's not the worst news."

"Why? How can you get worse than that?"

"Isaiah, not only are they unaware that she's dead, but I think it's quite possible that they don't even know she existed at all. That's where you come in. You'll need to call and tell them."

"*What?* And these two women suddenly need to be contacted out of the blue by me—a total stranger—about the death of another total stranger, because …?"

"Because … because Salome and Zoie are, uh … oh, sweet Jesus," she said, the pitch of her voice rising and falling as she gripped her hands together and squeezed her eyes shut in readiness. "They're Abby's *children*, Isaiah," she blurted out. "Her *daughters*," she added, her words scarcely audible.

A few moments of silence slipped by while he sat there staring at her and while the old woman uncoiled her body and peeked at him through squinting eyes. When he made no response, she reached for two of the corrugated file folders and handed them to him.

"Here," she said. "There's more information on each of the girls inside these. Of course, they aren't exactly *girls* anymore. They're your age, more or less. You'll find a lot of Abby's notes in there, along with some official documents and a few baby photos. I've been holding onto all of these things for her for so many years now."

Still without speaking, Isaiah pushed back his captain's chair, stood up, and walked into the kitchen, leaving the folders and letters on the table.

"I know this is probably a stupid question," she heard him say at length as she also heard a second bottle of wine being opened, "but when did the church start letting mommies into the convent?"

She bowed her head and made the sign of the cross, relieved that he was asking questions but a little ashamed of herself for suddenly finding him so amusing.

"Actually, there isn't a rule against it, Isaiah. It's just that it doesn't happen very often, which I suppose is a bit of an understatement. At any rate, Abby was never married, so there weren't any sacramental issues to deal with—just a number of rather major sins to confess and, I imagine, a number of hefty hours, or possibly weeks, spent in penance. As long as her children's best interests were protected, though—which they were, since both girls stayed with their fathers—she was free to follow God's calling, a force that had become *very* strong in her by then. Frankly, though, the truth of the matter is—"

"Uh-oh," he said, moving back into the living room and adding fresh chilled wine to each of their glasses. "I don't know if I can handle another round of truth so close to the last one."

"Yes, well, you might want to adjust yourself to the idea. At any rate," she continued, "the truth is that we didn't exactly *know* about the children in the beginning, when she first returned, I mean."

"I see. Can't say that I'm surprised. Who could blame her for wanting to keep the headline to herself? That's the sort of thing that would probably be hard to fit into a conversation, when you're a ... oh, let's see ... how about when you're *a nun*, for God's sake!"

Tess noted that he was clearly finding humor in the unexpected revelations, and she quietly forgave him for his irreverence, aware that her own sin of omission was one she continued to commit as she sat there.

"I'm sorry," he said. "I don't mean to be disrespectful. It's just that I need a few minutes to digest this. After all, we're talking about *Sister Abby* here! Our holy, wrinkled, little Sister Abby! Trying to picture her doing things that would result in *kids* is going to take some getting used to." Still standing, he placed one of his hands on her shoulder. Then he looked down at her as her eyes turned upward to meet his, while his facial muscles appeared to struggle against a laugh. "I can't believe that Dad expected me to help choreograph her funeral without filling me in—and without any warning. What could he have been thinking?"

"Indeed. I've been asking myself that same thing. But we're not likely to know, are we? And now the production appears to be our responsibility. I'll tell you what," she continued. "There's another tray of goodies in the refrigerator. Why don't you go get it, along with the crackers in the bread box? We'll sit together awhile longer, review a few more details, and schedule ourselves for the things we have to do tomorrow. Then we'll have our pie."

"Sure. Why not? I need to visit the men's room first, though. Splashing some cold water on my face and slapping myself silly would seem to be in order under the circumstances."

When she heard the bathroom door close, she exhaled after realizing that she'd been holding her breath. *Clearly, I have no choice*, she decided, *at least for the time being*, as she placed the third corrugated file folder underneath a pile of spiral binders and pushed the stack toward the back of the table. Then she moved around to the stove where she put a new log in the fire chamber. While she was there, she dropped down on her knees and took a moment to add yet another prayer to the day's mix, asking for help from Abby, whose spirit she believed was close at hand. *You need to pitch in here, my friend. I'm not so good at this by myself.*

CHAPTER FIVE

Miss Zoie Gerard would probably have been up early anyway, but the call that awakened her at 5:00 AM had derailed any thought she might have entertained about sleeping in a little later than normal. Isaiah Mellington told her that he'd only managed to get a couple of fitful hours of rest himself, and then he'd no longer been able to stop himself from dialing the number at two o'clock in the morning his time.

Now the orange and pink shadings of sunrise were just beginning to clear the trees on the Gerard farm. Zoie kept thinking about her conversation with him as she meandered along the north–south trail slicing through the center of her family's fifty-acre property in Harmony, North Carolina.

Even though she'd known for years that this contact would eventually be made, the sharp edges of reality had been more heartrending than she'd anticipated. After the call had ended, she'd thrown on her jeans, sneakers, and a sweatshirt. Then she'd filled her thermal mug with freshly brewed coffee and headed off toward Haven Hill, a man-made elevation in the center of the farm's acreage. Built by her dad, Zeke Gerard, when she was a young girl, the hill was where she frequently went to meditate and where she wanted to spend a little time this morning before her father woke up.

Few things were as comforting to her as this land. The ground's warmth had a way of opening up to her, surrounding her with a sense of safety and peace—and no source of strength was greater than the white brick, fifteen hundred-square-foot farmhouse that she'd shared with her father all of her life.

Moving away had been the primary goal for most of her classmates while growing up in the school system that drew from a dozen rural communities, and she'd given the concept of leaving the nest a try herself while earning her bachelor's degree in English literature at the University of North Carolina in Charlotte more than thirty-five years earlier. But she was quick to discover that she needed this land in order to breathe, and she couldn't walk away from the fact that, despite her father's protestations to the contrary, he had a hard time managing their tobacco and cotton crops without her help. The amount of land devoted to those two crops had been pared back during World War II to make room for the soybeans and corn the federal government paid farmers to grow to help offset the food shortage. But after the war was over, the Gerards weren't the only ones who once again increased the acreage devoted to tobacco and cotton, two highly labor-intensive crops.

Thus, after her college graduation in 1972, she returned to Harmony, where she worked long days beside her dad, and where she also began fostering a literacy program through the town council in her spare time. As an offshoot of that program, she wrote a book review column for the community's weekly newspaper and, within a year, her column had been picked up by larger publications in Statesville, Hickory, Gastonia, Salisbury, and eventually Charlotte, an achievement that brought in an extra two or three hundred dollars every month.

In the early 1980s, when she and her father decided to phase out of both the tobacco and cotton businesses, she capitalized on her column's reputation and launched her own public speaking and private tutoring enterprises within the surrounding counties, which she continued to pursue to this day, on an increasingly smaller scale. While she was working to establish her new business in those early days, she and her father began leasing their most fertile acreage to younger local farmers, who planted sweet potatoes and corn on contract for a large canned food company and returned a percentage of each crop's revenue back to the Gerards. For a small monthly fee, those same local farmers helped Zeke maintain the rest of his land, with Zeke doing a sizable share of the work himself, despite his advancing age.

In this manner, Zoie and her father had lived in simplicity and contentment, with Zoie never believing that she'd lost anything by declining the marriage invitations of two charming gentlemen. She'd been very fond of both men, but one had wanted her to move to New York with him, and the other had been almost obsessive about siring five or six children, which Zoie would care for as a stay-at-home mom while he advanced his career. She would have enjoyed a family of her own, but she didn't think she could manage more than one or two kids—and her southern sensibilities were offended by having the dynamics of such a personal decision as childbearing dictated to her by *anyone*. The other fellow had been quite tempting, but there was absolutely *no* possibility that she could have ever lived in New York. So both men eventually gave up their pursuit of her and went their separate ways, claiming their broken hearts would never heal. But she was confident they would survive and, indeed, she ultimately learned that each man had taken a wife within a year of their respective farewells to her.

Most of her friends believed she was going to have regrets, but she felt intensely fulfilled. She was so busy with projects and plans that she often wondered how millions of American women so successfully juggled the supreme triathlon of career, husband, and children. The wisdom of her personal choices became especially noticeable to her after she indulged in the purchase of a computer system, which she and her father soon discovered not only connected them to the world in ways their neighbors tried unsuccessfully to comprehend, but also consumed every breath of free time she'd previously had up to that point.

Zoie and Zeke took instantly to the technology, and they became shameless web surfers, online shoppers, and eBay power sellers. In 2004, as a result of satellite television's expansion into their area, they celebrated their new high-speed connection, and now they only turned their computer off during thunderstorms, and even then not until the weather Web casts clearly showed cells moving into their immediate area.

One of Zoie's most exhilarating discoveries had been the world of e-books, and she went a step further by figuring out how to build her own Web site so she could post book reviews online. She also created a Web site for her father, where he highlighted items from the Farmer's Almanac and other points of interest he thought might be of value to his neighbors. But with one or two exceptions, none of those neighbors had computers. So periodically, the group of elderly men, whose families and adjacent lands dated back a century or more, would assemble at Zeke's house to share sweet ice tea and cigars while Zeke updated them on the news available in his Web site, without any of them ever once looking at his computer. Always amused at this approach, Zoie had long ago stopped trying to interfere. She adored her father, and the symbiotic cadence between parent and child left little room for disagreement or pressure on any issue.

Now, on the morning of Isaiah's call, Zoie reached Haven Hill just as the sunlight was beginning to peek over the eastern tree line on the neighboring farm. After slowly climbing the brick staircase built into the hill's southern slope, she went inside the sixteen-square-foot gazebo, which had also been constructed by her father, on the center of the hilltop. There she stretched out on one of the two wrought iron chaise lounges covered with blue and white striped cushions.

Putting Isaiah's phone call aside for the moment, she surveyed her property, looking out through the floor-to-ceiling screens on all six sides of the structure. She could see the ten forested acres to the west, which she and her dad had never cleared in order to preserve the land's texture and the natural sanctuary for wildlife. There were trees on other parts of the land as well, but only in intermittent clumps amidst the chiseled crop acreage that spread out to the north and south like a pastel patch quilt. To the east was their closest neighbor's house, the only one she could see from the hill, and Zoie watched this morning as the smoke spiraled up from the chimney of that little red brick colonial.

About three hundred yards from the northeastern base of Haven Hill, separated from the main two-lane county road by a quarter-mile long driveway of crushed seashells, was the Gerard's tidy brick ranch house, which they'd painted white in 1999 just to be different. Surrounding the entire house was an eight-foot-deep screen porch filled with braided area rugs, wicker chairs and sofas crammed with pillows, a swing suspended from the ceiling, a small dining table outside of the kitchen, and ceiling fans placed about twenty feet apart. The wraparound porch nearly doubled the living and entertaining space of the house at least nine or ten months out of the year. Even during the icy, frozen parts of winter, Zoie and Zeke often bundled up and barbecued out there, primarily because no one was around to tell them they couldn't.

Smiling, she thought again of Isaiah and wondered if he'd ever been to a place like this. She'd been researching and following the Mellington family for years and, based on what she'd seen of the Seattle area on the Internet, she doubted that he'd experienced a farm like hers anywhere close to home. Where he lived did look quite beautiful, though, from what she'd seen online.

Still, she felt sorry for the man who'd inherited the task at hand—the man her father had mentioned in passing when he'd explained the source of the letter from Seattle ten years earlier. She'd wanted to call Sinclair Mellington way back then, to tell him she knew the whole story so things would be easier for him, especially since she had some idea about the hurdles awaiting him or his messenger when the time came to contact the Whitmores in San Francisco. Her father had insisted that she wait, however, until events played themselves out. Today she'd finally been able to have that conversation, albeit with Sinclair's son.

"Please forgive me for disturbing you at such an early hour," he'd said, his deep voice helping her awaken after she'd grabbed the phone from her bedside table. "My name is Isaiah Mellington, and I'm calling from Washington—the state—on an urgent legal matter for Mr. Zeke Gerard. Is he there by any chance?"

"Yes, he is, Isaiah, but I'm sure he's still asleep." Expecting that he might be surprised by her tone of familiarity, she had proceeded with the words she'd been saving for a decade. "If this is about Abigail, you can give the information directly to me. Dad filled me in a number of years ago, so you can stop worrying about how you're going to tell me."

"You're kidding!" he said after a brief pause. "That's about the only response I hadn't anticipated." Then he'd paused again and added, "If you don't mind my asking, Zoie, what exactly *did* your father tell you?"

"Isaiah," Zoie replied, the soft southern timbre of her voice slowly elongating the three syllables of his name. "Honestly, you can relax. The North Carolina end of your responsibility is easy. I hear your concern, but believe me, I do know the story, at least *my* part of it. In fact, I'm guessing that I have a better grasp of the situation than you do, because Dad still can't mention Abby's name to this day without growing tearful. Actually, I don't think he ever stopped loving her, and he tells me that I favor her. If you come across any pictures of her, by the way—of my mother—I'd love to have one. He says they only took a few photos while they were together, but those seem to have disappeared."

Isaiah was silent for a few moments.

"Are you still there?" Zoie asked.

"Yeah. Sorry. I was just thumbing through my files again. There aren't any pictures of Abby that I can find, although I do see a couple that are supposed to be of *you*. Cute kid."

"Why thank you."

"You're most welcome. *At any rate*, all this material is spread over my hotel room in sort of a mess. It's also two o'clock in the morning here, and I'm propping myself up on this bed. So it's possible I could be overlooking some of those tiny, old-time pictures they used to take."

"That's okay. I'm sure one or two will turn up eventually. Dad tells me that Abby had a thing about tucking personal mementos away for safekeeping."

"Really? He's talked that much about her?"

"Yes, he has. You probably find that surprising, but he's been pretty open about their situation, never making up any stories about her being dead or anything. He just said she loved me so much that she went away to make certain I'd be happy. There's never been another woman in his life—ever—so he felt free to share his memories of her with me, which have all been quite beautiful. Then, when the letter from Sinclair arrived ten years ago, Dad told me the rest. The fact that she'd become a nun was a little shocking, but easier for me to handle, quite frankly, than other options would have been, such as her leaving us for another man. It helped that I was a grown woman by then too. Part of me wanted to call your father, or even Abby directly, because I really wanted to meet her. But Dad helped me understand why that wouldn't be a good idea, by explaining how and why *he'd* let her go. Since then, I've been completely at peace, knowing this day was inevitable."

Once again, no response was forthcoming from the Washington end of the line.

"Isaiah?"

"I'm here, and I don't really know what to say. I guess I'm taken a bit off guard by how calm you sound. And I must confess that the vision of Sister Abby being *in love* with someone is going to require some adjustment. So, you've managed to shed a brighter—a more intriguing—light on this ... on this *assignment*, for lack of a better word. Also, the thought occurs to me that Tess might be the one to have some pictures of Abby. Do you know about her? About Tess, I mean? She used to be known as Sister Veronica?"

"Yes, I'm well aware of her. I don't think Dad ever met her, but according to him, if Tess hadn't already been at the convent, Abby might have been persuaded to stay here with us. He doesn't think she would have headed off into such isolation if her best friend hadn't been there, no matter how forcefully she heard God calling her," Zoie declared, her voice carrying a slight but unmistakable fleck of resentment as she emphasized the last few words.

"Well, there might be more about that theory in this pile of papers, which, by the way, I hope I can hand to you personally—and which sort of brings me to the next reason for my call. Abby left a written request that you attend her wake and funeral this week, if at all possible. I realize this is short notice, but how would you feel about flying out here to Washington?"

"I'll be there, Isaiah," she answered without hesitation. "And Dad will want to come too. Knowing this would be happening at some point, he's been praying he'd live long enough to go with me. Even though he's almost eighty-five, he still takes his tractor out into the fields every day and walks three miles after breakfast. I think he's had his eye on this goal for a very long time."

"That's quite remarkable, Zoie, and I'll look forward to meeting you both. Preliminary plans are that the private viewing for the local religious community will be held on Tuesday. The public viewing will be on Wednesday afternoon and evening. Tess tells me that Abby made quite a mark on a large number of people throughout this entire valley through her work in the hospital, and they're anticipating a big crowd. Then the funeral and burial will take place on Thursday, starting at ten in the morning. I'll know more and will be able to confirm everything I've just said after we visit the mortuary later on today."

"How nice to hear that she was widely loved. I guess I'm not surprised. So, when would you like us to be there?"

"By Tuesday night or Wednesday morning, if that works for you. You'll need to fly into Spokane and, if you'll call me with your arrangements, I'll have a car meet you at the airport. Kettle Falls is a good ninety minutes or more away, and I don't want you struggling with a rental car and directions. I'm pretty sure you won't find a direct flight out here, so the day will already be a long one. I'll also book rooms for you here at the lodge."

"Thank you, Isaiah. I appreciate that. But this being only Saturday, we could probably fly out on Monday, unless you think that's too soon."

"Uh, sure! Monday would be great, if you can manage it. There isn't much to do up here, though."

"Oh, please," she said with a chuckle. "I've lived my entire life in the middle of fifty acres, where our town's population is under a thousand residents, the closest general store is five miles away, and the nearest decent movie theater is an hour's drive. So, believe me, I'll be fine. Besides, *you'll* be there, and I have lots of things I'd like to explore about my mother and the place she called home for so many years. I also want to spend some time with Tess, even though Dad will probably want to pass on that one."

"Okay, then. I'll wait to hear back from you with your flight details—and I must tell you that, despite the circumstances, I'm really looking forward to meeting you."

"I can't wait to meet you too, Isaiah. What about the San Francisco part? Have you contacted them yet?"

"No, not yet. Got any tips? Or do you know very much about the Whitmores?"

"You mean, aside from the fact that they're inconceivably wealthy? Or that my older half sister lives there? Or that they may not be as happy to hear from you as I was?"

"Well, those are good for starters," he replied. "Truthfully," he added after a brief hesitation, "I'm sort of sorry I asked. The fact that you two are sisters hadn't really occurred to me. How do *you* feel about that?"

"I'm okay with it, in theory. But Dad's been pretty vague about Abby's history in San Francisco," Zoie continued, "which leads me to believe that she shared only the basics with him about Rosa and how she came to be."

"Who's *Rosa*?" he asked.

"Oh, of course. She's probably listed as Salome in your papers. But her middle name is Rosabella—Salome Rosabella. Pretty, isn't it? I'm told that Abby's the one who named us both, and a condition of the custody agreements was that the names remained unchanged. But I think that *Salome* might have been a bit too biblical for her family, or at least that's what Dad told me. So she was called Rosa, the last we heard."

"Thanks for letting me know. This madcap scenario is awkward enough without my sounding as if I don't know what I'm doing—which I really don't, I must admit, at the risk of ruining your impression of me."

"Isaiah," she replied with a soft laugh, "I know a few things about you and your family, and I'm quite happy with my image of you. Now, I suppose I should go. My father will be up soon and, after I fill him in, we'll obviously have much to do to ready ourselves for the trip."

"All right. I'll be in touch later. And thanks again, Zoie. You've helped make this a whole lot more comfortable than I'd expected it would be."

"My pleasure, Isaiah."

"Say—one more thing before you go. Do *you* have a middle name too?"

"I do, as a matter of fact. It's Evangeline. Zoie Evangeline. Both are biblical names, like Salome's. Zoie—which is technically spelled *Z-o-e*, but Dad changed it to *Z-o-i-e* because no one was saying it right—means 'life,' and Evangeline means 'bringing good news.' Interesting, don't you think?"

"More than I could have imagined." Then he gave her both his cell number and that of the lodge. "Take care, now, Zoie Evangeline. I'll talk to you soon."

*****

As Isaiah hung up, he felt as if he'd just been talking to an old friend, and he suddenly wanted to read every word inside the folder that had seemed such an imposition only a few hours earlier. He was also fascinated by whatever magical traits Sister Abby must have been hiding that would keep Zeke Gerard so emotionally tethered to her, sight unseen, for more than half a century. He'd never known a woman who'd even come close to having such an effect on *him*.

And, as for Zoie, he tried to envision the world she'd described in Harmony, North Carolina, feeling impatient at the thought of traveling an hour just to see a movie. Indeed, Zoie's unanticipated charm was lingering. Her voice had been mesmerizing—even her laughter sounded southern—and his imagination had her raising a hanky to her face to blot away unsightly moisture from the humidity after every sentence. Looking again at the two black-and-white baby pictures of her that he'd found in the file, he studied the long, curly dark hair, the square face, electric smile, and pale eyes that were probably blue or light green, and he wondered if the adult version was going to be a disappointment.

Transferring his focus to the Salome-now-Rosa file, he thought momentarily about making the second call just to get it over with. But he decided he needed a little more time to digest his conversation with Zoie. Leaning his head back against the pillows, he began replaying everything they'd said to each other and, within a few minutes, he fell into a deep sleep, fully clothed and entirely at peace, where he remained for nearly four hours.

When he opened his eyes again at seven o'clock that same Saturday morning, he needed a few seconds to remember where he was and what he was doing there. Once the curious circumstances came back to him, he threw his legs off the bed, raked his fingers through his hair, and walked over to the suite's small kitchenette where he made fresh coffee in the miniature brewing pot. Removing a carton of orange juice from the small, below-counter refrigerator, he poured a full glass, which he carried with him into the bathroom. After a shower and shave, he dressed in a pair of clean, ironed jeans and a crème-colored, V-neck cashmere sweater pulled over a white crew neck T-shirt.

With his wet, thick, and wavy hair brushed straight back on the sides and top, he slipped his bare feet into his scuffed brown loafers, placed his empty orange juice glass beside the sink, and helped himself to a hot cup of coffee. Returning to the bed, he put his coffee on the end table and eyed the two folders. With his mood decidedly improved after his nap, and his outlook uplifted by the unforeseen anticipation about meeting Zoie on Monday, he picked up the receiver and dialed the California phone number located on the first page of his Rosa file.

*****

San Francisco from any vantage point is breathtaking. But seen from the city's posh Pacific Heights, San Francisco is positively spellbinding. A twist of historical fate was responsible for this, to some degree. When the fires from the 1906 earthquake were burning furiously out of control, destroying the downtown area and the city's more eastern neighborhoods, a decision was made to include Van Ness Avenue, a main north–south artery, as one of the roads chosen to become an offensive barrier against the fire's further spread. Many splendid Van Ness homes were subsequently sacrificed in order to save structures in neighborhoods west of the avenue, and Pacific Heights was a beneficiary of that action. What survives today is an architectural paradise, where a wealth of nineteenth-century Victorian homes and mansions remain clustered, unscathed by the earthquake and the fire's destruction, and where Van Ness Avenue is considered the neighborhood's easternmost border.

Drawn by the views from one of San Francisco's highest points, the well-to-do began building their extravagant dwellings in Pacific Heights after the cable car lines enabled access to the area from downtown in 1870. Old-money families remain prominent in the area today, but they are blended liberally with the nouveau riche, whose presence has helped develop Fillmore Street into an upscale shopping paradise in the district's approximate center. There the willing and affluent can find high-end clothing and luxury items, gift boutiques, four- and five-star restaurants, and European-inspired sidewalk cafes. The less fortunate from other parts of the city, as well as visitors from around the globe, can sip lattes from those same cafes while observing the daily procession of impeccably groomed, designer-attired Pacific Heights residents moving blithely through their snug, picturesque world.

Two lush green areas—Alta Plaza and Lafayette Park—unfold across the neighborhood's peak elevations and, aside from their dramatic vistas of San Francisco Bay and beyond, the parks also offer tennis courts, playgrounds, wooded hiking trails, sunbathing spots, and plenty of paths for pet lovers. On this October Saturday morning, one block north of Lafayette Park on Jackson Street, between Laguna and Octavia, the sun illuminated the curves of beige stone and the ivory trim on the Whitmores' immense Victorian home. As on most weekends, the neighborhood was awakening late, with the Monday-through-Friday sights of pinstriped suits and chauffeured sedans giving way to buff joggers and new mothers pushing their own baby carriages in lieu of the weekday nannies.

By contrast, inside the Whitmore residence, the atmosphere was decidedly lethargic. The wide mahogany staircase, original to the house, emptied into the foyer in crescent curves from both sides of the second-floor landing. The twelve-foot ceilinged rooms, the meandering corridors, and the large, newly renovated island kitchen and breakfast room were blueprint-perfect. But amidst the beauty and elegant features, there was a cold, hollow aura and not the slightest indication that family experiences were being shared there.

Extending out from the bay window and French doors of the breakfast room, a deep, narrow deck overlooked a garden courtyard below, which was enclosed by tall walls built out of stone. Visible over the deck railing, beyond the walls of the backyard and the rooftops of houses directly behind the property, were the forested two square blocks of Lafayette Park. On the far side of the park, the familiar, postcard-perfect skyline of San Francisco unfolded from the lower edges of Pacific Heights.

Through the windows on the front of the house, in the main living areas on the second and third floors, the view was patently different from that in the rear, invoking images of a Hollywood movie backdrop. On all but the foggiest of days, one could see from left to right the Golden Gate Bridge, the Palace of Fine Arts, and the Marina Green, to name three of the many attractions standing out as if they'd been painted into the landscape. On the far side of the Golden Gate were the jade hills of fabled Marin County—passageway to the wine country—and the quaint waterfront communities of Sausalito and Tiburon, long ago captured in colorful Gold Rush legends and myths, and still bearing much of their original nineteenth-century charm.

This unobstructed *tableau vivant* was a main contributor to the hefty seven- and eight-figure appraised values of homes in the neighborhood.

And yet, sadly, the remarkable milieu showcased through the windows was rarely the subject of interest within the Whitmore household any longer, unless a Tall Ships Regalia or some other newsworthy event was taking place out in the Bay. This residence had been at the core of Whitmore family operations since the early 1900s, and every inch of history and architectural grandeur was now ignobly taken for granted.

On this particular morning, matriarch Anabeth Whitmore was outside in the rear garden courtyard, clipping a bouquet of fresh flowers for the breakfast table. She did not expect that anyone would wish to join her for the meal, as this day appeared to be no different from any other in recent memory. Nonetheless, as long as her two middle-aged children felt as if they were entitled to unlimited, open-ended return stays here in this house every time life dealt them a blow, she held out hope that a semblance of kinship might miraculously be reborn through the sheer force of personal contact.

"I'm afraid we didn't do a very good job with them, Danny," she whispered too softly to be heard as her clippers began snapping floral stems in time with her aggravation.

She placed the last few flowers in the flat wicker basket, along with the others she'd already gathered, buttoned her sweater up under her chin to block the early chill, and sat down on a white iron loveseat facing the rear of the house. The lattice arbor over her head was covered with the same ivy that draped the yard's stone enclosure, and the clusters of perennial shade trees in the relatively small space made her feel as if she were in a protective cocoon.

She used to love entertaining out here before Danny took ill, when their bevy of friends enjoyed sharing the beauty with her. But now Mrs. Anabeth Davis Whitmore, widow of Daniel Whitmore, was living out the last act of her life in near isolation, even though both of her children were housed under the same roof with her ... again. Yes, indeed. All those weekend sightseers being driven through the neighborhood on tour buses, who never seemed to tire of ogling her family's stately quarters, were only wasting their envy on *this* address.

Her face was still porcelain smooth, partially due to a good gene pool and otherwise credited to the practiced skill of her plastic surgeon. But her short white hair had thinned so much that her pink scalp was now visible all around her head, and her eighty-four-year-old body had become plump and saggy. Her most troubling ailment was the edema in her legs and ankles, which caused her considerable discomfort day and night unless she was propped up with stacks of pillows under her knees. She was determined to keep moving, though, appreciating each moment of being alive and afraid that if she stayed in bed for more than a few hours at a time, she might never get up.

In no rush to return to the kitchen, she closed her eyes and let herself feel massaged by the garden's fragrances and the luxurious early morning silence interspersed with melodies from birds flitting from branch, to rooftop, to stone wall. She felt her breathing deepen and her pulse rate slow down as a refreshing sense of peace displaced her vexation. At that moment, nothing could have seemed more inappropriate than the cacophonous ringing of the telephone inside.

"Who on earth?" she muttered, guessing that the hour couldn't be much later than eight thirty, as she waited for Miss Euleen to answer. Euleen, now seventy-five, hadn't been a "Miss" for more than fifty years, but the African American woman had been part of the family employed by the Whitmores long before Anabeth married Danny. And no one, especially Anabeth, had ever considered dropping the prefix.

The phone did stop ringing. But instead of hearing Miss Euleen make any sort of announcement, several minutes passed and then Anabeth's daughter, Rosa, emerged through the garden-level doorway. She was covered neck to knees in a pink terrycloth robe, with pink blobs of matching slippers on her feet, her platinum blonde hair pulled back from her jet-tanned face into a knot on top of her head.

"Mother," she said, her tone one of annoyance as she shuffled across the courtyard carrying a mug of hot coffee, "do you know someone named Isaiah Mellington?"

"No, I don't. Why? Is that who so inconsiderately dialed a private home at this ungodly weekend hour?"

"Yes. And he said you'd be familiar with his name. Actually, he first asked for Daddy when Miss Euleen answered the phone. That's when she came and got me, thinking it might be a prankster or something. He obviously didn't know that Daddy's not here anymore, which made me suspicious too. In fact, I almost hung up on him. But then he asked to speak with *you* and said he was calling with an extremely urgent legal matter he insisted you'd know about. Are you *sure* his name doesn't ring a bell? Isaiah Mellington? From Seattle?"

Anabeth's eyes briefly lost their focus as her mental tapes rewound to a point of clarity in the past. Moments later, she could only muster a small squeak of recognition in response to her daughter's question. In earlier years, she'd lived in constant fear that such words would worm their way into her reality. But a long time ago—and then again after Danny died last year—she'd reassured herself that the danger had all but diminished. So why was this happening now? Why couldn't they have waited just a little longer until she was dead too? Why should she be the one left to deal with this?

"Mother!" Rosa repeated, standing sternly in front of the loveseat with her mug-free hand defiantly pressed against her hip. "I can tell by the look on your face that you *do* know him. Who *is* he?"

Still seated with the basket of flowers on her lap, Anabeth was trying to find her way back to her voice when her son, Perry, appeared on the deck above them. He had no shirt on and, as she looked through the deck railing slats, she hoped her eyes were playing tricks on her since the rest of him seemed to be naked too. He was the younger of her two children and owned the true center of her heart, although she would never say such a thing out loud. But he was, after all, a man of fifty-three and should, she hoped, begin acting his age shortly.

"Hey, you guys," he said, peering down at his mother and sister and ruffling his bed hair with both hands. "What's all the commotion? Don't people know this is Saturday morning?"

"Oh, give me a break," Rosa said in exasperation, waving him away with her free arm. "*Every* day is Saturday for you, now that you've decided work is beneath you."

"Well, isn't *this* a freedom of speech moment!" he snapped, folding his arms across his bare chest as if he'd just noticed the chilly air. "I hardly think that *you*, Miss Serial Alimony, should be throwing any stones!"

"*Please*, children," Anabeth said with all the control she could rally. "Everyone on the street will hear you again."

"Oh, crap," Perry declared. "I don't know why I even try to be sociable." Then he turned around and disappeared, his naked backside clearly visible as he departed.

Rosa dismissed him with a disgusted sniff and shifted her attention back to her mother. Lifting the flower basket from Anabeth's lap and helping her up from the loveseat, she said, "All right, Mom. We need to go inside as well, so you can tell me whatever it is that's obviously upsetting the hell out of you."

Her breathing suddenly shallow, Anabeth held on to her daughter's arm as she let herself be guided toward the house.

"Yes, Rosa—*Salome Rosabella*—I'm afraid the time has come. And I can honestly say that, for some reason, all of a sudden, I really don't give a damn."

CHAPTER SIX

"Good morning!" Tess said to Isaiah, her intonation perking up from her initial hello as soon as she heard his voice. "How did you sleep?"

"Pretty well." He'd telephoned her after leaving a message for Mrs. Whitmore and then finishing off the remnants of his sandwiches, left over from the drive the day before. "Just wanted you to know that I made the calls."

"Already?"

"Frankly, I had a very pleasant conversation with Zoie, who was quite pliable and, much to my surprise, already knew about the whole thing. She seems like a very nice person."

"I'm sure she is. Did she say whether or not her father is still alive?"

"In spades. He sounds like a rock, and he's even coming out here with her ... Tess?" he prompted a few seconds later when she didn't respond.

"Sorry. I'm here. Thought someone was at my door. So ... I'm happy that went well. What about Salome?"

"She goes by Rosa now—short for Rosabella, her middle name—something Zoie pointed out to me. Surprise again. And I think Rosa's going to be a tougher nut. I'm only guessing, but I don't believe she has a clue. And *her* father is unfortunately deceased."

"Well, that is a shame. I suppose it would have been asking too much for both calls to be easy."

"Right. I think I can handle it, though, now that the ball is rolling. And, speaking of rolling, I was wondering if there might be a way to move our mortuary visit up a little earlier today. That experience doesn't sound like it's going to be very much fun, but apart from my desire to put the duty behind us, I'd like to have this afternoon to begin reading through all this stuff you gave me. Given the circumstances, I want to know as much as possible about Abby and these two women before people start arriving in a few days."

"Good idea, and I think I can change the schedule without any difficulty. By the way, Isaiah, I do appreciate your agreeable approach to this situation, not to mention your sense of urgency."

"If you want to know the truth, Tess, I'm beginning to be fascinated, although I'm more puzzled than ever now about why Dad never briefed me."

"Something we share, to be sure."

"Hopefully I'll understand more after reading the folders."

"Yes ... Well, I'd better go call Mr. Arthur at the funeral home. How early would you like to be there?"

"As soon as we can get in."

*****

After rearranging the appointment, Tess drove herself down from Kettle Falls to the lodge. Isaiah met her in the parking lot where she climbed into the backseat of the Jag as he held the front passenger door open for her.

"Why are you getting in back there?" he asked.

"I just want to see what it feels like. You know—to be chauffeured."

"Very funny. Now, please come sit up front with me."

She obediently switched places, and Isaiah pulled out onto 395.

"How far do we have to go?" he asked her.

"Down there, about three blocks."

"What? Then why didn't we just meet *there*?"

"Because I wanted to ride in your car."

He shook his head as he watched her looking at the Global Positioning System screen. Reaching out, he pressed a couple of buttons, and when the monotone computer-generated female voice issued the order to "Enter your destination," Tess let out a startled squeak as Isaiah started laughing.

"What's *that* for?" she asked.

"That's called a GPS. It enables a satellite to know where the car is and, if I don't know how to get where I'm going, I can enter an address, and the car lady will tell me how to get there."

"You can't be serious."

"Totally. It does lots of other things too—finds places of interest nearby, or restaurants, churches, that sort of stuff."

"How about mortuaries?"

"Sure. We just—"

"Turn right at the light. We're here."

While pulling into the parking lot, Isaiah switched off the GPS unit. "Good-bye," said the female voice.

Tess looked at Isaiah and shook her head in amusement. "They even gave her manners? Well I've seen everything now."

But as they got out of the car and began walking toward the entrance, her mood sobered. "I never pictured this, you know. I mean, having things happen this way. I always thought *I'd* be the first one to die, since I'm so overweight."

Isaiah didn't know how to respond tactfully so he didn't say anything as he opened the mortuary door for her and they walked into the cool stillness of the waiting area. Mr. Arthur, the day manager, was summoned via phone by the woman seated at the receptionist desk. He appeared moments later and, after Tess introduced Isaiah, escorted them into a barren, icy room to see Abby.

Isaiah had never fully appreciated the depth of friendship between Tess and Abby. But that relationship became heartbreakingly clear to him as Tess dropped to her knees, weeping and praying in an indecipherable whisper, beside the table where her friend rested.

Not yet prepared for any official viewing, the body was covered up to the neck with a gray blanket, and what immediately struck Isaiah was the youthfulness of the woman he'd never before seen without her headpiece and veil. She had thick hair, which was surprisingly long, almost to her shoulders, and mostly white but still layered with streaks of the original glossy charcoal. Her arms were outside of the blanket, and her hands, open and flat with palms down, rested on top of her chest. Woven in and out of her fingers was a rosary of blue faceted beads, the large silver crucifix balanced on her right wrist.

In her face, though waxen and ashy, he saw a beauty he could not remember in her, and he felt an unforeseen surge of sadness rush over him. The person laid out in front of him had been a part of his life, in some small measure, for as far back as he could recall. But when his father had said, "Let's go visit Sister Abby," the tone had always been the same as, "Let's go to a movie"—nothing out of the ordinary, just a longer drive. And now, as he looked at her, he realized that, after more than fifty years of visits, he was seeing her for the first time as a woman.

Trips to Kettle Falls had been excuses to spend rare weekends alone with his father. And over the past few years, those trips had become inconvenient promises he'd made at his father's bedside shortly before he'd passed away. Now the woman they'd come to see so many times was lifeless, unable to inquire about his interests and achievements, unable to laugh at shared moments with his dad, unable to wish Isaiah a tender "good-bye until the next time." Unpredictably, he was overwhelmed by a sense that his nagging desire to be somewhere else—*anywhere* else—whenever he'd been taken to see her had resulted in his missing something extraordinarily important while they were all together.

Suddenly feeling uncomfortable in a room where there was nothing to do but stare at a dead body, he touched Tess's shoulder, and then he and Mr. Arthur helped the old woman up from her knees. When they'd escorted her to one of the outer rooms furnished with a large desk, a sofa, two matching upholstered chairs, and a counter filled with coffee, juice, and ice water, she took a seat, had a cool drink, and regained her composure. Then she calmly asked about what her friend would be wearing for the services and, more importantly, when they planned on restoring her dignity by actually putting those clothes on her.

"Soon," Mr. Arthur replied, with the stiff, rehearsed compassion understandable in his line of work. "In preparation for the private viewing by the religious community on Tuesday, Sister Mary Abigail will be in a white habit and veil already delivered by the sisters from her convent, and the rosary she's holding will be exchanged for one with white beads."

"Very good," Tess said. "I'm sure she would agree with that choice, but please get her dressed as soon as possible. I can't bear to think of her the way she is right now. Also, Mr. Arthur," she continued, opening up the large gray woven satchel she'd been hauling around, "I'd like you to find a place for this somewhere close to the casket. Maybe even inside the open lid, if it wouldn't violate any of your procedures."

With that, she produced a photograph of Abby, in a black 8" × 10" frame. Isaiah thought of Zoie's request for a picture and asked if he could take a closer look.

"Of course," Tess replied affectionately. "This is from our senior year in high school in 1943. Wasn't she lovely?"

She was, indeed. He saw a stunning young woman, her rich black hair framing chiseled cheek bones, radiant eyes even in black and white, and a long graceful neck. Once again, he felt a pull at his heart as he handed the photo across the desk to Mr. Arthur.

"I know that picture is very precious to you," Isaiah said to Tess, watching her fight back more tears, "and I understand that you'll want it returned after the funeral. But this morning Zoie said she didn't have any photographs of her mother, and she asked me if I could find one for her. So, I—"

"I think that's very sweet," she interrupted, "and I do have others besides this one. Naturally, I'd like to keep one or two, but the rest of them rightfully belong with Abby's children."

Tess then smiled gently at Isaiah and leaned over to squeeze his hand, winking at him and tilting her head almost imperceptibly in Mr. Arthur's direction. Isaiah shifted his eyes, without moving his head, to look where she was directing him. There he saw the wide-eyed expression of shock replacing the frozen reserve on Mr. Arthur's face as he fiddled with some paperwork. The reference to "Abby's children" had been natural and inadvertent, but the words had clearly not been lost on Mr. Arthur, who must have been bursting with questions but dared not open his mouth. For the next few moments, Isaiah and Tess sat very still, looking straight at one another, and doing all they could to keep from laughing.

*****

Isaiah followed behind Tess as she drove her car from the lodge back to the yellow frame house in Kettle Falls. Once he'd seen her safely home, he made sure she had his cell phone number and then continued driving north on 395 another five miles to Barney's. The rustic restaurant and bar, in business since 1953, was just on the other side of a suspension bridge that towered over Lake Roosevelt, a 130-mile long body of water created when the Coulee Dam was built across the Columbia River in 1941. Named for President Franklin Delano Roosevelt, who was serving his third term in office at the time, the lake became the largest recreational feature in the Roosevelt National Recreation Area. Offering boating, fishing, swimming, camping, and hiking opportunities, not to mention tours of Fort Spokane and the Coulee Dam itself, the lake continued to afford—almost seventy years later—a majestic opportunity for residents and tourists alike to experience more of the Pacific Northwest's well-guarded treasures.

From a cushioned, burgundy leather booth inside Barney's, Isaiah looked out on the bridge and on the evergreens trimming the edges of the lake's brilliant protected waters. He was the only patron in the restaurant, although he could hear a few voices in the bar at the far end. And as he studied again the beauty outside the window—the air untouched by chemicals, the contrasting blue shadings of the October sky, the water, and the surrounding mountains, all distinct and unsoiled—he understood a little more clearly how someone could be lured into abandoning any other locale and lifestyle in favor of this one. Visions of his father also came into play as he recalled the many occasions when the two of them shared one of these booths together over platters full of chicken-fried steak.

Returning his attention to the menu, he realized how hungry he was. After leaving Tess last night, he'd stopped at a small restaurant near the lodge but had only picked at his food. Then he'd finished a beer while talking to Zoie. Otherwise, he hadn't put anything in his stomach for more than twenty-four hours, except for his coffee, juice, and sandwich remnants before leaving the lodge with Tess that morning. Looking down at his watch, he saw that the time was nearly one thirty in the afternoon.

"Hi! My name is Ava. What can I get for you today?"

The question was delivered by a sultry voice and, as his eyes followed the brown and white uniform upward, he discovered first a petite frame with a tiny waist accentuated by a white apron. Next he came upon full breasts trying to spill out from inside the uniform's brown buttoned bodice. And then he saw a cherubic face, with milky skin, round ruddy cheeks, and hazel eyes, all framed by a flounce of golden curls pushed back with a black headband. Perfectly manicured not-too-long nails were painted a pale, shimmering pink, and slender hands held her pen and pad at the ready. He guessed she was somewhere in her thirties, but he was notoriously bad at such estimates. Besides, he was completely thrown off his mark by the unexpected appearance of this beautiful young woman, in *Barney's*, of all places.

"I'm sorry. What did you say?" he asked.

"Well, let's see," she replied playfully. "I said, 'hi, my name is Ava,' and then I think I inquired about what you'd like to eat. Actually, that's probably not exactly what I said, but there aren't many variations on that theme in a place like this."

"No, I imagine there aren't," Isaiah responded, appreciating her good nature and still amazed that she was standing in front of him. "Are you new here, Ava? I don't remember seeing you before."

She smiled and tapped the end of her pen against her pad. "That's because you don't live around here. But nice try."

"Oh? And how can you be so sure?"

"Because if you lived here, your car—and you, too, naturally—would have been noticed."

"Ah, the car. It always seems to get top billing," he said, feeling a little flushed as he leaned back in the booth. "Well, I guess you're right. And now that you mention it, I *don't* live here, which is not my fault, let me hasten to add."

"Of course it's not," she said with a grin. "So, I won't hold it against you. To be completely fair with you, though, I've only been in the area for about a year myself."

"Really? Where'd you come from, and what brought you way out into this valley?"

"I was born and raised in Spokane. But when I was a kid, my family used to spend several weeks each summer at Kettle Falls Campground, over there across the bridge on Lake Roosevelt," she said, pointing through the window with a lean, toned arm. "And I always loved it. So, last year, when things … well, when I decided to relocate, this was the first place I thought of. Now," she said, straightening her posture and shifting her body back into business mode, "I suppose I'd better find out what you want to order before I get into trouble."

"Right. We certainly wouldn't want that to happen. And after careful consideration, I think I'll have your chicken-fried steak dinner, with a salad—French dressing—and a beer. Whatever you have on draft."

"Would you like your salad first or with your meal?"

"First."

"Coming right up, sir."

"*Isaiah*. Please, call me Isaiah, Ava. I've never been very good with the 'sir' thing."

"Sure … Isaiah," she added, trying out the name on her lips before smiling again and heading for the kitchen.

Whew, he thought after she left, lifting the two folders off the seat beside him and onto the tabletop. *How am I supposed to concentrate now?* Trying to usher his priorities back into place, he thought initially about starting with Zoie's story, because he found her the most compelling, not to mention friendly. But he decided to proceed chronologically and begin with Rosa. Turning past the first page containing her name, address, birth date, and phone number, he began reading a handwritten note dated September 19, 1971. Just then he felt his cell phone vibrating against his waist. When he removed the phone from his belt holster, the information flashing on his caller ID screen cut short his flirtatious thank you to Ava, who had walked over with his salad and beer.

"Mother!" he exclaimed after hurriedly pushing the TALK button. "Oh, my *God*! You must be ready to kill me!"

"Well, I'm not sure what I would gain by that, but the thought *has* crossed my mind over the last twenty-four hours. I'm happy to hear your voice, though, since I thought you might already be dead."

"Please forgive me! There's absolutely no excuse for my not calling you. But after I got to Tess's house last night, circumstances sort of carried me off my normal track. I am *so* sorry."

"I know. And it's okay. I'm better now. So make up for it by telling me what's going on. How's Tess doing?"

"Remarkably well, to be honest. But you're going to be blown away by what I've learned!" He lowered his voice and dropped his head down to keep his words from traveling across the empty room, recalling Tess's paranoia about the town's gossip mill. "Dad knew all about this, and he arranged for me to be in charge. But why he never said anything is beyond me."

"Said what about what?"

"You'd better sit down, Mother. How's this for openers? Sister Abby had *two children*!"

He wasn't surprised at the pause, but after about ten seconds, he thought the call might have been dropped.

"Mother?"

"Yes, Isaiah, I'm here."

"Pretty astonishing, isn't it?"

"You say she has two ... two children?"

"Right. Two daughters, by two different men, no less. One lives in San Francisco, and the other is in North Carolina. Can you believe it? Part of the reason I was asked to come here is to get them both to attend the wake and funeral this week. The girl, or I should say woman, in North Carolina already knew about Abby and wasn't any problem. But the other one is going to be a challenge. I don't think she even has an inkling yet. So, if she ever calls me back, I'll be the lucky one who gets to tell her that her biological mother became a nun."

"I see," Sarah replied, her voice cutting in and out because of what Isaiah assumed was the shaky connection in the mountains. "Well, you obviously have your hands full, dear. Will you be seeing Tess again anytime soon?"

"Probably not until tomorrow, or maybe not until Monday. We just finished making all the arrangements at the mortuary a little while ago. Why?"

"Oh, nothing. Please give her my regards."

"I will—and I promise to check in with you at least once a day."

"That will certainly be appreciated. How long do you think you'll have to stay out there?"

"Until next weekend, I guess. The funeral's on Thursday, and I'm not sure what all will be involved once Zoie and Rosa get here."

"Of course. Zoie and Rosa."

"Abby's daughters."

"Yes, Isaiah. I *heard* you."

Her sharp edge was evident, but he couldn't blame her for being aggravated with him. "Are you all right, Mother?"

"Perfectly fine, and thank you for asking. But I'd better let you go now."

"Okay. I'll call you tomorrow."

"Very good. Take care, Son."

"Love you, Mother." But she was gone before the words were out of his mouth. Feeling buried by guilt for having neglected to call her, he was relieved to see Ava approaching the booth with his chicken-fried steak platter as he put his cell phone down beside his untouched salad.

"Uh-oh," she said, noting his clean silverware still resting on his napkin. "Would you like me to keep this under the warmer for a while?"

"That's probably a good idea. In fact, I have a lot of work to do this afternoon, and I think I'd prefer to do it here rather than back at my hotel room. Would you mind if I take up space for a few hours?"

"Not at all. My shift doesn't end until six. Just let me know whenever you're ready for this steak."

"Will do." And then on an impulse, as she was turning to leave, he added, "Ava, are you doing anything after you get off work?"

She stopped and looked back at him, his platter balanced on her left arm, her right hand cupped at her waist as her hip slanted upward with an attitude.

"I don't know. Why?"

"I was just wondering if you'd let me buy you a drink."

Her smile opened easily as her body language softened, and her blonde head of curls took on a halo effect from the backlighting of the kitchen glare behind her.

"Sure," she said. "I think I'd like that—especially if you'll take me for a spin in that amazing car of yours."

"I guess that could be arranged," he replied, trying to remember if he'd left any garbage on the passenger seat.

"Great! Meet you down in the bar a little after six."

He wanted to say more, but two new sets of customers came in. Ava welcomed them, seamlessly shifting her attention away from Isaiah and back into her work.

Gratified to know he'd have company later on—someone he could talk with who would help get his mind off the peculiar circumstances unfolding all around him—he took several bites of salad and a dinner roll, and drank a few sips of beer. Then he refocused his attention on the Rosa folder, reading the handwritten page again, which had been fastened by a rubber band to a stack of a half dozen journals.

September 19, 1971

My eldest child, Salome Rosabella Whitmore, was born on July 12, 1948. Salome means "peace," and Rosabella means "a fair rose"—and I still pray each and every day that her life has had an abundance of both.

When I was a young girl dreaming about love and being grown up, I imagined the birth of a baby to be a miraculous, joyful occasion—and, for a short time after this baby was born, I was allowed to feel that miracle. But I wasn't prepared for the part about growing up, nor was I ready to hear God's voice calling me through the misery that was to follow.

If only I could have been certain about His summons before the whole cycle began spinning in the first place ...

CHAPTER SEVEN

September 1947

Abby stepped off the trolley bus at the corner of Franklin and Washington Streets in San Francisco's Pacific Heights neighborhood. After carefully folding her September 15 issue of *Life* magazine, which she'd been reading during the ride from her residence hotel, she slipped the magazine inside her handbag next to her steno pad. Then she looked again at the directions Caroline had written down for her on an index card.

The Whitmore residence, where she was headed to cover a major society party on her own for the first time, was one block north and two blocks west of where she stood. So she opened her umbrella to shelter her new dress and coat as much as possible from the fog and light drizzle that seemed to have blanketed the city almost continuously since her arrival six weeks earlier. Her co-workers at the *Chronicle* and the girlfriends she'd made at the hotel all complained incessantly about the weather, but Abby loved the rain and the acoustic magic of fog that cushioned the clamor of city sounds and reminded her so much of her beloved Seattle.

The many similarities between the two cities had been an unexpected and welcome surprise. Aside from the weather, there was San Francisco Bay, which evoked memories of Puget Sound. And the landscape that put neighborhoods and hotels on steep inclines like Nob and Russian Hill was so much like Seattle's, stirring up images of a walk she'd taken with Sinclair on top of Queen Anne Hill that past July. Seattle's fog had been so dense that evening that they couldn't see from their shoes to the corner.

Sometimes the cities' parallels were comforting to her and kept her from feeling homesick. At other times, as she would look out the front window of her two-room apartment—or on evenings like this one, as she walked alone beneath her umbrella—her sense of longing and loneliness was almost unbearable. But this job at the *Chronicle* had been a godsend, and she was careful to remind herself, whenever she felt moods of melancholy threatening to overtake her, that she had been immensely blessed.

*****

After leaving Lady of the Valley in July of 1945, she had returned to the University of Washington and her journalism studies in Seattle, taking as full a course load as the school would allow so she could make up for the time she'd spent at the convent. She'd contacted Sinclair shortly after starting her first semester back, intent on repaying him for her train fare a little each month. They'd quickly become friends.

Although their families were from dramatically different social and economic circles, Abby was bright and well-read and had no trouble keeping up with Mellington conversations. More importantly, though, the trauma surrounding Abby's first meeting with Sinclair in Kettle Falls had created a bond between them and had served as a bridge between their backgrounds. His parents became quite fond of her as well, and she spent many comfortable evenings sharing dinner with them in their stately Queen Anne home.

"They think we're a couple," Sinclair said to her several months after her introduction to them.

"Well, we are, sort of. A couple of great pals. Right?"

"Right. But, Abby, have you ever thought—"

"No," she'd interrupted. "I can't. Please, Sinclair. Don't do or say anything that might change what we have."

"All right," he'd answered, although his unwillingness to look at her as he spoke let her know that he would have preferred a different response. Nonetheless, he'd remained true to his word and had made no further mention of moving their relationship to another level, agreeing to let her set the pace.

In addition to her maxed-out course load, Abby had been working at two jobs. The fact that she was living at home with her parents in the University District, just a short bus ride away from the campus, had helped with her budget. But she felt obligated to contribute money for food, and she paid for all of her own clothing and shoes, not to mention year-round necessities, such as coats, boots, gloves, and scarves—and umbrellas frequently left on buses or elsewhere.

Adding in the costs of tuition, books, and other expenses that seemed to pop up daily, her finances were pushed beyond the wherewithal of a single part-time job. So she worked as a secretary in the university's admissions office for four hours each afternoon during the week, and she waited tables at a popular student hangout on "The Ave" on three rotating weeknights plus one night on the weekend. The rest of her time was spent in class, in the library, or studying at home, leaving increasingly rare opportunities for time with Sinclair, while also testing the limits of her physical and mental stamina.

When she was nearing the end of her second semester with that schedule, the Mellingtons invited her over to their home for dinner one Sunday afternoon. The meal and conversation were both extraordinary, as always, and when the table had been cleared, Abby gathered with Sinclair and his parents in the library, in front of the radiating fireplace that also opened into the living room on the opposite side. On a mahogany coffee table in front of the raised hearth was a silver tray containing four cut crystal brandy snifters and a matching decanter filled halfway with a tawny liquid that reflected light from the crackling logs burning a few feet away.

"Dad has something to share with you, Abby," Sinclair said as he poured a small amount of brandy into each snifter and then replaced the teardrop-shaped stopper on the decanter.

"Oh?" she replied, taking her glass from him and pretending to sip.

"Yes I do," Mr. Mellington said. "Sinclair tells me that you're going to kill yourself with the schedule you're keeping, between your university studies and the two jobs you're working. Is that right?"

"Actually, I'm holding up quite well," she answered, sending a sharp glance in Sinclair's direction. "But I do appreciate your concern."

"Of course," Mr. Mellington said. "And we wouldn't want to interfere. I have an old college buddy, though, who is the production manager at the *Examiner*, and he tells me that he's looking for a part-time assistant. With your journalistic aspirations, I thought I should at least mention the opportunity to you. I'm not sure how much you're earning in your two jobs, but I believe there's a good chance you could equal or exceed that amount in this one part-time job, with fewer total hours. Do you think you might be interested?"

Abby could not believe what she was hearing and was only slightly annoyed at the widening grin on Sinclair's face.

"Mr. Mellington, I don't know what to say. I've been sending letters to every department at the *Examiner* for months, trying to find some sort of work there. This is amazing, and *of course* I would be interested! How can I ever thank you?"

"Save your thanks, Abby," he said, "until the job is officially yours. Then we'll celebrate. Meanwhile, give my friend Adam Dresney a call tomorrow to set up an interview—and good luck!" he added, clinking his brandy glass against hers with one hand and sliding a business card across the coffee table with the other.

The next week was something of a blur for her as she went through the interview process, secured the job, and then put her notice in at both the admissions office and the restaurant. She was going to miss those people, *but not all that much*, she thought.

Her employment at the *Examiner* continued throughout the balance of her undergraduate work, part time during school months and full time during the summer of 1946. While the production department was where she spent a good percentage of her time, Adam and his counterparts on the management team began rotating her through other functional areas as well, giving her valuable exposure and introducing her to a variety of reporters. Several of the reporters began to mentor her and take her along with them when they covered events around the city, even letting her draft stories with increasing frequency, which were subject to their sometimes brutal critiques.

But she learned quickly in this apprenticeship and responded favorably to input. More importantly, her eagerness to both please and achieve endeared her to those who worked with her and caused them to be genuinely interested in contributing to her development. Consequently, given her professional growth and the quality of her work, she was hoping that there might be an offer for a permanent position forthcoming after her graduation. But although everyone assured her that she was welcome to stay on in her current status, there were no regular salaried positions opening up in the foreseeable future.

Still optimistic in May of 1947, and knowing that she'd be working full time anyway in her present capacity during the summer following her graduation in less than a month, she decided to hold onto the job rather than look for something else. *Besides, where would I go?* she thought.

"Perhaps a staff position will become available in the fall," Sinclair said, while they were discussing her situation over a hamburger and fries one night. "I could talk to Dad and see if he might be able to nose around through Adam."

"No, I'd rather you didn't say anything. They all know what I'm looking for, and I trust them. But thanks for offering. You're such a dear, as always."

She suspected that he had ignored her request, however, when Adam called her into his office right before Memorial Day, just one week ahead of her commencement ceremony at the university, which was scheduled for June 7.

"Have a seat, Abby," Adam said, removing a stack of books and papers from the only extra chair in the cluttered room. He then sat down at his small wooden desk, folded his hands on a pile of file folders, and smiled at her. His face looked like a caricature, with his large brown eyes and dark bushy eyebrows widely set beneath a hairline that didn't exist anymore.

A tall, narrow window behind him was covered with a gray metal Venetian blind that was pulled up at a crooked angle and anchored at the window's midpoint, with the bottom edge of the blind dipping down haphazardly to the right. A murky light from the rain-drenched afternoon seeped in through the blind's open slats and the exposed bottom window pane, while a soft buzz from the ceiling's florescent light offered up background noise.

Abby thought the scene would be great in a movie or a novel, perhaps one about a haggard reporter trying to sell his editor on the merits of a story centered on local government corruption and greed, maybe even a murder—and then she smiled back at him, keeping the fictional imagery to herself.

"I asked to speak with you," he continued, "because I know you've been hoping for a permanent job once you graduate, and an opportunity has been brought to my attention."

Her heart rate abruptly accelerated with anticipation, and she realized that she didn't care at all if Sinclair had broken his promise about not saying anything.

"I do think the job will be perfect for you" he continued, "at least as your first staff position, and I feel obligated to tell you about it, even though there's one problem with it."

His tone was troubling, but she couldn't imagine any problem big enough to derail this moment. "Why? What job is it?"

"The *what* isn't the issue, Abby, because the opening is for an associate staff reporter on the city's society pages."

She could not believe what she was hearing. Post–World War II society had become a bustling business in response to the economy's positive upturn and the lingering jubilance over the war's end. Society coverage had expanded from a single short column into an entire section of the newspaper, and there were few better ways to become knowledgeable about the city's issues and luminaries than being assigned to cover major social events. *What could possibly be wrong with that?*

"The issue," Adam continued, "is the *where*."

"I don't understand."

"No, you don't. That's because I haven't told you yet that the job opening is with the *San Francisco Chronicle*."

"Excuse me?"

"The job is *in* San Francisco."

She didn't know what to say as she stared back at him, his balding head framed by the window and crooked metal blind behind him.

"Ah-ha!" he said with a broad, warm smile. "I see that we've finally found a way to make you stop talking,"

"I'm sorry, Adam. You've completely thrown me. Why on earth would someone in San Francisco be interested in *me* for such a position?"

"Because I gave you a fabulous reference, that's why."

"But how did the subject even come up in a conversation?"

"Abby, our news business may cover the world, but the internal network we create in the process is really very small and tight. Notices come in every week, sometimes daily, about available jobs in cities of all sizes across the country. When I saw this one, I immediately thought of you and gave them a call. Although I hate to lose you, I believe this is an opportunity for you to learn and grow in the business, and I'm hopeful that, if it works out, we'll get you back here one day."

She nodded and whispered "thank you" as an overwhelming sense of trepidation stopped the thrill and excitement from coming through.

"If you're interested," Adam continued, "the society editor—a woman by the name of Caroline Potrero—is waiting to hear from you to set up an interview. I've already received approval to cover your train fare and lodging for the trip. So what do you think?"

"I'm not *sure* what to think, frankly. I left Seattle once before, several years ago, and that didn't turn out very well for me. The idea of leaving again—especially since this is so sudden—has pushed me a bit off balance. What do *you* think, Adam?"

"Naturally, the decision is completely yours, but I have to say that this is a set of circumstances you won't likely see again anytime soon. I wish I could tell you that something was going to open up for you here, and you never know. At the moment, however, there's nothing on the horizon, and this plum in San Francisco will undoubtedly be plucked quickly by someone else if you hesitate too long."

"Well," she said after a quiet moment, "I'm sure you're right about that. And I suppose I have nothing to lose by at least going down there for an interview."

"Precisely." He turned to look at the two-foot-square monthly calendar that hung from a nail on the wall to his right. "Let's see. A week from tomorrow is your graduation. How would you feel about taking the train to San Francisco the next day? That would be Sunday, June 8. You could be there for an interview by Monday afternoon, or Tuesday morning at the latest."

"I guess that would be okay. Not sure how my parents are going to feel about this, though, or how ..." She stopped herself from saying Sinclair's name. After all, he was just a friend.

* * * * *

At the end of a whirlwind month following her interview, Abby was settled into her furnished two-room apartment in San Francisco, in the Women's Residence Hotel on Jones Street, a four-story white stucco structure that took up most of the block. Although her apartment was small and identical in layout to all the others in the hotel, she had managed to add personal touches that made the place feel like home, an accomplishment she had worried would be impossible when she'd first been shown the uninspiring quarters.

Her apartment, like all the others, had a large bay window in the living area, a feature that added much needed floor space and light. Included as part of that same room was an indented alcove kitchenette with a two-burner stove, a white porcelain half sink, and a refrigerator underneath the four-foot-long stretch of countertop finished with tiny white ceramic tiles. A row of three shallow cupboards was mounted above this arrangement, and a two-panel curtain was gathered onto a rod that extended across the alcove opening, to close off the kitchenette when not in use. Just outside the alcove, against the wall, was a small chrome dinette table with two matching chrome chairs sporting yellow vinyl seat cushions.

The first day Abby was there, she'd rearranged the room's other furniture to create a better sense of balance and coziness. She pushed the two armchairs into the bay window space and placed them at slight angles, with the room's sole end table in between. The room's only electric shaded lamp was centered on that end table and plugged into the room's only electrical outlet on the wall next to the bay window. Then she pushed the brown sofa into the center of the room, with the sofa facing the bay to form a conversation area with the two armchairs. The door to the apartment was behind the sofa, and the kitchen alcove was to the right of the door. So whenever she was snuggled on the sofa with a novel from the library or a new *Life* magazine, the front door and the poor excuse for a kitchen were out of sight, leaving the bay window as her view, with the light streaming in to soothe her.

The apartment's tiny bedroom, which had a narrow sash window centered on the outside wall, was thankfully at least a separate room with an actual door. But the space was filled to capacity with only three pieces of furniture. This configuration left scarcely enough room to walk without stubbing a toe. The double bed, with both a headboard and footboard fashioned out of chrome, was pushed up against the window where the headboard blocked out most of the light. There was one small bedside table in the corner and a three-drawer dresser with an attached oval mirror on the wall facing the foot of the bed. Abby measured a scant twenty inches of walking space separating those two pieces of furniture. And the apartment's only closet, which was big enough to hold about a half dozen items plus her coat, was also in this room, along with access to the microscopic bathroom equipped with a miniature sink, a toilet, and a shower in which Abby could barely turn around without bumping her elbows.

Four blocks away on Geary Street, at a furniture shop owned by an elderly couple that reminded her of her parents, she found two inexpensive three-shelf bookcases, each three feet high by five feet wide. She also purchased four large and highly functional oil lamps with dark green frosted glass bases, as well as a dark wood coat rack with several branches on which to hang things. When the man who owned the shop personally delivered her new items the next day, he helped her place one of the bookcases up against the back of the sofa. They put the second bookcase on the wall to the right of the sofa, in line with the kitchen alcove and the dinette table. The coat rack was positioned to the left of the door as one entered the apartment. Two of the oil lamps were set on top of the bookcase behind the sofa; the third was placed on the bedroom dresser to the left of the mirror; and the fourth was centered on the bedside table.

Privacy roller shades were mounted inside the frames of the bay window in the living room and the sash window in the bedroom, while thick folds of gathered sheer ivory drapery panels were hung on wrought iron rods in front of the bay window shades, adding acoustic softness and diffusing the outside light when the shades were open.

Several weeks after Abby left Seattle, four large boxes that her parents had helped her pack were delivered. The night they arrived, she unwrapped a collection of framed family photographs, along with some of Tess and a few of their friends. In the other boxes were a blue and white quilt for her bed, a half dozen decorative pillows, and several crocheted and knitted throws. Once she'd arranged the familiar, treasured items throughout her apartment, she finally felt a sense of order and normalcy return, in tandem with a resurgence of energy to begin her life's new adventure in earnest.

*****

The fall of 1947 had spawned an exceptionally intense social and political schedule. For starters, Mayor Roger Lapham's plan to remove the famed and fabled cable cars from the city, replacing them with buses, had fueled a firestorm of public opinion. A fellow by the name of Friedel Klussman, who was passionate about San Francisco's unique cultural history, found himself backed by thousands of supporters as he organized a ballot initiative for the November election that was designed to save the cable cars.

Ordinarily, Caroline would have attended the Whitmore event in partnership with Abby, but instead she had to cover a save-the-cable-car rally and fundraiser. So she gave Abby fifteen dollars to purchase a new dress and raincoat, understanding that her protégé needed something more appropriate and stylish to wear than the few skirts and sweaters Caroline had observed being rotated every two or three days. The girl had even admitted to owning her dark gray raincoat, with the worn collar and fraying cuffs, since her freshman year in high school.

Caroline Potrero had turned out to be not only an impressive business woman, reporter, and editor, but also a kind and generous friend and mentor, which wasn't the first impression left by her blunt, earthy manner. She was thirty-six years old, about five foot nine and thus a good five inches taller than Abby. Her physique was stocky but curvy, and her thick auburn hair was typically wrapped in a chignon and often hidden beneath one of the stylish wide-brimmed hats she collected to complement her always-in-fashion wardrobe. Almond-shaped indigo blue eyes peered over the tiny round lenses of her wire-rimmed glasses that usually rested on the bridge of her nose, unless she was holding them in her hand and jabbing at the air with them to help punctuate a point she was making.

Abby had grown extraordinarily fond of Caroline and trusted her instincts, but she wasn't at all certain that this latest decision to dispatch her to the Whitmore event alone was in the best interests of all concerned, most particularly her own.

"You'll have a fabulous time," Caroline had said one evening two weeks earlier, "and the experience will introduce you to a number of influential people who will prove helpful on future assignments."

The two women were having dinner together at a secluded downtown restaurant on Maiden Lane, which was patronized by Seattle's power crowd, who Caroline wanted Abby to observe in action. They had finished their first martini cocktails and a round of appetizers when Caroline first informed Abby of the change in plans that would send Abby to the Whitmores' by herself.

"Honestly," she insisted, "you have nothing to worry about. I have complete faith in you."

"But I don't think I've been in this town long enough to handle such an important event without you," Abby said, taking a sip of the second cocktail just placed in front of her. "I've been following the press notices about the home for disabled veterans that the Whitmores will be launching, and everyone who's *any*body is going to be there."

"Undoubtedly. This fundraiser is quite the noble cause, and Marcella Whitmore is certainly the one to get it done. Never mind," she added, lowering her voice, "that there's been not a shred of prior evidence indicating a single vein of philanthropic blood in *Admiral Whitmore's* starched body."

"Caroline!" Abby whispered, looking around to see if any of the other patrons had picked up on the remark. Speaking ill of luminaries who had the authority to grant interviews and access to information was a taboo drilled into her since her first day on the job, especially in any sort of public setting.

"Please forgive me, dear," Caroline said. "You caught me in a moment of weakness."

"Doesn't sound as if you like him very much."

"He's an arrogant, boastful, self-righteous prig."

Abby smiled and relaxed into the high-back red velvet dining chair. "But other than that, he's a prince, right?"

Caroline returned the smile and took another drink of her martini. "Other than that, he's a cad, and so is his son, Daniel."

"Oh, I see—and you want to send me into this den of wolves by myself?"

"Marcella will take care of you. I talked to her and told her about my conflict with the Klussman rally, which she thinks is just as important. She's looking forward to meeting you."

"You two are friends?"

"We've grown to know each other over the years and have developed a mutual respect. I'd never tell her this, of course, but I think she's a saint for putting up with the men in her life."

"I thought the son was a war hero," Abby said, leaning in across the table and doing her best to keep her words from traveling. "Isn't that why the new veteran's home is being sponsored in the first place? In honor of Daniel's service in Europe?"

"That's the story. And Marcella is his mother, so who am I to muddy the image? She honestly *does* care, though, about the veterans who have no place else to go, and this project is extremely ambitious. She deserves a thorough, positive piece that will create awareness of what she's trying to do. The city's bluebloods will be at the Whitmores' on September 27 with their money, but Marcella is also hoping to attract volunteers and people of lesser means who might want to help as the project begins to develop. And I believe you're the perfect person to give the story the proper balance."

"Well, thank you ... I think," Abby said, following suit as Caroline raised her glass in the air, offering a toast to confidence, journalism, and fresh opportunities.

"You'll be fine," Caroline added, turning her attention to her menu. "Just fine. Trust me."

*****

As Abby walked the last half block from the bus stop toward the Whitmore house, she was drawn to the lights and music mingling with a din of voices coming from the beige stone mansion midway up the street on the left. She double-checked the address on her index card, as if her destination weren't already obvious, and then she ascended the steps to the home's deep, covered front porch. Before ringing the doorbell, she closed her umbrella, shook off the excess mist, and placed the handle over a hook on the overflowing umbrella stand. Then she removed her mirrored compact from her handbag for one final look at her reflection.

Her thick, silky black hair fell just above her shoulders and held up amazingly well in this weather with her new pageboy cut. The top was combed over from a side part and fastened near her right ear with a black barrette dotted with rhinestones. The ends of her fresh haircut curved under ever so slightly and moved with a bounce whenever she turned her head. Her fair, flawless skin was brightened with a touch of pink rouge blended into her cheeks. Her lips were filled in with a pale cherry color, and her emerald eyes were surrounded by long, dense black lashes that required nothing manmade to make them enviable.

Replacing her compact in her bag, she unbuttoned her raincoat and ran her hands over the skirt of her new light teal long-sleeved dress. The bodice crisscrossed in soft pleats around her bustline above fabric that smoothed and narrowed over her thin waist and then pulled asymmetrically into a single draping front pleat that fell with the rest of the skirt to a point several inches below her knees. Her black pumps coordinated with her black handbag, but other than the barrette in her hair, she wore no jewelry or adornments.

This is who I am, she thought, *and I pray to God that it will be good enough to get me through whatever is waiting on the other side of this threshold.*

Shortly after she pressed the bell button, the door was opened by a gray-haired, dark-skinned man dressed in a black-and-white uniform. He was massive, well over six feet, and broad about the shoulders and arms. The two stared at each other for a moment and then they both smiled.

"Hello," she said. "My name is Abigail Ryan, and I'm a reporter with the *Chronicle*. I believe Mrs. Whitmore is expecting me."

"Yes, of course, Miss Ryan." His large brown eyes seemed to twinkle as he gestured for her to enter. "Please, may I take your coat?"

"Oh, sure. Thank you. I left my umbrella outside, since it looks like that's what everyone else has been doing."

"Yes, ma'am," he said, the twinkle now paired with a grin. "Everyone brings one, and everyone leaves with one, but not always the *same* one."

"I was wondering about that."

"No one ever seems to worry too much about which is which."

"Thanks. I appreciate the tip," she said, slipping out of her coat, which was already in his hands. "And what is *your* name, sir?"

The gentleness on the face of such a Goliath of a man was compelling, and he seemed surprised that she was even asking.

"Most people call me Mister Ben, Miss Ryan. Now, if you'll just make yourself comfortable on that settee over there, I'll let Mrs. Whitmore know you're here."

As he turned and left through a side door, she did not sit down but instead took notice of where she was standing. Twin staircases curved upward on opposite sides of the foyer, coming together on a second-floor landing that towered above her. Over her head hung an immense crystal and brass chandelier that looked like ones she had seen in pictures from the Russian palaces she'd studied in her high school World History class. Straight in front of her, between the staircases and behind a pair of closed, carved French doors, she heard swells of voices, laughter, and music.

Mounted on the wall at the base of the staircase to her right was a rectangular gold framed mirror that must have been fifteen feet high and about six feet wide. Almost the entire foyer was reflected in the glass, not the least of which was Abby's own image, looking small and insignificant in her new dress and pageboy haircut. She had come here tonight to do her job. But as she saw herself in that mirror, she had the strangest sense that when she'd walked through this home's front door she had somehow crossed into another world.

Unexpectedly swept with a rush of foreboding, she thought about leaving, about paying attention to her instincts that warned of something creeping up behind her again. But before she could act on her intuition, the pair of carved French doors swung open, and two people swished toward her.

"Abigail! What a pleasure to meet you! I'm Marcella Whitmore, and this is my son, Danny."

"How do you do," Abby said twice as she robotically shook each of their hands.

Marcella was stunning, much thinner and more compact than Abby had envisioned for a woman who had to be at least in her midforties. She wore a sleek and flowing ankle-length gown in a pale gold satin. A shoulder cape in the same fabric was gathered softly and secured to the dress just above the outside curve of each breast with starburst pins of clear sparkling crystals.

Marcella's hands and arms up to her elbows were covered in black satin gloves, and around her right wrist was what appeared to be a diamond cuff bracelet that stood out brilliantly against the black satin. The bracelet matched her teardrop earrings, which also looked like they might be diamonds, dangling and twinkling next to the line of her jaw. Pulled back from her face, her platinum hair was twisted and braided around the crown of her head, and shiny red lipstick outlined her broad smile.

"Caroline told me all about you, Abby," Marcella gushed. "But she neglected to mention how lovely you are."

Recalling the single black barrette in her own hair, and her new dress that had seemed so perfect a few minutes ago but now seemed almost dowdy, Abby felt anything but lovely. And what had happened to her voice? Where were her words? How could she get out of this?

"As you know, we have a large number of guests here tonight," Marcella continued without taking a breath. "So Danny will be your escort, showing you around, introducing you to everyone, and filling you in on the essentials of what we'd like to have covered in the article. My husband, Alan—Admiral Whitmore—will be addressing the group later on, and you'll want to take notes while he's speaking. And your newspaper's photographer is already here, so I assume the two of you will be coordinating your efforts. Otherwise, I do hope you'll make yourself comfortable. Help yourself to food, if you like, and to a cocktail, if you wish. Caroline always does, and we certainly don't mind. Now, I must really return to my guests. Danny, she's all yours."

With that, Marcella Whitmore floated out of the foyer, and Abby turned her focus for the first time to Marcella's son. He was nearly as tall as Mister Ben, and he was staring down at her with mesmerizing eyes that appeared to be a deep violet beneath the chandelier lighting. His full head of thick blond hair was neatly combed straight back on the sides and top, with every strand lacquered in place. His boyish face, etched with an intriguing cleft chin, bore the bronze tan of one who had perhaps spent all summer on a sail boat. Threaded beneath the collar of his crisp white shirt was a perfectly knotted black satin bow tie; the shirt's French cuffs and gold cuff links peeked out from the sleeves of his tuxedo jacket, his entire presentation reminding her of Cary Grant in the movie *Night and Day*.

"I'm very happy to meet you, Mr. Whitmore," she said, feeling as if she were repeating herself, but relieved that at least something was coming out of her mouth.

"It's Danny," he insisted. "And I know you're supposed to be here on a job assignment, but I'm hoping you'll let me show you a good time anyway. I promise that you'll have all the information you'll need before you leave." Then he held out his arm for her to take, as if he were actually her date.

"I'm afraid I feel a bit awkward about this," she blurted, her words blessedly freed but her feet seemingly frozen in place. "And I'm terribly underdressed for this occasion. Perhaps there's a way I could just—"

"Don't you worry that gorgeous head of yours, Abby. All of the women in there have to work very hard to look reasonably human, and they use their dresses to hide things I'd prefer not to mention. But you, on the other hand, radiate a natural beauty that is rare and refreshing, so what you're wearing doesn't make any difference. Besides, I think your dress is perfect. Come. Let me show you off."

This time, when he held his arm out to her, she found herself willingly placing her hand on the inside of his jacket sleeve. But her plain black handbag, which contained her steno pad and *Life* magazine, remained gripped in the fingers of her other hand. Consciously holding on to the handbag's handle, she almost felt as if she were trying to keep one side of herself grounded in the *other* world, where she lived in an insignificant two-room apartment way across town and had to travel on a bus to reach this fantasy setting.

Despite her discomfort with the extremes, she let Danny Whitmore lead her through the carved French doors, into the buzzing, well-heeled crowd she'd been overhearing since she'd rounded the corner at the end of the block. As she and Danny moved together, she was surprised that she actually did feel comfortable with him and, while the evening progressed, she discovered that completing this assignment and enjoying herself were not as mutually exclusive as she'd initially believed they would be.

Several hours later, just before ten o'clock and after Mister Ben had retrieved her coat, Danny escorted her down the front steps of the mansion and out to the sidewalk, where they both stood beneath the umbrella she was holding.

"Would you mind if I gave you a call later this week?" he asked. "Maybe we could have lunch?"

"I'd like that very much," she answered, her sense of trepidation having been stilled as she found no similarity whatsoever between this charming man and the unsavory cad Caroline had described.

"Good," he said as he gently kissed the top of her free hand.

Then they smiled at each other, and she walked away from him down the sidewalk toward the bus stop. Sensing that he was watching her, she felt a bit like a waif from a Dickens novel who'd wandered into the wrong neighborhood.

While she'd been at the party, the fog and mist had given way to a soft, steady rain. She'd already boarded the bus, however, before she became aware that the umbrella she'd mechanically opened over her head when she left the house was stylishly accented with a silver point and a rounded leather handle, neither of which had been part of the one she'd brought with her. Fortunately, the memory of Mister Ben's words kept her from feeling like a thief, although she did have a tinge of guilt about the poor person who'd ended up with her old and slightly bent model. Yet those thoughts were quickly pushed aside in favor of the magic she'd been introduced to that night. Caroline had at least been right about one thing: *I'm going to be fine. Just fine.*

Abby watched through the bus window as the cars and people made their way slowly along the shimmering rain-slicked streets and sidewalks. For the first time since her train had arrived in San Francisco, this city was finally starting to feel like home. Perhaps her next letter to Tess would come across a bit more buoyant than some she'd written of late. Perhaps there'd be fewer references to her longing for the tranquility and sense of purpose she'd had at Lady of the Valley, which she'd been trying to replicate outside of the convent setting. Maybe she was getting closer to finding the path she was supposed to follow. Maybe tonight had been a turning point.

CHAPTER EIGHT

Isaiah leaned back in his booth at Barney's, feeling slightly anesthetized from his immersion in Abby's words, which he'd been experiencing over the last four hours through her notes, letters, and journals. Originally stacked neatly inside the black corrugated folder from Tess, the collection of papers was now spread in random chaos across the tabletop, along with three empty beer mugs and the remains of his lunch. There was still almost as much left to read in the Rosa file as he'd finished, and his curiosity about the rest of what had happened in San Francisco was compelling. But he needed to stretch, and he really wanted another beer.

Checking his watch, he realized it was already 5:45 and remembered he was supposed to meet Ava in the bar shortly after six. With a resurgence of anticipation, he scooped all the materials together and dropped them back in the file, trying to lift himself out of Abby's story. When he'd made his way to the word "LOUNGE" on a flickering yellow fluorescent sign mounted above an arched doorway at the far end of the restaurant, he found a dozen men in the pub, several sitting alone and others huddled in groups of two or three. They all stopped their conversations and turned to look at Isaiah as he entered. Nodding a self-conscious greeting to no one in particular, he took a seat at the bar rather than at one of the tables.

"Hi!" said the bartender, a tall, thin-haired man, probably in his late thirties, who sported a scruffy patch of beard beneath his lower lip and wore a name tag that read *Eddie*.

"How's everything?" Isaiah asked.

"We're good down here," Eddie replied. "Want another draft like the others you been having?" Isaiah's surprise at the apparent familiarity must have been visible on his face. "Not very often a stranger stays in the barn all afternoon," the bartender continued, "and working the whole time too, without hardly lifting his head."

"In the *barn?*"

"Oh," Eddie said, smiling so broadly that the large wad of chewing gum smashed between his back teeth became clearly visible. "We call that end of the building *the barn* 'cause that's where all the animals get fed."

"Ah. Well, that certainly makes sense," Isaiah said, delivering his trademark charm across the counter instead of commenting about Eddie's cheeky perspective on the restaurant's dining patrons. "I appreciate your keeping an eye on me and, sure, another draft will be fine."

"Coming right up. And Ava said to tell you she'll be down shortly."

Oh great, Isaiah thought. *A date under a microscope in a small town.* "Thanks," was his only response as he took a few pages out of the folder and pretended to read again, just to avoid any further idle chatter or uncomfortable questions from Eddie.

Only a few minutes had passed when a slender hand with shimmering pale pink nails touched his arm.

"Hi, Isaiah," she said. "Are you still at it?"

Turning, he saw her short blonde curly hair freshly fluffed and framing flawless fair skin and lightly blushed cheeks. Her smile this close to him revealed orthodontia-perfect teeth, and her large almond-shaped hazel eyes transfixed him. She wore a baggy white turtleneck sweater over faded straight-legged jeans tucked into camel-colored cowboy boots, and hanging from her right shoulder was a brown leather saddlebag of a purse. Folded over her left arm was a furry tiger print jacket.

Once he caught his breath he said, "The only thing I'm *at* is full attention. So lead the way."

✦✦✦✦✦

They had been settled in a corner of the lounge for about half an hour, as far away from Eddie and the other customers as possible. Throughout the room, tiny flames from clusters of votive candles in the center of each table cast a soft yellow warmth over the stark, rustic wood floors, walls, and furniture.

Isaiah was drinking his beer too fast, and Ava was nursing a glass of white wine, as they took turns getting through the small talk.

"Ava is the perfect name for you, you know—simple yet refined," he said, noting her smile and a beguiling twinkle in her eyes turn on at the same time. "And I'll bet your last name is the perfect complement."

"Thank you, Isaiah. I appreciate that, but I recognize 'laying it on thick' when I see it, so let's skip that part. Okay?"

"Okay."

"My last name is Lindsey. Ava Louise Lindsey. What's yours?"

"Mellington. Isaiah Benjamin Mellington." There was a brief pause while they studied each other. "Can we get married now?"

She laughed, and he was relieved that she seemed to appreciate his sense of humor. After they'd completed his "I'm here for a funeral" and her "I'm here because of a long story" question-and-answer segment, there was another lull in their conversation, and then Ava was the first to speak again.

"Please forgive me, Isaiah, but I have to ask you something before I finish this drink. Sort of a rule I made for myself."

"Ask away," he said, eager to find out about this girl and uncharacteristically willing to share things about himself in kind.

"Are you married?" she asked bluntly, her eyes fixed intently on his. "Or in any sort of committed relationship?"

His first impulse was to laugh, but he allowed a few well-timed moments to pass. "I suppose a yes answer would make for a very short evening," he said.

With the feathery ends of her curly blonde bob glistening in the candlelight, she didn't respond or give any indication that she thought this particular comment of his was amusing. And he noticed that her shoulders dropped, almost imperceptibly, although her eyes never left his.

"Well, I admire your principals and your courage for asking," he went on. "And *no*, I'm not married—and I'm not in any relationship, committed or otherwise."

She leaned back in her chair and brought her wine glass to her lips, breathing in and out deeply before taking a sip. Then she smiled and slowly shook her head from side to side.

"How is that possible?" she asked.

"Just hasn't been in the cards, apparently."

"Wait a minute," she said, leaning forward again and placing her glass back on the table. "Are you saying you've *never* been married?"

"Sort of pitiful, isn't it?"

"Are you gay?"

Now he laughed. "Nobody's ever asked me that before," he said, feeling a little uncomfortable all of a sudden. "And no, I'm not, as far as I know anyway."

"I think you'd probably have that answer by now." Her face and entire demeanor appeared instantly more relaxed as she took another sip of wine. "What are you, about fifty?"

"Hey! Isn't that supposed to be impolite?"

"Sorry," she said with a coy smile, removing a smudge of lipstick from the rim of her wine glass with her thumb. "Well?" she added after a well-timed pause. "Am I close?"

"I must say that your straightforward approach is rather refreshing. Certainly leaves no room for misunderstandings or getting off on the wrong foot."

"That's the idea."

"Okay. If you insist, I'm fifty-eight. Is that close enough?"

Her brow furrowed slightly as she seemed to be studying his face. "I would have guessed younger, but fifty-eight is great. And," she added, her smile returning, "thanks for humoring me."

"My pleasure, believe me. *So*," he said, deciding to find out just how two-way this street was actually going to be, "what about you? I'm thinking you're thirty-five, maybe thirty-six or thirty-seven. Somewhere in there."

She held a sip of wine in her mouth for a few seconds then swallowed and moved in as far forward as she could across the table, looking from side to side around the room as if worried someone would hear her. "I'm forty-seven—forty-eight in December," she whispered. "But you have to promise not to tell anyone."

"Wow!" he said, surprised that he was so far off. "No one would believe me. You look absolutely amazing!"

"Why, thank you," she said, relaxing back in her chair.

"And have *you* ever been married?" he asked, hoping he wasn't pushing too far, despite the tit-for-tat precedent established thus far.

"Yes," she answered, without hesitation. "I waited a long time before taking the plunge, until I was almost forty-four. Then it only lasted two years. The whole thing ended in an unpleasant blur about a year and a half ago, which is part of my long story—and one I'd rather not go into just yet, if that's okay."

"Sure," Isaiah said, grateful to have learned this much. "We'll have plenty of time, I'm hoping."

Her smile hinted that he might be right, and then the expression on her face became more serious. "I'm sorry, Isaiah. I was so obsessed with getting to my test questions for you that I completely glossed over your saying that you're here for a funeral. That was very insensitive of me, and I apologize. Did you lose someone close?"

"An old friend of the family—of my late father, actually. She was a nun he met right after he came home from the war in 1945. There used to be a convent off 395, just south of—"

"I remember."

"Really? I thought you said you're from Spokane?"

"I am, but as I told you this afternoon, we used to spend a few weeks each summer at the Kettle Falls campgrounds."

"Oh, right. But how did you know about the convent?"

"*Everybody* knew about that convent, Isaiah. Some thought the place was sort of odd, mostly because no one understood that way of life. My family was—*is*—Catholic, and I remember my dad and mom trying to explain what the nuns and monasteries were all about to the local kids who hung out with us down at the lake. Didn't seem to help much, though. And when I was about nine or ten, the place got sold or something, and then we stopped coming to the campgrounds a year or two later, and that was that. So where did your father's friend go after they closed down?"

"Just to Colville. A buddy of hers, who stopped being a nun at that point, stayed in Kettle Falls. Dad and I used to come up and visit both of them a couple times a year—father-son road trips, togetherness stuff, you know."

"How nice. Sounds like you had a great relationship with your dad."

"Uh, *that* would be another story," he said, raising his eyebrows. He glanced down at his watch and then back up at the cherubic face he could not believe was only ten years younger than he was. He was thoroughly enjoying this woman and wasn't anywhere near ready for their date to end. "How much time do you have, Ava? Do you have other plans tonight?"

"Are you kidding?" she said, folding her arms across her chest. "I'm not going *anywhere* until I get that ride in your Jag."

*****

Despite the fact that they'd both been in Barney's most of the day, they decided to stay and have dinner in the lounge, just to keep things simple. She had her car in the parking lot too, and the nearest possible dining alternative—a little café that was only open until eight o'clock—was at least five miles away in Kettle Falls. If they went all the way into Colville, she'd either have to follow him, or they'd have to ride together and then drive the ten miles back up to Barney's to get her car at the end of the evening. So they chose the least complicated option of staying put. They also agreed that taking a quick trip later over the bridge, to the lake's edge inside the campgrounds, would serve as their nightcap and the fulfillment of Isaiah's promise to give her a ride in the Jag.

After a shared appetizer of hot spinach dip and homemade chips, she picked slowly through a grilled chicken salad while he savored the surprisingly gourmet poached salmon. And Eddie the bartender remained attentive, coordinating the food order himself with the kitchen and delivering another round of drinks as soon as he saw their glasses emptied. For three more hours they continued to talk.

Isaiah filled Ava in on as much as he knew about Tess and Abby's story, his phone call with Zoie, and the general plan for the week ahead. Then he briefly covered the basics of his life, growing up in Seattle, his Catholic school education through high school—which turned out to be similar to hers—and his undergraduate and law school degrees at the University of Washington. The changes he'd been trying to make in his life since his father's death were summed up by saying, "About a year ago, I left my dad's law firm, where I'd been working since I finally passed the bar at the age of thirty-five. And now I'm frankly embarrassed to tell you that I guess I don't know *what* I want to be when I grow up."

"Is there something you really love to do that doesn't feel like work?" she asked. "They say we should pay attention to any sense of passion we have regarding a hobby or outside interest, because that's where our intended life's work often lies."

"Really? And who are 'they'?"

"Oh, you know," she said, blotting a blob of salad dressing from the corner of her mouth with her napkin. "The all-important pontificating 'they.'"

"Of course. That's who I thought you meant, and I wouldn't dream of ignoring *them*." He leaned back in his chair and took a sip of the pinot grigio he'd ordered to go with his salmon. "I don't know if I'd call it a passion, but I've always enjoyed writing mystery stories."

"How fun! Murder mysteries?"

"Not necessarily. They could be about crimes, but just as easily about things that happen between people living regular lives. I actually wrote my first story when I was in the ninth grade. Won first place in the school's writing contest."

"A belated congratulations! I taught grades nine through twelve for twenty years, and I would have *loved* to come across a boy like you!"

"Not nearly as much as this boy would have loved to come across *you*! Sorry," he added, "but I cannot tell a lie. So what did you teach?"

"English grammar and lit."

"You have to be kidding."

"Nope," she said, rounding off the word with the smile he was finding so infectious. "*That* was *my* passion."

She went on to tell him that she'd wanted to be a teacher for as far back as she could remember, conducting classes in her bedroom with her dolls before she'd ever been inside a school herself. With her goals clearly mapped out, she'd ultimately earned her master's in education from Washington State University at Spokane.

She was the eldest of three daughters, her younger sisters being forty-two and thirty-eight, both married and with five children between them. Ava had no children herself, and although she mentioned that fact without any visible emotion, Isaiah certainly did not feel comfortable probing the issue further.

Her parents were still living and in their early seventies, and they presided over what sounded like an extremely close-knit and geographically tethered family, except for Ava, who had wandered from the pack for some reason she still didn't want to discuss. Something significant had obviously caused her to move away from Spokane, and the teaching career that she had so clearly loved, to Kettle Falls where she was waiting tables in Barney's Restaurant. But rather than being impatient to know, Isaiah took quiet pleasure in this nonfiction version of a mystery, hoping he'd be spending enough time with her to find out further details.

Shortly before nine thirty, they were finishing their dessert and coffee when Isaiah felt his cell phone vibrating on his belt. Concerned that the caller might be Tess, or even his mother again, he removed the phone from the holster but didn't recognize the number on the screen.

"Would you mind if I answer this, Ava? I'm not sure who it is."

She waved okay with a flutter of her fingers as she finished the last of her coffee.

"Hello?"

"Is this Mr. Isaiah Mellington?" a woman's voice asked.

"Yes it is."

"I'm Rosa Whitmore, and I'm calling you back only because my mother is insisting that I do."

"Thank you, Ms. Whitmore," he said, looking at Ava, who began listening with interest after recognizing the name from Isaiah's story. "I really appre—"

"There's nothing to thank me for," Rosa interrupted, "and there's no way in hell I'm coming up there. Mother confessed all the sordid details to me this afternoon, so you can consider me informed. But I have no interest in becoming involved any further. Whether there's a biological connection or not, I only have one mother, and she's here in San Francisco. I don't mean to be rude, but there's no point in dressing up the pig."

"Your position is certainly understandable," Isaiah responded, sorting his words carefully, "and I would not even attempt to put myself in your shoes. But if you'll give me just another minute, I'd like to make sure you have all the information."

"I don't *need* any more information. But all right. Go ahead."

"I'll be very brief. Did your mother tell you that you have a sister—a half sister? Her name is Zoie, and she's two years younger than you. She lives in North Carolina, and she'll be arriving here in Kettle Falls on Monday." He waited for a reply from her. "Are you still there?"

"Yes, I'm here. And no, Mother didn't tell me about a sister. Good Lord. How can this get any worse?" she added, her voice fading.

Isaiah felt oddly comforted by Ava's presence, watching her sit across from him, looking so composed and supportive as he tried another approach with Rosa. "I would never presume to suggest an outcome, Ms. Whitmore. But I'd like to offer the possibility that the situation *could* look different to you, if you agreed to fly up here. Abby left a file of information for you—handwritten letters and journals, pictures, and some other stuff—and the thought occurs to me that having a chance to see everything in the file and to meet Zoie, and even see Abby, might actually be helpful to you."

"Right. And the thought occurs to *me*, Mr. Mellington, that a better time for the woman named Abby to have been helpful to me was back in 1948 when I was born. Frankly, dropping this sort of bombshell on someone my age seems rather inhumane. So you can do whatever you want with the file of information. I don't care about Abby or any of it, and I have no interest in meeting my so-called sister either."

"Okay. I hear you," Isaiah said, not wanting to push her any further. "If you should change your mind, though, for any reason, please call me on this number. There will be a wake on both Tuesday and Wednesday.

Abby was quite revered in her community, it seems—just so you know. The funeral is on Thursday. All the services are in Colville, Washington, about ninety miles east of—"

"Don't bother with directions. Thanks, Mr. Mellington. Now I really need to run."

"Ms. Whitmore, wait." But she was gone already.

"Tough conversation," Ava said as Isaiah dropped his phone back into his belt holster.

"Yeah. And I'm not sure I handled it very well."

"You did fine," she said, folding her napkin neatly on the right side of her coffee cup. "From what I could tell on this end anyway."

"You should have heard her voice. She sounded *so* angry, and I can't say that I blame her. Not finding out that you're adopted until you're in your sixties would be bad enough. But adding in the facts that your biological mother became a nun after having a second child, who happens to be your half sister, would be hard to process, to put it mildly. Sort of like, 'Other than that, Mrs. Lincoln, how was the play?'"

Ava laughed softly and looked a little tired. "It's not your fault, Isaiah. You're just doing what's been asked of you. Remember that."

"Thanks. And you're right. I shouldn't take this personally. But the difference between Rosa's reaction and Zoie's is huge. I guess I should be grateful that at least one of the girls—excuse me, *women*—wants to be here."

"Everything will be fine. You'll see. Now, I hate to say this, but the long day is starting to close in on me all of a sudden. Could we take that ride pretty soon?"

"I thought you'd never ask."

He stood up to help her on with her coat, which looked like real fur, but he didn't dare ask. Then he slipped his own leather bomber jacket on, tucked the file folders under his arm, and left a one hundred dollar bill, which was forty-five dollars more than their dinner total, under one of the votive candles.

As they made their way out of the lounge toward the restaurant's front door, Eddie said, "Hope you guys enjoyed your evening."

"Everything was perfect," Ava replied. "Thanks so much, Eddie."

"You workin' tomorrow?" he asked.

"No, not until the Monday afternoon shift. How about you?"

"Yeah, I'm here tomorrow *and* Monday."

"See you then," she said.

"I'll probably see you again too, Eddie," Isaiah added. "And I appreciate your taking such good care of us tonight." Then he leaned across the bar counter and lowered his voice. "I left money on our table for the bill. You keep the change."

*****

The less than ten minutes required to drive across the bridge from Barney's to the Kettle Falls campgrounds had apparently been long enough for the Jag's novelty to wear off for Ava. As soon as they parked, she jumped out of the car and walked ahead of Isaiah to the end of the dock that extended a good fifty feet into the lake. Tied to one of the vertical support beams was an empty rowboat that bumped against the moorings in time with each ripple of the water's movement.

"Somebody just left that here?" Isaiah asked, keeping pace behind her and startled that the normal tenor of his voice sounded like it was amplified through a megaphone in the park's stillness.

"It probably belongs to a fisherman who'll be back in the morning," she said in a whisper that somehow felt more appropriate.

"What if somebody else takes it?" he asked, whispering too, but still hearing his words linger in the calm night air.

"That's not likely to happen unless some evil-minded stranger happens to stumble across it. And, even then, what would the average evil-minded stranger want with an old rowboat?"

"I guess you're right. Seems sort of strange to me, though, coming from a place where everyone locks everything up."

"I noticed that," she said, "when you locked your car. Worried that some wild animal is going to climb into it?"

"*Wild animal?* You have wild animals just wandering around out here?"

"Yeah. Mostly bears. But don't worry. They won't bother us if we don't bother them."

"Well, that's certainly reassuring."

"Come on," she said with a laugh, taking his hand and pulling him back down the dock. "Let's go over there."

She led him to a wrought iron bench bolted to the asphalt where the campground's parking lot met the beach sand. Once they were seated, Isaiah wanted to put his arm around her but settled for his leg touching hers, which she didn't seem to mind. As he squinted to bring the scene into focus, he couldn't recall ever being anywhere this dark. The streetlamps in the parking lot were off, and there weren't even any cars with headlights traveling across the bridge that towered over them to their right.

Now that he and Ava weren't moving or speaking, he could hear the soft pulse of Lake Roosevelt's water lapping against the shoreline, and he could see intermittent flashes of white as the small, gentle waves broke on the sand, providing the only sound, other than his and Ava's breathing. Even the crickets and companion night creatures seemed to have gone underground, leaving behind a hush as imposing as the darkness. And spread out above them, the black sky provided the perfect backdrop for the brilliantly clear array of stars—some appearing to be in motion, others fixed in place—that literally twinkled like something out of a Walt Disney movie.

"I've always been amazed at the night sky in this part of the country," he said.

"I know. It's remarkable what happens when you take away all the city lights and pollution. All this land is protected too, so nothing changes. That's one of the reasons I decided to move here, to regain my bearings."

Isaiah waited for her to say more, and when she didn't, he decided to change the subject.

"Even though I've been coming here since I was a kid, I never had much interest in learning about this valley. Dad and I were usually in and out overnight. Do you know if that bridge has a name?" he asked, looking up at the shadowy arch of steel that enabled Highway 395 to cross over the water.

"It does, but it's not very romantic. It's the Columbia River Bridge at Kettle Falls. There are several Columbia River bridges, actually, each named for the town they're either in or closest to."

"But I thought this was Lake Roosevelt."

"It is, but it's also the river. Confusing, I know. The Columbia River starts way up in Canada, winds down here, and then makes a turn west a little farther south from here and heads out to the Pacific Ocean, near Portland. Are you familiar with the Grand Coulee Dam?"

"I've heard of it but wouldn't exactly say that I'm familiar with it."

"It's really sort of interesting. The town of Grand Coulee is about a hundred miles away, kind of on your way back to Seattle. During the Depression, in the early 1930s, President Roosevelt authorized the construction of the dam there. The project was similar to the stimulus package we're dealing with now, to help jump-start the economy. The original purpose was for irrigation and electricity, but it also put thousands and thousands of people back to work."

"What's that old saying? 'The more things change, the more they remain the same.'"

"So true. Well, anyway," she said, "when the dam was finally finished in 1942, Lake Roosevelt was created right in the middle of the Columbia River. The lake is huge—one of the largest in the state, I think—and stretches all the way up from the Coulee Dam, past Kettle Falls and north to Canada. The lake serves as a flood control reservoir on the river. And you know something else?"

"What?"

"This whole area was originally settled by the Indians, and there actually used to be waterfalls called Kettle Falls next to an old town with the same name. But when the dam opened, the river backed up against the dam and flooded over the town *and* the falls, which are all buried out there now under that lake."

"Seriously? Were people killed?"

"No, thank goodness. They had lots of advance notice and basically moved the entire town, buildings and all, up the hill next to a place call Myers Falls. Then, eventually, the whole area was named back to Kettle Falls. When you hear people say '*old* Kettle Falls,' they're talking about the town that's under water."

"That is fascinating! And at least there's a happy ending."

"Some would say so. But a lot of folks living around here remember 1942 when the dam opened. Talk to them and you won't hear all about happy endings. Sure, there were good things that happened, like the electricity and the help to farmers from the irrigation. But the old-timers still mourn the loss of the waterfalls and the huge chunk of the valley's land."

"That may be true. But I have to tell you that someone like me, coming here without knowing any of that history, sees what looks like a hidden, untouched paradise. Everything is so beautiful and seems so unspoiled that you'd never believe *anything* had been lost or destroyed."

"Now *there's* something you could write about. I'm sure the longtime locals would appreciate your perspective. And believe me, they *love* to talk about it."

"Not a bad idea. I'll give it some thought."

They sat there on the bench for several more minutes, their legs still touching, as Isaiah considered the darkness, the softly breaking water, and the soaring shadow of a bridge, all with a newfound appreciation. He was also beginning to understand the love that Abby and Tess had developed for the area and the narcotic effect of a prolonged stay.

"Maybe I'll come back here for a vacation," he mused, giving serious consideration to the idea.

"Well," she said, abruptly standing up and stuffing each of her hands inside the opposite jacket sleeve, "it's really getting chilly now. And as much as I'm enjoying being with you, I'm ready for a return ride in that incredible car of yours so I can go home and crash. Would you mind?"

"Of course not." He looked at his watch as he rose to his feet but wasn't able to see anything. "It must be getting close to midnight anyway."

They walked quietly back to the car while the clunking sound of Isaiah's remote unlocking of the doors echoed throughout the parking lot, and the automatic illumination of headlights cut through the blackness.

"How quickly the spell is broken," he said, helping her into the passenger seat as the fragrance of the Jag's calf leather upholstery commingled with the crisp night's evergreen scent.

"The good news," she said a moment later as he slid in on the driver's side, "is that the spell is easily rekindled any time you want down here. I can't tell you how many hours I've spent in this spot over the last year, and each one has been *so* good for me. I'm strong again, and happy, and this place is a big part of *why*. And I'm not about to let anything, or anyone, set me back."

"Sometime I'd love to hear the story behind those words and that conviction, Ava," he said, noticing the sudden and distinct edge to her voice.

"Maybe you will, Isaiah, but not tonight."

He drove across the huge empty parking lot and onto the narrow, two-lane road leading out of the campground back to Highway 395. Fearful that he would wake up in the morning to discover Ava wasn't real, Isaiah didn't want the night to end without some sort of plan to see her again.

"You told Eddie you didn't have to work again until Monday, right?"

"Right."

"So, how would you like to have lunch with me tomorrow?"

"Really?" she said, sounding surprised that he was asking. "Actually, that might be fun. Where would you like to meet?"

"If you'll give me your number, I'll call you. I'm hoping to find a way to get into the old convent tomorrow afternoon, if possible. Apparently, a lot of the original convent's structure and grounds have been maintained, and I thought Zoie might enjoy seeing it while she's here. But I need to find out if the current owners would be willing to meet with us. If I can get in, would you like to go with me?"

"Oh, yes! That would be incredible!"

"Great. I'll see what I can do in the morning, and then I'll give you a jingle."

When they arrived back at the restaurant, she wrote her phone number on a Barney's business card pulled from her purse. He put the card in his wallet then got out and walked around to the passenger door. After helping her from the Jag, he escorted her to her own car, which was the only other vehicle in the lot at this late hour. As she removed her keys from her handbag, she looked up at him.

"Thank you for an absolutely magical evening, Isaiah. I can't tell you how much I enjoyed myself."

"I don't think you could possibly have had a better time than I did."

He moved closer to her and placed his hands on her elbows. Applying a gentle pressure against her arms, he edged her body in toward his and leaned down to kiss her. She made no attempt to stop him as his mouth parted slightly and met with hers, caressing first her upper lip and then her lower lip between his own. There was no force or sense of urgency, just the soft supple movement of lips exploring lips while their breathing accelerated. Then he kissed her cheek and put his arms all the way around her, holding her securely as he felt her full, firm breasts against his chest and her fingers kneading his back.

"Good night, Ava," he whispered in her ear. "I can't wait to see you tomorrow."

"Good night, Isaiah."

As he eased himself away from her, he placed his hands on her shoulders and gave her another soft kiss on her forehead. "Be careful going home."

"I will. You can follow me to Juniper Street in Kettle Falls, if you want. That's where I'll be turning off."

"Good idea." He opened the car door for her, waited while she started the ignition, and returned to the Jag. He knew this was the right thing to do but still wished he could be with her for the rest of the night.

Five miles later when she made the right turn onto Juniper, he flashed his headlights at her and continued south on 395 to Colville. By the time he arrived at the lodge ten minutes later, he had reviewed the entire day in his mind and could not believe that only twelve hours had passed since Ava had walked up to his table and into his life. The way he was feeling about her, he could just as easily have known her for years. No woman had ever made him feel this comfortable so quickly.

Once inside his suite, he dropped the two file folders on the coffee table in front of the small sofa. Then he stripped off his clothes and took a hot shower. A bit chillier than he'd expected to be after drying off, he pulled on a pair of sweatpants and a long-sleeved T-shirt and climbed into bed, falling into a deep and comforting sleep, with the light still on.

*****

By seven the next morning, Isaiah had already finished breakfast and had read the local newspaper at the diner a few blocks from the lodge. After engaging in a few minutes of flirtatious banter with the waitress as a means of gaining access to small town information, he learned that one place he might find out about the old convent's current owner was at the feed store in the center of Kettle Falls. The proprietor was apparently from an old valley family, and he was supposed to be a really nice guy, in addition to knowing *everyone*.

"Even though this is Sunday," the waitress said, refilling Isaiah's coffee cup for the third time, "there might be somebody at the store if you get there early, before folks are going to church."

He thanked her and left her a ten dollar tip then headed back up 395, with Rosa's folder—the only one he'd brought with him that morning—silently nagging at him from the passenger seat on the other side of the console. When he arrived at the corner of 395 and the main drag in Kettle Falls ten minutes later, a single pickup truck was parked in the gravel lot, and a cluster of bells rang over his head as he opened the store's thankfully unlocked front door.

What the waitress had called a "feed store" was actually a general store containing a variety of farm equipment and supplies, hardware, bags of flour, and other sundry items. And next to the cash register, on a long counter, was a tall, multishelf glass container with heat lamps warming an assortment of scrumptious looking and smelling cinnamon buns and pastries.

"Freshly made an hour ago in the bakery down the street," said a square block of a man coming through a door behind the counter. He was taller than Isaiah, with white hair that was thin but still covered most of his head, and a bulbous nose the same shade of pale red as his cheeks. Steely blue eyes peered out behind large, black, square-rimmed glasses, and a well-rounded tummy helped fill in his denim overalls paired with a long-sleeved white turtleneck shirt. The man could have been in his seventies, but Isaiah no longer had any confidence in his ability to assess such things.

"They look delicious!" Isaiah said, pulling out his wallet even though he'd just finished breakfast. "How much are they?"

"Fifty cents for the small ones. A dollar for the large."

"I'll take two of those large cinnamon rolls."

"Good choice. My favorite. You just passing through town?"

"Actually, no. My name is Isaiah Mellington, and I'm here for the funeral of a nun who used to live at the old Lady of the Valley convent."

"Ah. Sister Abby," the man said, removing the cinnamon rolls from the heated container with what looked like a piece of waxed paper. Then he placed the rolls in a small cardboard box and closed the lid. "She was really something."

"You knew Sister Abby?"

"*Everybody* either knew her or knew about her in these parts. She did great work for people who was dying and their families—and plenty of folks died in the last twenty-five years. Any of those who was in Sister Abby's hospital left this earth as peacefully and prepared to meet our Maker as possible. Lots of families have lots of stories, and none of 'em is bad."

He handed the box of cinnamon buns to Isaiah.

"How much?" Isaiah inquired again.

"Two bucks."

"That's it? No tax?"

"Yup and nope."

"What's your name, sir?" Isaiah asked as he handed him the two dollars.

"Richard."

"Nice to meet you, Richard."

"Same here. Now, what else can I do for you? Don't think you came by this early on a Sunday morning just for some rolls you didn't even know was here."

"You're right about that, Richard. My father, who passed away four years ago—"

"Sorry for your loss. That's tough for a young fella."

"Thanks. It's never easy, is it?"

"Nope. Never is. 'Specially for young folks."

"I'm not really all that young, you know. Fifty-eight, actually."

"Naw! Don't kid a kidder!"

"It's true."

"Well, I'll be! You need to box up whatever you're doing and bring it here for me to sell. I'll even buy some myself!" Richard laughed and slapped his hand on the counter. "No fooling? *Fifty-eight?*"

Isaiah was beginning to think that the Disney-like nature of last night's sky was a quality sprinkled over the entire valley.

"No fooling, Richard. You're a kick. I like you."

"Think I like you too. Now, what were you saying about what you're doing here?"

"My dad was an old friend of Sister Abby's. In fact, he and I used to drive here from Seattle a couple times a year to visit her and a friend of hers when I was growing up."

"I bet that friend was Tess."

"You know her too?"

"Sure do. She's a great gal. In fact, I think she would have made some man a real good wife, God help me for saying so. My brother taught her how to drive when she first stopped being a nun. Yup. We go way back."

"She told me about that," Isaiah said, recalling his conversation with Tess when he arrived on Friday night. "This is really a small world out here."

"You're tellin' *me*? I could lay some tales on you!"

"I bet you could. And I'd love to hear them. But today I'm trying to find someone who could introduce me to the owners of the old convent. I'm involved with coordinating Sister Abby's funeral arrangements, and I'd like to refresh my memory about the old place from when I was a kid. Got any suggestions about how I could do that?"

"Hold on a sec."

Richard picked up the phone next to the bun heater and dialed a number. "Hey! Richard here. Sorry to bother you so early, but there's a young fella here ..."

By the time Richard hung up, Isaiah had an appointment to meet the owners at the convent site at three o'clock that afternoon.

"Perfect," Isaiah said, thanking Richard and telling him he'd try to get back for more cinnamon rolls during the week.

"Do the best you can, son. But I'll see you at the funeral for sure."

As Isaiah was driving away from the store back toward Colville, he called Ava's number on his cell phone.

"Good morning," she said after only one ring. "I was waiting to hear your voice."

Knowing she was on the other end of the line felt like a tranquillizer. "Still up for having lunch with me?" he asked.

"You bet. How do you want to do this?"

"Would you feel like driving down to the Colville Lodge around eleven thirty or twelve? We could head out from there for a bite to eat and then go up to the old convent. The owners have agreed to see me at three."

"Perfect. I'll be at the lodge by eleven thirty."

"I'll meet you in the lobby."

Instead of going back to his suite, he decided to return to the diner where he'd had breakfast. He'd spotted a crescent shaped booth in the back of the restaurant earlier and thought that would give him enough space to spread out the material in Rosa's folder. He wanted to finish this part of Abby's story so he could also complete Zoie's before she and her father arrived the next afternoon.

The waitress who'd been so helpful before was still there and happy to see him, and his target booth was empty and waiting for him. The room was filled with the aromatic tease of freshly brewed coffee. He would have preferred one of the scrumptious cinnamon buns out in his car as an accompaniment, but he settled for the poor substitute the waitress brought him from the diner's selection.

Easing into the curve of the faux leather booth cushion, he sipped on his coffee while organizing the things from Rosa's file, stacking notes and labeled photographs in chronological order and grouping the journals together. Secure in the knowledge that he would see Ava again soon, he put his thoughts of her aside, eager to understand what had happened to Abby in San Francisco, how Rosa had come to be, and how North Carolina had then become part of the picture.

Talk about a mystery, he thought, picking up the journal where he'd left off and turning again to September 1947.

CHAPTER NINE

Abby hopped off the cable car on Powell Street, about a block from the top of Nob Hill. Then she walked the steep incline for a dozen yards to the small restaurant where Danny had told her to meet him. She'd decided not to tell Caroline where she was going, instead just mentioning that she had a personal appointment during lunch and might be gone a little longer than normal. Fortunately, the accolades over her Whitmore article, which had run in the Sunday edition three days earlier, were still flowing and seemed to award her more freedom, however temporary, from Caroline's customary scrutiny.

"Take as long as you like," she'd said to Abby. "There's nothing pressing here that I can't handle without you—for a few hours anyway. Enjoy your lunch."

Danny had called her at the *Chronicle* on Monday morning to tell her how deeply appreciative both Admiral and Marcella Whitmore were for the thorough and professional coverage of their party and the veteran's home project that had now been launched in such grand style. He said he wanted to extend the family's gratitude in person and had invited her to lunch. Tiny voices that she worked hard to silence were whispering that this meeting might not be appropriate. *But what harm can there be in one lunch*, she'd countered as she fought to ignore the tingling expectation about seeing him again.

Upon entering the restaurant, the maître d' greeted her as though he knew her and led her to a secluded booth in the far back corner of the narrow room where Danny stood waiting for her. He immediately took her hand in his and pressed a gentle kiss against her knuckles.

"I'm so honored you could join me, Abby," he said, motioning for her to slide around the deep maroon leather seat shaped in a semicircle, which had enough space to accommodate six people. He slid around the other way, establishing his place in the center on the back side of the booth, ensuring that she wouldn't be very far away from him no matter where she sat. So she stayed as close to the outer edge of the table as possible, trying not to appear rude.

"I'm the one honored with the invitation, Danny. But I was only doing my job."

"Well, let's not debate the reason why we're here. Let's just enjoy that we are. Now, what sort of cocktail would you like to order?"

"Oh, none for me, thank you. I have to go back to work. And I've never had a drink in the middle of the day before anyway."

"You're kidding!" At that point, he summoned the waiter and ordered a Manhattan for her, since that's what she'd asked for at the party. He had not yet finished the scotch on the rocks he'd been nursing when she arrived, but he ordered another nonetheless. "You wouldn't want me to drink alone, would you? Besides, I insist on being the one to share your first luncheon cocktail with you."

"All right," she said, with deep feelings of misgivings that she continued to disregard.

But as the alcohol took effect, tempered only slightly by the few bites of her lunch that she managed to eat, any qualms that had lingered were fully cast aside. And the more she relaxed, the more she began to talk. He asked her questions about where she was from and what brought her to San Francisco, and before she knew what she was doing, she found herself telling him about Tess and Lady of Valley, avoiding any of the details about why she'd left. She was surprised at how attentive he was and, at one point, when he placed both of his hands over hers and gave them an affectionate squeeze, she realized that she had somehow moved farther inside the booth's bench and was sitting right next him.

"We're all Methodists in my family," he said. "So I've never seen any nuns in person—just in the movies," he added with a grin that grew more captivating by the minute over that cleft chin. "And as far as I know, I haven't met anyone before today who *used* to be a nun. I think your story is intriguing, though, and quite admirable. You should use your journalistic talent and put all of that on paper."

"Oh, I could never do that. And I've probably said too much already. That part of my life is very personal, and private ... not to mention holy. And I still sometimes wonder if I made the right decision when I left."

"Seriously?"

"Oh yes. I pray about it all the time."

"Well, for whatever it's worth, I think you're in exactly the right place, and I'm feeling lucky that you are."

"Why, thank you, Danny. That's very sweet."

"Right," he said, his attention diverted by the waiter bringing the check.

As they finished their coffee, Abby felt as if they'd reached some sort of unseen time limit. Danny was busy paying the waiter and joking around with him and seemed to have suddenly lost interest in her. But while they were walking out of the restaurant together, he placed his hand on the small of her back and guided her through the door. Under the awning outside, he turned to face her.

"Have you ever been out to Grand View Park or Ocean Beach in the Sunset District?"

"No, I haven't. Frankly, I'm afraid I haven't seen very much of the city at all, except where I live and work."

"How about letting me show you? Maybe on Saturday afternoon? Are you busy then?"

She hesitated a moment, trying to decide if this was another bad idea. "No, I don't have any plans."

"Great! I'll pick you up at your place around one o'clock. Don't eat lunch. I'll bring a surprise."

He waited with her until the cable car came back down the hill and, after she boarded, she watched him walk back up Powell Street toward the Fairmont Hotel. *Caroline was so wrong about him*, she thought, as all the tiny voices once again grew mute.

*****

September and early October in San Francisco are typically the warmest months of the year, and the thermometer mounted outside Abby's living room window on Saturday, October 4 read seventy-five degrees just before she left the apartment. Unobstructed by even a single cloud, the sun's rays reflected off the white and pastel buildings spread up and down San Francisco's hills, making the city look like a collection of jewelry.

Standing inside the enclosed vestibule of her hotel lobby, in the only nice outfit she owned for a warm-weather date, she hoped she'd be appropriate for the day ahead. Her dress had been a gift from her parents last Easter, an early college graduation gift, they'd said. Fashioned from a crisp bright yellow seersucker fabric, the skirt fell in soft folds, with vertical ruffles sewn from about two inches below her waist down to her midcalf. The cap-sleeved bodice had a square-cut neckline, and a row of ruffles matching those on her skirt extended down from each shoulder, curving over each ample breast and ending just beneath her bust line. The ruffle-free midsection of the dress accentuated her narrow waist and flat tummy, although her white cardigan sweater hid most of those attributes from view.

In one hand, she held a bright red, wide-brimmed straw hat, which she didn't want to put on yet for fear of messing up the smooth, glossy black undercurves of her pageboy haircut. In her other hand was a straw purse that matched her hat, and on her feet, in the same shade of red, were canvas peep-toe wedge shoes.

Two of her neighbors had come downstairs while she was waiting, each of them telling her how lovely she looked, and she was beginning to believe them. Attempting to catch her image in one of the front door's side-panel windows, she ended up watching instead as a deep purple, four-door Buick sedan pulled to the curb. The angular, aerodynamic lines of the vehicle's body structure were at odds with the massive dimensions, making the car appear to still be moving, even at a full stop.

In those first few moments, she never considered that the appearance of this bigger-than-life vehicle might have anything to do with *her*. The grill and bumper embellishments were fashioned from shiny chrome, adding further to the wow factor of the purple paint. And both the oversized white sidewall tires and a hood ornament right out of a Captain Marvel comic capped the spectacle that she assumed had arrived for someone else. But then she saw Danny sitting behind the wheel, smiling broadly and waving as he spotted her.

By the time she got out to the curb, he was standing on the sidewalk, holding the passenger door open for her.

"Hi there," he said, looking quite pleased with the impression he seemed to be making. "And don't *you* look gorgeous!"

"Thank you, Danny," she said, holding her hat over her head to shield her eyes from the glare, which she wasn't sure was coming from the sun or the car.

"Thought you might enjoy the afternoon in style," he added as she slid onto the soft, sand-colored fabric of the front seat. "You and I will be sharing in the inaugural outing of this new beauty, and I'm delighted to see that you've dressed for the part." Then he pushed the car door closed as the sound of heavy, intricately engineered metal became one with the car's frame, in a solid, secure thud.

As he made his way around the front end, with the lower half of his body obscured up to his chest by the height and scope of the automobile's lustrous hood, Abby took a quick inventory of the lavish interior. The dashboard was a blend of more chrome and polished wood filled with gauges, dials, and a futuristic radio. Over her left shoulder, she noted that the rear seat, which was covered in the same soft taupe fabric and located a good yard of leg room behind her, was almost as big as her living room sofa.

"Well, what do you think?" he asked as he opened the driver's side door and moved in behind the steering wheel. His thick blond hair was less lacquered and had more of a windblown look than she'd seen previously, making him look younger somehow and even more handsome than she remembered.

"I *think* this is incredible! I've seen pictures of cars like this in my *Life* magazines, but I never thought I'd be riding in one! Sure does beat the bus."

He laughed and shook his head as he started the engine. Then he moved the gearshift lever down a notch on the right side of the steering wheel, which must have been at least sixteen inches in diameter. As the massive automobile began inching forward, Abby actually felt a bit nervous and realized that her hands were gripping the piping along the edge of the upholstered seat.

"I told you I'd bring you a surprise," he said, his words suddenly mingling with the tiny voices in her head that were unexpectedly making their presence known again. "But that isn't all."

"Really? What else could there possibly be?"

"Take a look on the floor behind you," he said, glancing over at her and then back out the immense front window.

She turned and pulled herself up on her knees to peer over the seat back, discovering a large brown wicker basket with double handles and lids that lifted up from each end.

"What's in it?" she asked, sitting back down and tucking the skirt of her dress in around her legs.

"Miss Peel's specialties."

"Who's Miss Peel?"

"Remember meeting Mister Ben the night you were at my house? Our butler?"

"Yes, of course. What a sweet man."

"Right. Well, his wife also works for my family, and her name is Philippa. But when I was little, I could only say Peel. So it stuck."

"Philippa is such a beautiful name. Does she mind you calling her Peel now that you're an adult?"

A sharp twist of his head in her direction revealed a look in his eyes that startled her. "I don't know if she does or not, Abby," he said in a harsh tone. "I never asked her. She *works* for me, remember?"

"I'm sorry," she said, feeling herself pull inward.

"Never mind." His voice softened as he patted her arm. "But as I was starting to say, she's a great cook. Makes the best deviled eggs in the world, and the best sandwiches too. So I asked her to put our lunch together, and she packed the basket up to the brim."

"That was certainly very nice of her."

Abby was doing her best to ignore the jabs of apprehension, and she kept telling herself to relax and enjoy the experience. After all, she was going to Ocean Beach for a picnic on a perfect fall day, with a prince of a date from a good family, in an automobile right out of *Life* magazine. *Just think how many girls would love to trade places with me.*

Danny piloted the massive Buick Super Sedan from Abby's hotel west on Geary Boulevard across the city.

"Since you've never been out on that end of San Francisco," he said, "I thought you might enjoy touring around for a little while before we stop and have lunch."

"Yes," she replied, thinking that sounded quite normal and enjoyable. "I'd like that very much."

"The sights and history on the northwest corner of the city are really spectacular," he went on, beginning to sound like a travel guide. "Have you ever heard of the Sutro Baths or the Cliff House?"

"No, I'm embarrassed to say that I haven't. But I'm sure they'll be amazing."

"They are indeed, Abby. And you shouldn't feel embarrassed. I'll bring you up to speed in no time."

The six-mile ride on Geary Boulevard was in a straight line from the downtown area out toward the ocean, passing through several of the city's neighborhoods. The largest of those was the Richmond District, directly north of Golden Gate Park, which began where Geary crossed Stanyon Street, the eastern border of the park. Then the neighborhood extended westward for forty-eight avenue blocks, all numbered consecutively, beginning with "First," and northward for five long street blocks that ran perpendicular to the avenues. As the car motored past block after block of narrow, two- and three-story stucco houses and stocky apartment buildings on both sides of the street, Abby and Danny rode in silence the entire way.

At Fortieth Avenue, he angled the steering wheel slightly right and then slightly left to continue going west, as Geary turned into Point Lobos Avenue. By the time they reached Forty-third, Abby could see the Pacific Ocean out in front of them in the distance. They were not at sea level, however, but high on a bluff. And as Point Lobos Avenue continued in a straight line, Abby imagined momentarily that they were going to keep driving in that line, directly over the edge of the bluff, with the huge car plummeting, flashy hood ornament first, into a messy, purple demise. Instead, the Buick followed Point Lobos as the road curved gently to the left, heading south, at which point the Pacific and the spellbinding Ocean Beach came into full view.

"Oh dear heaven!" she gasped. "How *beautiful!*"

A big white building on the right side of the road was marked by a sign that read "Cliff House," and Danny abruptly swung the Buick into a vertical parking slot in front.

"Let's stop here for a minute," he said. "I want to show you something."

He got out first and came around to the passenger side to open the door for her, which she thought was very polite. Taking hold of his outstretched hand, she emerged from the car, only to be blown into his arms by an unexpectedly powerful wind.

"You have to get used to that on this end of the city," he said, chuckling as he put his arm around her shoulder and began guiding her to the north end of the Cliff House. "It's always windy out this way and, more often than not, it's so foggy that you can't even see the ocean. We're lucky to have such a clear day for all the special things I have planned."

She wanted to reply, but she was preoccupied with using one hand to keep her blowing hair out of her eyes and mouth while holding her dress down around her legs with the other. When they reached the end of the Cliff House, she saw the most incredible thing she'd ever witnessed—a gargantuan structure made entirely of glass rising up like a behemoth from the beach and rocks hundreds of feet below them.

"What *is* that?" she managed to ask against the force of the wind, giving up on her hair and struggling with both hands to keep her dress from blowing up over her head.

"*That* is the Sutro Baths," he said, standing with his back to the wind and almost looking like he was laughing at her. "It's the largest swimming facility in the world. Supposedly accommodates about twenty five thousand people, hard as that is to imagine. And there's a museum in there too. Built sixty or seventy years ago by a fellow named Adolph Sutro, who used to be mayor of San Francisco. He owned all this land around here and built the Cliff House too, although this is the third rendition. The last one was the best—looked like a castle. But it burned down. Sometime we'll have to come here to—"

"I'm sorry, Danny," Abby said, turning away from him and hurrying back toward the car, while she leaned over and gripped the hem of her dress tightly around her knees with both hands. "I have to get out of this wind," she shouted over her shoulder.

When she reached the Buick, she pulled the heavy passenger door open herself and climbed inside. The door blew closed behind her, just missing her fingers and the edge of her dress. As she watched Danny approaching, the silence and the blessed absence of wind came as a huge relief. She was also grateful that she'd left her divine red hat in the car. Otherwise, the gorgeous thing would surely be flying out to sea by now. Removing her comb from her pocketbook, she began smoothing the tangles out of her pageboy as Danny opened the door on the driver's side and slid onto the seat.

"Please forgive me," she said. "I hope I wasn't rude, but I'm not dressed properly for such fierce wind. If I'd known we'd be walking around like that, I would have worn slacks instead. I hope you're not upset with me, Danny. I was really very uncomfortable."

"No problem," he replied, looking straight ahead as he started the ignition. "I just thought you'd find the place interesting."

"Oh I do! And I'd love to hear more. I've never seen *anything* like the Sutro Baths building in my life! Now that we're out of the wind, please tell me about the history and how something like was ever built in such a spot in the first place."

"Maybe later," he said, swinging the Buick around and heading back up Point Lobos Avenue. "I'm getting hungry, and I want to find a place where we can have our picnic, somewhere *out of the wind*," he added, glancing over at her with narrowed eyes and lips closed in a tight grin.

"Okay," she said, not feeling at all hungry herself and suddenly wishing she'd paid more attention to Caroline.

*****

The spot Danny chose for their picnic was more spectacular than he'd described. He'd turned left off Point Lobos Avenue onto El Camino del Mar, a narrow two-lane road still high on a bluff that wound through a parklike setting, with the ocean visible again a short distance away on their left.

"This area is called Point Lobos," he said, reverting to his instructional tone. "We're on the far northwest corner of the city, and that compound over there," he continued, extending his arm in front of her and pointing out the window to their right, "is Fort Miley. Six years ago, after Pearl Harbor, the fort began serving as the main defense site for San Francisco's own harbor. In a few minutes you'll see the Golden Gate Bridge, which everyone worried might be another target for a Japanese attack, especially after we joined the war effort. So Fort Miley was—and still is—a pretty significant military base, even with the war over. But there's also an incredible museum in this park, which we'll be passing shortly. And most importantly for us today, there are special places where people can have private picnics while still taking in the view."

"That sounds wonderful, Danny, and I'm looking forward to more of your stories about the history. I guess I've been so preoccupied with learning my job over the last couple of months, and with finding my way around, that I've neglected to learn about the city's ... well, its résumé, for lack of a better word. But you've been very inspirational, and I'm going to take what you're giving me today and follow up with some in-depth study. Understanding San Francisco's past will help me cover current stories more effectively. I should have figured that out sooner, on my own."

"You sound like I've just counseled you out of a life of crime," he said, glancing over at her briefly with that tight grin again. "But I'm glad I could help you learn something new about yourself. Hopefully, that'll be just the beginning of what I can teach you," he added, returning his eyes to the road ahead.

"Right," she said softly, not really sure what he meant by that.

They passed the museum Danny had mentioned, and a few minutes later he turned left off El Camino del Mar into a gravel parking area where theirs was the only car.

"We'll unload the basket and blanket here," he said, bringing the Buick to a stop, with the hood ornament inches away from a thick hedge at least six feet tall. "On the other side of those bushes, there's a nice area of grass and trees, with sort of a postcard view of the harbor and bridge. And because we're on the north slope, we'll be shielded from the wind, so you should be more comfortable." His tone of voice sounded sincere rather than sarcastic this time.

He gave her an easy, natural smile, reminding her again how good-looking he was. She began to think that they'd only veered off in an awkward direction for a little while earlier and that the afternoon might still be as enjoyable as she'd originally hoped.

Once they were both out of the car, Danny opened the back door and grabbed the handles of the oversized picnic basket, revealing a large quilted blanket underneath, which he partially unfolded and tossed over his shoulder.

"All right," he said, closing the car door. "Let's get to it!" Then he walked ahead of her toward an opening in the hedge.

She followed behind him, carrying her red straw purse in one hand and her red hat in the other, because she trusted his word about the wind.

*****

The surroundings far exceeded any of Abby's expectations, with the San Francisco Harbor and Golden Gate Bridge in their direct line of sight, and only the slightest breeze present to refresh the afternoon's above average warmth. The quilt, which had been constructed with blue and red fabric patches and heavy crème-colored blanket stitching, was spread out on the grass beneath a colossal shade tree. Danny unloaded the picnic basket in a buffet style arrangement on the end of the quilt running parallel to their view of the harbor.

Their conversation was congenial while they ate, as Abby asked questions about the places they'd seen thus far, and Danny showed off his impressive amalgamation of San Francisco lore, both factual and folk. His disarming manner, first evident the night she'd met him at the Whitmore mansion, was operating at full throttle, and she was captivated once again by the way he made her laugh, by his muscular build, and by his tousled blond hair and boyish face that only added further to his charm.

Miss Peel's lunch was a winner as well. She'd included a cut up chicken fried to perfection without any lingering trace of grease, a recipe Abby knew she absolutely must have.

"Do you think she'd be willing to share her technique with me?"

"I have no idea, and I doubt anyone has ever asked her for one of her recipes before. But I can find out. Euleen might have to write it down for her, though."

"Who's Euleen?"

"Mister Ben and Miss Peel's daughter. She's about thirteen or fourteen now, I think, and she's the only one of the three who knows how to read or write."

Abby had never met anyone who was illiterate, and she certainly did not want to risk embarrassing Miss Peel.

"Don't worry about it, Danny. If I ever have a chance to meet her, I'll just ask her myself, and she can explain it to me in person. Sure is the best fried chicken I've ever tasted!"

"And you become easier to please by the moment."

In addition to the chicken, the basket was also filled with potato salad, coleslaw, and the largest, fluffiest biscuits imaginable—even surpassing those at the convent—and a jug of red Kool-Aid. All of this had been more than sufficient, but Danny had tucked a bottle of wine in the basket as well, and Abby's insistence that she didn't care for any was ignored as he poured a glass for each of them. She took a small sip and, when he wasn't looking, emptied a little on the grass. Yet he still kept pouring more for her. An hour later, despite her best efforts, she was feeling light-headed, but admitted to herself that she was having a nice time after all.

She'd been sitting facing him, with her legs folded sideways and tucked demurely beneath her dress throughout their meal and conversation, periodically shifting her weight whenever she felt her feet start to tingle.

"Why don't you just stretch your legs out in front of you?" Danny asked at length, after he'd haphazardly replaced all the remnants of food, plates, trash, and utensils back in the basket. "You don't look very comfortable at all," he said, moving next to her and placing his hand on the dress covering her knees.

"I'm fine, really. Besides, we'll be leaving soon."

"What's your hurry, Abby? Aren't you enjoying yourself?" His words had taken on that sarcastic tone again and were spoken as he nuzzled his nose in her hair. Then, without any warning, his lips were on her cheek, and then his hand was on the back of her head, pressing her face into his mouth, which was all over her.

"Please, Danny, don't," she said, managing to push a few inches away from him as the little persistent voices that had been whispering warnings to her were now blasting at an ear-shattering pitch.

"I know you don't really mean that," he said, wrapping one of his arms around her back and the other behind her knees as the mass of his body pushed against hers and lowered them both onto the quilt.

"Yes I do!" She spoke as loudly as possible with his weight against her lungs. "Please stop, Danny!" Now she was crying, struggling to wedge her hands between his chest and hers. Old images began flooding her mind as his upper body strength completely immobilized her from the waist up while she felt his powerful legs pushing hers apart.

"No!" She tried to scream, but she couldn't get any air. "Please, Danny! Don't *do* this!" But her pleas emerged as mere whispers.

Then he lifted his shoulders and chest up slightly, grabbing her wrists with one of his hands and holding them down above her head. Beads of his sweat were dropping onto her face, and he looked like a rabid animal.

"Don't play little Miss Innocent Nun with me, Abby. You've wanted this just as much as I have ever since you told me about your *former career*."

"No! *Please*! I'm sorry if I ..."

But she stopped speaking when she saw and felt what he was doing with his free hand and when she realized that he'd pinned her legs with his so she couldn't move. She closed her eyes and felt again the spinning of the gazebo floor at Lady of the Valley. She fought to wrench her legs free so she could kick him in the face. She remembered the relief she'd felt when she'd staggered to her feet and when she'd seen the faces of the soldiers after they'd saved her from the attack. She remembered the gentleness of Sinclair. She knew she'd screamed back then, and she thought she was surely screaming now as an unimaginable pain shot through her.

Someone will be here soon, she thought. *Someone will be here soon.*

And yet, this time, no one came.

*****

Caroline wanted to stop by the residence hotel for a visit after Abby called her at home on Sunday to say she was ill and wouldn't be in the office the next day. But Abby couldn't bear the thought of seeing anyone, least of all Caroline, whose wise counsel, if heeded, would have most likely prevented this nightmare from taking life. What Abby needed now was an interval of peace. She also needed time for the bruises to heal and a quiet period of devotion for the substantial penance and introspection the priest had imposed upon her.

On Saturday, in the first few minutes after the horror had ended, Abby had been afraid that there might be more of the same to come, or maybe even worse. She really didn't know *what* to expect from him once he'd rolled off of her and began straightening himself up. So she behaved compliantly, hoping to minimize the risk of any further violence, until she could get away from him.

Danny, on the other hand, had started—inconceivably—to behave like a gentleman, as if nothing had happened. He even offered his assistance as Abby tried to wash the blood out of her dress with water from a drinking fountain near their picnic site. Once he had loaded the quilt and basket back into the Buick, he returned and escorted her to the car, with one arm around her shoulders for support and the other holding her hand. Disgusted as she felt, she was too stunned, too weak, too frightened, and in too much pain to refuse his help.

But she offered no response, other than a nod or a one-word mumble, to his attempts at inane conversation on what seemed like an interminable return drive. Instead, she hugged the inside of the passenger door to remain as far away from him as possible. Only a few hours earlier, the same trip had been so enjoyable, with San Francisco looking magical and promising to her. Yet now the city appeared stained and strewn with filth. And before the gaudy, kitschy purple vehicle—*after all, let's be perfectly honest*, she thought—had come to a complete stop in front of her hotel, she pushed the car door open, jumped out, and ran into the safety of the lobby, without so much as a word of good-bye.

Inside the cocoon of her apartment, she stripped off her beautiful yellow dress and her undergarments, wound everything together into as tight a ball as possible, and dropped the wad into the wastebasket beside her bedroom bureau. Her adorable peep-toe wedge pumps and her red sunhat might be salvaged, she thought, if she could find a way to disconnect them from the memories. For the moment, she simply tossed them in the closet, the shoes on the floor and the hat on the upper shelf.

After washing her hair under free-running water in her claw foot bathtub, she wrapped her head in a towel, put the rubber stopper in the drain, and filled the tub with a hot bubble bath. Sinking down so only her face was exposed, she let herself float and soak and steam and disinfect, while guilt and shame and mourning for an innocence never to be recovered poured relentlessly out of her soul.

Two hours later, with the marks on her body covered as completely as possible in a pair of unseasonably warm black trousers and a white cardigan buttoned up to her neck, she rode the bus to Old St. Mary's Church on California Street between Grant and Kearny, where she'd been attending Mass since shortly after arriving in San Francisco. She'd already missed the five thirty evening service, but she desperately needed the comfort of the sanctuary, and she knew that one door of a Catholic church was always open, no matter what time of day or night.

Once the bus let her off on the southwest corner of Grant and California, she crossed the street and walked the half block to the church where she slowly pulled herself up the front steps. But the massive wooden doors were locked.

The rectory was next to the church, and in between the two buildings was a beautifully landscaped courtyard filled with two flowering plum shade trees, lavender hydrangea bushes, a variety of annuals, and an eight-foot-tall sculpture of the Madonna and Child overlooking a small pond. A recirculating fountain fed softly tinkling water down the face of a curved rock wall behind the statue and over the edges of a rock garden encircling the pond. Abby usually spent a half hour in that courtyard after each Mass, sitting on the stone bench facing the Madonna statue and pond, while she finished saying her rosary. She remembered that a door opened onto the courtyard from the church, and that one she found unlocked.

Nothing made her feel closer to God than being inside a church when no one else was there. When parishioners filled the pews, she often wondered how God managed to decipher and prioritize all the prayers and thoughts bombarding Him at the same time. But when she was alone in a church, when her footsteps echoed throughout the nave as she walked down the center aisle toward the altar railing, she felt as if she were the only one God had to deal with or to worry about in that moment.

Kneeling down on the velvety altar rail padding, she made the sign of the cross and looked up at the ornately carved crucifix covering most of the wall above the altar. But nothing else was forthcoming from her—no words, no prayers, just the tears that began flowing again. Then she heard someone else's footsteps on the center aisle behind her. *Oh no*, she thought, feeling exposed and vulnerable.

"Is there some way I can help you, my child?"

The voice was unmistakably that of Father Moynihan. He was an Irish priest, who reminded Abby of a youthful version of Father Fitzgibbon, a character in the Bing Crosby movie *Going My Way*, which she'd seen with her mother in 1944. The Irish brogue was the same. And Father Moynihan's full head of dark hair was already dotted with the flecks of white she suspected would dominate his entire head by the time he was an old man, assuming he would have any hair left at all by then.

"I don't mean to intrude, miss," Father Moynihan continued, "but I saw you enter the church while I was looking out the rectory window. I couldn't help but notice that you seem to be troubled, and I just wanted to see if there was—"

"Thank you, Father," Abby interrupted, rising to her feet. "Frankly, I'm glad you're here. I need to speak with you."

She introduced herself to him, and then they sat on the front pew together rather than going into the confessional. For the next hour, she talked while he listened. She told him about Lady of the Valley and what had taken place there. She told him what she'd been doing with her life since then. And she told him what had happened that afternoon, in halting sentences fractured by moments when the sickening imagery made her feel as if she were going to vomit.

What she really wanted, she realized, was her mother, someone she knew would console and support her, no matter what she did. But she also understood that what she really *needed* was absolution and freedom from the unyielding shame and self-reproach that she was feeling. Father Moynihan was the only one who could help with that objective, and Abby struggled to get through her confession. She believed God had purposely led her and the priest into the sanctuary at the same moment so this could happen.

But gentle as he was with her, Father Moynihan fell short of comforting. "I'm so sorry that you've suffered today, Abby," he said. "Sometimes people misjudge or misinterpret another's intentions, and it seems that's what this young man did with you. For some reason, he thought you wanted the same thing he did."

"Yes, Father. That's what I've been thinking. But I can't for the life of me put my finger on what I did to mislead him. We were only out on a picnic, and I—"

"Did you let him kiss you?"

"Yes."

"Well, there you go." The words virtually dripped through his Irish brogue.

"What?"

"Young women have to be very careful about the signals they send out to young men, and kissing your young man obviously sent him a message that you didn't intend to deliver."

"He's *not* my young man, and it was just a kiss. Can't people kiss someone they like without that other person deciding that the next natural step is intercourse?"

"Only if that point is made very clear, and even then there's a risk."

"I *did* make it clear. I said 'no' and 'stop' over and over again."

"Well, my dear, for some reason he didn't believe you. But God knows your true intentions, and I think I do as well. So forgiveness is at hand. Come. Let's go to the confessional and help you find some peace."

She wanted to say more, but the conversation was obviously over. So she followed him, made her confession, and bowed her head when he gave her absolution. After Father Moynihan said his good-bye, she remained in the sanctuary alone, kneeling at the altar again while saying the five rosaries he'd given her as one element of her penance. As she prayed, though, the peace he'd promised her wasn't forthcoming yet.

In her heart, she believed she was basically a good girl and, more importantly, a good Catholic girl. So there could be no greater hell for her than the brutal invasion that had bloodied her body just hours earlier, obliterating virtue, trust, and virginity in one cruel, violent sweep. Father Moynihan clearly felt sorry for her and had attempted to offer a measure of solace. Yet he was also clear in his belief that she bore some responsibility for the outcome. Consequently, she needed to figure out what she'd done to trigger Danny's behavior and then construct the balance of her life so she was certain never to repeat the mistake. Perhaps *that* was the path to peace.

For the next two hours, she bowed in repentance in the stillness of the darkened church, gradually moving the beads of her rosary through her fingers five times. But despite her reverence, along with her attempt to feel hopeful again on the heels of Father Moynihan's encouragement, she grew increasingly fearful that she had somehow fallen into step behind the devil.

CHAPTER TEN

"But she was *raped*! Why didn't anyone call the police?"

Isaiah's voice had carried a little farther than he'd intended. He and Ava were beginning their lunch in a garish, red and gold Chinese restaurant about a mile from the Colville Lodge. He'd planned to give her a methodical and chronological summary of the Rosa file but had jumped immediately to the episode with Danny, driven by an unexpected emotional surge that caught him off guard. Luckily, the two of them were the only patrons in the place, save for one other couple that either didn't hear him or pretended not to.

"Believe me," Ava answered, "if more *men* had been asking that question in 1947, the whole subject of rape might not have carried so much gender bias for the next half century." She rested her chopsticks on her plate, with a whole pot sticker appetizer still balanced between them, as she leaned back into the black lacquered dining chair. "The truth is," she continued, her tone sober and her eyes fixed on Isaiah's, "that proving a negative is impossible, and the absence of consent falls into that category. In those days, if a woman claimed that she'd said 'no' or 'stop,' one of two things was sure to happen next: either no one would believe her at all, or the next phrase thrown at her would be 'yeah, but he didn't think you really *meant* no.'"

"Makes me feel embarrassed, Ava," Isaiah responded, setting his oval ceramic spoon down on the plate beneath his wonton soup bowl. "I know I've been guilty of those feelings—those suspicions—myself. When I was a sophomore in college, I had a fraternity brother who was accused of assaulting a girl at a party, and the common belief was that drinking had made *her* memory rusty. Either that or she was just plain lying to try to get something out of him."

"Didn't any of you ever consider that she might have been telling the truth?"

"I talked with some of the guys about that at one point. But none of us was there at the time it supposedly happened, so we decided to let matters take their own course. I'm not sure how the thing was settled. It just sort of went away, eventually."

"That's because the fight was too tough and too lonely for most women to pursue in those days. So they *did* just sort of *go away*. Things are better today, although men do still try that approach even now, claiming a misinterpretation of a woman's cues, or worse. But if she says that she said 'no' or 'stop,' that's given far more credence now than ever before. Sadly, Abby was living in a time when, unless there was an eyewitness to a rape, the benefit of the doubt was *always* given to the male—and generally *by* a male as well, since lawyers and judges were all men too. Not to mention priests and ministers and rabbis. Just think about the tens of thousands of women who suffered like her, without any recourse."

"Seems we've hit a nerve, Ava, for both of us. My mother told me that respecting and protecting women was supposed to be part of my DNA, although not in so many words. So I have a hard time imagining that kind of violence."

"What about your dad? I'm sure he was gentle too, seeing how you turned out."

"Well, the word 'gentle' doesn't leap to mind when I think of him, and he never talked about such things. But he was basically a good man— tough and stern and not a lot of fun, but good—and I never saw anything but love between him and my mother."

"What's your mother's name?"

"Sarah."

"Maybe I'll have a chance to meet her someday?"

"Maybe," he said, reaching across the table to squeeze one of her hands. "I've been trying to get ahold of her since yesterday morning, but she hasn't answered at home or on her cell."

"Will she be coming here for the funeral?"

"No. She didn't know Abby or Tess, but she was very supportive of Dad keeping in touch with them. Now I'm starting to wonder, though, if she knew more about Abby's story than she let on. Or maybe Dad didn't tell her."

"Tell her what?"

Isaiah had finished reading everything inside the San Francisco folder while passing the morning in the diner, not only discovering the details about Rosa but also a new dimension about his father. He'd been looking forward to this lunch with Ava where he could share what he'd learned with her. Having someone he could talk to while moving through this peculiar set of circumstances was proving to be a surprising comfort.

Thus far, he'd summarized for her the story through Abby's meeting with the priest, including Isaiah's own abhorrence of what had happened to her. Although he'd spent relatively little time with Abby throughout his life, his connection to her was strong enough to make him feel angry and almost sick to his stomach over what she'd experienced. Yet he had not anticipated Ava's shared and piercing response. Before he let her in on the rest of the Rosa file, he wanted to see if she would let *him* in on a little more about herself.

"I'll tell you everything," he said. "I promise. But first I have a question."

"And that would be?"

"That would be a curiosity about your passion concerning what happened to Abby and others like her 'in those days,' as you say. I know you're sensitive to the issue as a woman, but you seem to be exceptionally riled up about someone who's a total stranger to you."

"Yes," Ava said, her pot sticker still untouched and her arms folded across her chest. "Actually, I'm a bit touchy on the whole subject of domestic violence."

He took a sip of his hot tea, which was now cold, and then looked at her with a sideways glance. "Feel like telling me why?"

"No, I don't—but I guess I will."

Realizing that some of the mystery she'd been concealing was about to be disclosed, he leaned forward, his arms resting on the table, as he prepared to listen. Her blonde pouf of hair was feathered softly around her face and reflected highlights of the room's red and gold ambiance. Her naturally ruddy cheeks grew rosier as he watched—*an emotional giveaway*, he thought, *on this amazing woman*.

"Long story short," she said, "my husband and I had control problems. We were *both* sort of bullheaded and should never have been together in the first place—and I was as much at fault for that pairing as he was. But

I pushed for control using my *words* which, I admit, were pretty raw at times. He, on the other hand, used his fists."

Isaiah's adrenaline surged through his body at the mere thought of anyone battering her. But she continued speaking before he could say anything.

"Let me be clear. He never raped me or even attempted to do anything like that. But there were plenty of bruises and one black eye during the two years we were married, marks that I always tried to justify and explain away, like you see people do on Oprah. I finally packed up and left him. But one day, not too long after I moved out, he stormed into the school where I was teaching. I don't really think he would have hurt anyone there. But he was acting crazy—loud, and threatening—and he had a knife with him."

"Oh my God, Ava! That must have been terrifying for you!" Isaiah was leaning in farther across the table as he tried to visualize such a scene at her school.

"You can't even imagine. I'm sure he'd been drinking or was on some sort of drug," she said. "The police were called, and they arrested him. He's in jail now—still. I resigned my teaching job at the end of that term," she added, making no attempt to stop the tears that swelled out of her hazel eyes and down those rosy cheeks.

"But why did you leave? None of what happened was your fault."

"I know, and I loved my job so much … and those kids." The words were catching in her throat. "Nothing was the same, though. And after I testified against him at his trial—because he refused to take a plea, which would have been the sensible path—I was nervous about being so close to the children. Not that he was any kingpin or anything, with any sort of power. He just simply snuffed out the light in my career. Worse, he stole the sweet innocence from those kids who witnessed him breaking into my classroom, screaming at me like a madman. That's when I decided to move here. And I'm happy to report that this valley has helped make me whole again."

A pause lingered between them for several moments.

"I don't know what to say, Ava."

"There's really nothing *to* say. It is what it is. But I'm deeply touched by Abby's story because, more than sixty years later at my husband's trial, his attorney was still lobbing questions at me about what *I* might have done to provoke his client. As if *any* answer I could have given would have justified that sort of behavior. We've come a long way since 1947, but not

131

far enough. So," she said, unfolding her arms, picking up her chopsticks, and dipping the pot sticker into the brown liquid perched over a candle warmer, "now you know."

"Right," he said, returning his focus to his own food as well, after realizing that the subject was being irrevocably shifted.

"So what happened next to Abby?" Ava asked. "And where did Rosa come from, as if I can't guess at this point?"

"Hmmm. Beautiful *and* intuitive," he said, smiling when he saw the glint of mischief appear in her eyes in place of the sadness. "I've been thinking that you might find Abby's actual notes of interest rather than hearing a summary. Listening to her describe things in her own words is very compelling, including things about my dad that I never knew. So I have an idea. We still have almost two hours before we're supposed to be at the old convent for our tour. Why don't we stop by the lodge after we finish here so you can see the file for yourself?"

"Sounds like a *wonderful* plan!" Then she put her chopsticks down again. "Are you really into this meal?"

"Not exactly."

"Why don't we split the bill and just leave?"

And that's precisely what they did, followed by a run through McDonald's drive-in window on their way back to the lodge.

*****

Fortunately, the housekeeping service at the lodge had already visited his suite while he'd been out.

"Ah, nice and tidy," he said as he opened the door and let Ava go in first. "Just the way I left it."

"Well, I'd be impressed if I believed you," she said, looking around at the surprisingly well-appointed room.

In addition to the kitchenette on the right wall as they entered, there was a sitting area straight ahead, with a sofa and end tables, two armchairs, a coffee table, and several lamps. A work area was on the wall to their left and, at the far right end of the room, beyond the kitchen, a king-size bed fluffed high with cushy bedcovers and at least a half dozen pillows was next to a large bathroom. The floor of the entire suite, except for the bath, was covered with a soft beige Berber-style carpeting.

"I must have driven by this place a thousand times," Ava said, taking a seat on the crème-colored velveteen sofa as she crossed her legs and looked around, "and I never would have guessed that these rooms were so lovely."

"I know. The building looks sort of old and weathered from the front," Isaiah replied, dropping two large McDonald's bags on the coffee table and sitting down in one of the dark brown upholstered armchairs facing Ava. "Truthfully, it wasn't always great inside either. I've been staying in this exact room since I was a kid, with my dad. And believe me, you wouldn't have felt this comfortable back then. But they renovated the place in about 2002 or '03, I think, and did a nice job. Of course, Dad died a couple of years later, and I'm sorry to say that I've only been back a few times since."

Ava smiled at him and nodded at the bags of food. "Hungry?" she asked.

"That I am. But would you mind if I took a minute to call my mother again? Then we can eat and go through Abby's stuff."

"Of course," she said, starting to unload and arrange the food, utensils, and napkins.

Isaiah first called the Queen Anne house and left a voice mail when there wasn't any answer. Developing a concerned look on his face, he tried Sarah's cell and left another message when she didn't answer that one either.

"I *cannot* figure out where she is," he said, the furrow lines in his brow becoming visibly deeper. "She called and gave me hell yesterday when I was up at Barney's—right after I met you, as a matter of fact—because I didn't check in with her when I got here Friday night. I promised her I'd be better about staying in touch, and I've been trying to find her since early this morning."

"She's probably just out with friends."

He looked off into nowhere, sighed, and shook his head. "You're probably right," he said, returning his focus to the coffee table, to Ava, and to the McDonald's spread. He started to raise his hamburger to his mouth but stopped and connected his eyes with hers. "You know something *else* I cannot figure out?"

"Tell me."

"I cannot figure out how it was *only yesterday* that I met you. I swear I must have known you in another life or something, because I've never been this comfortable with someone I've only known for one day."

She put a french fry in her mouth but started talking anyway. "I'm feeling the same way, Isaiah, although I'm not going to analyze it. Let's just be happy that we're relaxed with each other and leave it there for now. Okay?"

"Okay. So, how are your chicken nuggets?"

"They're *Mc*Nuggets—and they're the best."

"Terrific! Now, while you're savoring your meal," he said, pulling a letter-sized envelope out of a black file folder and removing several pieces of paper that were folded in thirds, "I thought you might also want to feast on this."

Ava took the letter from him and began to read.

November 26, 1947
The day before Thanksgiving

My dearest Tess—

Despite my endless prayers of late, I've been unable to find my way to giving thanks for much of anything that's happened in the last two months. I've been hoping that the clouds would part so this letter would be more uplifting than my last one, which I realize in retrospect would not take much effort. I fear upon reflection that learning of my entanglement with Danny Whitmore must have been very upsetting for you. And I'm so sorry about that.

Unfortunately, I'm not yet able to bring you any news that will make you feel better. In fact, just the opposite is true, if you can believe that's possible. And I'm hesitant to begin telling you the latest, but I know that I must. So, my friend, here's what's going on.

During the month that followed what I'm only able to refer to as "the incident," I slowly began to come to grips with what had happened to me. Caroline was (and remains) more helpful than there are words to describe. You would love her!

As you know, I had to confess the situation to her because my strange behavior and frequent absences from work were beginning to place my job in jeopardy. But once she knew the story, Caroline became an ally, a blessing, a true Godsend— and those three qualities were what I needed desperately. I still do, since I can't seem to find the end to this unthinkable catastrophe ...

*****

Father Moynihan's absolution and the penance he had assigned to Abby provided her with some reassurance that she wasn't going to hell, at least not over her most recent transgression. But Caroline had begun to play an even more essential role than the priest in Abby's recovery, because Caroline actually knew Danny. More importantly, she understood things from a woman's perspective and from a legal standpoint as well, something Abby hadn't even considered.

"Do you know an attorney?" Carolyn asked one Saturday morning while sharing coffee and sweet rolls in Abby's apartment.

"Yes I do," Abby said, her thoughts immediately turning to Sinclair. "Why do you ask?"

"Sometimes it's better to be too prepared than not at all, and this situation sort of cries out for that kind of caution."

"But it's over, Caroline."

"Is it? Then why are you still suffering?"

"Because I haven't completed my penance."

"Perhaps. Or maybe it's because Danny Whitmore committed a crime against you and should be in jail!"

Abby smiled. "My dear sweet Caroline. I understand that's how you feel, and I love you for it. But if a crime was committed, then I am partially responsible. So there will be no need for an attorney, unless you want me to go to jail too."

Abby felt a little stronger, due in large part, she knew, to the indestructible, absolute support that Caroline continued to provide.

By the end of October, Abby was consistently back at work and beginning to feel close to her old self again. She was also feeling God's presence more powerfully than ever before, and she was daring to believe in the possibility that she might one day be ready for a return to Lady of the Valley.

She understood that there was still more penance to undergo, however, despite the fact that she'd completed everything on Father Moynihan's list. *I'll know when I've done enough*, she continually reassured herself. *God will find a way to tell me that atonement has been accomplished.*

On November 4, 1947, a huge election was held in San Francisco, in which a number of candidates for various offices were on the ballot, as well as several initiatives to be decided by the voters. The most significant of those initiatives was the one designed to save the cable cars from extinction. In vibrant opposition to Mayor Lapham's plan to remove the cars and replace them with buses, Friedel Klussman had been successful in getting the initiative on the ballot. Throughout that process, the topic had consumed the city with heated controversy and ugly campaigning for months.

In the end, the initiative passed, protecting the cable cars from developers and professed "visionaries" who wanted to modernize the transit system. Modernization would still be part of the system's future, but all plans going forward would now need to include, and be worked around, the cable cars—those iconic symbols so inexorably linked with San Francisco.

Covering the social events leading up to that election had kept Abby extremely busy. And her presence at fundraisers had helped her regain her confidence and her emotional footing as she interviewed and mingled with people on the city's "Who's Who" list.

> *I'm sure that was Caroline's design when she assigned the stories to me. I didn't cover all the parties, of course, but enough to keep me on the go and distracted—and I had fun and really loved what I was doing, Tess. I truly did ...*

Her work was being well received by other editors too, according to Caroline at least, who called Abby into her office the day after the election.

"We've all decided to award you with the opportunity to accompany me when I cover the Klussman celebration this weekend," she said, looking up from her high-back swivel chair.

"You're joking!" Abby replied as she stood just inside the office door. Her first reaction was a thrill she could scarcely contain, because there's no way she would have ever been invited to an affair like that on her own, without Caroline's influence. But a familiar insecurity immediately tried to smother that excitement, since the Klussman gala on Saturday, November 8, in the Garden Court at the exclusive Palace Hotel, had been widely heralded in the society column as an elegant black-tie affair. And Abby certainly had nothing appropriate to wear, as usual.

"I've already thought of that," Caroline said, glancing down briefly at some papers on the desktop in front of her.

"You've thought of *what?*"

"Oh honestly, Abby. Stop being so serious for a minute. I can read your face, you know—*and* your mind—like you had the words written all over your forehead."

"Is that right? And just exactly what were those words saying?"

Caroline leaned back in her chair and smiled softly. "They were saying enough. And don't worry. We'll go shopping for a dress tomorrow over lunch."

Abby closed the door to keep from being overheard. "But you can't keep buying clothes for me, Caroline. I'm starting to feel like an orphan."

"So pay me back after you get a raise."

"I'm getting a raise?"

"Not if you keep hanging around here instead of doing your work. Go on now and get busy!"

The shopping excursion the following afternoon at one of Caroline's favorite boutiques produced a long black satin dress, simple and sleek with an empire waist, a scoop neck, and long sleeves. The accessories were simple and uncomplicated as well—matching black satin pumps, rhinestone button earrings, and a silver and rhinestone bracelet.

By the time Abby had applied a little more makeup than normal while getting ready on Saturday evening, and after she'd pulled her glossy jet-black hair up into a French twist, she looked supremely elegant and a far cry from simple.

"You certainly don't look like an orphan tonight," Caroline said when she picked Abby up in front of her apartment. "In fact, you look rather like a blue blood, if you want to know the truth."

"Thank you," Abby replied as she settled into the front passenger seat of Caroline's car. "If not for you, though, I would certainly—"

"Hey! I thought we agreed to stop going over that same ground."

"Right. Sorry." And then, after a pause, Abby added, "Can we talk about my raise yet?"

"No."

Then they both looked at each other and laughed, and their lighthearted mood was sustained throughout the rest of their short drive to the party at the grand Palace Hotel, one of San Francisco's crown jewels that Abby had studied in preparation for this night.

When the Palace originally opened in 1875, the space now occupied by the Garden Court Restaurant had been the hotel's carriage entrance. Then, despite the fact that the hotel had managed to survive the earthquake in 1906, the entire structure had subsequently been destroyed by the fire that swept through and decimated most of the downtown area in the aftermath of the quake.

Rebuilding began almost immediately, however, and the newly restored Palace Hotel reopened three years later in 1909, this time with the former carriage entrance transformed into the captivating grandeur of the Court. Marble Ionic columns framed the length of the massive room on each side, and the entire space was covered with a spectacular stained glass dome, from which Austrian crystal chandeliers were suspended in rows running parallel to the Ionic columns.

As she and Caroline moved with measured grace through the hotel lobby and into the prodigious restaurant, Abby was thinking that she'd never seen anything as breathtaking. And when she wasn't standing in one spot, with her head tilted back as she stared transfixed at the domed ceiling and brilliant chandeliers, she found herself following Caroline around like a puppy on a leash amidst the throng of celebrities. At one point, she swore she saw Cary Grant across the room. But rather than dismiss her observation, Caroline told her that she was probably right, which left Abby speechless as well as starstruck while she peered around every tuxedo and evening gown trying to find him again.

After the first hour, the novelty hadn't exactly worn off, but Abby had begun to feel more like an adult befitting her regal appearance. Caroline had helped that image along by pretending that her protégé was playing some sort of important journalistic role at the gala each time she introduced Abby to one luminary after another. Many of the people were familiar to Abby from the business and sports sections of the *Chronicle*, and she recognized a number of them from their pictures in the society pages that had been taken at functions she hadn't covered.

When they'd first arrived and Abby had become aware of the company she was in, she'd been extremely ill at ease, feeling way out of her social and intellectual league, despite Caroline's reassurance that she blended in perfectly. Then gradually, while the two women had mixed with the crowd, Abby's confidence had begun to stabilize, as more and more people seemed to have an interest in speaking with her.

In the middle of one of those fortifying conversations, Abby spotted Marcella Whitmore heading straight toward them. She was well aware that Mrs. Whitmore and Caroline had known each other for a long time and, according to Caroline, had become friends on some odd, cross-pollinating societal level. In fact, when Abby first told Caroline about "the incident" with Danny, Caroline's instantaneous response had been, "Well, I need to call Marcella!"

Of course, no suggestion could have been more horrifying to Abby at the time and, after she pleaded with Caroline to keep her awful secret in confidence, Caroline agreed, "as long as Danny doesn't do anything else to hurt you," she'd said. But her knowledge of that verbal agreement did not stop the panic from rising in Abby's chest when she saw Mrs. Whitmore's outstretched arms closing in.

"How nice to see *you* again too, Miss Ryan," Marcella said, after her effusive, hugging hello to Caroline. "And don't you look positively divine this evening."

"Thank you, Mrs. Whitmore." Abby knew she was saying the words, but she couldn't hear any sound coming out of her mouth as the sickening thought crept into her mind that Danny might be somewhere in the room as well.

"Isn't this an absolutely magical night?" Marcella bubbled, turning her attention back to Caroline.

"Indeed it is! The whole city should feel proud," she called out as Marcella waved and danced off to embrace the next group waiting for her. "I can understand why she's so happy to have the cable cars for posterity," Caroline said to Abby in a lowered voice when Marcella was gone. "But she seems positively giddy. A bit much, if you ask me, from a woman who I doubt has ever even ridden in a cable car."

Abby heard what Caroline was saying, although her focus was elsewhere while she searched the room for Danny's face.

"What's the matter?" Caroline asked her. "You're pale as a sheet all of a sudden."

"I'm okay. Just a little worried that *he* might be here."

"Oh my God. That never occurred to me. And of course you're worried," she said, wrapping her arm around Abby's black satin shoulders. "But I doubt that he's here, dear. Otherwise, I'm sure we would have seen him or heard him by now."

"Yes. I suppose that's true."

"Well, why don't we unwind a bit! I say we let our hair down and enjoy a cocktail. Just one won't hurt us, and I also want to explore that spread of hors d'oeuvres over there on that side of the room. Come. We need to partake of this grand party for a little while before we get back to business."

For the next forty-five minutes, Abby and Caroline softly worked the room, mingling as guests, sipping one martini each, and exploring the virtual village of food that had been constructed on one side of the Court. Amidst ice sculptures and champagne fountains, an unparalleled feast had been arranged—mounds of chilled seafood, pyramids of miniature sandwiches, heated carving stations offering succulent beef and lamb, and tiers of mouthwatering desserts.

And Abby *did* see Cary Grant again, a pinch-me event that was still preoccupying her thoughts when a loud drumroll sounded from the bandstand, silencing everyone's conversation.

"Maybe Klussman is going to speak now," Caroline whispered.

But instead of Friedel Klussman, Admiral Whitmore walked up on the stage with the band, moving to the center and taking hold of the microphone with a swagger. A smattering of applause circulated among the guests as they watched him.

"Thank you all for being here tonight!" he said, speaking so close to the microphone that the sound reverberated. "Many of you worked tirelessly to ensure this victory for our beloved cable cars! *And—we—made—history!*" The polite applause erupted into cheers and hoots reminiscent of a high school sporting event. "Our honored host," he continued when the noise finally began to subside, "Mr. Friedel Klussman—" Another round of hollering and cheering broke out as soon as the name was spoken. "Friedel will be addressing us shortly," Admiral Whitmore blared into the microphone, quieting the crowd. "First, though, I have the esteemed and long-awaited pleasure of announcing something *else* we're celebrating tonight. This is certainly different from the cable cars, but no less amazing or historic, at least in my opinion."

At that point, Marcella Whitmore walked up the steps of the stage and stood beside her husband, followed by several other people who Abby hadn't met—and then by Danny, who was handsome and dapper in his tuxedo and who was holding hands with a beautiful woman.

"Ladies and gentlemen," the admiral said, "I know that many of you have been expecting this for some time, and that moment has finally arrived. With great pride and excitement, Marcella and I are thrilled to announce the engagement of our son, Danny, to Miss Anabeth Davis!"

One would have thought that the war had ended all over again, the way jubilation took over the room. But Abby felt as if she were going to pass out, and Caroline seemed to be worried about the same thing as she immediately put her arm around her protégé and ushered her out of the Court into the hotel lobby.

"I'm taking you home," she said. "And I'll stay with you as long as you want—all night, if necessary."

Abby didn't feel like protesting, knowing that the last thing she needed to be right now was alone. "But what about your coverage of the event?" she asked.

"I've seen enough," Caroline said. "And you're more important—*way* more important."

Once they were inside the car, Abby's composure collapsed, and the tears she'd been containing were unleashed.

"I *cannot* believe this, Caroline!" she cried. "The man who pretended to be interested in me and then defiled both my body and my soul was already planning to marry someone else!"

"I've been worried that something like this might happen," Caroline said softly.

"What? You *knew* about that woman?"

"I knew *of* her, Abby. Now please try to calm down. When we get to your place, I want you to lie down. I'll make us some tea, and then we'll talk."

"God help me," Abby sobbed, her head in her hands. "I don't think I can get through this."

"Yes you can, dear. And I'm going to help you."

An hour later, they were comfortably cocooned in Abby's apartment, sipping hot tea, with Abby stretched out on the sofa and Caroline in one of the armchairs in the bay window alcove. Gradually, Caroline began filling in the blanks, which also helped explain her unflattering assessment of Danny Whitmore from the beginning. She told Abby that Danny and Anabeth had been an item for several years, and that the anticipated "merger" between the Whitmore and Davis families promised to be the largest social event in the city in decades. But there was a widely held assumption that the couple had been delaying their nuptials because Danny wasn't quite ready to give up the plentiful sowing of his wild oats.

"That's disgusting," Abby said, grabbing another tissue to blot her eyes and nose.

"You're right. And perhaps the fact that I wanted to speak with Marcella as soon as you told me what happened on that picnic makes more sense to you now."

"And perhaps you won't be surprised to learn that I'm thinking about having the word 'fool' carved across my forehead."

Abby had some familiarity with the Davis family, and even recognized the parents from some of the events she'd covered. But she'd never heard a word about Anabeth, nor had she even seen a picture of her in any society story since she'd been in San Francisco.

"Why is that, Caroline? Where has she been?"

"On a four-month trip to Europe—her last *maiden* voyage, if you'll pardon the double entendre. Rumor has it that Danny agreed to move forward with the engagement, and the forced march of his fidelity thereafter, once she returned from overseas. And she finally arrived back in San Francisco the week before the election."

"So I guess I was the lucky winner chosen to be his last conquest," Abby said. Caroline just looked at her in silence as she sipped on her tea. "*What?*" Abby exclaimed. "There were *more* after me?" The ongoing silence answered Abby's question. "Holy Mother of God! How could I have been such an idiot?"

Caroline continued to sit with Abby and talk until almost two o'clock in the morning. After awhile, their conversation turned to other things besides Danny, more pleasant topics, such as their work and exciting functions scheduled throughout the city that they would be attending. And by the time Caroline finally said good-bye shortly before dawn, Abby had begun to think that, as upset and humiliated as she was, her future might be salvageable after all. She had made a huge mistake and had learned a painful lesson. But she believed her sin was in the process of being forgiven, and she was working on forgiving herself for her stupidity.

When she climbed into her bed and turned out the light, as hints of daybreak were peeking through the shades on her bedroom window, she was surprised that she was actually experiencing a little peace. She even dared to imagine that a return to Lady of the Valley might not be so improbable.

Then, two weeks later, after doing some heart-pounding calculations and trying to ignore things that were happening to her body, she did her best to pray her way out of a mounting fear and went to see a doctor. He examined her and did a blood test. The confirmation came the following week.

"I'm pregnant."

She and Caroline were at the Maiden Lane restaurant after work again, at Abby's request. But Abby's dinner sat untouched, and Caroline stopped eating as soon as the words were out of Abby's mouth.

"Are you sure?"

"I wish I could say no—that I was only making a bad joke. But yes. I'm sure."

"Oh Abby, I'm so sorry this is happening to you."

"I know. Me too."

"What are you going to do?"

"Well, once I stopped throwing up—a feeling I have all the time now, by the way—I went to see Father Moynihan and explained my plight. I asked him if he could help me find a Catholic Charities home in this area that would take me in until the baby is born. Then I'll put the child up for adoption. He agreed to assist me, so I'm just waiting to hear what he suggests. I have to tell you, though, that this is all very frightening, and it's not such good news for my job either, is it?"

"No, but let's not worry about that right now. You'll have your job until you can't work anymore. And then you can come back later, if you still want to."

"Caroline, you're unbelievable, and I don't deserve you. But knowing that I can still work, for a while anyway, makes me feel a little more secure."

"If you *really* want security," Caroline said, leaning in toward the center of the table over her dinner plate, "then what *I* think you need to do is tell Danny."

"Oh right. That would be just terrific!" Abby answered, astonished at the thought. "Let's see. How would that conversation go? Uh, excuse me, Miss Davis. Would you mind if I borrowed Danny for a minute? I have something I need to tell him."

"I'm not suggesting that Anabeth be involved. Just Danny. He's responsible for your predicament, and he has an obligation to help pay for whatever these next several months are going to cost."

"You're very sweet, as always, Caroline. But there's absolutely no way I could ever confront him with this. It's completely out of the question."

Caroline did not give up, however. Over the next week, she managed to convince Abby about the importance of at least telling *someone* in the Whitmore family.

"If you can't bring yourself to speak with Danny, which I do understand, then I will help you arrange a meeting with Marcella. And I'll go with you."

"And what good would that do? Assuming you could get me there without tying me up and putting me in a box."

"You have no idea how much difference that single meeting would make. I know her—and I know she understands her son. Trust me, Abby. Let me help you."

*****

Abby couldn't remember ever shaking the way she was when she and Caroline arrived at the Whitmore mansion on the afternoon of Friday, November 21, 1947. Abby had not been back to that house since the whole disaster had begun brewing in September. But Mister Ben seemed to remember her when he opened the door, and he clearly knew Caroline.

"Good afternoon, ladies," he said as he ushered them into the grand foyer. Then he layered their coats over his arm, his kind eyes and wise face somehow connecting with Abby's soul and making her feel more comfortable. *It's almost as if he knows why we're here*, she thought. *Perhaps he's watched this scene play out before in this house.* "Mrs. Whitmore will be down shortly," he said. Then he escorted them to the library and closed the doors.

Marcella made her appearance about ten minutes later and took a seat across the reading table from Caroline and Abby after a perfunctory hello to each of them. Thankfully, Caroline did most of the talking, because Abby was so terrified that she was convinced she'd be mute if she opened her mouth. Despite the tension, however, there was obviously a warm relationship between Marcella and Caroline, who did an amazing job of keeping the message informational rather than confrontational— "we thought you should know ..." and "we thought you'd want to be advised ..."

Abby was equally as impressed with Mrs. Whitmore, who remained calm and civil, and who didn't seem at all shocked to hear her son being accused of rape. At one point, she turned to Abby and asked very matter-of-factly when and where "the event" had taken place and how far along in her pregnancy she was. After Abby had squeaked out the answers, Marcella stood up, thanked both women for coming, gave Caroline a kiss on the cheek, and said she would be in contact within a few days. Then she turned and left the room.

Once Mister Ben had retrieved their coats and they were on the sidewalk in front of the house, Abby began to find her voice again.

"But, Caroline, you never even mentioned anything about financial assistance to her. So why did we put ourselves through this torture? I thought the reason we came here was to ask for help with the pregnancy expenses."

"Believe me, Abby. Marcella Whitmore understood very clearly what we wanted, although I'm not sure how she's going to respond. If the whole thing were left up to her, I'd have a better idea. But unfortunately, she'll be consulting with the admiral, and with Danny as well, I imagine. So, my dear, this would be a good time to contact that attorney you said you know. It's possible that you're going to need someone to help you negotiate things."

With fear and humiliation rising again to new levels, Abby called Sinclair that night, using the telephone in Caroline's house rather than the communal phone in the hallway of her hotel floor. When she heard his voice, she started shaking and began to cry before she'd scarcely spoken a word.

"Abby! What's happened?" he asked, the concern in his voice such a comfort, as always. "I had a feeling something was wrong when I didn't hear from you for so long."

"Yes, I'm sorry," she said, struggling to gather her composure. "I thought that things were going to be all right—that I could manage the situation on my own."

"Well, I don't know what you're talking about, and I don't really care. I think I need to make a trip down there to see you."

"Truthfully, that might not be such a bad idea. But first you need to let me tell you the sordid details because, once I do, you might never want to see me again."

"I find that highly doubtful," he said. "But go ahead."

With great difficulty as she fought back her tears, she stumbled and bumped through the explanation of all that had transpired since she'd first arrived at the Whitmore mansion to cover the veteran's home fundraiser. And when she finished telling the story, instead of sounding angry or judgmental, Sinclair continued to be gentle.

"I just feel terrible that I haven't been closer, so I could have been of help sooner," he said. "On second thought, the distance is probably a good thing. Otherwise, I'd probably be in jail for assaulting that *as ...* that sniveling excuse for a man. But I'll be there on Monday, so you try to get some rest in the meantime. And please try to stop beating yourself up."

"Thank you, Sinclair. You always seem to be there in the worst of times, you know. And I doubt that you'll ever understand how grateful I am. I'm looking forward to seeing you too. Hopefully, by the time you get here, we will have heard from Mrs. Whitmore, although Caroline doesn't think there will be any word before Monday. Apparently, the Whitmore and Davis families are up in Napa Valley for the Thanksgiving weekend at the Whitmores' country home. So we shouldn't expect them to contact us until after they return."

"Well, whether you've heard from them or not by the time I arrive, *they* are going to hear from *us* very shortly."

> *So, my dear Tess, I'm praying for strength to get out of this mess. Take care, my friend. Write to me if you can, and I'll send off another letter to you as soon as I know what the next step is going to be. I miss you and love you!*
>
> *Abby*

*****

Ava rested the letter in her lap and looked up at Isaiah, who was still seated in one of the suite's armchairs, facing her across the coffee table.

"I'm exhausted," she said. "That poor woman! Is there more in those file folders that tells us the rest of what happened to her?"

"There's plenty. In Rosa's file, at least. Zoie's is the one that's sort of skimpy by comparison, but I'm hoping she and her father will be able to fill in the blanks after they arrive tomorrow."

"What time will they be here?"

"Their flight gets into Spokane about one o'clock, and I've arranged for a car service to pick them up. So they should arrive at the lodge by three-ish."

"Shoot! I have to work the three-to-eleven shift tomorrow," she said, the disappointment visible on her face.

"Don't worry. I'll make sure you meet everyone. What's your schedule on Tuesday?"

"I'm supposed to work the same shift again. But I have a lot of vacation time that's been building up. I think I'll call my boss and see if I can take a couple of days off."

"That would be great, Ava. Then we could all have dinner together on Tuesday night."

"I'll see what I can do. Meanwhile, what happened to Abby after your dad flew down to San Francisco?"

Isaiah scooped up all the McDonald's containers and wrappers and dropped them in the wastebasket next to the work desk. Then he opened the Rosa file and began removing the contents. Ava watched as journals, steno pads, more letters, and several 11" × 14" manila envelopes began covering the surface of the coffee table.

"We don't have time to go through all of this before we leave for the convent tour," he said. "But we still have about half an hour. According to Abby's notes, Dad flew down from Seattle the Monday after Thanksgiving and met her at Caroline's house that evening. After he got there, Abby and Caroline informed him that the initial response from the Whitmores was an offer to pay to send her overseas for an abortion."

"*What?* You have to be kidding!"

"Nope. Can you imagine coming at a young, naïve Catholic woman, who'd been in training to be a nun, with something like that?"

"No, I cannot. And putting the social and moral issues aside, abortions were illegal in the United States back then."

"That's why they wanted to ship her overseas."

"So, what was Plan B, since Plan A obviously didn't come to pass?"

"The details are very clear in the agreement here," he said, pointing to one of the manila envelopes, "although Abby's journals indicate that Dad's negotiation of that agreement might have included some mild threats."

"What kind of threats? From whom to whom?"

"From Dad to the Whitmores. Threatening to go to the police—*and* the newspapers—with the rape allegation."

"But that would have been so hard to prove. Especially in those days."

"I don't think that was the point. Dad was raised in pretty much the same social structure as the Whitmores. He would have understood the power of just *threatening* to put something like that in the newspaper. Two elite families getting ready to combine their scope of influence through the marriage of their children—and then this meteor hits them? Just the *idea* of a well publicized accusation of rape against Danny—whether anything could have been proven or not—would have been horrifying to the Whitmores. And knowing Dad, he would have been very skilled at painting a picture for them of what was likely to happen once Anabeth and her family got wind of what was going on. Even the *hint* of a scandal that huge going public—with the truth being irrelevant at that point—would have probably derailed the wedding."

"So, what did they do?"

"They paid her to go away. Here—take a look at this."

January 7, 1948 / 11:15 PM

Dear Tess—

This letter is being written from Napa Valley, where the Whitmore country place will be my new home for the next six months. If I didn't feel like I was in a prison (of my own making, sadly), I would be soaking up the beauty of this massive house and the acres of lush land all around. We're up on a hill, and the peacefulness reminds me of Lady of the Valley.

We arrived this afternoon. Admiral Whitmore and Mister Ben drove us up here—"us" being me and Euleen, who is Mister Ben and Miss Peel's fifteen-year-old daughter. She'll be my companion for the duration, and she's as sweet as her parents. I'm grateful she's the one they chose.

This is all part of the agreement Sinclair worked out with the Whitmores, who decided after I refused to end my pregnancy that they could not permit their blood grandchild to be adopted by strangers. So they'll be taking the baby themselves. Or, more accurately, Danny and Anabeth will be the ones taking the baby, in the strangest plan imaginable.

Their wedding will go forward on schedule in March, and then they'll take their honeymoon in Florida, where Anabeth will supposedly strike up an unconventional friendship with a young female employee at the hotel who confesses to Anabeth that she is pregnant. Long story short, as far as their friends and the public will know, Anabeth will be the one who wants to adopt the baby, and Danny will finally agree because of his "deep and abiding love for his new wife." Almost makes me want to throw up.

I cannot understand why Anabeth would consent to such a charade. Caroline says that she thinks the woman actually loves Danny, which is incomprehensible to me. When I first brought up the idea of adoption to Father Moynihan, never did I dream that a series of events like those engulfing me would come to pass. And Marcella Whitmore has turned out to be so very clever—protecting the reputation of her son and, by default, her family, while still managing to have her blood grandchild close at hand, even though that truth will be a carefully crafted secret.

Nonetheless, whatever my feelings might be about Danny, growing up as a Whitmore will bring a far more promising future than anything I will ever be able to provide. There is some hope for me, though, Tess. Sinclair's agreement with the family will include a lump sum of money that I will receive when I release the baby—a payment large enough to take care of my needs for a long time to come, and one that will eliminate any excuses for my not figuring out what to do with myself.

I will also be guaranteed a job at a newspaper somewhere, although the "somewhere" must be far enough away from California to assure the Whitmores that I will not become a problem. I'll let you know where I end up.

First, though, I must complete this pregnancy, which, at the moment, feels like an unending case of the flu. I've brought with me a supply of empty journals that I'm hoping to fill and, of course, there will be many letters to you and Sinclair. I've always been on the lookout for an interesting story to cover, and I guess I might as well start with my own.

Well, Euleen has just knocked on my door to tell me that the local Whitmore doctor is here to see me. I don't think I want to see him right now, but I suppose I have no choice.

Oh, Tess, how I miss you—and how I'm praying that you'll forgive me for this disaster.

Always your dearest friend (and trying to make amends with God),

Abby

"Every letter to Tess and my dad is copied word for word into her journals," Isaiah said, now sitting next to Ava on the sofa inside his suite. "Abby must have been worried that the letters would get misplaced, and she wanted to make sure the story didn't get lost as well."

"She must have been worried about so *many* things," Ava replied, resting her hands on top of the letter in her lap. "And what a lonely, scary situation."

"I wish you could have known her the way I did, Ava, as little as that might have been. Even though she was sequestered in that convent, she always seemed like a tough, feisty lady. So she came a long way from the young woman in that letter. And speaking of the convent," Isaiah said, looking at his watch, "we'd better get going. We're supposed to be there for our tour in ten minutes."

He stood up, walked around the coffee table, and began pulling on his jacket while Ava straightened the piles of journals and papers.

"I'm dying to read the rest of this," she said, rising to her feet and picking up her sweater and pocketbook. "Does she mention anywhere how much money the Whitmores paid her?"

"Nope," he answered, placing his hand on her back and guiding her toward the suite's door. "Not that I've found. In fact, there isn't very much information at all after she headed east."

"East? East where?"

"As far away from them as they could send her without shipping her overseas," Isaiah said as they made their way down the hall to the lobby. "The job the Whitmores arranged for her was at the *Washington Post* in Washington DC. And that was just the beginning. Somehow she then ended up in North Carolina, with Zeke Gerard."

"And then there was Zoie," Ava added.

"Right. And then back here to the convent. You know, getting through all of this could end up taking a lot of time, with you and me together." Isaiah grinned and put his arm around her shoulders, giving her a squeeze as they walked through the parking lot toward his Jag.

"Well, I'm in—as long as we keep going for rides in this car."

CHAPTER ELEVEN

"This room, which we use as our formal living room and is where we put our Christmas tree, used to be the chapel." Mrs. Baldwin had welcomed Isaiah and Ava with an obvious eagerness to talk about the former convent that she and her husband had called home since 1989.

They made a handsome couple, appearing to be in their mid-to-late sixties and in lean physical condition. He was about five foot eight, and she was a good six inches shorter. They both had gray hair—hers still salt-and-peppery and fastened in a braided wrap at the crown of her head; his close to white, thin and receding, and combed neatly with a side part. And they seemed to move and speak in perfect rhythm, the way those rare couples do when they're still really in love with each other, even after decades of marriage.

The four of them sat on matching brown leather sofas—Isaiah and Ava on one, and Mr. and Mrs. Baldwin on the other—facing each other across an oversized square mahogany coffee table. Mr. Baldwin had poured a deep burgundy wine into four delicate crystal goblets from a crystal decanter shortly after Isaiah and Ava's arrival, and he was already refilling his and Isaiah's glasses not yet thirty minutes into the visit.

A realistic gas log fire on the raised brick hearth was complete with an authentic crackling sound. The fire burned behind smoky glass fireplace doors that gleamed with brass trim and ornate brass door pulls. The exposed brick chimney extended upward through the full height of the open two-story room and was flanked on either side by rectangular windows that extended down about three feet beneath the ceiling.

"When the nuns lived here," Mrs. Baldwin continued, "the chapel had a low ceiling, and that upper part of the chimney and those two windows up there were part of the room that used to be above us. The family that owned the property immediately prior to us did a massive renovation, and that's when the ceiling in here was removed to make this an open two-story room. The upper part of the staircase," she added, pointing to the soaring flight of stairs leading to the second floor, "was also exposed at that time. The handrail and spindles on both the stairway and the landing are all originals, dating back to the early 1900s when this place was first built as Sacred Heart Academy. After this became a convent in 1934, the hearth and chimney were covered over, and the chapel altar was positioned flush against the fireplace wall."

"*That's* why everything looks so different to me," Isaiah said.

"Oh? You've been here before?" Mr. Baldwin asked.

"Yes, many times when I was a boy, starting when I was five or six, I think. My dad used to bring me here twice a year to visit one of the nuns—a friend of the family."

"How interesting," Mrs. Baldwin said. "Then you probably noticed a number of changes when you drove down our driveway today."

"If you mean the original buildings that are gone now, my father and I actually saw that demolition happening in the mideighties. We were still coming up here, even after the nuns moved out, when I was in college."

"How much was torn down?" Ava asked.

Mrs. Baldwin opened a large manila envelope that had been resting on the coffee table and removed several letter-sized black-and-white photocopies that she handed to Ava across the table. "As you can see," she said, "the original structure, most of which was dormitory space but also included the part that is now our house, was three stories in height and extended back about three times again the length of this building we're sitting in."

Looking at the massive scale of the former convent in the photographs, Ava shook her head. "Why would they have destroyed so much?" she asked.

"Well, they wanted to turn the place into a private family home," Mr. Baldwin replied. "And hundreds—perhaps thousands—of feet of old dormitory rooms weren't nearly as appealing, I guess, as the open land they gained once the majority of the main building was gone. After all, the property did belong to them, so they could do whatever they wanted."

"I know," Ava said. "But I can't stop thinking about all that history suddenly gone."

"Frankly," Mrs. Baldwin said, "the surviving sisters weren't very happy about it either. Having lived in a cloistered environment for most of their adult lives, they were pretty tight when they went their separate directions. Most of them stayed in touch with each other and with what was going on in the valley—even those who relocated to Spokane. But fortunately," she added, "we have lots of pictures of things as they were during Lady of the Valley's thirty-six years—and, believe it or not, a lot of history still remains. When we bought the property in 1989, we met and built friendships with a number of the sisters who'd lived here. And we took great care to preserve and restore whatever was left of their convent—especially the gymnasium, which the sisters called Saint Thomas Hall, along with the cemetery and the gazebo. For many years, we operated a bed-and-breakfast here, and Lady of the Valley lore—including things like the legend of Sister Ladolpha, the ghost, who some say still appears in the cemetery—was something that drew a large number of our guests here. Of course, the sheer beauty of this valley, which many believe is almost mystical, added to the appeal."

"My family used to come to Kettle Falls to camp when I was little," Ava said, "and I moved here a year ago on my own. So I know what you mean. The local kids playing with us down at the campgrounds every summer would tell the story about the ghost nun to scare little girls like me—with great success, I might add. And then, once I grew up, there was just *something* about the valley that pulled me in every time I came back. It truly is a magical, secret place in this big country of ours."

Mrs. Baldwin leaned back into the folds of the leather sofa, looking first at Ava and then at Isaiah. "Would you two like us to show you around the property?" she asked.

"We'd like that very much," Isaiah said, "but we don't want to trouble you or take up any more of your time." He felt Ava's elbow nudge him gently in his side.

"Nonsense," Mrs. Baldwin said, rising to her feet at the precise moment her husband did. "We've been looking forward to this, especially since we learned of your close association with both Sister Abby and Tess." In an apparent response to the look of surprise on both Isaiah and Ava's faces, she smiled broadly. "This is a *very* small town, Mr. Mellington, and I must confess that word about your lengthy history in our little part of the world has preceded you."

"Uh-oh," Isaiah said as he and Ava also stood up.

"Don't worry." Mr. Baldwin smiled and gently patted Isaiah on the back. "It's all been good, all the gossip and crazy tales we've been hearing about you." Then he laughed good-naturedly and filled everyone's wine glasses one more time from the decanter. "Just kidding! Now, grab your drinks. Nothing deserves a bold toast like this little forty-acre plot of land, and we'll offer a hefty one up for Lady of the Valley and for Sister Abby—and for Tess too—when we're outside."

The tour took another hour. On the back edge of the property, they saw the ravine that had once been full of water and had frozen over every winter, supplying the sisters with their own ice skating rink. Inside the gymnasium, they were asked to imagine the sisters playing basketball. In another part of what had been Saint Thomas Hall, they were shown the room where the sisters crafted works of art for sale in the outside world as well as functional items required inside the convent.

Then they wound their way around the grounds, past the quarter-acre vegetable garden, which Mrs. Baldwin explained looked much like the one the sisters would have planted. Back in the far corner of the property was the original maintenance building where equipment was stored and where the men who took care of the estate would have lived. Retracing their steps, they passed spectacular evergreen trees well over one hundred years old as they headed toward the cemetery, located in the center of the forty acres.

The entrance to the graveyard was marked by a stone grotto, in which a white statue of the Madonna was mounted. On either side of the grotto were archways constructed of the same stone. As the Baldwins, Isaiah, and Ava walked beneath the archway on the right, all of their casual conversation ceased. Immediately in front of them were graves marked by identical marble headstones, in the shape of crosses, positioned on concrete slabs. There were twenty headstones in all, commemorating sisters born as early as 1877 and as late as 1932. The first to be buried were three sisters in 1942, the oldest of those being Mother Mary Bonaventure, OP, age sixty-five, who was the convent's foundress, according to the epitaph. The youngest sister buried was the one born in 1932—Sister Mary Cecilia, OP, who died in 1964 when she was only thirty-two. The last to be buried was Mother Mary Seraphica, OP, who died in 1967 at the age of ninety.

As Isaiah studied the headstones, he realized with a rush of emotion that Abby and Tess could just as easily have been buried there as well—but he'd been lucky enough to know them both and, remarkably, to still have Tess around. He needed to call her when they got back to the lodge, to let her know what he'd seen, what he'd learned, and what he was feeling. The scope and magnitude of her life, and of Abby's, was suddenly overwhelming to him as he stood in the midst of the graves. Telling Tess about his newfound understanding and appreciation of what she'd been through was an unexpected priority.

Ava's arm was linked in his as they followed the Baldwins back under the stone archway and out of the cemetery. He thought his visualizations of the past could not become more vivid than what he'd just experienced. But then he realized that they were approaching the gazebo, and once they'd stepped inside, Abby's words from her journal began spinning through his mind.

> *But my moment of tranquility was abruptly shattered, and the pamphlets flew out of my hands as an overpowering force plowed into me from behind, viciously shoving me to the ground. Somehow a scream managed to escape my lips just before my nose and face slammed into the gazebo's stone floor . . .*
>
> *Suddenly a wild commotion erupted as other voices were being added to the mix. Staggering to my feet and raising my hand to catch the blood dripping from my nose and mouth, I turned and saw four figures in olive green fatigues drag the two attackers out of the gazebo and throw them face down on the grass. Once the pair had been subdued, with their wrists somehow tethered behind their backs, one of the olive green figures came into focus—the soldier who'd given me the pamphlets.*
>
> *"Oh my God, Sister, are you all right?" he asked me, his anxious voice and expression both blessings to behold . . .*
>
> *He placed his hands on my shoulders and gently lowered me to the built-in bench encircling the inside of the gazebo. I felt his arm wrap around me, and as I realized I was going to pass out, I believed that God was speaking to me through this calamity and through this handsome warrior . . .*

The "he"—the "handsome warrior"—had been Isaiah's father, and although he'd already come to grips with this part of Abby's story, minus the explanation about why his dad had failed to mention a word, Isaiah felt a chill when he realized where he was standing. But before he could whisper "I'm in the exact spot where Dad met Abby" into Ava's ear, another voice caught his attention.

"I mentioned earlier that we'd have a toast outside," Mr. Baldwin was saying, raising his glass in the air, "and we think this is the best place to do that. Our tour is now complete, having led us to the gazebo where the sisters, we're told, spent a lot of their free time. We often come out here and believe we can feel the spirit and intent of their mission in this spot, as we do in the cemetery. So, in memory of Sister Abby, who became a sainted soul in our community—and in honor of Tess, who we're still blessed to have with us and who endeared herself to people in this valley through her years of teaching—let's raise our glasses to toast two very remarkable women. May God wrap his arms around the one who's already up there with Him and watch over the one we so love down here. Please watch over the rest of us too, by the way, and help Tess be strong during the next few days."

"Here-here!" Mrs. Baldwin, Isaiah, and Ava all said in unison. Then, while the others moved out of the gazebo and made their way across the grass toward the house, Isaiah looked around one more time before downing the rest of his wine in a single swallow and hurrying to catch up with Ava. She and the Baldwins had reached the back wall of the house, which had once been connected to the long dormitory buildings.

As Isaiah approached, Mr. Baldwin looked at him and pointed to a place in the wall where a doorway appeared to have been bricked over. "This was most likely the approximate point," he said, "where you and your dad would have been taken to see Sister Abby. The visitation room supposedly started right here, forming the transition from the public rooms into the dormitories."

Isaiah knew that the cloistered nuns had been completely sequestered, even from the other sisters who had chosen not to be monastic. The two groups didn't even attend Mass together in the chapel. But the cloistered sisters *were* allowed brief visits a few times a year from special people. Isaiah remembered being led with his father from the convent's front door, past the chapel, past a living room with a fireplace, and down a long hallway. A door would then be opened for them, and they would enter a room only about six feet deep but twice as wide from side to side. There they would be seated at a counter that ran the full width of the room, in front of closed wood panels that rose from the top of the counter to the ceiling.

After a few minutes of waiting, some nun, who was never introduced and always seemed to appear from nowhere, would walk up behind them, slide the heavy wood panels open, and then disappear. Isaiah and his dad would be looking through a thick wire mesh screen, which was called a grille, and on the other side would be Sister Abby, seated, with her head covered in her black veil and her hands folded on the counter in front of her. Even though they couldn't touch her, and even though her image was a little fuzzy through the grille, he remembered that the radiance of her smile always came through clearly. And the melodic tone of her voice was soothing, almost as if she were singing to them, as she exchanged pleasantries with Sinclair and asked Isaiah questions about his schooling.

Then abruptly and too soon, the other nun would appear again and begin to slowly close the wood panels, first one side and then the other. As this was happening, Abby would whisper something Isaiah couldn't hear to his dad right before she would say, "Remember how happy I am and that I'm praying you'll find your way to the same peace. 'Bye for now, and God bless you."

Then his father would lean forward and press his hand against the grille. "Good-bye, Abby," he would say, just as the other nun was pushing the second wood panel shut tight.

"Isaiah?" Ava was holding his left hand, and he realized that his right hand was flattened against the outside back wall of the house. "Are you okay?" she asked him.

"What? Oh," he said, removing his hand from the cool brick and turning to look at her and the Baldwins. "Sorry. Guess my memories got the best of me for a minute. Must have something to do with the giant building that's missing," he added with a forced laugh, trying to bridge the odd discomfort of the moment.

"Would you like to come back inside for a little while?" Mrs. Baldwin asked as they all began walking on the concrete path again toward the front door.

"Thank you so much," Isaiah replied, "but we really do need to get going. I can't tell you how much we appreciate the time you've taken with us, though. This has been an amazing experience and one I had honestly not anticipated."

"I agree," Ava said. "Being here with you, and learning so much about the history, has fulfilled a secret wish I've had since I was ten years old when my parents and I first drove by this place on the way to camp. And meeting you has been such a bonus!"

"The pleasure has been ours, my dear," Mrs. Baldwin said.

After handing their wine glasses to Mr. Baldwin, Isaiah and Ava headed toward the Jag, turning to wave good-bye to their hosts.

"We'll see you Thursday at the funeral," Mr. Baldwin called out.

"Great!" Isaiah answered back, realizing how far away Thursday seemed in that moment as he opened the passenger door for Ava. "I haven't even been thinking about the funeral," he said, lowering his voice so only she could hear him as she slid into the front bucket seat. "Guess that's because we've been talking about Abby like she's still here."

"Maybe she is. Lots of people believe—"

But Isaiah closed the door before she could finish her sentence.

*****

Ava apparently understood that he wasn't in the mood for any discussion of afterlife theories because they rode without saying a word for the first mile back to Colville. Their silence was being serenaded by Rod Stewart singing "The Very Thought of You" from his *Great American Songbook* CD playing in the Jag's entertainment system. Then Isaiah and Ava both began speaking at once.

"You go first," he said, laughing along with her.

"Okay," she agreed, turning down the stereo volume without asking permission. "I was just going to say that I think your father would be proud of the way you're handling this whole situation for him."

"I'm not so sure about that." He kept his eyes fixed on the road ahead as he struggled with an odd mixture of vexing tears and an unanticipated surge of anger bubbling up just beneath the surface of his control. "Dad was never very liberal with his praise. And besides, he's the one who dumped all of this on me without any warning or explanation. So I don't think he's earned any brownie points or any right to an opinion."

"You sound upset."

"Yeah. I guess I am."

She reached across the center console and placed her hand on his shoulder, patting him gently without comment. He returned the gesture with a quick glance and a smile.

"Can I ask you a question about Abby?" she said, keeping her hand in place on his shoulder and softly moving her fingers back and forth on his sweater.

"Sure," he replied, returning his focus to the road.

"Were your visits with her different after the convent closed? I mean, that would have been a big change, with her being out in the open instead of behind that screen."

He took a moment to rewind his memory tapes. "Well, I was in my sophomore or junior year of college—can't remember which—the first time we went to see her after the move. The one picture that does stand out was the clarity of her face. She'd always looked sort of blurry behind the grille, so seeing her without any distortion was a big change. She was really quite beautiful. And she did shake our hands when we walked in. That was the first time I'd actually touched her, which was a little uncomfortable, now that I think about it. But otherwise, there wasn't much difference. She sat across a big table from us in a little meeting room in the hospital, and we went through the same Q and A session that we always did. I do recall Dad asking if she was happy in the new place, and she said yes, of course. I don't think I *ever* heard a word of complaint out of her. Then she gave us both a hug when we were leaving, which also felt strange, and that was it."

"How did your dad feel about seeing her in the new setting?"

"I don't know. He never said, and I never asked." Isaiah glanced over at Ava because he thought he could guess what she was thinking. "That's just the way we were with each other."

"I didn't say anything, Isaiah."

"You didn't have to." Then he reached back, took her hand from his shoulder, and brought her fingers to his lips.

"Did you visit Abby regularly after that?"

"Not like we used to. I was older and busy with my own stuff, and sometimes I even lied to Dad, telling him I had something going on when I didn't."

"So, how often *did* you go?"

"Every year or two. I tried to convince him that making the trip by plane might be more efficient. Instead of taking three days, we could have flown from Seattle to Spokane in less than an hour, so we could have completed the travel *and* the visit in the same day. But he was stuck on the old routine, and I just didn't want to do it anymore. Funny thing, though. Last Friday I never even considered flying."

"That is kind of odd. Why do you think that was?"

"Probably because I hadn't made the drive since my dad died, and taking the trip in the Jag sort of appealed to me, I guess."

"It's been four years since you saw Abby?"

"No. I flew out a few months after Dad's death and then again about a year ago. Both times I visited with Abby and then spent some time with Tess. And I was pretty good about answering their letters for a while. Naturally, I couldn't convince either one of them to get a computer and graduate to e-mail. So my letters were short, but at least I wrote."

"That was very thoughtful of you."

"Don't give me too much credit. Remember, Dad made me promise not to forget about those women."

"And through all those years, he never explained why they were so important to him?"

"Nope. Of course, as I mentioned before, I never asked him any questions either. And yes, you're right," he said. "I'm as much to blame for being blindsided by this situation as he is."

"Isaiah, you're trying to put your own words into my mouth."

He didn't respond, and they rode the remaining three miles to the lodge in silence, their hands resting together on top of the console.

* * * * *

"Why don't you make yourself comfortable," Isaiah suggested when they were back inside his suite. "That is, if you still feel like staying for a while."

"Yes, I'd like to very much," she replied, taking her now familiar seat on the sofa.

He just smiled as he hung up her sweater in the closet. "You want to go out for dinner later? Or we could order a pizza or something."

"Let's have pizza. I like everything except anchovies."

"Okay. Tell you what. I know you want to read more of Abby's files, and I need to see if I can find my mother. I also want to call Tess. Why don't I run out and pick up a pizza and a bottle of wine. I can make my calls while I'm out, and you can read without me talking over you."

"You won't bother me if you're on the phone, but please do whatever you'd like. I'll be fine either way."

"Great," he said, walking over to her and leaning down to kiss her cheek. "I'll be back in about forty-five minutes."

As soon as he'd closed the door, Ava got up and brought two of the oversized pillows from the bed to the sofa where she stretched out her legs and propped the pillows behind her back. Picking up the Rosa file from the coffee table, she thumbed through the pages until she found the group of letters that Abby had written to Tess after she'd arrived at the Whitmores'

160

country home in Napa. The first letter was the one she'd already seen earlier that day. As she scanned the others, her attention was drawn to the last one in the stack. When she began to read, she felt as if she actually knew the woman whose writing she held in her hands.

Saturday, July 31, 1948 / 8:30 PM

Dearest Tess—

Right now I'm feeling numb, but not quite as bad as I did this morning. The separation was a thousand times worse than I'd anticipated. As I was being driven from Napa back to San Francisco, I wrote everything in my journal while the visions and emotions were fresh. Sometime during the next few days I'll copy that entry for you. Right now I can't even think about it. But I'm hopeful that time and distance will enable me to revisit this day—which seems without beginning or end at the moment.

As I write this to you, I'm sitting in the club car on a train that left San Francisco about three hours ago headed for Chicago. I'll have about a twelve-hour stopover there before changing to a different train that will take me the rest of the way to Washington DC. Yes, our nation's capital is where I'll be in exile. I was finally told the destination about a week ago.

My parents don't know yet, and I don't want to worry them. So I'll wait until I'm settled, and then I'll call them. They still think that all is well, that I'm working at the Chronicle *and having a wonderful time on my little adventure. I know I'm committing a sin by lying to them— even if I'm lying more by omission than directly, in case God makes a distinction and deducts points accordingly. But until I'm on the other side of this nightmare, I won't know how to even begin explaining everything to my parents. Instead, I've been writing to them regularly, with newsy tidbits from the newspaper, and then, whenever Mister Ben or Caroline would come up to visit me, they would take my letters and mail them in the city, so there would be a San Francisco postmark. Cowardly, I know.*

161

The job promised to me as part of the agreement Sinclair worked out will be with the Washington Post, *but I haven't been told my exact assignment yet. And I'll be staying in another residence hotel for women. I won't be arriving in DC until Wednesday morning, and the following Monday is Labor Day, so I'm not scheduled to be at work until Tuesday. That gives me almost a whole week to get situated! There are certainly lots of new pieces in the puzzle that has become my life, and once they are all in place, I will write to you with a thorough update.*

Meanwhile, I'll add to this letter in installments, reporting to you on the scenery and whatever I might learn about my fellow passengers as this train chugs along the tracks. The scheduled arrival in Chicago is day after tomorrow, in the morning, so I'll mail whatever this has developed into while I'm there on my stopover. 'Bye for now.

Love,
Abby

Rather than continue reading the rest of the addendums to that particular letter, Ava began looking for the journal entry that Abby had referenced, the one she said she wrote while being driven from Napa to San Francisco. But there were more than two dozen journals, which were actually thick composition notebooks that looked like they might have been purchased in a university bookstore. Each was the same size, about eight by ten inches, bound with a black-and-white cover, with approximately one hundred pages. Many were filled exclusively with the handwritten copies Abby had made of all her letters to Tess and Sinclair. The rest contained more typical journal entries that were summaries of events or expositions about Abby's feelings and perspectives, all recorded in chronological order. Labels on the front of each cover were marked with "from" and "to" dates, indicating the first and last entries inside the book.

The earliest "from" date that Ava could find was "August 8, 1943," and even though that wasn't what she was looking for, she started reading anyway. *"Tess has still not returned from her retreat."* But Ava immediately realized how easily she could become sidetracked. There would be plenty of time, she hoped, to explore all of the entries eventually. Right now she wanted to find July 31, 1948. After a few more moments of searching, she found the journal labeled "March 3 to October 25, 1948." With a heightened sense of expectation, she opened the book and turned to July 31.

July 31, 1948 / 10:45 AM

In the backseat of a limousine, en route from Napa to San Francisco's train station.

After I gave birth to Salome Rosabella on July 12, I was blessed with what I thought at the time was a miracle—almost three weeks to spend with her. But as each day passed, I came to realize more and more that, rather than a blessing, the three weeks were a form of carefully crafted torture. The deeper I fell in love with my child, the closer the moment drew when she would be taken from me. Had I known what I was going to feel, I'm not at all certain that I would have let Sinclair make this agreement. But I didn't know, and the agreement was made. And now the one thing I'm sure of is that my heart was cut from my body and left on the Whitmore driveway in Napa a short while ago ...

*****

Abby sat beside Salome's crib all night on July 30, 1948, waiting for those moments when the baby would awaken and cry to be fed or changed. Each of those moments was cherished. And in between, she stayed awake to watch her daughter sleep. The child's breathing was relaxing and helped Abby forget, however briefly, what was going to happen after daybreak.

By eight thirty the next morning, Abby, Euleen, and Salome had been waiting in the front parlor, in a depressing silence, for about forty-five minutes. Everything was packed as agreed, and the baby was resting peacefully in her rocking cradle. Then Abby watched through the window as the long black car pulled up the circular driveway and swung around to a stop at the bottom of the front steps. The driver got out and opened the back passenger door facing the house. A woman dressed in a white uniform—complete with a white hat, white nylon stockings, and white shoes—emerged and walked up to the front door of the house. Abby had been told that a nurse would be coming, but somehow she thought that one of the Whitmores—maybe Anabeth or Marcella—would also be there. Not so.

After the nurse rang the bell, Euleen looked at Abby.

163

"If you're thinking about a last-minute escape," Abby said with a weak smile, "I am too. But I'm afraid there's no way out at this point."

The fifteen-year-old daughter of Mister Ben and Miss Peel had been sent along to Napa as a maidservant. But she and Abby had actually become close friends over the nearly six months they'd spent together in isolation from the rest of the world. Save for occasional visits from Caroline and Mister Ben, they'd been completely on their own, without even a telephone call from the Whitmores. They'd checked dozens of books out of the library and had played cards so often that they'd learned how to tell when the other was bluffing.

And now there was the odd confluence of events that would take Euleen back to San Francisco with the baby and send Abby away to the other side of the country without her child. As many times as they'd discussed the inevitability of this day, neither of them was ready for the separation to actually happen. So they let the doorbell ring several times before Euleen finally responded with a reluctant shrug of her shoulders and eyes that were filling with tears.

When the door had been opened, the nurse bustled in with a huff, more abrupt and rude than businesslike.

"I'm here for the Whitmore child," she said, as if Abby and Euleen could have possibly been thinking she was there for any other reason.

Euleen lifted Salome from the cradle and brought her over to Abby, who leaned down to kiss the little pink cheeks she'd grown to love so much. As she opened her arms to hold the baby one more time, though, the nurse intervened, grabbing the child away from Euleen and heading straight for the door.

Immobilized, Abby just stood there watching as Euleen picked up the two suitcases of baby clothes and the diaper bag. "I'm so sorry," Euleen said in a voice scarcely above a whisper. "I promise to watch over her and sing her all the songs you taught me."

"Thank you. Knowing that you'll be there makes me feel a little better. And please thank your mom and dad for all they've done. Tell them I'll miss them too."

With that, Euleen turned and followed the nurse outside. Abby watched through the window as they all got into the car, first Euleen and then the nurse, who said something to the driver before sliding onto the seat with Salome in her arms. After the driver came back inside to get the cradle and Euleen's suitcase, which he proceeded to carry out to the car and put in the trunk, Abby continued to watch through the window as they all drove away. Just like that. They simply drove away.

Moments later, she fell to the floor, pounding her fists on the rug as if someone had just died. And someone had. The Abby everyone had known prior to that morning no longer existed. All along, she'd been waiting for her punishment to be delivered in full. But she never could have anticipated the agony that became hers to bear, not just in that instant but, as she now understood, for the rest of her life. For the next hour, she lay prostrate on the expensive Oriental rug she'd been admonished to treat with care, hysterically weeping and retching until she was so exhausted that she could no longer move.

Then she heard the second limousine arrive. After the bell rang, she slowly rose to her feet and answered the door, politely asking the driver if he could wait a few minutes. He very kindly said yes, giving her plenty of time to wash her face and do a minimal job of cleaning the mess on the rug. Then she opened the door again, and the driver carried her things out to the car while she locked the house. The next thing she knew, she was in the cushioned leather luxury of a limousine and was being whisked away. Rather than leaving the nightmare behind her, however, the agony was riding *with* her, *inside* of her, tearing her apart.

Once they'd been en route to the city for nearly an hour, she was still numb but felt her heart rate beginning to slow down as she wrote in her journal, doing her best to capture every nuance, image, and rupture embedded in the parting. She didn't believe that God could have asked her to endure all that had taken place that morning without also forgiving her, finally, for her sin. So at least she began to find some peace in that thought. Her task from there on out would be to listen and pay attention, in order that she might discover, at last, the life the Lord had in mind for her.

She was also taking some comfort in knowing that, while she'd been obedient in all the primary areas of the agreement Sinclair had negotiated with the Whitmores, she hadn't exactly complied with *every* element. In her pocketbook, she had the cross-country train ticket that would take her to Washington DC. She also had the savings passbook from the Riggs National Bank in Washington that showed the money the Whitmores had deposited for her. But there were a few other things as well.

According to the agreement, she was forbidden from taking any of Salome's memorabilia with her, and since the original birth certificate was being sealed and reissued naming Salome as a Whitmore, the agreement forbade her from having a copy of the original. *Well, my sin this time is not against God but against a piece of paper drawn up by lawyers*, she thought.

She had a handful of baby pictures that Mister Ben and Caroline had helped her take and get developed during their visits. She also had a small bottle of baby lotion that would enable her to remember Salome's delicate fragrance. And lastly, she did have a copy of the original birth certificate. Caroline had been able to enlist the service of a local Napa printer, who made the copy on his mimeograph machine right after the certificate arrived in the mail.

That was the biggest mistake the Whitmores had made by never coming up to Napa to see Abby. The address she'd listed on all the hospital forms was that of the country home, not the house in San Francisco. Caroline was the one who'd pointed out the hole in the plan to Abby. And by the time the Whitmores had figured out where the birth certificate had been sent and had dispatched Mr. Ben to retrieve the document, the copy had already been made.

Abby knew she shouldn't have been so sneaky. But she just couldn't visualize leaving her baby behind without taking along at least some small measure of the truth. Now, after what she'd experience that morning, she was very grateful for what she had in her possession.

> *Salome may never know about any of this and, if she ever does, she will probably never forgive me. But I need to do whatever I can to record what really happened here and how I really feel about everything, in case the day ever arrives when she does care.*
>
> *Well, I can see the spires of the Golden Gate Bridge in the distance, so I guess I should begin preparing for the next leg of this journey. As I struggle to hold myself together and put one foot in front of the other, I'm finding it very odd that, in the midst of this madness, my memories of Lady of the Valley and Tess are the only things that seem grounded and sane. And yet, I'm afraid that the window of opportunity for my ever getting back there might just have been closed forever.*

*****

Ava leaned her head against the pillows and closed her eyes, letting the tears slip unattended down her cheeks. "What a tragedy," she whispered out loud. Then, after digesting Abby's words for a few minutes, she flipped the pages of the journal back to the entry written on the day Rosa was born.

Monday, July 12, 1948 / 4:30 PM

In my room at the hospital in Napa Valley

This morning about six o'clock I brought into the world the most beautiful creature I've ever seen. She weighs seven and a half pounds, and her name is Salome Rosabella Ryan, for the moment at least. The "Ryan" will change to "Whitmore" in a few weeks, but her first and middle names cannot be changed, according to the agreement.

In the months that I've been spending up here, I've had a lot of time to write, but more importantly, I've renewed my devotion to the daily study of scripture. And, in the process, I found my way to my child's name. Salome means "peace," and Rosabella means "a fair rose." Having seen her at last, she is certainly the fairest of roses, and peace is what I pray will become the hallmark of her life.

Thank God I will have some time to get to know her a little bit. Now that she's here, I can honestly testify that I have witnessed a miracle.

Isaiah returned to the suite shortly after Ava finished reading.

"Did you get in touch with Tess?" she asked.

He was opening the wine while she cleared off the coffee table to make room for the large pizza with sausage and mushrooms, the container of steamed mussels in marinara sauce, and the double order of tossed salad.

"Nope. Tess wasn't there again, so I left her another message."

"How about your mother? Did you find her?"

"I did not. Zero for two. But she's apparently still alive," Isaiah said as he poured wine into two juice glasses taken from the small cupboard and carried them over to the coffee table. "I called our neighbor, Edna, across the street, who's lived there as long as we have and who's always taken in the mail and watched over things whenever we went out of town. She said she saw Mom get into her car this morning and drive off somewhere. So I asked Edna to leave a message in the mailbox asking my errant mother to call me right away. I can't figure out why I haven't heard from her yet, but when I finally do, she's going to get some of her own medicine about not checking in."

"Maybe she tried to call your cell but couldn't get through."

"Maybe. But I'm willing to bet there's another reason. This just isn't like her."

"Well, at least you know she's okay," Ava said as she sat down on the sofa. "Great idea, by the way, getting these mussels. I *love* them!"

"I had a feeling you would." Seated in his now traditional spot—the armchair—he took a sip of wine.

She dished a scoop of mussels into one of the Styrofoam bowls included in the bag from the pizza store. "I have another question," she said.

"Okay."

"Did you ever try to contact Rosa again?"

"Was I supposed to?"

"Maybe it would be a good idea. While you were out, I read some of Abby's journal entries that she wrote after Rosa was born."

"Did you see the one on the day she left Napa?"

"Yes, that one too. And I don't know how anyone could read those without being moved. When you spoke with Rosa last night, you said she sounded so angry. I think she might feel differently if she could see what we've seen."

"Fair enough," he said, taking his cell phone out of his pocket after a brief pause and searching the call log for the San Francisco number Rosa had used to reach him the previous night.

"Boy, are you ever easy," Ava said after she swallowed another mussel and wiped a drip of marinara sauce from her chin.

"Hey! I live to please." Then he pushed the SEND button and waited.

"Hello?" an elderly woman's voice said after such a long string of rings that Isaiah was expecting to hear a voice mail greeting.

"Hi. Is Rosa there?"

"May I ask who's calling?"

"This is Isaiah Mellington."

Isaiah was certain he heard an extended sigh, and he wondered if he might be speaking with Anabeth.

"She isn't here."

"Well, could you please take a message asking her to call me?"

"That won't be necessary, Mr. Mellington."

Now he was convinced that the woman was Anabeth. "But I'd really appreciate your—"

"I *said* that a message *won't be necessary*. Now, I don't mean to be rude, but there isn't anything else to say. Good evening, Mr. Mellington."

He knew she was gone even before he saw "call disconnected" appear in the cell phone display. Leaning forward, he placed the phone on the coffee table.

"And?" Ava said, looking at him expectantly.

"*And*," he answered, taking another sip of wine and lifting a large slice of pizza from the box, "something tells me that Rosa has already changed her mind about coming up here."

*****

Ninety minutes later, they had finished eating and had cleaned up the mess, cramming all the trash that would fit into the only wastebasket in the room and stacking the rest neatly on top of the microwave. Isaiah was stretched out on his back on the sofa, with his head in Ava's lap as she stroked his hair. The sun had already gone down, and the suite was dimly lit by only the green-shaded banker's lamp on the writing desk.

"What time did you say you have to work tomorrow?" he asked.

"The three-to-eleven shift."

"So that means you don't have to get up too early?"

She stopped rubbing his head. "I guess not. Why?"

He sat up and looked in her eyes and then brushed his lips across hers. "I was just wondering if you might want to stay here tonight." She didn't say anything. "I'm sorry. I shouldn't have—"

"Sh-h-h," she said, placing her fingers on his mouth. "I've sort of been thinking about the same thing, and I'd love to stay here with you. But only if we sleep together without *doing* anything. Do you think that would be possible?"

"Uh ... sure," he said, trying to process the improbable imagery. She started laughing, prompting him to say, "Oh, I thought you were serious."

"I am," she said, still laughing. "I'm *completely* serious. Being together all night would be wonderful, if all we do is snuggle. I'm just not ready yet for anything else, Isaiah. But I'll understand if the idea is a problem."

He considered the options, weighing the degree of pleasure he'd have in his bed alone against the thought of having her next to him.

"I'm a big boy," he said, placing his hands on either side of her face and kissing her on the forehead. "I think I can handle it."

"Maybe we could watch a movie," she suggested. "Let's see what's on," she added, getting up from the sofa and walking over to the desk to look at the "What's Showing?" offerings next to the TV channel listing.

They decided on *Analyze This*, which started at seven thirty. With both of them wearing their underwear paired with a matching set of Isaiah's white T-shirts, they climbed into the king-size bed and propped three pillows each behind them. Isaiah used the remote control to fire up the television and order the movie as they sipped wine from the glasses he'd refilled to finish off the bottle.

When the movie started, they were huddled next to each other, holding hands with their legs and feet touching. At first, Isaiah wasn't sure if this was going to work. He was feeling an almost painful desire for her building in every part of him, even before Robert De Niro's mobster character and Billy Crystal's psychiatrist persona had met in the story. The sensation of Ava's bare skin against his, and the tantalizing scent of her as her curly blonde head rested on his shoulder, were more than he thought he'd be able to endure or resist.

But before the movie was over, they were both sound asleep, with Ava's back nestled against the front of Isaiah's body, in spoon fashion—and unbelievably, he had survived.

CHAPTER TWELVE

Isaiah had already been awake for twenty minutes at nine o'clock the next morning, just watching Ava and marveling at his willingness to let her have power over him.

"Want to go out for breakfast?" he asked when she finally opened her eyes. He was lying on his side, his elbow on the pillow, his chin in his hand, and a Cheshire cat grin was blazoned across his face.

"Well, aren't *we* cheerful this morning!" she said, lifting herself up to kiss him on the cheek. Then she threw off the covers and climbed slowly out of bed. "You know I'd love to have breakfast, but I really want to go home and get cleaned up. I also have some errands to run," she added, "since I didn't get anything done on my list yesterday."

"Okay," he said, rearranging his expression into an exaggerated pout as he put his head back down on the pillow.

"You're a very bad actor." She laughed as she traded his T-shirt for her own clothes. "Besides, you have a really big day today, with Zoie and her dad arriving."

"Maybe we can talk later?"

"I'll call your cell when I take my break this afternoon," she answered, running a brush through her hair. "If that turns out to be a bad time for you, I'll try again when I get off work—assuming you'll still be up at eleven tonight."

He got out of bed and stood in front of her, placing his hands on her waist. She smiled as she wrapped her arms around his neck.

"Oh, I'll be up," he said. "If I haven't talked with you yet, I'll *definitely* be up."

"Great," she said after he leaned down to kiss her. "And I'll do my best to get some time off over the next three days. The only problem will be the late notice. Otherwise, I have plenty of vacation coming. So we'll see."

After he dressed in his clothes from the day before, he walked her out to her car in the parking lot, kissed her again, and watched her drive away, as if someone he'd known his entire life was leaving. By the time he returned to his suite, the message light on his cell phone was flashing. His call log told him that the call he'd missed was from Tess. But when he dialed her number, he got her voice mail again.

"Hi, Tess," he said in his message, doing his best to hide his frustration. "Sorry we keep missing each other. I'm anxious to talk with you because a friend of mine and I visited the folks who own the old convent yesterday. Also, Zoie and her dad will be here in few hours. So try me again when you get this."

He poured himself a glass of juice from the tiny refrigerator, stripped off his clothes, and stepped into the shower after placing his cell phone on the edge of the sink. He spent a couple of minutes just letting the strong, steady pulse of water fall on his head and body, trying to keep his mind from playing hopscotch over the odd mixture of people and events he'd encountered during the last three days.

But although the water and steam were soothing, his thoughts would not be quieted. So he let them tumble around in his head as he washed his hair using shampoo from the tiny hotel bottle, lathering the rest of himself as much as possible with the tiny hotel soap bar. He had just finished rinsing off and was standing with his face turned up directly into the stream of water when he heard his cell phone ringing.

Quickly turning the shower off, he grabbed a towel to blot his face and dry his hands then picked up the phone without looking at the caller ID.

"Hello?"

"Good morning, Isaiah."

The woman's voice on the other end had a husky tone. Isaiah briefly took the phone from his ear to look at the display and see who this was.

"Tess?"

"Yes, it's me."

"Are you okay? You sound like you're sick." There was a pause. "Tess? Talk to me!"

"Okay," she said, sniffling and then blowing her nose. "Isaiah, someone broke into my house this morning."

"*What?* Are you all right? Did you call the police?"

"Too many questions in a row, dear. But yes, I'm fine."

"I'll be right there."

"No, you really don't need to—"

"I said I'll be right there."

He finished drying off and took his last pair of clean underwear out of his duffel bag. "I need to find a laundry," he mumbled, realizing for the first time that he'd only packed enough basics for the two days he'd originally thought this trip would entail.

After pulling on the T-shirt that Ava had worn overnight and, in the process, igniting her scent, he dressed again in the same jeans and sweater from the day before, and slipped his black loafers on over his last pair of clean socks. Then he brushed his thick, wet hair straight back on the sides and top; grabbed his bomber jacket, wallet, cell phone, and car keys; and left the suite thinking, *Could this situation possibly get any more dramatic?* Halfway through the lobby, he turned around and went back to his suite where he put his dirty clothes in the plastic laundry bag hanging in the closet. *At least I can do some wash while we're filing a police report.*

*****

The little yellow house in Kettle Falls didn't look any different to him than he remembered from Friday, which was a relief. Nothing appeared to have been ransacked, as he noted the same neat stacks of papers and files on the large table in the tiny living room and the seemingly untouched books and knickknacks on the bookcase along the wall.

But Tess was clearly a mess. Her face was red from crying, and clumps of her short gray hair were sticking out every which way around her head. She wore a pair of baggy black pants and an oversized, long-sleeved blue work shirt that came down to her midthighs, the combination making her short pudgy body look sort of like a box. Well-worn, heavy-duty black sneakers were on her feet, and when she walked she lifted each foot slowly, as if the soles were sticking to something on the floor.

"*Please* sit down in your chair," Isaiah said after Tess insisted on pouring coffee for him from the percolator she'd removed from the wood-burning stove. "Tell me what happened."

She obediently took a seat in her black leather recliner and faced Isaiah, who was sitting in the captain's chair at the large table.

"I'm sorry, dear," she said, sighing deeply. "I'm afraid I overreacted. Everything is fine. Really."

"Not from this angle, it isn't. *Something* happened here to make you so upset. You said on the phone that someone broke into your house."

"Yes. Well, I should have been more careful about blurting that out."

"Tess, *did* you have a break-in here or not?"

"I … I thought I did, after I got back from my walk this morning. I was gone longer than normal because I stopped at the feed store to visit and have a cinnamon bun. Everyone in town is talking about Abby and the funeral, and I—"

With mounting annoyance, Isaiah interrupted her. "When you got home, was your front door open?"

"Not open, but unlocked, like it always is."

"Are you telling me that you never lock this place when you leave?"

"That's right, Isaiah. There's never been any need to around here."

"Okay. So what made you think you'd had a break-in?"

"I'm … I don't really know now," she said, her eyes looking off to the right and then up at the ceiling. "I guess I thought some things had been moved, and that's when I called you. But I shouldn't have bothered you. I acted in haste, and I'm sorry."

"Nothing's been moved? Nothing's missing?"

Her eyes turned away from him again. "No. Nothing."

She's lying to me. "Look, Tess. I get the feeling that you're not exactly being honest with me, and I'm not sure why. I want to help you, and I certainly don't want to leave a suspected break-in unattended. But if you're not going to tell me what *really* happened, I don't know what I can do. Would you like me to call the police?"

Her focus abruptly returned to him. "Oh no! Please forgive me for worrying you and making you drive up here. Everything's all right. Honestly."

"Okay," he said, shaking his head and looking at his watch. "Zoie and her dad will be here in a couple of hours, but I'll stay with you a little longer, if you'd like. In fact, would you mind if I use your washer to run a load of clothes?"

"Of course I wouldn't mind. And I'd like very much to have you stay a little while. Thank you," she said, her demeanor brightening as she stood up. "Let's have more coffee, and then you can tell me about your visit to the convent. And by the way, who's the friend that went with you?"

He stayed for another hour while his clothes washed and dried in the dungeonlike basement laundry room, telling her first about Ava, how they'd met, a little bit about her background, and the fact that she'd been an elementary school teacher like Tess.

"She sounds lovely, Isaiah."

"Yes, she is. And I know this is going to sound ridiculous three days after meeting her, but I've never felt so comfortable with anyone in my life. *And* I can't believe how lucky I was that she was working that shift on Saturday. She could just as easily have been off that day."

"My faith tells me," Tess said, pouring more coffee into his cup, "that there isn't any such thing as luck, or accidents of fate, or coincidence. Everything that happens is by divine design, although we often don't understand the plan for a while … or ever. So I'm confident that you were *supposed* to meet her on this particular trip."

"Right. Why couldn't I just as easily have met her on my *next* visit here to see you—or on my last one?"

"And when exactly would that next visit of yours have been, Isaiah, if Abby hadn't died?" A surge of guilt shot through him. "And how long has it been since your *last* trip? More than a year, I know that—and according to what you just told me, Ava didn't even live here then."

"I'm sorry I didn't come more often," he said, embarrassed that he had no reasonable excuse. "And you're probably right about destiny," he added, simply to bring that part of the conversation to an end.

"So, what did Ava think of the convent?" Tess asked, easily moving to another subject.

"She was as fascinated as I was. And I must confess, with all due respect to you, that I never understood someone making the choice to be a nun. I probably still don't. But walking around those grounds, looking through the photographs, throwing in my own memories, I have more of an appreciation now for what was involved with that commitment."

"I'm glad, Isaiah. Your understanding is a nice change … and one that will be very important," she said, her voice and focus both trailing off, as if all but her body had momentarily left the room.

"All right then!" he said, slapping his hands on his thighs and standing up, having reached the point where he'd had enough. "If you're okay, I think I should be going."

"Oh my goodness, yes. I didn't realize the time. You have such a big day ahead of you. And I'm perfectly fine, so don't you worry that handsome head of yours."

She put her arms around him and patted his back. "Will you and the Gerards be at the wake tomorrow?" she asked, pulling away from him.

175

"Tomorrow? I thought that was supposed to be for the religious community."

"It is, technically. They scheduled a separate day because people will be arriving from all over the place. I think there might even be a couple of sisters still surviving from Lady of the Valley days who'll be coming from Spokane. I haven't seen any of those women for more than thirty years, and if they do show up, that will be quite a reunion. But the viewing will actually be open to anyone who wants to be there. Please stop by with the Gerards, if you feel like it, or by yourself—or with that *new friend* of yours," she added with a cocked head and mischievous grin.

"Okay. I'll let them all know—and I'm guessing we'll be there at some point in the day. But will you do me a favor in the meantime?"

"Of course, Isaiah."

"Please start locking your house when you go out *and* when you're home."

"We'll see. That would be a big change for me, losing trust like that."

"Just think about it. Okay?"

"Okay."

"And call me right away if anything else happens!"

"Aye-aye, Captain."

After giving her one more squeeze around her shoulders, he picked up his bag of clean clothes and went down the porch steps. As he was walking toward the street where his car was parked, he heard the deadbolt latch and the chain lock being fastened on the door behind him. *Now I know something happened in there*, he thought, *if she's locking that door before I'm even gone. But why won't she tell me?*

He started the ignition in the Jag and drove up Kettle Crest Drive to the corner, where he turned left on Evergreen. Two short blocks later, as he was approaching Kalmia Street on his left, he saw Ava's car parked in the driveway of a neat white frame house near the corner. Pulling over to the curb, he couldn't help himself as he took his cell phone out of his pocket, found her number in his directory, and pressed SEND. She answered after only one ring.

"What are you doing, Mr. Mellington?"

"Frankly, I think I'm parked close to your house, if you live on Kalmia."

"Are you telling me that you followed me home?"

"No, but I might have if I'd thought of it."

"So what *are* you doing?"

"Tess had a little emergency, so I drove up. Turns out that she lives two blocks away from you on Kettle Crest. I just happened to see your car as I was heading back."

"Is she okay?"

"I think so, although I get the feeling that something a little odd is going on. I'll fill you in when we have more time to talk. I know you're busy, and I need to get back to the lodge."

"Well, hearing your voice so soon has been an unexpected pleasure, Mr. Mellington."

"Same here, Ms. Lindsey. Call me later when you get a chance."

"I will—and if there's anything I can do for Tess, let me know, especially since I live so close."

As the call ended and Isaiah turned right on Juniper and then right on 395 heading to Colville, any lingering concerns he had about the strange incident at the little yellow house were completely pushed aside by his thoughts of Ava. *I don't know about any divine design—but I must have done something right somewhere along the way to be this lucky.*

Reminding himself of Zoie and Zeke's imminent arrival, he did his best not to dwell on his thoughts of Ava. But shaking his mind and heart free of her was turning out to be a challenge.

*****

Isaiah had been seated in a lobby wing chair for about half an hour when he watched through the floor-to-ceiling plate glass window as a black town car pulled up under the covered entrance to the lodge shortly after three thirty. He had just walked outside when the back passenger door opened, and a tall, lean woman stepped out. Her long dark hair was pulled back in a simple ponytail, and she wore crease-ironed jeans over brown cowboy boots. A hip-length brown suede jacket was buttoned up to her neck.

She looked at him with Abby's piercing jade eyes and smiled broadly as he approached her. Even though her face was tan and a bit weathered, her overall appearance was of a woman at least ten years younger than he was, although he knew they were approximately the same age.

"Well, hello at last, Isaiah Mellington," she said, with the same southern lilt that had charmed him on the phone.

They opened their arms to each other, and their embrace felt more like one of old friends or former lovers to Isaiah rather than complete strangers.

"Hi, Zoie," he said, stepping back from her as he held her hands and took another good look at her. "I can't get over how much you look like Abby!"

"So I've been told."

Just then, the limo driver walked around the back of the car from the other side, his arms gently supporting an elderly man, who was well over six foot, even though he was slightly hunched over. Lean like his daughter, he had a full head of thick white hair, and his skin bore a much deeper tan than Zoie's. Marked with deep lines and wrinkles, his face was that of a man in his eighties who'd worked his land for a living his entire life.

When Zeke saw Isaiah, he stopped walking for a moment and eased his arms and shoulders free from the limo driver's assistance. Then he extended his large right hand in greeting as he began moving forward again on his own. Isaiah stepped in to meet him and took his hand, struck by the old man's perfectly round cobalt blue eyes that were reddened and filled with what looked like pools of tears somehow being contained.

"Mr. Gerard," Isaiah said, "I'm so happy to meet you, and I appreciate your bringing Zoie all the way out here for this."

Zeke cleared his throat and seemed to swallow his tears as his eyes began to clear up. "I been waiting close to sixty years for this, Isaiah," he said, his voice deep and strong, and his southern drawl even thicker than Zoie's. "So there's no call for thanking me. And please," he added with a wide smile, patting Isaiah's upper arms with his huge hands, "I'm not Mr. Gerard, or sir, either. Just plain Zeke is how I'm known." Then he stepped back and looked Isaiah up and down. "*You're* a fine looking boy!"

"That's very kind of you, sir ... uh, Zeke—and you're in great shape yourself!"

"Well, I hate to interrupt this fan fest," Zoie said, laughing and linking her arm in her father's as the limo driver unloaded their luggage. "But we've had a long day already, and I think this fine specimen and I need to spend a couple of hours resting and getting cleaned up. Would that be okay? Or did you have other plans for us?"

"I thought we'd go out to dinner tonight, but other than that, nothing's on the agenda."

"Great," she said, leading Zeke inside as Isaiah and the limo driver followed behind with the bags. "We'll be new people by dinner," she added, turning around and flashing another one of those magnetic smiles.

Isaiah paid the limo driver while Zoie and Zeke checked in, and then he helped them get their bags to their rooms, which were on the corridor off the lobby and at the opposite end from his suite. Zeke immediately sat down in the upholstered chair inside the room he'd decided was his, while Isaiah made sure that the connecting door leading from Zoie's room into Zeke's worked properly. He also pointed out to her the platters of fruit, cheese, and crackers that he'd had delivered for both of them.

"I thought you might be hungry," he said. "And there's water and soft drinks in each of those little refrigerators. I also have wine in my suite, in case you're interested."

"This is so nice of you, Isaiah! You really shouldn't have gone to all this trouble."

"Well, *I'm* grateful he did," they heard Zeke call from the other room. "All they gave us on that airplane ride was a bag a nuts and a cold ham san'wich." Isaiah and Zoie followed his voice through the connecting doors and found him sitting on the side of his bed, taking off his shoes. "And," he said when he saw them, "I don't care much for wine, but I *am* planning on having a nice glass of cognac when we go out tonight."

"Oh, really?" Zoie asked, looking at him incredulously. "Since when do you drink cognac?"

"Since I been planning this!" he said, leaning back against the pillows and pulling the bedspread up around his legs and stocking feet. "You think you know everything about me, girl, and mostly you do. But some things you don't." Then he closed his eyes and folded his arms across his chest. "Abby and I shared cognac," he said, his voice falling to almost a whisper, "the night before she left. And now, at long last, I'm finally gonna have another." As Isaiah and Zoie watched, he fell immediately to sleep.

"That's not the first strange thing he's said or done since I told him you'd called on Saturday," she whispered when they'd walked back into her room.

"Is he okay?"

"Yeah, I think so. I'm doing my best to make sure he gets plenty of rest, though. He's been waiting so long for this that I don't want him to get overtired. *And* ... I must admit that I'm a little worried about him seeing Abby. I hope it won't turn out to be too much for him. But there was no way I could stop him from coming."

"How about you, Zoie? How do *you* feel about seeing Abby?"

She looked up at Isaiah. "She was my mother, Isaiah, and I feel very blessed that I'll have the chance to touch her and replace all the years of imaginary pictures with the real thing. Sometimes, though," she said, all pretense of a smile fading beneath the tears slipping down her cheeks, "I wish I hadn't listened to Dad after he told me about her. I wish I'd come out here *then*—so I could have seen her and talked with her." Wiping her cheeks with the backs of her hands, she added, "But I was a big girl. And deciding to stay away was my decision alone. Sorry," she said, a weak smile coming through again. "I guess that actually being here might be opening up some feelings I didn't know were there."

Isaiah wanted to put his arms around her and comfort her, but he wasn't sure if that would be the appropriate thing to do or if she would receive the gesture as intended. So he opted for restraint.

"My suite is number 101, at the end of the hall right off the lobby. If you want to talk, or if there's anything I can do for you, please just pick up the phone and call me."

"Thank you so much," she said, throwing her arms around his neck and tucking her head underneath his chin.

Okay, he thought. *Hugging doesn't seem to be a problem.*

"If you weren't here," she went on, "if someone else had been the messenger, I'm not sure how bearable this would be." Then she gently pulled away from him, her eyes locking on his with such intensity that he actually felt uncomfortable. "But Dad always told me he was sure that, if Sinclair didn't live long enough, you would be the one to contact us. So I feel as if I've known you for years—and I want to thank you for making our trip out here so easy."

"You're welcome, Zoie, but no thanks are necessary. That's all part of the job my dad left for me. And *I'm* glad I'm here too." Feeling at ease with her again, he wrapped one arm around her shoulders. "Now, why don't you take a nap while he's sleeping? There's no timetable either. It's only going to be the three of us for dinner, so we can head out whenever you're ready. Just call me when you guys wake up."

Back in his suite, his first inclination was to give Ava a call, but he decided not to bother her again—yet. His second thought was to spend these unplanned free hours working on his book, which he hadn't even removed from his briefcase since he arrived. The fictional story he'd outlined, however, seemed sort of anemic compared to the real one about Abby that had overtaken his life during the last four days.

After flipping on the wall-mounted heating unit below the window to cut the fall chill in the room, he slipped off his shoes and leaned back on the bed. Then he sank into the layers of pillows, pulling the bedspread up around his legs and feet just as he'd watched Zeke do. *Great idea*, he thought. *Hardly messes up the bed at all.* Before his thoughts about Ava had time to crystallize in the room's stillness, he was drawn into the deepest sleep he'd experienced since he'd left Seattle.

*****

By seven that evening, Isaiah, Zoie, and Zeke were seated at a small round table in the most upscale restaurant Isaiah could find in Colville. Zeke was directly across from Isaiah, and Zoie was between them, to Isaiah's left. They'd already enjoyed an artichoke dip appetizer while Zoie and Isaiah began sharing a bottle of Australian Shiraz and Zeke nursed his long-awaited snifter of cognac. Their conversation had been mostly light, with a brief flare of passion while the presidential campaign was debated, even though all three of them were supporting the same candidate and celebrating the historic nature of the upcoming election.

"Would you mind if I poked around your memories for a little information?" Isaiah asked during a conversational lull, directing his question to Zeke while they awaited delivery of their entrees.

"Nope," Zeke said, lifting his cognac to his lips for another sip, his riveting blue eyes peering at Isaiah over the rim of his glass.

"I think he would have been disappointed if you *hadn't* asked," Zoie said with a soft laugh as she leaned back in her chair.

"Well … okay then," Isaiah said. "I guess my main question is why Zoie's file is so thin compared to Rosa's, which has a birth certificate, plenty of letters, journals, and a bunch of other stuff that really helped piece that part of Abby's story together. But Zoie's file is practically empty. There are a couple of baby photos and a few notes about things like what the weather was doing. But no journals or anything. Not even a birth certificate."

"Oh, *I* have a copy of that," Zoie interjected. "And I brought it with me. It's in my room, if you want to see it later. Although I'm not sure what it would add at this point."

"I'm not either," Isaiah said. "But Abby was so diligent about taking a copy of Rosa's original certificate with her that I'm a little surprised she didn't take a copy of yours. Do you have any ideas about that, Zeke?"

The old man sipped on his cognac and shrugged his shoulders. "Next question," he said.

Isaiah studied Zeke's face, bronzed and leathery but giving away nothing of what Isaiah suspected was being left unsaid. "All right. I know that Abby went from San Francisco to Washington DC for a new job once the Whitmores took custody of Rosa. After that, though, there's nothing about how she got from DC to North Carolina, or how you guys met, or how she ended up back at the convent."

"If I'm not mistaken," Zeke replied, resting his elbows on the arms of his chair and rolling the bowl of his snifter between his palms, "that's *three* questions. Which one you want first?"

"How about in chronological order?" Isaiah asked, trying not to sound frustrated at the obvious.

At that moment, their waitress arrived with their entrees—a grilled chicken salad for Zoie, poached salmon again for Isaiah, and a rare ten-ounce porterhouse steak bleeding all over the plate for Zeke. Before Isaiah and Zoie had fully surveyed their own selections, Zeke had cut into the filet mignon end of his meat and had taken a couple of bites.

"I had a feeling this was gonna be good," Zeke said, "after driving by the cattle ranches 'round here this afternoon."

Isaiah nodded, feeling heart-healthy but a bit like a wuss as he lifted his fork full of salmon flakes to his mouth. Then he waited several minutes while they all ate in silence before he took the reins of their conversation again.

"So, Zeke, as we were—"

"The whole thing was a setup. A cheap, dirty, reneging setup."

Zeke's declaration caught Isaiah off guard. "Care to elaborate?" he asked the old man after a moment's pause.

"Yeah, Dad," Zoie said, sounding surprised herself as she touched her napkin to the corners of her mouth before taking a sip of wine. "You never mentioned anything about that before."

He turned to look at his daughter, the expression on his face still unchanged. "Didn't come up." Then he continued, shifting his focus back to Isaiah. "You say you want this in chronological order?"

"It doesn't really matter, Zeke. Whatever's easiest for you. I just appreciate your being here and—"

"Her job was supposed to be in Washington DC," Zeke said, his eyes still fixed on Isaiah's and his jaw visibly tightening. "That was the deal Sinclair made with the Whitmores. She didn't have a car or even know how to drive, so she needed to be in a big city where she could get around on the bus. But she'd only been there a couple a weeks when they sent her to the *Washington Post*'s Charlotte office to cover some cockamamie made-up *feature story*, they called it."

"What makes you think it was made up?" Isaiah asked, feeling full already and watching in awe as the meat continued to disappear from Zeke's plate whether he was speaking or not.

"Figured it out once I got to know her. Didn't take *much* figuring neither."

"And how *did* you get to know her?"

Zeke stopped chewing and fixed his eyes on Isaiah's. "You can be kinda pushy, son."

"Sorry," Isaiah said, suddenly feeling like he was five.

Flashing a smile so broad that the meat was visible between his teeth, Zeke said, "Just joshing you." Then he stared off into the air. "Chronological order, huh? Well, that might not be as easy as you'd think. But I guess the front end musta been on Saturday, October 23, 1948."

Isaiah put his fork down on his plate and studied Zeke's face. "You remember the date *and* the day of the week?"

"That's what I said. You got a hearing problem?"

"Is that when you met Abby?"

"Yup. Everybody's got a fork-in-the-road story, you know. And that was mine. Got up that morning, just like always. Ate breakfast just like always too. Didn't wear my overalls, though, 'cause we was going into Charlotte. Put on my go-to-meeting jeans and a clean shirt that I even ironed. Guess I should a seen it coming, but I didn't. All I know is that nothing 'bout my life—and I mean *nothing*, not even the color of the damn sky—was ever the same after that day."

CHAPTER THIRTEEN

Saturday, October 23, 1948

Abby sat perfectly still behind the long table in front of the hotel conference room in Charlotte, North Carolina. Attendees were beginning to arrive, and she was so nervous that she wasn't at all confident she'd have a voice when the time came for her to speak. Dede had suggested that Abby spend a few minutes sitting there, to try to help her relax into the surroundings.

"Take a few deep breaths," she'd said, "and introduce yourself to people who wander up front to say hello. You'll be fine."

Dede Marsden was the editor who'd been assigned to Abby after the whole North Carolina thing had come up so suddenly. She was only a few years older than Abby and had been immensely helpful and supportive, not to mention creative. And she'd been just as surprised as Abby about the sudden relocation and the abrupt shift in assignments.

Extremely petite at five foot two and maybe a hundred pounds, if wet, she'd been engaged to be married, but her fiancé had been killed during the Normandy invasion. Yet she still wore her engagement ring more than four years after the fact and openly spoke of her Billy and how much the two of them had loved each other.

Her long blonde hair was usually braided and pinned up in a twist at the crown of her head, and her fair skin and pale green eyes made her look like Heidi in the classic children's story by Johanna Spyri that Abby and Tess had read countless times together as young girls. *What a different picture Dede paints*, Abby thought with a smile, *than my tall, broad, loud, and bold Caroline, who I love and miss so much.*

Deciding to remain up in front of the meeting room for a few minutes longer, Abby sat with her hands folded in her lap and her ankles crossed demurely, showcasing her new black leather pumps visible beneath the white tablecloth. She smiled again, looking down at those shoes on her feet. Her battered heart had not yet mended from San Francisco, and unwelcome whispers at night denied her complete comfort in the decisions she'd made. But she was grateful for the agreement that now provided her with enough money to buy a new outfit and a new pair of shoes when needed, without having to borrow cash from someone like Caroline or skip meals for a week.

Today she felt both businesslike and fashionable in the fitted steel blue jumper suit that she'd found in a department store not far from the hotel. The skirt fell in soft folds to her midcalf, and the long-sleeved peplum jacket buttoned up the front to the collar where a scarf in the same fabric was tied in a soft flouncy bow. And after a full day of shopping, she still had $384 left out of the $400 she'd withdrawn from her new savings account before leaving Washington.

With her jet-black hair brushing her shoulders, still in the pageboy cut she'd begun wearing in San Francisco, she was confident about her appearance, believing she looked proper and professional. But she did *not* feel ready for this presentation, or this assignment. *And why should I expect myself to be ready for this,* she thought as she watched two more men sign in at the table along the room's back wall. After all, she was supposed to be working in Washington DC, not Charlotte, North Carolina. And that relocation from California to Washington a month and a half earlier had been challenging enough, without this new one being added to the mix.

She'd believed that the move to DC had been part of her penance, and consequently, she'd tried not to complain, even in the privacy of her own mind. But arriving in that strange city where she didn't know a single person, and where she was totally dependent upon an unfamiliar system of public transportation, had been both difficult and frightening.

Then a strange thing had happened. Because she'd arrived in town the Wednesday before Labor Day weekend, she'd had the luxury of not being required to report to work until almost a week later, on Tuesday, September 7. So she started to use the time to settle into her residence hotel apartment, which was only a studio and smaller by half than her place in San Francisco. A couple of colorful plants from the floral shop down the street had added a little warmth and texture to the tiny single room furnished with only a sofa, a small coffee table, two straight-legged chairs, and another narrow sofa in the corner, which was actually her bed. Very little effort was required to make an improvement in the place that featured only one window overlooking the brick side of the building next door.

Guess the Whitmores figured this was good enough for me, she thought when she'd initially opened the door. *Perhaps they're right, but I think I'll find my own place, after I get going in my job.*

That was the first moment she'd begun to appreciate the existence of the money, because she realized that she actually *could* move to a different apartment, even to a different part of town, if that's what she wanted to do. There was an unexpected comfort and security in that knowledge, and other than the two plants, she decided not to invest any further time or expense in the veritable dump the Whitmores had rented for her.

Caroline had kindly offered to store all of Abby's personal belongings at her home in San Francisco. "When you're settled," she'd said during her last visit to the Whitmore country home in Napa, "I'll have them shipped to you. That way, you won't have to worry about hauling any of that stuff with you on the train." Now, given her decision to look for another apartment, Abby would just write to Caroline and ask if she'd mind holding onto everything a little longer.

Free of any desire to decorate, she spent the balance of the week exploring Washington DC. She'd never been to the nation's capital before, and she quickly discovered that the district's bus system would take her directly to all of the monuments, to the capitol building, and even to the White House. She toured them all with the rapt delight of a child, standing fully immobilized when President Truman actually walked up to her tour group in the White House and welcomed them to what he called "the people's house," as he shook hands with every single visitor in the line.

That night, beneath the light of a dim bulb in her gloomy apartment, she wrote a letter to Tess, describing the events of her remarkable day.

> *... and he's a much smaller man than you would suspect from photographs in the newspapers and even in my* Life *magazines. In fact, I was wearing my heels, and I'm sure I was taller than he was. But his eyes actually twinkled, Tess, and the power of his office was something you could feel, as if it had its own energy, despite President Truman's best efforts to act ordinary with us. I have no idea where or how he found the time to say hello to us while he's running for reelection and trying to deal with all the maddening extremes*

in Congress. But there he was, nonetheless, in the flesh, in our midst. Honest to goodness, the memories I have from this unbelievable day will surely last for the rest of my life.

And you know something else, my dear friend? I believe I've changed and grown already, in the short time since I arrived here. I've been wandering through the hallmarks of this historic place—through the Lincoln and Jefferson Memorials, and the Washington Monument, where I climbed and descended every step (oh yes I did, despite the skeptical look I'm visualizing on your face). I also visited both the House and the Senate, where elected officials were following parliamentary procedure as they worked on "the people's business." In the Senate, there was a debate underway on the merits (or not) of repealing the Taft-Hartley Law. I'm not sure if you're able to follow such things, but last year the Republican Congress passed that law, which limits the unions' right to strike and dilutes their political power. Truman has called for the repeal of that law, a move that is ripe with controversy. Watching and listening from the Senate gallery, as several different senators blustered their way through their perspectives on the subject, was fascinating and absorbing.

You and I studied together in school all the things I've observed this week, but the words on those textbook pages have really come to life for me now. And, more importantly, I have a much clearer and deeper appreciation of the liberties and way of life that our soldiers fought for—and that so many thousands died for—during the war.

Three years have passed since the free world celebrated the end of that war and the victory over such unspeakable evil. But I know I've been guilty of complacency, slipping into today's life, wallowing around in today's problems, forgetting the trauma of what this country went through for so long, and why. I suspect that I'm not alone among Americans in this forgetting, and I'm grateful that God's plan for me has sent me here to this awe-inspiring city, in order that I might be reminded of the recent history and sacrifice that have kept us free ...

She wanted to tell Tess that she'd also been exploring neighborhoods in search of a different apartment, but she knew her friend would end up worrying about why such a move was necessary in the first place. Instead, she decided to wait until she was resituated.

Good thing, too, because less than three weeks after she'd reported to her new job, she found out that her apartment wasn't the only part of her new circumstances that was about to change.

*****

Still sitting in front of the Charlotte hotel's meeting room, as more people kept arriving and signing in, Abby continued to be amazed at the speed and creativity her superiors in Washington had used to get rid of her. Of course, "get rid of her" weren't the words they'd used. Apparently thinking she was an imbecile or a vegetable, her supervising editor at the *Washington Post* had gushed over the "fabulous opportunity" that had just come up for her in North Carolina.

"We have an office in Charlotte," the editor said, sitting behind her desk while Abby perched rigidly on the edge of a steel, straight-back chair next to the office door. "And they need someone there to research and write a feature story on how the southern agricultural community has changed since the war ended. Has the impact of peacetime been a positive one on them economically? What crops are important to them now? And I'm sure there are many other elements to this story that will come to light once you get down there."

Abby was in shock for what felt like several minutes before she found her voice. "I see," she said. "And how long will I be gone?"

"Well," the editor hedged, peering down at the papers in front of her rather than at Abby, "I can't really answer that right now. This story will take you some time to write, since a substantial amount of research will need to be completed first. We'll be paying for your accommodations at a nice hotel—your room, meals, laundry, and anything else you need. And after you've submitted the story," she continued, leaning forward and resting her arms on the desk as her eyes finally lifted to meet Abby's, "we'll see where we are by then. But I recommend that you either take all of your belongings with you or leave some things with a friend. The room you're in now at the residence hotel will be freed up for someone else in your absence."

"Oh." Abby couldn't produce any other words as she tried to imagine how she was going to explain *this* to Caroline, or to anyone else, for that matter. And a surge of fear caught in her throat. Rising to her feet in an attempt to regain some small sense of control, she managed to say, "I ... I haven't really been here long enough to make any friends, as I'm sure you know. And I—"

"I'm sorry, Abby," the editor said, standing up as well. "But we think you'll be perfect for this assignment. When you come in tomorrow morning, we'll have all the details ready for you, and then you can head down to Charlotte next week."

That was on September 23, and Abby's train arrived in Charlotte on September 29, at midnight, which actually made the date the thirtieth. Dede Marsden had been dispatched to pick her up at the station, and both women knew the whole situation had been contrived without having to say a word to each other. But Abby was determined to make the best of the circumstances, and Dede pitched in to help, without probing for information.

"I don't know what's going on here," she said to Abby on the drive from the train station to the hotel. "But I do know a raw deal when I see one—or better yet, when I smell one. If you feel like talking about anything, let me know. Meanwhile, I want to assure you that I'll do everything in my power to assist you with this assignment and make the story a success."

"Thank you, Dede. I appreciate that, especially since you don't even know me. But the truth is that I don't think anyone, besides you perhaps, *wants* me to make the story a success."

"Even more reason to knock it out of the park," Dede said, glancing over at Abby with a compassionate, welcoming smile.

And the next day, Dede came up with the idea. "I think we need to start with a meeting that brings in farmers from all around this area. We'll advertise in the newspapers and on the radio, explaining that we're looking for as many as possible to interview about how the post-war economy and the political climate are affecting them. We'll hold the meeting in the hotel where you're staying, and we'll offer them free coffee and rolls in the morning plus lunch. If we get a large enough attendance, you should be able to get a solid start on the preliminaries of your story, with all those farming resources in one room together. How do you feel about that approach?"

"I *love* it!"

That was on Friday, October 1. Three weeks and one day later, on Saturday, October 23, Abby continued to watch Dede manage the sign-ins at the table in the back as the room with a seating capacity of more than one hundred filled up. Feeling much calmer—more at ease with her surroundings, as Dede had assured her she would be—Abby stood up and began making her way down the center aisle to see if she could be of assistance. Her slim figure and long legs were accentuated by the curves of her peplum jacket and the heel rise of her pumps.

The assembling audience was mostly men, many of them dressed in overalls and long-sleeved shirts. A few women were scattered among the rows, *probably wives who talked their husbands into taking them to the city,* Abby thought. Some of the people were still mingling around the coffee setup on the side of the room, but everyone else had already taken a seat.

One fellow in particular caught her attention. He was sitting on the aisle about halfway back and was dressed in crease-pressed blue jeans, black cowboy boots, and a blue plaid flannel shirt that had obviously been ironed as well. He had a head full of thick, black hair combed back Frank Sinatra style, and his stunning sapphire eyes were especially striking surrounded by the bronze coloring of his face.

"Howdy, miss," he said, standing up as she approached his row, revealing a height well over six foot. "I'm Zeke Gerard, and this here is my older brother, Andy," he added, extending his right hand to Abby and pointing with his left to a man in the next chair who looked rather grumpy and not a thing like this charmer.

"Hello," Abby said, using the handshake as an excuse to stop walking. "My name is Abigail Ryan, and we're very grateful that you and your brother—and all of these other fine people as well—have taken time out of your busy days to come here this morning."

"We're happy to do it, miss. A lot of these folks is our neighbors. We all caravanned into town today in our trucks, and we're sure looking forward to hearing what you got to say. Ain't that right, Andy?" Andy just shrugged his shoulders. His arms were folded across his chest and rested on a very round belly as he sipped from a coffee cup held in one hand. "Don't mind him," Zeke said with a grin. "He's usually like that till lunch."

Abby smiled and nodded politely at the brother. "Well, Mr. Gerard, I hope I have a chance to talk with you more later on. But now I need to go help my associate, before I get into trouble."

"Sure wouldn't want that to happen, especially on account a me," Zeke replied.

As she walked away from him, she could feel those blue eyes following her.

*****

Three hours later, Abby and Dede's expectations regarding input from the group had been far exceeded. They'd learned more than they'd imagined possible in such a short period about the history of U.S. agriculture in general and the specifics about the geographical area surrounding Charlotte. In the early twentieth century, the industry had been highly labor intensive, with the human labor being manual, supplemented by somewhere around *twenty-two million* work animals. That massive effort took place on a large number of small farms in rural areas. Close to fifty percent of the American workforce lived on those farms, producing an average of five commodities nationwide, two of which were tobacco and cotton in the southern states.

But World War II had brought changes of titanic proportions to the entire country, and especially to the South where, as part of the war effort, the Federal government had introduced new industries and military bases. People moved to the South from all over America to work in those industries and on those bases. At the same time, the emphasis on farming tobacco and cotton crops shifted to soybeans, corn, and other foods to help support the massive military operations in both the European and Pacific war theaters and the subsequent food shortage in the homeland. To increase production as much as possible, technological advances—such as gasoline- and electric-powered machinery and the widespread use of pesticides and chemical fertilizers—were introduced to the farmers, gradually replacing the need for manual labor and those millions of work animals.

"Now that the war's been over for three years," one man in the audience began telling Abby and Dede, "our production is way up, but we got no place to send half the crops we harvest."

"That's right," said someone else. "Soldiers are all home now, and there isn't enough demand stateside for everything we can accomplish with all this new-fangled equipment and sprays that keep the insects under control."

"And big companies are starting to buy up little farms," came another voice.

"And those of us who want to hang onto our family farms that been here for a hun'erd years," said yet another man, "are having a hard time competing with the big businesses."

"Some of us are starting to talk about leaving the land."

"More 'n *some* of us."

"Yeah," came a collective voice, sounding more like a groan across the room.

This commentary continued all morning, with Dede officiating and Abby taking copious notes. Then shortly after twelve thirty, Dede offered a summary of what had been learned, thanked them all for their participation and their honesty, and suggested that they conclude and have lunch.

"If you haven't already done so, please leave your mailing addresses and telephone numbers for us on the sheets in the back, in case we need to contact you. We'll also want to send you copies of the article when it comes out. And *our* office information is available for each of you on the table in the back, in the event you think of something else you'd like to share with us. Now, we know that many of you have driven long distances today, and we want to make sure you're back out on the roads with plenty of time to get home before dark. So enjoy your lunch, and thank you again for coming. Miss Ryan and I will be here until the last of you leaves, so please come and talk to us, if you'd like."

With that, everyone in the audience applauded and then stood up at the same time and began heading like a herd toward the luncheon buffet table. Abby and Dede spent several minutes speaking with a few men and a couple of their wives who came forward to shake hands and offer their personal gratitude for being invited to the meeting. Then Abby followed her mentor as they threaded their way through the crowd to the reception area in the back.

"I think that went quite well," Dede said, not worrying about whispering, with the loud hum of conversation in the room absorbing her words.

"I agree," Abby replied. "And I have pages and pages of notes. The next step will be to go to the library and begin supplementing what we learned today with facts and information that I can reference with documented sources."

"Sounds like *one* thing you might wanna do," said a deep male voice approaching the table from the side. Both women turned and saw Zeke Gerard standing there, holding a plate piled high with sandwich halves, fruit, and potato salad in one hand, and a glass of ice tea in the other.

"Does that mean you have another idea, Mr. Gerard?" Abby asked.

"Yes, miss, I sure do. Mind if I pull up a chair?" He set his plate and ice tea down on the table next to the sign-in sheet, which Dede immediately scooped up as if she anticipated something spilling on the valuable collection of names and numbers.

"Please, Mr. Gerard, make yourself comfortable," Abby said, but Zeke was already sitting down before she'd finished her sentence.

"I was just talking to my brother and some of our neighbors over there, and we think you should come out to see us where we live. Walk with us on our farmland. See firsthand what we do and what our problems are. That's the kind of stuff for your story that you won't be finding in no library. And we'll take good care a you too. Give you some *real* food," he said, grinning as he took a bite of his turkey sandwich on limp white bread.

"And where is it that you live?" Dede interjected.

"Out in Harmony. 'Bout ninety minutes straight north a here, depending on how fast you go." He might have been answering Dede's question, but he was looking and smiling at Abby.

"Well, that's a very kind offer, Mr. Gerard," Abby said. "But I don't have a car, so I'm afraid that won't be possible."

"But I got a truck. And my neighbors got 'bout a dozen more, if mine don't work. I'll pick you up and bring you back. My pleasure."

"Thank you, but I—"

"Actually, Abby," Dede said, with an unmistakable look of mischief on her face, "that might not be such a bad idea. I doubt that our associates in Washington will be expecting such an in-depth and personal perspective. Could make your story quite compelling."

Filled with mixed feelings about heading off with a strange man in a truck versus the thought of blindsiding the Washington editor with a story that would leap off the page, Abby sat still for a moment, contemplating the idea. But only for a moment.

"All right, Mr. Gerard," she said. "I accept your kind offer. When would you like to do this?"

"How 'bout next Saturday, the thirtieth? Folks'll be doing Halloween hayrides for the children, picking punkins, and all sorts of other stuff that might be fun. You can be working and having a good time all at once."

"That sounds wonderful, Mr. Gerard. How many children do you have?"

"What? *Oh.* No, not me. Not *mine.* I ain't never been married. And my brother Andy and his wife Belinda never had any neither. No, I was talking 'bout my neighbors' children. We all kind a blend in together on holidays, you know. How 'bout you? You married with kids?" he asked with a hesitant tone in his voice.

"No," Abby said, looking down at the table when she felt the memories rise along with the blush on her cheeks. "I'm not married." Then she decided to try out the words, just to see how they felt. "The truth is, I'm hoping to become a nun one day."

Expecting that there might be a forthcoming question, she waited. But when she looked up, she saw Dede and Zeke staring at her with numb expressions and making no apparent attempt to speak. *This is really quite funny*, she thought. *I'll bet they think I'm kidding.*

"So, Mr. Gerard, what time would you like to pick me up next Saturday?"

*****

He picked her up at nine thirty. The weather was in the upper fifties and cloudy but with no rain, and the next ninety minutes were filled with a little small talk and a lot of silence. Shortly after eleven o'clock, Zeke made a right turn onto a long driveway paved with seashells. As the truck bounced forward, with the shells crunching beneath the tires, she saw in front of them a graying single-story farmhouse, with a wide screened-in wraparound porch encircling the entire structure. About thirty yards off to the right side was another house, much smaller, and almost looking like an enclosed single square room. But the little house had a chimney, which suggested a fireplace and raised Abby's curiosity about what might be in there.

As Zeke pulled the truck to a stop next to the farmhouse, a side door opened and a woman walked through the screened porch and down the steps to greet them. She looked like she might be in her thirties, about Abby's height, around five foot eight or nine, and her body was a little round. She was wearing brown slacks and a white pullover sweater, and her caramel-colored hair was tied back in a simple ponytail.

After Zeke walked to the passenger side of the truck, he opened the door to help Abby step down as he made the introduction.

"This here is my sister-in-law, Belinda Gerard. Belinda, this here is Abby Ryan, the one I been telling you 'bout."

"How do you do," Belinda said, taking both of Abby's hands in hers and smiling broadly, as if she were receiving a gift. "And welcome to our little corner of America."

As Abby got a closer look at her, she could see that the woman's rosy cheeks and the shaded lids over her large brown eyes were completely natural, with not a hint of makeup or rouge evident.

"Belinda's been mighty excited 'bout you coming out here today," Zeke said, leading the way into the house through the same door she'd come out. "She sees the same old people all the time and is looking forward to something fresh. Ain't that right?"

"That's right, Zeke," Belinda said through a warm smile as she wrapped a nurturing arm that felt absolutely wonderful around Abby's shoulders.

"Where's Andy?" Zeke asked, holding the door open for the women.

"He's giving the Holder, Johnson, and Bayner kids a hayride. Been gone about an hour. The next group's due to arrive after lunch, around one."

"How many in that bunch?"

"I'm not sure. It's a smaller group, I think. Maybe six or seven."

Once they were all inside, Abby saw that they were standing in a combination living, dining, and kitchen area, comfortably decorated and furnished in earth tones, with thick, plump cushions on the sofa and easy chairs, and plenty of pillows and throws everywhere. A blazing fire crackled from a massive stone fireplace at the far end of the multipurpose room, heating the entire space. Lacy curtains were hung on all the windows, even on the door, and hand stenciled swirls, fruits, and farm animals, in shades of blues, reds, and greens, had been painted along the top edges of every wall, just below the ceiling.

"Wanna go on the next hayride with me?" Zeke asked Abby, looking down at her with those remarkable blue eyes as he hovered uncomfortably close.

"Well ... I ..." Abby stammered, taking a couple of steps back.

"Nothing to be scared of, little lady," he said, walking over to the stove and lifting the lids on three pots simmering there, peering inside each one. "Andy'll do the driving, and I'll sit back on the hay with you and the kids. It'll be a great way for you to see the farm and for me to show you some of what we do here. And then we'll head into the woods, of course, where it's darker 'cause of the trees, and where Andy and me set up a haunted area to scare the crap outta—"

"Zeke!" Belinda interrupted.

"S'cuse me, Miss Ryan. Well, you get the point. That's the part the kids live for 'round here every year at this time. And we do one ride after dark, for those with strong hearts," he added with a smile that was irrepressible.

Warming immediately to the ambience and love evident in this house, Abby began to relax.

"Okay," she said. "I'd love to go on a hayride after lunch. But I think I'll leave the one after dark to the younger crowd. Besides, I'll need to get home by then anyway."

"Oh? We thought you might want to spend the night with us," Belinda said, sitting down on the sofa in front of the fire and gesturing for Abby to join her. "I fixed up our little guesthouse for you, and I'm making a roasted chicken for dinner."

"Belinda, that's very kind of you. But I'm not prepared to spend the night. I didn't bring anything with me, and tomorrow's Sunday, so I have to get up early for Mass."

Zeke turned away from the pots on the stove and exchanged a look with Belinda. "Guess I wasn't too clear with my invitation," he said to her.

"Apparently not. Well, Miss Ryan," she said, returning her attention to Abby. "Perhaps next weekend you—"

"Perhaps, but not before all of you stop calling me Miss Ryan. Your hospitality is overwhelming, and I would be very happy if you'd call me Abby."

Zeke's smile broadened as Belinda patted Abby's hand. "Why don't we spend some time getting acquainted and showing you around," Belinda responded, "and then maybe you'll feel more comfortable about the idea of spending the night down the road."

"Thank you," Abby said, sensing again that nurturing mantle of warmth that seemed to be part of Belinda's nature.

"I *would* like you to think about staying for dinner today, though," Belinda added. "We'll be eating early, before the first evening hayride. So Zeke can still get you back home before it's too late."

"All right," Abby acquiesced. "But please don't go to any trouble."

"Believe me, it's no trouble. I do this every day."

"Yes she does," Zeke said, still standing next to the stove. "And I'm guessing that, if you're making chicken for dinner, then this here stew's what you got in mind for lunch."

"You're too clever for words, Zeke."

"You got cornbread to go with this?"

"Don't I always?"

"Well, I'm in heaven just thinking 'bout it," he said. "And you're gonna be too, Miss Ryan ... I mean, Abby." He took a sip of the stew with the tasting spoon Belinda left beside the pot. "Yup. You're gonna be too ... *Abby*," he added, speaking her name in almost a whisper.

*****

"Our land stretches out as far as you can see from this point," Zeke said, his voice a little jerky as the truck bumped along the rough ground.

They'd headed out shortly past one o'clock, after savoring what was, indeed, heaven in the form of stew and cornbread, followed up with hot coffee and three different kinds of pie, with ice cream. *How do these people stay so trim?* Abby wondered, feeling the pressure of her waistband against her tummy after only one meal.

She was seated on a bale of hay, leaning back against another, with an extra jacket from Belinda pulled on over her sweater and a blanket wrapped around the gray wool slacks she was glad she'd had sense enough to wear. Three young children—half the group they'd expected—were seated on bales above and behind her.

Despite the choppy ride, she felt like she was sitting in a straw easy chair, breathing in the sweet, clean farm air, and letting the peace of the land wash over her. She'd felt like this at Lady of the Valley, and again when she'd allowed herself a few moments to appreciate the beauty of the Whitmore estate in Napa. Somehow, there seemed to be a more unobstructed connection to God out in countryside like this versus a big city like Seattle, where she'd been raised, or even Washington DC or Charlotte.

"And one day," Zeke continued, "I'm gonna build a huge hill over in that area, with steps going up the side, so I can stand on top of something and be able to see all of our land from one end to the other. That's a dream a mine, and I *am* gonna make it happen."

"That's an impressive goal, Zeke," she said, calling him by his first name now as well. "But how do you build a hill?"

"We'll have'ta haul in tons a dirt, pack it all down hard, like cement, and then haul in tons more. I figure the job'll take a year or two, by the time the rains and winter freezes help us do the packing. But it'll be done right, and then I'm gonna build a screen house or a gazebo or something on top a the hill, so I can sit up there and look out over our place and do nothing, if that's what I feel like doing."

She closed her eyes and tried to visualize what the hill would look like. "I'd love to see that when it's finished," she said, glancing over at him on the hay bale next to her.

"Maybe that'll happen, Abby. Do you think you could still come and look at it, if you're a nun by then?" he asked with a grin.

She could feel the blush rising in her cheeks again. "Maybe we could talk about that another time."

"Well, as long as I know there's gonna *be* another time, I'm happy to wait."

Andy finished driving them around the core of the farm and then headed into the woods where a crude assembly of scarecrows, skeletons, and rubber spiders in cotton candylike webs did not disappoint the three children, based on their squeals and screams. Then they went back to the house, and after the neighboring parents departed with the children, they shared Belinda's roasted chicken, mashed potatoes and gravy, fresh green beans canned from their garden, and hot biscuits with more gravy, all followed with coffee again and remnants of the three pies.

"Next weekend," Zeke said, when the dishes had been cleared and they were sitting around the table with a second cup of coffee, "our neighbors that was at the meeting in Charlotte, and some that wasn't, would like to come over and talk to you some more. They've been thinking 'bout stuff they want to tell you that didn't come to mind when we was at the hotel. So, we was wondering—Andy, Belinda, and me—if you'd like to be our guest for the weekend. Belinda fixed up the guesthouse real nice. It's just one room, but there's a fireplace and a little bathroom. We could have all the folks come over on Saturday."

"Thank you, Zeke," Belinda said. "Now *that* was a proper invitation." Then she turned her attention to Abby. "The wives of everyone who comes will bring their favorite dishes," Belinda interjected, "so we'll have plenty to eat all day, but we won't have to do much of the cooking here."

"And there's a Catholic church 'bout five miles away," Zeke went on. "I can take you there on Sunday morning. Then we can come back here and all have supper, and then I'll drive you back to town."

"We'd so love to have you here," Belinda said. "I can't tell you how much I've enjoyed the company of another woman on just this single day. The thought of you being here for a whole weekend makes me feel like a child again."

"And if my Belinda is happy," Andy said, finally speaking up and actually producing a smile, which made him look years younger, "we're *all* gonna have a good day!"

Thus the routine began, starting with the "next" weekend that turned into months of weekends. Zeke would pick Abby up at her hotel on Friday afternoon and bring her back on Sunday evening. The guesthouse became her second home, a private retreat where she felt safe and protected.

The square room's plank floor was covered with a brown braided rug, and on the full-size bed pushed up into one corner was a patchwork quilt in shades of brown and blue. An end table topped with an ornate oil lamp was beside the bed. Another corner of the room had been sectioned off as a bathroom, with running water in the sink, a functioning toilet, and a gilt-edged oval mirror mounted over the sink. On the wall opposite the fireplace was a large armoire; and two upholstered armchairs were positioned in front of the fireplace, with a small round table in between them. Every time she stepped foot into that guesthouse, she felt at peace and at home.

On most of the weekends, she spent Saturdays on neighboring farms, listening and taking notes while being shown the operations, which were remarkably different from farm to farm. Then, on Sunday mornings, Zeke drove her to the little Catholic church five miles away and waited for her outside in his truck during Mass, except for one Sunday when she was able to coax him to join her. But that was the *only* time.

"The pastor seems like a nice enough fella," he said on the way home after attending the service with her. "And I liked most a what he had to say. But—and I mean no disrespect, Abby—all that standing and sitting and kneeling is a bit much for me, and I don't really know what it's for in the first place. So I don't mind waiting in the truck."

And that's what he continued to do, even during the extra Masses she attended over the Thanksgiving and Christmas holidays, when she spent a week or more on the farm rather than just a weekend.

Each Monday upon her return to work, she would type up her notes and review them with Dede. And the more time she spent living the farming life, walking the grounds, and growing to understand the issues and personalities of the farming community in and around Harmony, the more texture she was able to add to her story. She wasn't just writing about agriculture any longer. She was telling a story about the lives of real people affected by that agriculture, not to mention all the attendant challenges and crises brought on by post-war politics and swelling shifts in the economy.

"This has the potential now of being quite excellent," Dede said after one review of Abby's work in early December. "And you look very happy, I might add."

"I've made some wonderful friends, Dede, and it's such a different outcome than I would have predicted two months ago."

"I agree—and I absolutely cannot wait until we submit your story to Washington. When do you think you'll have it finished?"

"Well, most of the research is done now, although every weekend one family or another seems to add a new vignette or issue. But I'm going to start pulling the whole thing together over the Christmas holidays when I'll be out there for ten days. By the time you and I get through all the necessary edits, I'm guessing we'll be at the end of January."

"That sounds realistic. I think I'll tell Washington that the first of February will be our deadline, since they don't seem to want to set one *for* us. We'll see what happens after that."

*****

On Christmas morning, Abby and the Gerards exchanged a few gifts with each other. Abby bought a bright yellow full-body apron, with white ruffles around the neckline, for Belinda. She also bought her a copy of *The Joy of Cooking*, an incredible cookbook written and compiled by Irma Rombauer, which was not only filled with hundreds of pages of recipes but also with history and stories about the foods and seasonings used in those recipes. With as much time as Belinda had spent helping Abby learn her way around a kitchen in the last few months, Abby felt these were appropriate gifts for her newfound friend—and the presents were, indeed, received with great enthusiasm.

For Andy, Abby purchased a white turtleneck cotton shirt and a sea blue wool cardigan sweater, because he always dressed like an old man. And Abby thought Belinda deserved him to look like the handsome man he *could* be, with just a little effort and perhaps more than a little weight loss.

Zeke's gifts were the most difficult for her to select. She knew how he felt about her, and she didn't want to buy him anything that might lead him to believe those feelings were mutual. As fond as she'd grown of him and his family, she was marking the time while she lived through what she believed was her remaining penance, and while she continued to ready herself for her return to Lady of the Valley.

But she'd looked out the window of the guesthouse on many cold nights, only to discover Zeke bundled up on one of the rocking chairs on the screen porch. She suspected that he was waiting for her, hoping that she would see him and decide to come out and join him. Her heart ached because he was such a good and gentle man, and she didn't want to hurt him. Yet she was on a mission to restore her vocational path, and she did not want to make any more mistakes.

So for Christmas she bought him his own radio to keep in his small bedroom, because Andy liked to listen to different shows on many evenings, and they only had the one radio in the living room. She also bought him a small oil painting that she found in a shop not far from her hotel. The artist had created a pastel green hill in the middle of a field, with vistas that seemed to extend for miles. On top of the hill was a white gazebo. When he opened the radio, he was laughing out loud. When he opened the oil painting, his eyes filled up with tears.

"Thank you, Abby," he said. "This is just what I'm hoping my hill will look like."

"I'm glad, and I know you'll make it happen."

Two packages remained under the tree, which Zeke pulled out and placed in front of Abby. One was quite small and turned out to be a bottle of French perfume from Zeke. The second was the size of a breadbox and extremely heavy. Abby wondered what in the world this could be as Zeke, Belinda, and Andy stood over her like expectant parents while she removed the wrapping paper.

"Oh dear heaven!" she gasped when she saw what was inside. "I cannot believe my eyes," she whispered as she stared at the brand new typewriter.

"We wanted you to have your own," Belinda said, "so you can get more work done while you're here. We see you writing everything with a pen, and we thought this would help you get your story done faster."

"But this is way too much," Abby insisted. "No one's ever given me a gift like this before."

"It's not as much as you think," Andy said. "I got a good deal through our bank."

"Right," Zeke added. "So don't you worry one bit. And I'll carry it over to the guesthouse later on where it'll always be there for you."

"I don't know what to say or how to thank you."

"And we feel the same way about your gifts," Belinda said. "So let's all say a prayer of gratitude and then have breakfast."

"Are you gonna heat up that ham to have with them eggs and potatoes?" Zeke asked.

"Yes," Belinda answered, smiling at Abby and shaking her head. "That's the plan."

*****

By the end of January 1949, Abby and Dede had edited Abby's article into what they believed was as close to perfection as they could get. "Finding Harmony—A Study of the People and Their Challenges in a Southern Post-War Farming Community" combined educational, political, and humanitarian elements in a riveting piece that read like a short story. Characters were developed to such a depth that the deeply troubling issues they faced struck emotional chords throughout the newsroom in Charlotte. Everyone who read the draft agreed that Abby deserved the byline that would surely be forthcoming in the *Washington Post*'s southern feature section.

Late on Friday night, February 11, ten days after the package had been mailed to Washington DC, Abby was in the guesthouse on the farm getting ready for bed when she peeked through the curtains and saw Zeke on the porch. He'd been uncharacteristically melancholy during the drive from Charlotte that afternoon and during dinner, and she thought she knew why. When she couldn't bear watching him any longer, she put her slacks and sweater back on, pulled on her coat, and walked over to join him, amazed at the brightening of his expression and the straightening of his body when he saw her.

"Hi," she said.

"Hi."

"Mind if I sit with you awhile?"

"Now what do *you* think, Abby?"

"Yeah. I guess that was a stupid question."

"Not stupid. Just overdue."

"I'm sorry, Zeke," she said, pulling up another rocking chair alongside his and taking a seat. "I know we should have probably had this conversation a long time ago, but I—"

"You don't have to say nothing. I understand. You'll be going back to Washington now that your story's done."

"What?"

"That's the only reason you came here, ain't it?"

She paused a moment before answering. "Well, yes. That's why they originally sent me to Charlotte. But that's certainly not the reason I've been spending so much time here on the farm."

"No?"

"No. Other than my family and my best friend Tess, I've never felt as comfortable and loved with anyone as I do with you and Belinda and Andy. I've grown extraordinarily fond of all of you—and frankly, I'm not sure if they *will* call me back to Washington after my article is published. They might want me to stay in Charlotte."

"Why would that be?"

"It's a long story, Zeke, and one I'd rather not get into now. But there *is* something I do want to talk about."

"What's that?"

"My plan to become a nun."

He leaned forward in his chair and put his head in hands. "Damn it, Abby! I can't believe you're serious about doing something crazy like that."

"I know you can't, and that's why I want to talk with you about it. You see, I was in the convent once already." He sat up and looked at her as if she were speaking another language. "But I thought I'd made a mistake," she continued, "so I left. Then I finished school, started working, and ended up taking a job with the *San Francisco Chronicle*. That move didn't turn out too well for me, though, and that's when I was sent to Washington. But all the while—since not too long after I left the convent, actually—I've believed that I'm supposed to follow that original path. I belong there. I just wasn't ready the first time, and then things got pretty mixed up, and I've been working hard to get myself to the point where I'm ready to go back. Now I think I'm getting close. Maybe another year."

"I really don't understand, Abby."

"I realize that, Zeke," she said, reaching out to take his hand. "But I want you to know how deeply I care about you and that, if this calling weren't so strong and so consistent, I would have no trouble seeing things the way you'd like me to see them. The truth is, though, that I can't deny the path God has set out for me, and I'm hoping you and I can still be friends, even if we want different things from our relationship."

"Abby, I love you," he said, his voice as strong as his conviction. "You must know that by now. I will *always* love you, much more than a friend. And I'm telling you right now that I'll never be able to accept what you're doing as God's plan, or anyone else's plan either. It just ain't right."

"I understand your feelings, Zeke. Can we agree to keep talking about it, though?"

"It won't do any good, but if it'll keep you coming out here, I'll talk about it."

"Thank you," she said, getting up and leaning over to kiss him on top of his head. "You are the most gentle man I've ever known. And you know what else?"

"What."

"I believe that God sent me here so I would be exposed to the love of a gentle man before I return to the convent."

"Oh really? And what do you think his plan is for *me* after you leave? What does he 'spect *me* to do then? See, there's *two* people in this plan you're talking 'bout. But so far God only gave thought to one of 'em. Ain't that right?"

She didn't respond immediately, but after a minute said, "You know, Zeke, that's an excellent point. And I'm going to pray about that tonight, to see if there's a better answer than any I can think of right now."

"You do that, Abby." He waited a moment before continuing. "And how quick you think the good Lord is gonna get back to you? 'Cause if he's planning on letting me meet someone else 'fore you go—just to make things fair and even—then I'm gonna need a new shirt."

She started laughing, which made him laugh too, and the heaviness of the moment passed. Then he stood up and put his arms around her, holding her close to him for the first time.

"I'm gonna keep doing everything I can," he whispered, "to make you change your mind."

"I know," she whispered back, putting her arms around him too. "And that's okay."

*****

More than a month had gone by without any response from Washington regarding Abby's article. Dede finally called up there on Thursday, March 17, and she received the answer later that day. But she didn't tell Abby the devastating news until the next morning.

When Zeke picked her up at her hotel that Friday afternoon as usual, she knew her face was blotchy and her eyes were red, but somehow she thought he might not notice if she added more rouge to her cheeks.

"What's wrong?" was the first thing he asked her, though.

When she started to answer him, her voice caught, and she began crying again, despite her best efforts to hold the tears back. That caused him to pull the truck over to the curb and stop.

"What the hell happened, Abby?"

Still unable to get any words out, she let him bring her into his arms where she began sobbing on his shoulder. Several minutes later, after using up two handkerchiefs from her handbag and one from his pocket, she started to regain her composure.

"They killed my story," she was finally able to say.

"What does *that* mean?"

"It means the story is dead. Buried. Never going to see print. And bless her heart, Dede's as upset as I am."

"But how is that possible? Everyone told you how good it was!"

"The people in Washington never had any intention of printing it, Zeke. They just wanted to get rid of me."

"Why would they want to do that?"

"It's a long story, and one that I *am* going to tell you. But I want to wait until we get to the farm. It's something I need to explain to all of you, together."

"Somehow I feel like slugging somebody all of a sudden, Abby."

"Me too."

*****

Two hours later, Abby was sitting on the porch with Zeke, Belinda, and Andy as the sun was beginning to set on an unseasonably warm early spring day. Dinner had been immediately put on hold as soon as Zeke announced that "Abby has something she wants to tell us," and after Belinda had taken a look at Abby's face.

She began with the day she'd arrived at the Whitmores to cover their gala, and then she proceeded with the rest of the story, in as much detail as she could stomach. Through the first series of events—even through the rape, which was the only thing she told with abbreviation—her voice was strong and steady, as if the cathartic revelations were emboldening her. But when she reached the part about Salome, Sinclair's deal, and the money, she began to break down, ending up in Belinda's arms while the two men sat speechless and immobilized. Several minutes later, when she'd regained her voice yet again, she sat up and looked at each of her dear friends, slowly, one at a time.

"I'll understand if you think I'm a horrible person," she said softly. "And I won't blame you if you want me to leave and never come back to your wonderful home."

"*You*, my dear," Belinda responded without hesitation, clearly trying to maintain her own composure, "are *not* the one who's horrible! I know how

205

hard that story must have been for you to tell us, and your courage has only made me love you more. So don't you think for one minute that we want you to leave. You can stay here with us for as long as you like."

Zeke stood up and shocked everyone by slamming his fist into the side of the house. He didn't leave so much as a mark on the brick structure, but he shook his hand and grimaced in pain as he paced up and down the length of the porch.

"I'm not really sure what I'm going to do," Abby said, resisting the urge to get up and take a look at Zeke's hand. "They've told me I still have a job, and they're still going to send me my paycheck, but they said they don't have any assignment for me right now. And Dede, as much as she'd like to, hasn't been authorized to give me anything either."

"Why don't you just quit?" Zeke asked, finally stopping his pacing and standing in front of Abby as he massaged his sore hand with his good one.

"I did think about that. But where would I go? And what would I do to support myself? I'm certainly not ready to go back to the convent yet," she added, ignoring the frown lines that immediately deepened on Andy's forehead in response to Belinda's sideways glance at her husband. "Especially not with such heaviness in my heart."

"What about the money you got from those *people* in San Francisco?" Zeke was sitting down beside her again. "You should have plenty there to support you for a long time, without even needing a job."

"But it's in a savings account in Washington. I only have a few hundred dollars left in the bank account I opened here."

"I'll drive you up there to get it," he said. "Nobody said you had to keep it there, did they?"

"No, I guess they didn't. That's just where the Whitmores put it."

"Well," Andy piped in, "if the account's in your name, you can put it wherever you want to."

"And I think you should move out of your hotel and stay with us for a while," Belinda added. "Just until you figure things out. The guesthouse is yours already, and maybe you could write a book in there or something." She smiled and reached across the rocking chair arms to pat Abby's hand.

"Thank you so much for the offer, Belinda. But that would be such an imposition on all of you, having me around all the time. Weekends and holidays are one thing, but every single day would be—"

"A gift," Belinda said, finishing Abby's sentence. "And if you're worried about earning your keep or staying busy, I could always use some help in the house, or in the kitchen trying out those mouth-watering recipes in that *Joy of Cooking* book you gave me."

Abby looked at Zeke, who was resting against the high back of his rocker with his hands clasped behind his head and his lips pressed together, clearly trying not to smile.

"You *know* how I feel, without even asking," he said, looking back at her. "So I'm not saying nothing. You need to decide whatever feels best."

As she studied the faces of these three kind and generous people, who had opened their hearts and home to her and made her feel like part of their family, she knew her decision had already been made.

The following Monday, on March 21, 1949, Abby submitted her resignation to Dede, who understood but accepted the letter with regret.

"I feel terrible about all of this, Abby. If there was something I could do, I—"

"Please don't worry about it, Dede. I believe this is all happening for a reason, and I just need a little time to understand what I'm supposed to do next."

"Well, I'm going to miss you very much—you and your special magic with words. I hope you don't give that up, because you have a great deal to offer. And if you ever think I can be of help to you, please write to me."

The two women exchanged an extended embrace, and then Abby returned to her hotel where Zeke helped her load her things into his truck.

On Wednesday of that week, she and Zeke left the farm at dawn for the drive to Washington, arriving just as the sun was setting. They stayed for two days, in separate hotel rooms, while Abby withdrew the balance of the Whitmores' original deposit—$20,000 less the $400 she'd taken to Charlotte, which left $19,600 plus a little interest—in the form of a check from the savings bank. Since that was enough money to buy a whole house, a new car, and plenty of other necessities, they immediately put the check in the hotel safe.

Abby then spent the better part of Thursday and Friday touring Zeke around the district, showing off her newly minted knowledge about the history, the monuments, and the operation of the government. He'd never been to DC before and was duly impressed by the city, but not nearly as impressed as he was by Abby, which he mentioned every time they moved from one historical site to another.

On Friday night, they had dinner in a small Italian restaurant within walking distance of their hotel. Lounging in the candlelit booth after they'd finished their meal, Zeke ordered an Amaretto liqueur for Abby and a snifter of cognac for himself, and then he insisted that they clink their glasses in a toast.

"Here's to a fresh beginning, and to possibilities, Abby."

But before she clinked, she said, "Zeke, I'm uncomfortable with the way that sounds. Nothing has changed, you know. I *am* going to return to the convent. I'm just not sure when I'll be ready yet."

"Girl, you're a handful, with the hardest head I ever saw. I know your mind's made up, but I told you I was never going to stop trying, and you said that was okay."

Abby looked at him across the table, his blue eyes glistening in the candlelight and his infectious smile reaching out to touch her heart.

"You're a handful too, Mr. Gerard."

"Good," he said. "Something we got in common—at last. Now, clink that glass a yours on mine."

And so she did.

*****

By mid-June, Abby had not only become part of the Gerard family but part of the Harmony community as well. She'd also begun to *really* learn about the hard, rugged life on a working farm. The time she'd spent there while writing her article had been mostly in the "off season," after the harvesting was complete and when the land had settled into dormancy for the winter. But for the past three months, she'd been witness to all the work involved with preparing the fields, planting the crops, and then keeping them safe from birds, insects, and weather so that the next harvest would be successful.

The days began before sunup, always with a big breakfast, which was usually the heaviest meal of the day. By sunset, everyone was so tired that early dinners and one or two radio shows was about all anyone could tolerate before falling asleep. But Abby adapted well to the routine, helping Belinda with the cooking and cleaning, and becoming even closer friends with her than she'd thought possible. She wrote consistently in her journals, attended Mass every Sunday and on every Holy Day of Obligation, and felt herself growing stronger spiritually and emotionally. All the while, the seemingly unlimited love and support of the Gerards continued to insulate her from further pain and disappointment.

She also wrote to Tess several times a month, including one note over the 1949 Memorial Day weekend.

I feel certain I'll be ready to return to Lady of the Valley soon, perhaps early next year. Your words that last day at the convent have never been far from my heart, you know.

You said you wanted me to remember that you were there. First, though, you told me I'd need to believe, from the very depths of my soul, that life behind those cloistered doors would not represent confinement or oppression. Instead, you said that life at Lady of the Valley offers an unimaginable freedom, coupled with a purpose so powerful that the biggest challenge for each sister is to remain humble. You also said that, if the day comes when I am drawn there because I'm convinced that your words are true—and if I have no doubt that I've been called there—then your open arms will await me.

I've been carrying those words with me for nearly five years now, my dear Tess, and I've worked hard to listen for God's voice and to see His plan in all that's happened to me. Finally, I'm feeling strong, and I have no doubt that I've been called. I'm just trying to figure out how and when I can get back there ...

On Thursday, June 30, 1949, Abby and Belinda were in the kitchen preparing lunch about eleven thirty. Summer had arrived with a vengeance, blanketing North Carolina in a sweltering siege of heat and humidity. Both women were constantly blotting their faces despite the fact that all the windows were open and electric table fans were doing their best to keep the air moving inside the house.

The hum of those fans made the voice outside difficult to hear at first, but then they both heard the shouting at the same moment and ran through the kitchen door to the porch. There they saw Zeke sprinting through one of the soybean fields, calling out something they could not yet understand. In the distance behind him, they could see the yellow tractor. But they didn't see Andy anywhere.

As Zeke drew closer to the house, his words suddenly became clear. "Call Doctor Jake!" he was yelling at them. "Call Doctor Jake!"

Abby and Belinda rushed down the porch steps to meet him.

"What's happened?" Belinda asked anxiously. "Where's Andy?"

"He fell off the tractor," Zeke said breathlessly as he kept running toward his truck. "I'm driving back out there to pick him up and take him to the hospital. Call Doctor Jake and tell him to meet us there!"

Without ever breaking his stride, Zeke reached the truck, climbed inside, and sped off in a dust cloud on the path alongside the soybean field toward the tractor. Belinda seemed paralyzed with fear and wouldn't move.

"I have to go with them," she kept repeating.

"No," Abby insisted. "We need to go inside and call the doctor, like Zeke said. If you'll tell me where the number is, I'll do it."

Abby had to literally pull Belinda back into the house, and as they were dialing the doctor's number, they watched through the window as the truck raced past the field, the house, and onto the road, the tires squealing and the truck fishtailing as Zeke wrestled to maintain control of the wheel at such a high speed. When the truck straightened out and flew away, Belinda handed the phone to Abby and collapsed on the sofa.

"Hello? Doctor Jake? This is Abby Ryan over at the Gerard place. Zeke asked us to call you because something has happened to Andy, and they're on the way to the hospital right now. Thank you, Doctor Jake. Please have Zeke call us."

"Oh my God!" Belinda kept crying, her hands covering her face as she hysterically rocked back and forth. "Oh my God! Oh my God!"

Abby sat down and put her arms around her friend, trying to calm her while her own fears were rising. *Dear God in heaven*, she prayed silently. *Please help us, and keep Andy in your protective care—and Zeke too.*

*****

Andy Gerard died at the age of thirty-one, before his brother got him to the hospital. He'd had a heart attack in the heat while driving the tractor, and he'd fallen off and hit his head. But the doctor insisted that Andy was probably dead before he'd reached the ground, trying to assuage the guilt that Zeke was feeling about not getting to the hospital in time. Nothing anyone did or said, though, even came close to easing Zeke's pain, or that of Belinda, who'd just had the center of her life ripped away from her. She'd been married to Andy since she was eighteen, and because they'd never had any children, they'd lived for each other—inseparable soul mates. Without him, she didn't know how to breathe.

Despite the efforts of the Gerards' remarkable neighbors, who delivered comfort, support, and food in an unending stream over the next three days, Abby was unable to find even a spark of the light she'd come to love so much in Zeke and Belinda, or the intrinsic warmth that had been so consistently captivating in the little farmhouse. Andy was gone, and through the pall of sorrow, Abby had no trouble seeing that every meaningful aspect of life in the Gerard household had come to an end. She knew that time was a great healer, but she could not visualize any way that Belinda could recover from this tragedy and move forward on her own. And she wasn't sure about Zeke either. All she knew was that she needed to be there for both of them, for whatever amount of time would be required.

Getting through the funeral was a blur, and there was great concern about Belinda because she had stopped speaking and refused to eat. The following week, her sister and brother-in-law took the train down from Boston to take her home with them.

"We're right by the water," her sister said, "which she's always found very soothing. We also have our children—her three nieces and one nephew—whom she loves deeply. And our other sister and brother are nearby, with their families. So we think she'll have an easier time getting through this up there than she would here, with all of Andy's memories so close. When she's better, we'll bring her back home, if that's what she wants to do."

Zeke agreed, but his heart seemed to be breaking all over again the day Belinda's family took her away. Abby sat with him on the porch that afternoon, holding his hand as they rocked side by side in silence. Then he spoke while looking straight ahead rather than at her.

"And I'm guessing, Abby, that you'll be leaving soon too. Going to the convent, like you been planning all this time."

Abby closed her eyes, listening for God's voice again while knowing full well that she'd never be able to leave Zeke alone like this.

"*Eventually* I'll be going, Zeke," she said softly. "But not for a while, I suspect. I'll stay here with you for as long as you need me. I promise. And after Belinda comes home, we'll see where we are by then."

He turned to look at her, his normally animated blue eyes clouded with grief and filled with tears.

"I'm sorry, Abby," he said, his voice hoarse and breaking. "This sure wasn't how I was wanting you to stay."

"I know," she whispered, squeezing his hand. "But we're going to be okay."

211

CHAPTER FOURTEEN

"How's *that* for chronological order?" Zeke asked, looking across the table at Isaiah with a weak smile.

"Come on, Dad," Zoie said, pushing her chair back. "We're taking you to the lodge now, and I don't care how much you think you have left to tell us. I know how tired *I* am, and I can only imagine how you must be feeling after sharing all of that."

"You always think you know more 'n you do, girl. Gets a little irritating."

"Whatever," Zoie replied as she and Isaiah each took one of Zeke's arms to help him up.

As much as he wanted to hear the rest of the story himself, Isaiah kept quiet. He could see how exhausted and emotionally drained Zeke was, and besides, how much more could there be to tell anyway? Zoie's path into the world seemed pretty obvious at this point, and all that remained unanswered were the questions about Abby's return to the convent.

Isaiah still had a couple of days to satisfy his curiosity, although if he never learned anything else beyond what he already knew, what would be the difference? His job had been to get Zoie and Rosa to Kettle Falls. At the moment, he was batting .500, and he was hanging on to his hunch that Rosa was going to show up, no matter what she'd said on the phone. So, all of Zeke's yet-to-be-learned details, while compelling, were peripheral to the main task. *I'm accomplishing everything I've been asked to do*, he assured himself.

After they'd returned to the lodge and he'd escorted Zoie and her dad to their rooms, they agreed to meet in the lobby at nine the next morning.

"We can go to the diner for breakfast," he said, "and then head over to the mortuary, if you'd like. The wake tomorrow will be largely for nuns and priests, who I guess will be coming from as far away as Spokane. But Tess tells me that anyone can attend, and she'll be there all day."

"I don't care much 'bout meeting Tess," Zeke said, his voice sounding fatigued as he sat on a chair, taking off his shoes. "But I do want to see Abby."

"Me too," Zoie echoed.

"Then I'll meet you guys at nine. Get a good night's sleep."

"I don't think that's going to be a problem," Zoie said, exchanging an air kiss with Isaiah.

"Wait!" Zeke called out. "I forgot to give him the letter! It's in my jacket pocket."

"Hold on," Zoie said to Isaiah, returning moments later with an envelope in her hand. "This is the only letter Dad ever received from Abby after she left. We'd like to have it back, but we thought you might want to read it."

"Thanks. I'll bring it to breakfast."

When she'd closed the door, he returned to his own suite and immediately changed out of his jeans into black sweatpants and a long-sleeved gray T-shirt. Then he sat down on the sofa, put his feet up on the coffee table, and opened the envelope.

October 8, 1950

My dearest Zeke—

Please forgive the time that has passed. There aren't many opportunities to focus on people and things outside of the enclosure, but believe me when I tell you that you remain daily in my prayers.

I do hope that everything is all right with you, and that circumstances aren't too difficult. Despite my conviction that the best decision was made, there are moments in solitude when I drift out of conversations with God and into images of what was left behind. You'll be happy to know that, on this end, Sinclair has been helpful and accommodating, which under the circumstances, remains quite amazing to me. So everyone's minds should be at ease regarding the security of the arrangements.

Whenever I speak with him, he says he will stay in touch with you as well. But he never mentions that you have spoken, so I suspect that you have not. No matter. One day, everything will come to light, when the Lord is ready.

Although I'm sure you still question my sanity, I wish there were sufficient words to help you understand the fulfillment and liberation awarded to me when I finally surrendered to the Lord's call. Never before have I felt the freedom and purpose that greeted me within these walls. Please take comfort in the fact that I have, at long last, done the right thing.

Blessings to all of you, and may you each be granted a full and joyful life. When I am able, I will write again. Meanwhile, I remain humble in the love and forgiveness of the Almighty.

Sister Mary Abigail (Abby, always, to you)

Isaiah was struck again by the effect of seeing his father's name in yet another piece of Abby's writing. He also noted that Zoie was about six months old when the letter was written—maybe a month or two older than Isaiah, based on the chronology of Zeke's story. The timing suggested that Abby's return to the convent had happened very shortly after Zoie was born. He understood now the power of her calling to the religious life, but this letter had rekindled his curiosity, convincing him that something significant about Abby's story was still missing.

Feeling restless, he wanted to talk to Ava and wondered what she was doing. He looked at his watch—ten thirty. Her shift would be over soon, and she probably wasn't very busy at this hour on a Monday night. So he took his cell phone out of his jacket pocket and called her mobile number. She answered on the first ring, which led him to believe that she was carrying her phone in her uniform pocket, a thought that made him smile.

"Hey there," she said. "I was just thinking about you."

"Funny. I haven't *stopped* thinking about you."

"Not possible, Isaiah. You've been too busy."

"Well, I guess you're probably right. But you've been on my mind every *spare* minute. How's that?"

"More believable—and very sweet."

"Isn't your shift about over?"

"Supposed to be in another half hour. But I think I'll be leaving in a few minutes. Nobody's here, not even in the bar."

"Were you able to get tomorrow off?"

"Yup. In fact, I don't have to be at work again until the three o'clock shift on Friday."

"Wow! That's terrific! Um … what are you planning to do after you leave tonight?"

"Gee, Isaiah. I don't know. Got any ideas?"

"Well, I thought there might be a chance that you'd … um … want to come visit, maybe … *me*?"

"Hmm. That's strange. I was sort of thinking the same thing."

"Really?"

"Yeah. But only if we can have the same deal we had last night. You know …"

"You mean … *the torture*?" He laughed lightly to let her know he was joking.

"I'll understand if you'd rather not."

"Ava, I was trying to be funny. Of *course* I want you here, no matter what we do or don't do."

Within an hour, she was walking into his suite, still wearing her Barney's uniform and pulling a wheeled bag behind her, with a smaller matching bag fastened to the handle.

"Do you always carry suitcases around in the car with you, in case you decide to go on a trip after you get off work at midnight?" he asked.

She smiled as she lifted herself on her tiptoes to kiss him on his cheek. "No, I do not. But in this case, call me presumptuous. Or call me an optimist. The truth is that, before I left for work this afternoon, I packed enough stuff to last me until Friday. Is that too scary for you?"

"A little bit," he said, putting his arms around her and raising her feet off the floor with the power of his embrace. "But I think I'll live."

When he'd kissed her and put her back down, she excused herself for "just a minute" and pulled her bag into the bathroom. A short time later she emerged wearing pink flannel lounge pants, a baggy white flannel sweatshirt printed with pink flowers, and pink furry slippers. A black headband pressed her blonde curls away from her shiny, moisturized face that had been scrubbed free of all makeup.

"All right," she said, her arms outstretched as she made a slow 360-degree turn for his inspection. "This is as bad as it gets. I promise."

He was sitting on the sofa, sipping from a can of ginger ale. "Come over here. I need to get a closer look before I decide if I can stand it." She moved eagerly into his arms. "Guess you'll do in an emergency," he said, smiling as he held her face between his hands and kissed first her forehead, then her nose, and finally her lips, teasing them open for just a brief, tantalizing moment. Then he eased away. "Want some ginger ale?"

"Sure. Sounds good," she said, taking in a huge breath and exhaling slowly.

That's a healthy sign, he thought, hoping she hadn't seen him smile as he popped open the second can of soda already on the coffee table. They talked for the next two hours, facing each other as they leaned against opposite ends of the sofa, their legs stretched out, hers resting on top of his. When they could no longer keep their eyes open, they went to bed, fully clothed in their "jammies"—and Isaiah fell asleep having a hard time believing that his overwhelming desire for her could be so comforted by the abundance of pink and flannel in his arms.

★★★★★

His room's oppressive air hung thick with the smoky haze and sour odor that typically collect in places denied open windows and sunlight. Dressed in dark, threadbare clothing, his skeletal body remained seated in a frayed and faded upholstered rocking chair that squeaked back and forth with a numbing rhythm. Facing the doorway, his eyes were glassy and unfocused, appearing to have sunk even farther into their shadowy sockets. The room offered no sound except a crackling static from the radio that had slipped out of tune, the red line on the dial hovering between stations that had once delivered music to his life.

When the doorway opened, a much younger man stepped in, one adorned in the finest of contemporary fashion and appearing to have been groomed by a lifetime of gracious example. His stance was tall and elegant, his skin taut and tan, his black hair full and enviable. Flickering with animation, his luminescent green eyes studied his surroundings at first, and then he saw the figure facing him from the rocker.

Stopping his forward motion, the man who'd just arrived struggled to catch his breath in the atmosphere drained of energy and oxygen. Yet

216

some force kept urging him deeper into the room to get a closer look at the one who'd summoned him, the one who just kept staring and made no attempt to rise from the rocking chair.

"Who *are* you?" the newcomer asked the old man as he always did, feeling the bile of fear back up in his throat so predictably. "Why have you asked me to come here? What is it that you have to say?"

But the cadaverous stranger remained silent and seated, his empty eyes fixed ahead at nothing. Then he took all the answers with him as he slowly began to disappear from the chair in sections, as if unseen hands were dismantling a human puzzle, piece by piece.

*****

Isaiah's thrashing awakened Ava just before he sat up in bed drenched in a cold sweat.

"What's wrong?" she asked, her voice heavy with concern as she switched on the bedside lamp and put her arms around him. "Were you dreaming?"

"Yeah," he said, his elbows resting on his bent knees and his head in his hands. "Same damn dream I've been having for months."

"What's it about?" She posed the question as she got out of bed and headed into the bathroom.

"Some dead guy in a rocking chair wants to talk to me. At least I *think* it's me he wants to talk to."

"What does the dead guy want to talk about?" she asked as she returned with a cool wet washcloth that she placed on the back of his neck.

"Thanks. That feels wonderful."

"Here. Lift up your head," she said. "You need to put this on your face too."

He wiped his forehead and eyes and then leaned back against the pillows propped against the headboard.

"So?" she asked him, sitting on the edge of the bed beside him.

"So *what?*"

"What does the dead guy want to talk about?"

"I have no idea. He always dissolves into thin air before I find out."

"Sounds kind of creepy."

"You're telling me. There was something different this time, though—something different about *him*."

"Different how?"

217

"Nothing I can put my finger on. And it's all starting to fade anyway. If I don't write things down as soon as I wake up, I lose the picture." He looked at her sitting beside him as she blotted the washcloth across the front of his neck. "You sure are cute, Ms. Lindsey."

"Why, thank you very much, Mr. Mellington. But you're obviously delusional. I just saw myself in the mirror."

"Then you're not seeing yourself the way I do," he said, reaching up to touch her face.

"Hmm. Guess I should count my blessings. Now, what's the plan for today?"

"Is it *today* already?"

"Almost seven o'clock."

"You have to be kidding," he said, rolling over and wrapping one of the pillows around his head. "We have to meet Zeke and Zoie in the lobby at nine."

"And then what?"

"And then we're going out to breakfast," he said, throwing off the pillow and sitting up again. "And then we're going to the mortuary. Today's the first viewing."

"Okay. But before I get cleaned up, I need to spend a few minutes doing my exercises since I didn't do them yesterday. You can take your shower first."

Isaiah remained still on the bed behind her, feeling his pulse increase as he watched her stretching and bending over to touch the floor.

"Good idea," he said, moving into the bathroom.

"Save some hot water for me," she called after him.

"Don't worry, Ava. I won't be using any *hot* water."

*****

Isaiah read the newspaper in the lobby while she finished getting ready, the two of them having agreed that emerging from his suite together would feel a bit awkward. She appeared at eight forty-five, looking crisp and glowing, wearing a long, straight gray knit skirt, a white twin sweater set, and black knee-high boots visible through the slits on both sides of the skirt. A red leather hobo handbag was hanging from her right shoulder, and a black leather coat was folded over her left arm. Her freshly washed blonde curls were glistening, and her porcelain skin and rosy cheeks had been skillfully elevated to perfection with the virtual drug store of products she'd lifted out of her second luggage bag.

218

"Girls have to take care of their skin," she'd said when he started laughing at the array of jars and tools spread over the top of the work desk. "And the older we get, the more effort it takes to look youthful. Fifty is just around the corner for me, you know. So if you like the end result, you shouldn't make fun of the process required to get there."

"Yes, ma'am," he'd responded with a salute, still having a hard time believing that she was pushing fifty. And now, as he watched her walk across the lobby toward him, with the brilliant October sun that streamed through the plate glass window appearing dull and ordinary in her presence, he swore he'd never tease her again about that bag full of stuff.

"Hi," she said, sitting down in the chair next to him. "You look very handsome."

He wasn't sure how that was possible, this being the fourth day in a row that he'd worn some combination of the same clothes. But at least they were clean.

"Thank you very much," he said, putting the newspaper down on the end table between his chair and Ava's, absorbing her fragrance, which smelled like fresh melons. "And you look lovelier than I remember, if that's possible."

She gave him a smile and a nod of appreciation. "I've decided I'm no longer going to interfere with your delusion. What have we been missing in the news?" she asked. "I haven't even looked at a paper since Saturday."

"Just a lot of political insanity. I cannot *wait* for this eternal campaign to finally be over."

"Me too. But I have a feeling that some new cycle of craziness will start up again after the election, no matter who wins."

"Maybe. Still, I'd like to believe that if—"

"Good morning, Isaiah." The woman's voice was coming from behind them.

Both Ava and Isaiah stood up at the same time and turned around. Zeke was dressed in a black suit, white shirt, and skinny black tie. Zoie wore a black cable-knit pullover sweater, black pants, black loafers, and socks. Her only jewelry was a pair of what looked like diamond stud earrings and a silver chain-link watch—and the puzzled expressions on both her face and her father's were hard to miss as they looked at Isaiah and Ava standing together.

"Good morning," Isaiah said after clearing his throat. Then he placed his hand on Ava's elbow and guided her around the chairs. "I'd like to introduce a friend of mine," he added when they were all standing next

219

to each other. "Zeke and Zoie, this is Ava Lindsey. Ava, please meet Zeke and Zoie Gerard."

Ava immediately extended her hand, first to Zeke, who responded right away, and then to Zoie, who seemed to hesitate a moment before she reached out. Isaiah watched the exchange. He hadn't considered that there might be any sense of personal intrusion, but that's exactly the feeling he was getting, at least from Zoie.

"I've been sharing Abby's story with Ava for the past four days," he continued, hoping that further explanation would diffuse any tension, "and she's been kind enough to indulge me. She even went with me to visit the old convent on Sunday. Since she's come to appreciate Abby and to anticipate your arrival along with me, I invited her to join us today. I hope you don't mind."

"Of course we don't," Zeke responded. "I'm glad to see you with such a lovely friend."

"Yes," Zoie said, acquiescing to her father with a weak smile and little of the warmth she'd been sharing since her arrival. "How long have you and Isaiah known each other?" she asked, still smiling as she stared at Ava.

"An eternity that seems like only yesterday," Isaiah interjected. "Say," he kept going without pausing for a breath, "would you guys be interested in seeing the old convent yourselves? I could call the owners and arrange something for this afternoon."

"I'd like to drive by it," Zoie said. "But I don't think there's much point in going inside. Supposedly, at least according to information I've found online, the place doesn't look anything like it did when Abby was there."

"I don't even care 'bout driving by it," Zeke said, folding his arms across his chest.

Isaiah noted the odd mixture of emotions roiling around. *I should have expected this*, he thought as he considered how many years this day had been a point out in the future for both of the Gerards. Now that the future had become "today," *I can't imagine what they must be feeling, each in such different ways.*

"Okay," he said. "Why don't we just take a drive after we leave the mortuary? We could go by the convent and then see some of the sights nearby."

"Sounds all right to me," Zeke answered.

"I'm flexible," Zoie added crisply, linking her arm in her father's and leading him toward the lobby door.

Ava held Isaiah's hand as they followed close behind the Gerards. "Everything's going to be fine," she whispered to him, as if she'd been reading his mind.

*****

Breakfast didn't turn out to be the problem that Isaiah had anticipated. After the typical weather small talk, the conversation inevitably migrated to the ubiquitous presidential campaign, and to everyone's surprise, they discovered that they shared the same politics. This solidarity led to a lightening of the mood, and even to a few laughs that carried them through their meal and the drive to the mortuary. By the time Mr. Arthur greeted them when they walked through the double front doors of the long, flat building's covered entrance, they were a far more cohesive group than they'd been ninety minutes earlier.

Mr. Arthur directed them to a room at the end of a long hallway to their left. But they would have been able to find their own way without his help, given the dozens of priests and nuns coming and going in their distinctive black-and-white suits, dresses, collars, and veils. Isaiah had expected to see more sisters than priests, but there was an equal number of both mingling in the lobby and the hallway.

The viewing room was set up like a church sanctuary, with chairs arranged on both sides of a center aisle. As Isaiah and his guests entered, they were astounded by the sea of religious professionals filling nearly every chair. Others stood along the sides of the room in clusters, and all were speaking quietly among themselves. The confluence of conversations between those standing and seated, along with the soft classical music playing in the background, made Isaiah feel as if he and his companions were slightly less conspicuous when they walked in, even though he sensed eyes turning toward them from every direction.

To their left as they entered, there was a small altar up at the front of the room, with sprays of floral arrangements on stands—two layers of arrangements deep, with at least eight or ten individual sprays in each layer—extending out from both sides of the altar and down to the point where the seating began. Easels holding poster boards filled with photographs were arranged along the walls, and in the middle of everything, directly below the altar, was Abby's open casket.

Ava's arm was linked in Isaiah's, and her grip tightened as they both watched Zeke and Zoie begin heading up to the front. Feeling very protective of them, especially in this setting, Isaiah made certain that

221

he and Ava kept step right behind them as they wove their way forward, through the various clusters of people gathered along the side of the room, finally coming to a stop at the kneeling rail centered in front of the casket.

Isaiah caught his breath as Zeke and Zoie walked around the railing and right up to the casket. Zeke reached out and touched the veil covering Abby's head, and Zoie placed her hand on both of Abby's, which rested on her chest with a rosary threaded between her fingers. Father and daughter stood there, unmoving, for a couple of minutes that seemed more like an hour. When they finally turned around, the pain and tears from nearly six decades of anticipating this moment were awash on both of their faces. Isaiah was struggling to restrain his own emotions, and when he looked down at Ava, he saw from the unchecked streams rolling down her cheeks that she'd lost her struggle to do the same.

"Isaiah." Someone was whispering his name and touching his arm. Turning, he saw Tess standing there, dressed in a dark gray shirt dress that came down to her ankles, a black sweater, and heavy black shoes. She reminded him of a monochromatic version of the fairy godmother in Cinderella—roly-poly body, round cheeks, Benjamin Franklin glasses, and a kind, all-knowing face.

"Hi, Tess," he whispered back, leaning down to kiss her on the forehead.

At that moment, Zoie and Zeke rejoined them, leaving Isaiah with a number of introductions to be made. But Tess lifted the burden.

"Hello," she said, extending her hand to Zoie and keeping her voice low. "I knew who you were the minute you walked in. You look so much like Abby. In all the pictures we've arranged around the room, you'll see her from the time she and I were little girls together, until just a few months ago. Your resemblance to her is truly remarkable."

"I'm happy to meet you, Tess," Zoie responded.

"Oh my goodness," Tess said. "I forgot to introduce *myself*, didn't I? Please forgive me."

"Don't worry." Zoie was subdued, her voice gentle. "I believe I'd know you anywhere too. And Tess, this is my father, Zeke Gerard."

"I didn't think I'd want to meet you or shake your hand," he said, looking at Tess with unspent tears still hovering in his eyes as he accepted her welcoming gesture. "But now that I'm here—now that I've seen Abby again—I guess I'm happy that all the pieces is starting to come together."

222

"Yes," she said, patting him on the wrist. "I'm sure that will be a comfort to you." Then she abruptly turned her attention to Ava. "And *you* must be the friend Isaiah was telling me about."

"Ava Lindsey," Isaiah said, "please meet Tess McDowell."

"Hi, Tess," Ava said, accepting the old woman's hand. "Isaiah tells me that you and I are Kettle Falls neighbors—only a couple of blocks apart."

"Is that right?" Tess said. "Well, you need to come by for coffee sometime—once all of this is over." Then she stopped speaking and seemed to be resetting her bearings. "Oh dear," she continued. "I don't know what's happening to my memory. There's someone else here you need to meet. I took her to a private room once I realized who she was."

"Is it Rosa?" Zoie, Isaiah, and Ava asked the same question, almost in unison.

"Yes. Come with me."

They all followed Tess, threading their way through the assembly of nuns and priests that watched the small procession with great interest. When they reached the hall, Tess led them back up to the lobby, across to the other side of the building, and down another corridor to a closed door on the right. Then she turned the ornate brass door handle, and the small group entered a bright meeting room with a large picture window on the opposite wall.

To their left, a tall, slender woman was standing at the far end of a dark wood conference table surrounded by ten chairs. Her face was deeply tanned, her platinum hair pulled back and twisted into a chignon. She was wearing a navy blue straight skirt that fell just below her knees, with a short matching jacket buttoned up to her neck. And her hands were clasped together beneath her chin, making her appear both expectant and fearful.

From across the room, Isaiah saw the large violet eyes that Abby had described about Danny. All of a sudden, the merging of past and present—a story he'd been reading that had morphed into reality—was sobering to him. Looking at Rosa, who seemed almost childlike in her vulnerability despite her age, he realized that people's lives were being ripped up by the roots as a result of this situation. And in that moment, his perspective on this "task" began shifting from a fascinating exploration, which had been sort of fun up to this point, into a sequence of events that was causing hearts to break.

Zoie was the last to enter the conference room behind Tess, Isaiah, Ava, and Zeke, but she made her way around everyone else and then slowly began walking toward the sister she'd been dreaming about meeting for the last ten years.

"Hi, Rosa," she said softly, "I'm Zoie."

"I know," Rosa replied, not moving from where she stood.

When Zoie reached the end of the table, she opened her arms and brought Rosa into her embrace. Rosa's arms remained at her sides for a few moments, but then she wrapped them gently around the younger sister she'd never known existed until a few days earlier. As Isaiah, Ava, Zeke, and Tess watched, the two women buried their heads in the curves of each other's necks and began to sob. Unleashed at last, the depth of their shared emotion spilled over into the room, taking the breath away from the four people who witnessed the exchange.

*****

Once everyone had introduced themselves to Rosa, Tess excused herself, and the remaining five individuals engaged in small talk for another half hour. Then Isaiah suggested that Zoie and Rosa might want to spend some private time together in his suite at the lodge. But both women said they'd prefer the second option, which had been presented by Ava when no one else came up with an alternative—and that was an early lunch with the entire group together.

Since Rosa had a rental car and was staying at an inn several miles from the lodge, she followed behind the Jag as Isaiah drove to the same restaurant where he'd had dinner with Zeke and Zoie the previous night. At his request, the five of them were shown to a rectangular table in a back corner of the room where he thought things would be quieter, even though there weren't many other luncheon patrons in the place yet. Zoie took a seat between Rosa on her left and Zeke on her right, while Ava and Isaiah faced the three of them across the table.

"I'm not really hungry," Zoie said after the waitress left the menus with them. "It's only been two hours since we finished breakfast."

"Speak for yourself, girl," Zeke replied, putting on his reading glasses and beginning to study the specials.

"Do we have to order right away?" Rosa asked softly. "Can't we just sit here for a little while first?"

"Sure," Isaiah said, aware along with everyone else of the awkward need to bridge a half century. "Let's take our time." After a short pause, he asked, "Would anyone like a drink?" Looking at his watch, he said, "It's officially noon—uh, wait. Six ... five ... four ... three ... two ... one ... okay—*now.*"

They exchanged stiff smiles that did little to ease the tension.

"Yes," Rosa said, "I'd love a glass of wine."

Everyone except Zeke chimed in with the same request.

"What would *you* like?" Isaiah asked him.

"I'd like another glass of cognac. But I'm not sure if I should. What do you think, Zoie?"

"Don't ask me, Dad. Until last night, I've never seen you drink anything besides an occasional beer. So you're on your own."

"Okay," he said, looking across the table at Isaiah. "I'll have a cognac. No sense in letting the rest of you zone out and leave me behind."

"Zone out?" Zoie asked, turning toward her father. "What's that supposed to mean?"

"Heard it on the radio. Means taking a mental vacation in the middle of something uncomfortable."

"Seriously?" Isaiah asked, opening his arms wide, as if to embrace the entire group. "Is anyone here uncomfortable about anything?"

They looked around the table at each other for a moment and then began laughing.

"I suppose there really is an amusing side to this, if you dig deep enough," Rosa said a minute later, sliding the tips of her ring fingers under her lower eyelids to remove any smudged mascara.

"And Abby would *want* us to see the funny part," Zeke added, using his napkin to blot his face.

When the waitress returned, Isaiah ordered Zeke's cognac and a bottle of the same Australian Shiraz he and Ava had enjoyed at dinner. He also requested the three appetizers that he'd suggested as a compromise for their varying levels of appetite. The beverages arrived within minutes. The familiar artichoke dip, fried calamari, and a raw vegetable platter were delivered shortly thereafter. Half an hour later, the mood around the table had mellowed decidedly, and the questions begging for release began to flow.

"Rosa, you sure don't have to answer this," Isaiah said, scooping more calamari, red sauce, artichoke dip, and tortilla chips onto his plate. "And I don't really have the right to ask. But what made you change your mind about coming up here?"

Rosa finished chewing a carrot from the vegetable platter then took a sip of her wine and leaned back in her chair.

"My mother," she answered. "I mean, the woman I've always known as my mother. She knew how angry I was—at her, at my father, at everybody really. After all, the lies they told and the secrets they kept were pretty unforgivable. Even my brother, Perry, who's been like oil to my water our whole lives, was on my side, for once. I couldn't bear being in the same house with Mother any longer and was packing to leave for a hotel when she started knocking on my door. She just wouldn't stop. I do love her very much, and I worry about her now that she has so many health issues. So I let her in."

Everyone at the table had stopped eating, their focus fixed entirely on Rosa and what she had decided to share with them.

"She put her arms around me—always a real anger buzzkill for me," she continued with a fragile smile. "Then she sat down on my bed and apologized, for the hundredth time, trying to explain the forces that had been at work in her life in 1948. But when I told her that no explanation could possibly justify keeping the truth from me, she said I was right. And *that*, she told me, was why I needed to make the trip. She said that denying me the truth about who I really was had been the overwhelming regret of her life. But now that the secret was out, my refusal to face the truth would end up torturing me the way her decision had tortured her. And if I didn't come up here, this little window of opportunity for me to connect with my beginnings would be closed to me forever. Those words hit me like a sledgehammer. And here I am."

"I'm so glad you are," Zoie said, squeezing Rosa's hand. "I never used to think that I'd missed anything by being an only child. But even though I don't really know you, just sitting next to you and understanding that you're my sister has filled in a part of me that I didn't even realize was empty. I feel like I've been given a great gift."

"Thank you," Rosa said, putting her arm around Zoie. "It's funny that you should mention an empty space, because I've always felt like something was a little off in my life. There must be an instinct inside us that tells us a key piece of our life's puzzle is missing. Of course," she said with a smile, "I always thought that whatever was missing was supposed to be filled in by *a man*. But four marriages later, the missing part was *still* missing, and I decided to call off the search. Now, all of a sudden, I don't feel anything gnawing at me anymore. Very strange, and rather peaceful. Guess Mother was right."

No one seemed to know what to say, so they helped themselves to more food to fill the silence. Then Ava spoke up for the first time since they'd been at the restaurant.

"Do you have any children?" she asked Rosa.

"Yes. Two girls from my first marriage."

"Really? So I'm an aunt too?" Zoie's unfettered excitement about her newly discovered extended family was breaking out all over her.

"Well, I guess you are. Telling *them* about this is going to be interesting," Rosa added, taking another sip of wine.

"Do they live near you?"

"One is in Santa Barbara. The other—the oldest—is in New York. Both of them have careers instead of marriages, so far. Now, Zoie," Rosa said, "what about *you*? Are you married?"

"No I'm not. Never found the right one," she answered, looking briefly across the table at Isaiah, then at Ava, and then back to Rosa.

"Wow. That's amazing," Rosa said. "I would have thought that someone as beautiful and sharp as you would have been run over with suitors."

"Oh, she was," Zeke interjected. "She just turned 'em all down."

"As I was saying, I never found the right one," Zoie repeated, patting her father on his arm. "But I've had a good life anyway."

"I'm glad about that. So tell me," Rosa said, lowering her voice. "When did *you* find out about Abby?"

"About ten years ago. My dad told me."

Rosa leaned around Zoie to look at Zeke. "That must have been very difficult for you, Mr. Gerard," she said to him as everyone at the table watched his eyes tear up. "I'm sorry. I didn't mean to upset you."

"It's okay." He choked out the words as he caught the tears with his napkin.

"I just think you were pretty courageous," Rosa went on. "*My* father left the job to his wife. Of course, even though he was a good *dad*, for the most part, he was never the best of husbands. Mom told me a few stories the other day—her version of what happened between my father and Abby, among other anecdotes. She thought she was telling me something I didn't already know about him. But I observed plenty on my own about his moral character, or lack thereof, while I was growing up. So his leaving Mom with the responsibility of telling me isn't surprising. I just wish he'd had the guts to do it himself."

Their waitress came by to see if she could get them anything else since the three appetizer platters had been picked clean. But they each declined the offer.

"You know, Rosa," Isaiah said, "Abby left a collection of letters and journals and other memorabilia from her time in San Francisco."

"She did?" Rosa asked, the eager look on her face impossible to miss.

"Yes, and all of it belongs to you now."

"I had no idea," she said. "Is there anything in there about when I was born?"

"There is. If you'd like to follow me back to the lodge when we leave here, I'll be happy to give you everything I have."

"I'd like that very much," she said, the composure she'd been exhibiting throughout lunch starting to give way to what Isaiah imagined were sad thoughts of a child left behind.

When the waitress brought their check, Isaiah pulled out his credit card over Zeke's objections.

"But you paid for dinner last night," Zeke said.

"And I'll be paying the whole time you're here, my friend. So just relax."

"But I *need* to do *something*!" The pleading tone in his voice was alarming as everyone watched him mop his face again with his napkin.

Zoie had been so focused on Rosa that she hadn't been paying attention to her father.

"Hey, Dad," she said. "Are you all right?"

"Just tired, I think."

"You know, Isaiah," she said, "I think we'll pass on that drive around the valley this afternoon. It feels like it's been a long day already. Would you mind if Dad and I bow out until tomorrow?"

"Whatever you think is best, Zoie. Would you like to meet up for breakfast again in the morning?"

"That would be fine. How about ten instead of nine, though, since we don't need to pay our respects at the mortuary again until the afternoon? And maybe we could take that drive afterward?"

"Rosa, would you like to join us for all of that?" Isaiah asked.

"Yes, I would. And thank you for asking. I'm also thinking about switching from the inn where I'm staying to the lodge where all of you guys are."

"I think that's a great idea," Zoie said. "If we're in the same place, maybe I could even touch base with you later on while Dad's sleeping."

"I'd like that—very much."

Once the check was paid, the five of them left the restaurant and caravanned to the lodge. Everyone embraced in the lobby before Zoie and Zeke headed off to their rooms, and Isaiah and Ava took Rosa to the suite where custody of Abby's Rosa folder was turned over to the rightful owner. Then Isaiah went to the front desk and secured a room for Rosa. Afterward, he rode with her in her rental car back to the inn to pick up all of her things and check out. On the way, she asked him a few questions about his father, Sinclair.

"Abby did a good job in your file of explaining his role," Isaiah said. "Unfortunately, I didn't begin to understand the scope of his involvement until after I got here last Friday."

"You're kidding! You mean you were ambushed too?"

"Yeah. I guess you could say that. I knew that he and Abby were friends—and I went with him to visit her regularly while I was growing up. But that was about it. Of course, as I've been telling myself and everyone else, I never asked him any questions about how he met her, or why we kept visiting her. Maybe *that's* what he was waiting for—for me to ask."

"You know what *I* think, Isaiah?"

"No. What?"

"I think you and I should stop trying to figure out what our dead fathers were thinking."

He laughed. "You're probably right."

"And I also think we should be happy that Zoie still has *her* father. He's our only real living window into Abby's heart—and I still have some things I'd like to know about what kind of a woman she was. At least *he's* here to help answer our questions."

Isaiah looked over at the weathered yet still beautiful woman behind the wheel of her rental car. "Thanks, Rosa. And in case I haven't told you yet, I'm really glad you decided to come up here."

"Me too. And I truly mean that."

*****

After Isaiah had returned to the lodge with Rosa and her four suitcases and then helped her to her room, he discovered that Ava had fallen asleep on the sofa in his suite.

"What time is it?" she asked after he knelt down on the floor beside her and kissed her hand.

"A little past three."

229

"Hmm. What a gift we've been given—all these free, peaceful hours to spend together."

"I know," he said. "What would you like to do with them?"

"Well, I was thinking that maybe we could watch another movie."

"Ah. Good idea. I'll check the listing," he said, starting to get up.

"I already did. The only things playing this afternoon are some horror film and *Steel Magnolias*. We could see if there's something on one of the cable channels, or we could go out. Colville has a pretty decent movie theater."

"Actually, *Steel Magnolias* would be fine."

"You have to be kidding," she said, pushing herself up into a sitting position.

"No, seriously. I've always liked that movie."

"I cannot believe what I'm hearing."

"Why? Because it's a sappy chick flick?"

"Well, yes, frankly."

"But it also has a great cast. It's hilariously funny. And *then* it's a sappy chick flick. So if you want to watch it, I'm all yours. We have one bag of popcorn left, and plenty of soda."

"What more could a woman want?" After planting a kiss in the field of his thick salt-and-pepper hair, she got up and went over to the bed where she propped all the pillows against the headboard. "Mind if I put my jammies on for this?"

"Uh, sure," he said as visions of her body inside that pink flannel outfit began surging through his head again. While she was in the bathroom, he changed into his sweatpants and T-shirt, just to keep things even.

*****

When the movie's cemetery scene was over, where Sally Fields' character had come completely unglued, the tissue box was in between them on the bed, and Isaiah had shamelessly used almost as many as Ava.

"You really are something," she said, blowing her nose. "I've never met a man who's so open with his emotions."

"Comes with age, I guess. And I don't really care what people think anymore."

"Yes you do. You care a great deal—and that's the point." She turned to face him as the movie credits began rolling. "Showing emotion is about compassion, not weakness. People who don't let themselves cry are blocking out an essential part of who they are—of what we all share—as human beings."

"Oh really, *Doctor* Lindsey?"

"Yes. Really," she said, reaching up to touch his face. Then she fanned her fingers out in his hair and pressed his head slowly down toward her. "Kiss me," she whispered.

As the instrumental theme music from *Steel Magnolias* played in the background, Isaiah leaned in until his mouth was against hers. But his hands were on the bed, on either side of her, his arms extended to keep their bodies from touching, because he wasn't sure what she wanted him to do.

He teased and caressed her lips with his, moving down her neck and then back up to her lips again, noticing that her breathing was becoming deeper, heavier. Then he felt her arms encircle him, gently pressing him down on top of her. So he slipped his left arm behind her back, lifting her slightly off the pillow as his mouth traveled slowly down her neck again, until he bumped into her flannel rosebud shirt.

"Take it off," she whispered.

"What?"

"Take my shirt off."

"Ava, are you sure?"

"You are so sweet, Isaiah. And yes, I'm sure."

He could not believe how nervous he felt, like a teenager, like he'd never done this before, like he needed an instruction book. But when he pulled the flannel shirt over her head, everything came rushing back to him.

"Here," she said, putting her hand under one of the pillows and producing a small square packet. "I brought some of these with me, just in case."

"Why, Ava Lindsey!" he said, raising himself up. "You little devil!"

"I know. Presumptuous again. Can you ever forgive me?"

"I'm not sure," he said, taking his own shirt off. "I think I'm going to need some more time to mull that over."

Then he moved back down on top of her, and Ava inhaled deeply, closing her eyes when their bare bodies touched.

"Take all the time you want, Isaiah," she whispered.

CHAPTER FIFTEEN

Isaiah had been awake for half an hour. When he'd first opened his eyes, he'd checked his watch and had been surprised to learn that he was this alert at only eight o'clock in the morning. Lying on his back now in the suite's stillness, he felt unusually rested as he watched the hazy light from what was supposed to be a cloudy day filter through the semisheer curtains on the window. Next to him in the bed was the almost hypnotic cadence of Ava's deep breathing. *Unbelievable,* he thought, turning on his side to look at her. *She's even beautiful and sexy when she's sound asleep and snoring.*

He couldn't remember the last time he'd had great sex with someone he cared about so much. Maybe he'd *never* been with anyone like that, although he was certain he must have felt that way about his fiancée at some point in their relationship. But he could not reach back anywhere in his memories and find anything close to the way he was feeling at this moment.

"Ava," he whispered softly, just so he could hear her name. Her spray of blonde curls framed her flawless porcelain face on the pillow, her naturally plump lips were slightly open as an outlet for her cute snore, and her God-given, gorgeous chest was rising and falling in a soothing rhythm. Allowing himself to feast on the visions of the night they'd shared, his desire for her began to stir again, and he gently placed his hand on the sheet covering her tummy. "Ava," he whispered again, a little louder this time.

But a voice other than Ava's followed a knock on his suite's door.

"Isaiah? *Isaiah*! I know you're in there because your Jag is parked in the lot. So open up please."

He lay there for a few seconds as the voice registered, and then he sat bolt upright in the bed.

"Ava!" he said, no longer whispering as he nudged her. "You have to wake up!"

She stretched her arms up over her head, her mouth curving into a sly grin as her eyes slowly opened on him and her face radiated with a lazy, contented expression.

"Ava," he said, his tone low and sober, "I know you're going to think I'm kidding—but that's my *mother* knocking on our door."

She stared up at him for a moment or two, studying him while she processed his words. A split second later, the two of them vaulted from their respective sides of the bed, launching into a routine choreographed from the beginning of time that instinctively activates whenever lovers are confronted by an inopportune parental discovery.

"Hold on a sec, Mother," Isaiah called out, jumping into the puddle of his sweatpants on the floor and yanking them up over his naked body. "I'll be right there."

"Well, hurry up. I don't like standing out here in the hall."

As he was pulling his T-shirt over his head, he noticed that Ava was almost fully dressed already. *How did she do that?* She wasn't in her pajamas either, but in her jeans, silky white blouse, and leather vest that she'd unpacked and hung up the night before to let the wrinkles fall out. And she was standing at the foot of the bed, with both hands gripped on the bed covers.

In a single, snapping motion, she whipped the sheet, blanket, and coverlet up in the air as one unit, letting them float down over the mattress. After tossing the pillows in a neat line at the head of the bed, she fluffed and arranged her hair with her fingers as she sat down on the sofa. She looked poised and demure, and she smiled broadly, like a victorious character out of a Road Runner cartoon at the end of a crazed mountain chase. The only things out of sync with the rest of the perfect picture were her bare feet.

"How old are we again?" he asked rhetorically as he pushed his own bare feet into his loafers and shook his head at her. "I'm really sorry about this, Ava," he added, moving slowly toward the door and dreading what was about to happen.

"Don't be," she said, her smile widening. "Frankly, I think it's kind of funny."

"Oh really? Well, I'll check back in with you after this is over—and then, assuming I survive what's out in the hall, you can also tell me what part of your life taught you how to get dressed and make a bed so fast."

At that point, he unlatched the chain, released the deadbolt, and opened the door. Sarah Mellington was standing there looking pale, like she did when she wasn't wearing any makeup. *Must be the light*, he thought. Her silver hair was pulled back and wrapped in her familiar, stylish bun fastened with sparkling hair pins at the nape of her neck. And she was dressed completely in black—a black hip-length fur jacket, which Isaiah knew was faux but no one else would ever guess, black leather gloves, black slacks, and black leather low-heeled boots. Aside from giving the impression that she was going to, or coming from, a funeral, she was remarkably striking, and far younger in appearance than eighty-one years should have made her look.

"Mother, what a surprise!" he said, leaning down to embrace her and kiss her on the cheek. "I've been trying to reach you since Saturday. I even called—"

"Yes, I know," she said, raising herself up on her tiptoes to embrace and kiss him back. "I received all of your messages, and Edna's too, telling me you'd called. I'm sorry if I worried you."

He wanted to continue holding her, to obstruct her view of what was behind him. But she released her arms from around his neck and pushed her way into the suite, the lining of her black wool slacks making a swishing sound against the insides of her legs as she walked. Ava stood up as Sarah entered.

"Oh my!" Sarah said, looking first at Ava and then at Isaiah.

"Mother, this is Ava Lindsey," he offered as quickly as he could get the words out.

"How do you do, Mrs. Mellington," Ava said, walking around the coffee table and extending her hand, as if they were all assembling for some sort of business session. "I'm so happy to meet you."

Sarah offered her hand in exchange, but the gesture seemed more a rote product of her upbringing than anything else as she replied, "Yes, well, I—"

"Please forgive me, Mother," Isaiah interrupted. "This is not the way I'd hoped to introduce you."

"Ah, now *there's* an understatement, to be sure," Sarah said, her composure visibly returning and a look of amusement replacing her initial shock. "And I'm very happy to meet you as well, my dear," she said, placing both of her hands around Ava's. "Have you been keeping her a secret from me?" she asked, turning to her son and releasing Ava's hand after a final squeeze.

"Not intentionally, Mother. This is all a bit new ... to tell the truth."

"I see."

"Stop raising your eyebrows at me," he said. "This is different from what your first impression might make you think, but the story is sort of a long one."

"Well, it can't be *that* long. You've only been here since Friday."

"And I'll be happy to discuss the whole situation with you *later*," he continued, beginning to regain his emotional footing and feeling more like himself than the adolescent boy who'd opened the door moments earlier. "A more pressing question is what are *you* doing here? And why haven't you been answering any of your phones for the last *four days?*"

"Yes, I suppose that's fair," she said, moving over to the sofa and taking a seat, but making no attempt to remove her coat or gloves.

An unexpected surge of anxiety pulsed through Isaiah's body as he began to sense a solemnity in her that he hadn't observed since his father died, and as he realized after looking closer at her that she *wasn't*, in fact, wearing any makeup. After guiding Ava to one of the armchairs, he sat down on the sofa beside his mother, who fixed her eyes on his and then glanced over at Ava and back at him again, raising her eyebrows one more time in what Isaiah knew to be a question.

"Yes," he said, in answer to the unspoken query. "I'm completely comfortable with you saying anything you have to say in front of Ava."

"All right. Perhaps the Lord *does* open a window when a door closes."

"What?"

"Never mind. And I guess it's my turn to ask for forgiveness, for sounding so cryptic, because something has come up—something quite unexpected ... and most urgent."

"So stop beating around the bush, Mother. Just tell me."

"I'm afraid that's where the cryptic part and the forgiveness come in because I *can't* tell you. Not yet. I need to do this on my own terms. That's why I've arranged a meeting at eleven o'clock this morning, at Tess's house."

"*What?*"

"Please stop saying 'what,' Isaiah. Especially in that tone of voice. You're just going to have to be confused for a few more hours. I'm sorry."

"But how do you even know where Tess lives?"

"This is a very small place, and MapQuest works way out here too, you know."

"Since when do you use MapQuest?"

"It's in my rental car, and I'm not an idiot."

"Of course you're not. But I think that's probably a GPS unit, not MapQuest."

"Whatever. I didn't come here to debate technology with you. As I said, something of extreme importance needs to be addressed this morning."

"Unfortunately, I already have plans, Mother. Ava and I are supposed to have a late breakfast with Rosa, Zoie, and Zoie's dad before Abby's wake this afternoon."

"Yes, I'm aware of that, and I've spoken with them. They will all be joining us in Kettle Falls."

"What?"

"Oh, honest to God, Isaiah! Stop *saying* that!"

"But what could possibly involve *them* that also involves *you*? And why are we all meeting at Tess's house?"

"As I said, you'll have to wait, but only for a short while." Then she stood up and began making her way toward the door, a clear indication to Isaiah that the conversation was over. "And please bring Ava with you," she added, stopping and opening up her arms to her son, who entered her embrace without hesitation. She held him close to her, kissed him softly on his cheek, and then patted his arms as she released him. "I've never been one to deny serendipity," she said, shifting her attention to Ava and taking both of her hands.

"Thank you, Mrs. Mellington."

"You're welcome, my dear," Sarah replied, astonishing Isaiah by kissing Ava on her cheek as if she were an old friend. "I had not anticipated a ray of sunshine in the midst of this muddle." Then she opened the door and turned one more time to look at them both. "See you in a few hours." And as she spoke, Isaiah was certain that he saw tears welling up in her eyes.

When she was gone, he and Ava sat back down on the sofa.

"I'm so sorry," he said. "I have no earthly idea what this is all about."

"Please don't apologize," she said. "I'm fine—really. I'm just grateful that you've spent so much time making me a part of this. Your mother is obviously here about *something* connected to Abby."

"I know. But I can't imagine what that would be, and it's not like her to be so secretive. She's normally an open book with me. And she looked awful."

"Why do you say that? I thought she was lovely."

"I say that because I've never seen her leave the house without her 'face on,' as she says. In fact, when I was growing up, she used to be all put together by the time I came downstairs for breakfast. Sometimes I wondered if she slept in the stuff and *never* took it off. But today there was nothing."

"Well, she has beautiful skin for a woman her age. Maybe she's decided to start showing that off."

"Not a chance. There's something really wrong."

Neither of them knew what to say after that, but the silence wasn't uncomfortable for Isaiah. The passion of the previous night and the possibility of more this morning had receded, and yet he wasn't feeling any void, as he might have expected. Instead, he was experiencing a sense of safety, the peace of familiarity, and the security of a companionship that appeared to be adapting as the strange circumstances became stranger. *Unconditional,* he thought. *Maybe this is what that's supposed to feel like.*

"Since we're not going out to breakfast," he offered at length, "I have coffee, juice, and bagels in my little deli counter over there against the wall. Want some?"

"Sounds good. Why don't you go take your shower, and I'll put a bite together for us."

"Deal." Scooting close to her on the sofa, he gave her a soft kiss on her lips and put his arms around her. "Ava Lindsey," he said, whispering in her ear, "where *did* you come from?"

"From Spokane," she whispered back. "And my timing was perfect."

*****

Isaiah waited until nine thirty before calling Zoie to confirm that his mother had really spoken with her.

"Actually," Zoie said, "I was out taking a walk with Rosa when she called. But she spoke with Dad. And he's the one who told us about the change in plans. I asked him what your mother had to do with anything and why we all had to drive up to see Tess. But he just said that he wanted me to be quiet and humor him."

"Doesn't that seem a little strange to you?"

"Yes, but *everything* is a little strange right now, and I guess it doesn't really matter where we have breakfast."

"We're having breakfast up there?"

"Apparently. I don't think Dad would have agreed if food wasn't part of the plan."

"Well, I don't understand any of this," Isaiah said with an exaggerated sigh. "But I guess we'll find out."

"I guess we will. Okay if Dad and I ride with Rosa and follow you there?"

"Sure. Meet us in the lobby at ten forty-five."

"See you then."

*****

After they'd all pulled up in front of the little yellow house, Isaiah parked, got out, and was walking around to open the door for Ava when Tess came dashing out. She was wearing a pastel green long-sleeved shirtdress that came down almost to her ankles. A bright white full-body apron that matched her bright white sneakers was tied around her neck and her waist. She held a spatula in her right hand and was waving both arms over her head as she approached. *And* she was crying.

"Isaiah! Oh Isaiah," she said. "I am *so* sorry. I was only doing the best I could, and I didn't know. Please!" she sobbed, burying her head in his chest. "Please don't be mad at me."

He put his arms around her as Ava climbed out of the car and stood beside him, joined by Zoie, Zeke, and Rosa, who had parked right behind the Jag.

"Tess," he said, "I don't have a clue what you're talking about, but there's no way I could be mad at you about *anything*. Come on. Let's go inside."

"Your *mother's* in there."

"I figured as much."

When they all walked through the front door, the familiar aromas and sounds that Isaiah associated with this house wrapped around him once again—freshly baked pastries just out of the oven; coffee percolating on top of the potbelly stove between the front windows; wood burning inside the stove's chamber; the rhythmic movement of the pendulum on the wall clock in the hall; the popping and hissing of the water in the kitchen radiator. But this time something was different. This time his mother was here!

She was seated at the far end of the long table in the living room, in one of the eight captain's chairs that had all been arranged around the table instead of in their normal places. And she didn't even stand up as everyone came in, which Isaiah first thought was because the table and chairs occupied virtually every spare inch of space in the room. Upon taking a closer look, however, he saw that she had been crying too.

"Why don't you all grab a seat," Tess instructed as Isaiah was about to ask his mother what was going on. Then Tess lifted her apron and dabbed at her face while she walked into the kitchen. Moments later she returned with a platter full of cinnamon rolls and biscuits that she added to the center of the table.

"Let me help you," Ava said to her.

"No, dear. Thank you. You just sit down."

Then she went into the kitchen again and returned with a huge bowl of sliced fruit. Already on the table were a pitcher of freshly squeezed orange juice, a dish piled high with crisp bacon, and a chilled tin of butter pats, along with plates, forks, knives, spoons, juice glasses, coffee mugs, and cloth napkins at each place setting. And everyone except Sarah was still standing up.

"*Please*," Tess implored. "Find a chair and then help yourselves to whatever looks good to you."

Biting his tongue with mounting exasperation, Isaiah guided Ava through the small space between the back of his mother's chair and the wall. He then sat down on Sarah's right, with Ava next to him on his right. The wood-burning stove and the front windows of the house were behind them. Zeke took the chair directly across from Isaiah and to Sarah's left. Zoie sat down next to Zeke, and Rosa was next to Zoie. Tess was still standing under the arched opening leading into the kitchen, with the lower half of her white apron wadded up in her hands.

"You'd better sit down too, Tess," Sarah said, her tone signaling an order rather than a suggestion.

There were two empty chairs—one next to Ava, and the second option at the end of the table near the front door. Tess chose the latter, which was opposite lengthwise and seemingly as far away as possible from Sarah without actually leaving the house.

Zeke was already spooning fruit onto his plate out of the bowl he'd pulled over from the middle of the table. "Could you pass that plate a rolls down here?" he said to Zoie. "And the butter too?" But he was the only one who appeared interested in eating.

"All right," Isaiah said at length. "Enough with the niceties. I'm not alone in wondering what we're all doing here, Mother," he continued, looking into Sarah's puffy, bloodshot eyes. "What *is* this all about?"

She cleared her throat and began speaking in a nasally, raspy tone that he'd only heard one other time, shortly after his father had died. "*This* is why we're here," she said, patting the black file folder on the table beneath her hands, which Isaiah was just noticing. "I only became aware of what's in this folder the other day."

"That's because you *stole* it from me!" Tess shouted. "She *did*, Isaiah! She broke in here and *stole* it!"

"I didn't *break in* to anything," Sarah responded, raising her voice as well. "The door was wide open!"

"Mother, what are you talking about?" Then he turned toward Tess. "Is this the robbery you called me about on Monday?"

Tess nodded, nervously fingering the wrinkled lower half of her apron, which she had stretched up on top of the table.

"*Did* you break in here?" he asked, looking back at his mother.

"I did not *break* in."

"Did you *come* in?" he asked, clenching his teeth.

"Yes, Isaiah. I did."

"*What*? Do you mean to tell me that I've been trying to reach you for four days, and all the while you were right here in Kettle Falls—and you illegally entered this house?"

"Yes."

He just stared at her in disbelief. "But *why*? What possible reason could you have for doing that?"

She cleared her throat again. "All the answers are in here," she said, tapping her right index finger on the folder. "But under the circumstances, I think it's only fair that you be *told* rather than be forced to read about it."

"If this is about *me*, why have all these other people been dragged out here?"

"Tess?" Sarah asked with a frozen look on her face. "Would *you* like to answer him?"

"I didn't even *know* about this part!" Tess was still shouting, and both her voice and body were shaking. "Abby asked me to keep all the papers for her a long time ago, but I didn't *read* them. She finally told me everything right before she died, and since the moment she left this earth, I've done exactly what she asked me to do. But *this* part isn't my responsibility. *I* didn't have anything to do with it." Then she slammed her hands on the table, stood up, and pointed with unconcealed hostility down the table

240

at Sarah. "*You're* the one who should have told him. *You're* the one who's been lying all this time."

"But I didn't know everything either!" Sarah screamed back at Tess, as if the two of them were the only people at the table.

"Oh crap! Let me see that damn thing!" Isaiah exclaimed, grabbing the folder out from beneath Sarah's hands.

"Wait, Isaiah! Wait! *Please*. Let me try to explain." Isaiah had never heard his mother look or sound so desperate as she began to talk and sob at the same time. "I knew something was wrong when I talked to you on Saturday," she said. "I was going to tell you. I was trying to find the right time—but then I came here and learned that—"

"*Stop!* Everybody … just … *stop!*" Zeke's booming voice startled each person in the small room. Tess and Sarah both grew quiet, and Tess sat back down. "Tess is right," Zeke said, speaking slowly, his voice taking on a commanding tone that Isaiah had not yet heard from him. "None a this is her doing. And Mrs. Mellington, forgive me for saying so, but this has gotta end."

"Dad," Zoie said, "what are you talking about?"

"Hush, girl. Let this come out." Then he looked over at Isaiah. "Could you do an old man a big favor and let me see that folder for a minute?"

"Why?"

"Yeah, Dad," Zoie said, turning in her chair to face her father, the furrows of concern deepening on her forehead. "Why?"

Zeke held up both of his hands, one palm facing Isaiah, the other facing Zoie. "I said *hush*. Give me a minute to look at that folder without nobody saying nothing else just yet. Please, Isaiah."

"Shit!" Isaiah said, using his hand to propel the folder across the table. "This better be good!" he added as he felt Ava touch him supportively on his knee.

Zeke pushed his plate away toward the middle of the table and put on the reading glasses he'd taken out of his pocket. As he slowly opened the folder in front of him, he looked harshly at Zoie when she tried to peer in. Then he thumbed through the papers inside for less than a minute, removed a couple of pages, and closed the folder. After inhaling deeply and exhaling with a low moan, he placed one of the papers he'd removed on top of the folder and slid all of that back across the table to Isaiah, still holding another page in his hand.

"There," Zeke said to Isaiah. "That will explain part a what's going on here. And then you can kill me."

Isaiah didn't respond to that comment, yet another that made no sense to him. Instead, as Ava was reading over his shoulder, he stared down at the paper on top of the folder, which appeared to be a birth certificate. "Isaiah Benjamin Ryan," the typing read. "Born May 5, 1950 ... Male ... 5 pounds 14 ounces ... 18 inches ... Twin: Fraternal ... Mother: Abigail Louise Ryan ... Father: Ezekiel James Gerard ..."

"And *this* one is yours—the real one," Zeke said, handing the second paper he'd removed from the file folder to Zoie.

*****

The sheer brutality of the facts was the hardest part to assimilate at first. The "whys" would come later, but not until the full force of reality had hit those most deeply involved, unraveling the fabric of entire lives and leaving threadbare everything they'd believed to be true about who they were. No one had been spared. Each person had been deeply hurt and betrayed in one way or another.

Isaiah had been born a "Ryan" because the woman he now knew to be his biological mother wasn't married and thus gave him her name. The woman he'd been raised to believe *was* his mother—someone he'd venerated—had turned out to be a fraud. And his father was not Sinclair Mellington, the iconic figure who'd had such immeasurable influence on every aspect of his life. Instead, his *real* father was a kind, gentle old man, for whom Isaiah had already developed a deep affection, which had now been obliterated by this incomprehensible web of lies. And the lovely Zoie was his sister—his *twin* sister, for God's sake—making Rosa not only Zoie's half sister, but Isaiah's as well.

Overwhelmed by the punishing force of these truths, he grabbed the dreaded black file folder off the table and ran out to his car. He didn't know where he was going. He just knew that he had to get out of there. But Ava came running after him.

"I can't stay in there with those people," he said, pulling away from her when she took hold of his arm.

"Those *people* are your family, Isaiah!"

"Oh really? Which one? Exactly *which* family would that be, Ava? The one nobody bothered to tell me about? Or the fake one I thought I lived with that never really existed?"

"But don't you see? It's all *one* family. *They're* all one."

"And how do you figure *that*? Nobody in there even knows who *they* are anymore, much less each other, or *me*."

"Maybe so. But remember something, Isaiah. All week long you've been expecting Zoie and Rosa to deal rationally with their own discoveries. This sense of outrage that you're feeling now wasn't there until Abby's story suddenly hit you as well."

He stood beside the open door on the Jag's driver's side and looked at Ava, her blonde curls oscillating in the late October breeze like petals on a flower. "Are you suggesting that I *shouldn't* be feeling a sense of outrage?" he asked her in a low tone, his jaw tightened by teeth pressed together.

"No, of course I'm not. And I can't even imagine the pain you must be experiencing. What I *am* asking is that you stop for a minute. Call on the amazing compassion that I admire in you so much. Let yourself see that, as much as *you* are hurting, you are not the only one. You can tell that Zeke's heart is breaking just by looking at him. And what about Zoie? She has to be in shock like you are. And your mother—"

"She is *not* my mother."

"Yes, Isaiah, she is. She's devoted her life to you."

"But that life was a lie!" he shouted at her. "And what qualifies *you* to comment on this whole thing anyway? You don't even *know* any of those people in there—and you barely know *me*! So just stay the hell out of it!"

"Excuse me?" Ava stepped away from him, a stunned look on her face as she folded her arms across her chest.

He paused for a moment. "Ava, I—"

"Don't," she interrupted, turning her back to him. "You've said quite enough." Then she went inside the house while Isaiah leaned against his car door waiting—for *what*, he didn't know. A moment later, she reemerged wearing her sweater all buttoned up, with her handbag looped over her arm.

"Where are you going?" he asked in a lowered voice.

"Home," she said, huffing past him and down the sidewalk.

"But your car's still at the lodge, remember?"

"I'll have a friend drive me down there to get it." Her voice carried over her shoulder as she walked away from him.

Suddenly, his anger and his sense of betrayal reignited as he watched her leaving. "Damn it!" he shouted again. "I don't *need* this! *Any* of it! Or any of *you* either." Then he threw himself behind the wheel of the Jag, started the engine, and jammed his foot against the accelerator, launching the automobile down the street with the tires squealing. When he reached the corner, he slowed down a little before turning left and looked in the rearview mirror. Ava was still moving briskly toward the same corner, eyes to the ground, as if she hadn't even noticed him speeding by her.

*****

Fifteen minutes later, he pulled into the parking lot by the lake in the Kettle Falls campgrounds, recalling the night he and Ava had come here, which seemed a lifetime ago. *Someone else's lifetime*, he thought as he got out of the car and made his way out onto the dock. The same little orphaned rowboat was still moored there and was knocking against the concrete pilings with each rolling wave.

When he reached the far edge of the pier, he sat down, his legs dangling over the lake a few feet below. The sun had been slipping in and out of the clouds all morning, adding little noticeable warmth to the nippy mountain air. As a chill shot through his body, he realized that he was thankfully wearing his jacket, which he did not remember grabbing when he left the house. All he remembered was the sight of that birth certificate and the legion of truths that had crushed the pillars of his life as he'd known them in a single instant.

All the pontificating that he'd tolerated from Sinclair, the man Isaiah had believed was his father, had been delivered by an impostor. No wonder Isaiah had been unable to connect with anything close to the warmth he'd observed in his friends' relationships with their own fathers. And all those times Sinclair had put his arm around Isaiah's shoulders, calling him "Son," and pretending that what they had was real! *How could the man have done that? How could he have kept up such a lie, even on his deathbed when he was making me promise to stay in touch with Abby and Tess?*

"Did he ever even *think* about telling me?" Isaiah whispered to the lake. "He must have known I was going to find out eventually. How did he expect me to feel? Did he even care?" *Apparently not. And what about Mother?* "I can't believe she lied to me too," he said, still feeling the need to whisper, although there wasn't anyone else around.

Spinning the years of his life through his mind, he could see in retrospect, with the assistance of this new truth, how Sinclair had been sorely lacking in any sort of paternal gene. He'd been more like a military drill sergeant, treating Isaiah like a recruit. There'd been a lot of instructions and sermonizing, but no compassion, no physical proof of love through a touch, a knowing smile, or a genuinely heartfelt embrace.

As he thought about Sarah, though, he could not imagine her being any more of a mother than she'd been to him. She'd always played such a

244

commanding role in his life that he was having great difficulty accepting the fact that she had not actually given birth to him. *How could she have let herself be talked into something like that? And surely she must have wanted to tell me. So why didn't she, especially after Dad died?*

Isaiah lost track of how long he'd been at the lake, sometimes sitting on the dock, sometimes walking on the small beach. At one point, he found several large stones near the parking lot, which he hurled into the lake as an outlet for the rage and sadness competing for control. And there was a moment when he cried, dropping to his knees on the rough beach sand, mourning the death of the world and the family he'd known. But there was no relief in that catharsis as he struggled to absorb the *new* world that had so brutally overtaken his reality and his identity.

At length, after nearly two hours of riding emotional waves that swelled violently and then crashed, leaving him feeling weak, his fury began to level out. In the process, he slowly became aware of two things. First, Ava had been right about this place. The soft lapping of the water, the stillness broken only by the occasional call of a bird or the plop of a fish on the lake's surface, had eased his anger into something less volatile. And the downsizing of his passion was beginning to clear up his thinking, which brought him to the second thing he now realized. Ava was right about something else as well—about all the people gathered in that little yellow house. As incensed as he was, that collection of sorry characters offered the only hope of his getting answers to the litany of questions he now realized he needed to ask. And having those people all in one place, at the same time, might never happen again.

"Ava," he sighed, pulling his cell phone out of his pocket. He needed to call her, and he needed to call Tess as well. But after dialing the first number, which never rang, he realized that he wasn't getting any reception. "Shit!" he muttered as he stood up, brushed the sand from his jeans, and headed back to his car. Then he drove out of the campgrounds, clearly in a hurry again but much steadier at the wheel this time.

*****

He sat with the Jag idling for a few minutes, trying to come up with the best thing to say, before he finally turned off the ignition and walked up to Ava's door. He knocked and waited and then knocked and waited again, and he started to wonder if she'd decided she was completely through with him. *Or maybe she didn't come back to her house after all. Or what if something had happened to her? What if . . .*

"What is it, Isaiah?" she asked after opening the door a couple of inches against the latched chain. Her voice sounded hoarse and her nose stuffy, like she had a cold.

"I need to see you, Ava. I need to apologize."

"That would be a waste of time. And *I* don't need to see *you*."

"Please, Ava. Let me in for just a minute. After I've said what I need to say, if you want me to leave, I will."

She closed the door without responding, and he was just about ready to walk away when he heard the chain sliding free. Then the door opened again, as if by itself. When he entered the small living room, he saw her leaning against the wall behind the door, her eyes and face red and puffy.

"Oh, Ava," he said, moving toward her before she held her hands out to stop him. "I can't believe I did this to you," he continued, standing in place. "You've been so amazing and so supportive all week, and I turned my anger on you, of all people. When I drove off, I went down to the lake where you took me that first night. That's where I've been—thinking. I have a long way to go to get through this unbelievable situation, but in the process I hope I don't lose whatever special thing this is that I stumbled on with you. I'm so sorry about what I said to you. There's no excuse for hurting you. Can you please forgive me?"

She pushed the front door shut and walked past him to sit down on the sofa. He remained where he was.

"You know, Isaiah," she said at length, removing a shredded tissue from her pocket and wiping her nose, "sometimes you just can't apologize your way back in. Words thrown in anger can be very damaging, and I won't let myself be pulled into that kind of place again. I've worked too hard to regain my footing. And the hurt I felt when you told me to get the hell out of your life made me realize how easily I could lose all the ground I've regained. Considering what you have to deal with right now, you certainly don't need me around with that level of sensitivity."

"But that's not true, Ava," he said, sitting down next to her on the sofa. "I'm heading back over to that house when I leave here, and assuming anyone is still there, I want to find out how this nightmare got started and why no one ever thought about ending it before now. Hard as I try, Ava, I can't picture the scene over there without you in it. And I have no clue what's going to be in store for you and me after this week is over. But shouting and being angry is not normally part of who I am, in *any* relationship. And I am *so* sorry about what I said to you. I can't expect you to believe me, but I didn't mean it. I wanted those words back as soon as they came out of my mouth."

"I don't know, Isaiah," she said again, tears drizzling down her cheeks. When he put his arms around her, though, she didn't resist him.

"Just a little time," he said. "That's all I'm asking of you. Until I get through whatever explanations are waiting in that house. Will you come with me?"

At first there was silence. Then she whispered "okay" from inside the curve of his shoulder. "I'll go with you today. But I'm not promising anything about tomorrow."

*****

While Ava was redoing her face, Isaiah used her phone to call Tess.

"Hi," he said when she picked up on the first ring. "Isaiah here."

"Dear Lord in heaven! It's Isaiah!" she said to someone, which meant that at least one person was still there.

"I'm calling to see if everyone left."

"What? Oh my dear boy, you can't be serious. No! Absolutely *no one* left. Everyone's been worried sick about you."

"Ah. Well, better late than never, I suppose."

After a substantial pause, Tess said, "That's not really fair, Isaiah."

"Yes, I believe that's totally fair. But I don't want to debate the issue with you."

"Are you coming back here or not?" she asked, sounding uncharacteristically terse.

"In a few minutes."

"I'm glad to hear that. And the others will be too."

"Maybe not for long, though. You tell them that I'm coming back for answers—*all* the answers. And I'll try to remain civil, which is more than they deserve. You tell them that, Tess."

"You tell them yourself when you get here. We'll be waiting."

CHAPTER SIXTEEN

Isaiah and Ava took their original places next to each other at the living room table. As they did, Tess refilled coffee cups for Zeke and Sarah, who were also seated where they'd been earlier, as was Rosa. Zoie, however, had withdrawn to the little table in the kitchen, where she'd been for the last two hours, according to Tess.

After Isaiah and Ava had come back to the house, he'd said hello to Zoie, but she had refused to respond to his greeting. And when he'd placed his hand on her shoulder, intending a gesture of solidarity, she had pushed him away.

"She went for a long walk after you left," Tess had whispered to him when he'd emerged from the kitchen. "And when she returned, she sat down in there, and she hasn't spoken to anyone since—not even her father."

Now that everyone except Zoie was gathered around the table again, *no one* was talking. The combined tension and silence made the room feel heavy, almost oppressive, so Isaiah was relieved to see wine glasses and a newly opened bottle of merlot arranged in the center of the table. Apparently not the only one pleased to see this, he watched as Ava poured a glass for him and one for herself before gently pushing the bottle across the table to Rosa. After he took a sip, he looked very deliberately at Sarah to his left. He could feel the others staring at him, and he imagined that they were just waiting for him to say something, perhaps anxious about what those first words might be. As for Sarah, she looked positively terrified.

"All right," Isaiah said, to cut through the stillness he could no longer handle. His tone was soft and measured, his eyes still fixed on the woman who'd raised him. "When did you first find out that you weren't my mother?"

There was a distinct lag between the end of Isaiah's question and the processing of his words. Then Rosa burst out laughing, a fine spray of merlot involuntarily spewing out of her mouth.

"Oh dear heaven," Tess exclaimed from her spot at the end of the table. Then she got up to retrieve a towel from the kitchen, glancing over at Isaiah with a look of exasperation.

When Sarah started to cry, anything remaining of the light moment Isaiah had tried to create was extinguished completely.

"I'm sorry," he said, reaching out to squeeze her hand. "I thought a little levity might help." Sarah nodded but wasn't able to get any words out.

After handing Rosa the towel, Tess went into the bedroom and returned with a box of Kleenex that made stops at Rosa and Zeke before reaching the opposite end of the table. Sarah wiped her eyes and blew her nose and then looked up apprehensively at the man she'd loved as her son since infancy.

"Are you okay?" he asked, his inflection remaining soft but his words crisply enunciated. She nodded. "Then can you please help me understand what happened fifty-eight years ago? And can you tell me why, in God's name, no one thought that Zoie and I might benefit from knowing the truth?"

She started to respond to him, but when her words caught in her throat, Zeke raised his hand. "Can I try answering that?" he asked in a rough, scratchy voice.

"Sure, Zeke." Isaiah was sitting erect, his arms resting on the table, on top of the black folder that he'd brought in from the car. "Go ahead."

"*I'd* be interested in hearing your explanation too." Zoie's voice took them off guard as she stood in the doorway between the kitchen and living room.

"I know you would, girl," Zeke said, looking over his shoulder at her. "And I'm real sorry, like I said before. But I guess that don't mean much to you right now."

"No, Dad. It doesn't."

"Why don't you come over here and sit down?"

"Thanks, but I prefer to stand."

"Okay. That's the way it's gonna be then," he said, returning his attention to Isaiah as he took a sip of coffee. "Well, after my brother died and my sister-in-law, Belinda, went to Boston—and she never came back, by the way—Abby stayed on with me for several months, even though she kept talking 'bout going to the convent, and even though I knew she was dead serious. But we had something strong and good between us, her and me, and I'll always believe she felt it too."

He paused, looking over his shoulder again at Zoie and then back at Isaiah.

"Go on," Isaiah said. "We're listening."

"You stop me if you got any questions."

"I will. Trust me."

"I do," Zeke said. "Well, while I was still grieving over Andy—and I was pretty messed up, for sure—Abby kept on taking care a me. She was never more 'n a few feet away from me, fussing over me and cooking for me, like Belinda taught her how. And 'cause we was so close ... well ... *things* happened, and we ended up being together—in *that* way—if you get what I'm trying to say. Only two times, though. She went to confession after both of 'em, but even so, she told me she didn't want me to feel bad. Said she was real happy that the Lord had give her a chance to know what it was like to be with a *gentle* man 'fore she went home to the convent. That's what she called it—*home*—and that's what she called me—her *gentle* man."

Tess blew her nose so loudly at the end of the table that Zeke stopped speaking.

"Please forgive me," she said. "This is all so sad—and so much harder than I ever dreamed it would it be."

"That's because people kept kicking the truth down the road for more than half a century," Rosa said, speaking up for the first time. "And after being bottled up for so long, there's no *way* this could be easy."

"Any chance I can finish what I got to say down here?" Zeke asked.

"I'm sorry," Tess said. "I'll be quiet."

"And ain't *that* gonna be news!" Zeke replied, not bothering to look at her. "Now what was I saying?"

"That Abby called you her gentle man," Zoie answered softly, still standing in the kitchen doorway.

"Right," Zeke said, without turning around to look at her. "She did call me that. But my competition was stiff—way stronger than I could fight—'cause God kept on calling her and calling her. Finally, after watching over me for about three months, she told me she just couldn't wait any longer. She said she had to go, and she told me she believed I was strong enough to handle things on my own. Broke my heart and tore me up, but I knew I couldn't stop something big as God. So we was starting to figure out how to get her back to the convent when she got sick. I thought she was gonna die. Took her to the doctor and, well, about two weeks later we got the news. There was a baby coming. That's when I *really* thought she was gonna die. She was so upset and couldn't believe this was happening to her again."

Isaiah saw Rosa drop her head and then reach out to the middle of the table to grab a tissue from the box. He hoped she'd taken some time to read Abby's journals and letters so she would know by now that, despite the decision, Abby had loved her first child deeply. Then he stopped to remind himself that the same was probably true about him. All those visits to Kettle Falls while he was growing up—all those questions she used to ask him about what was going on in his life. Everything made sense now.

"But she was way far 'long before we knew that *two* babies was coming," Zeke was saying. "That's when she called Sinclair. He'd helped her before, and we needed help bad, 'cause I didn't think I could keep *two* kids by myself." He paused for a moment to look over his shoulder at Zoie again. "I do love you, girl, and I'm sorry I kept this from you."

Now Zoie was crying, and she walked over to the table to grab a Kleenex. "But why *did* you keep it from me, Dad? You always told me everything else."

"'Cause Sinclair told us not to. Said it would be better that way for a—"

"Sinclair said a lot of things," Sarah interrupted, causing all heads to turn in her direction. She was regaining control of herself and sounding more like the strong woman Isaiah had known all his life. "But he obviously left a lot of things *out* too," she went on. "Of course, I wasn't always completely honest with him either, if the truth be known."

Isaiah found himself reaching for Ava's hand beneath the table, and he was relieved to feel her lacing her fingers in his.

"Sinclair and I had been dating for about six months when I first heard Abby's name. He told me he had to fly down to San Francisco to give some legal assistance to her. I thought she might have been an old girlfriend, but he insisted she wasn't, and I believed him. When he came home, he suddenly asked me to marry him. I thought it was a little strange, but I loved him very much. Unfortunately, I hadn't told him yet that I had some … well, some physical problems that made the odds of my being able to have children very slim. I was a coward, and I didn't want to risk losing him. So I married him without telling him. About a year and a half after our wedding—in a nightmarish conversation that nearly killed me—he confessed to me that he'd had a long, ongoing affair with Abby and that she'd just given birth to his son."

Isaiah was speechless.

"That *bastard*!" Zeke said, sitting up board straight in his chair. "When he came out to North Carolina after the babies was born, he said he'd help Abby by taking one of 'em, but he wanted the boy. I didn't want to let you go, Son," he said, looking across the table at Isaiah, "but I felt trapped. Abby was leaving, and I could only handle one of you by myself. I thought keeping Zoie would help make me feel like part of Abby was still with me. But Sinclair promised Abby and me that he'd tell you the truth when you was old enough to understand—and he was supposed to call me when that happened so I could tell Zoie too. But that call never came, and then the years went on and on …"

"And the whole time he let me believe that you were *his* son," Sarah said, reaching for Isaiah's free hand, which he readily gave her. "I felt so guilty about keeping my own secret from him, and when he told me that he wanted to take custody of you because Abby was returning to the convent, I thought that if he had his own child with him, I would somehow be absolved. Plus, I loved you the minute I saw you. What I didn't know until just a few days ago was that the man I adored as my husband was so deeply in love with another woman that he chose to confess to an affair that had never happened and claim the paternity of a child that belonged to someone else. The images I had of him being with Abby tormented me for years, but I didn't tell him how I was feeling because of my own guilt. And all that time, the visions I lived with—visions of their being together—had never even taken place! I can't imagine how all those lies must have weighed him down. And it was so unnecessary. He never understood that my love for him was so strong I would have gladly taken you into our lives, even if he'd told me the truth."

"But why did you tolerate all those visits to the convent when I was growing up?"

"Because I sincerely wanted you to have some knowledge of Abby."

"Weren't you threatened by Dad's relationship with her? At least by the relationship you *thought* he had with her?"

"She was in a cloistered convent for more than twenty of those years, Isaiah. I figured that if she'd really wanted him, she never would have gone there. Yes, I believed he still cared for her, but given my own guilty conscience, I felt blessed to have as much of him as I did. Plus, you quickly became the brightest light of my life, and I thankfully lived with the circumstances I'd been given."

"And then," Isaiah said, "when Abby died ..."

"And then, when Abby died and you were suddenly called to Kettle Falls, I knew you were about to find out who your real mother was. But when I talked to you on Saturday and you told me that Abby had two children—two daughters, but no mention of a son—I knew something was very wrong somewhere. Your father—*Sinclair*, I mean—told me many years ago about Abby's friendship with Tess, about how they'd all met after the war. And I assumed that Tess would have some answers. So I flew here on Sunday, hoping to find out what was going on before you did. I only wanted to talk to Tess ... at first," she said, her eyes avoiding the old woman at the opposite end of the table.

"And the rest is history," Isaiah said.

"Yes. So it would seem."

"Ain't this the damndest situation you ever heard of in your whole damn life?" Zeke asked as he was blowing his own nose one more time.

No one offered an answer to his rhetorical question, but sat instead in complete silence for several minutes. Zoie eventually took the chair next to her father again and gently placed her hand on his arm, which caused him to drop his head and start sobbing. Without the slightest hesitation, she wrapped him in an embrace, holding onto him as if trying to keep him from slipping away. When he'd finally regained control, she coaxed him into taking a long drink of water. At that point, she looked across the table at Isaiah. "Surprise!" she said, opening her arms to him and doing her best to smile.

"Ditto from this corner," Rosa interjected. "I feel sort of like a fifth wheel here, though."

"But you're not, Rosa," Isaiah said. "We're all connected by a common thread—a common *force*, really. For better or worse, Abby is a part of all of us."

"And each of us is bleeding all over the table as a result," Rosa replied brusquely, after which another prolonged silence settled into the room.

"Well," Zeke said when several painful minutes had passed, "you young folks might have time to keep the bleedin' goin' on and on. But I don't." His voice was breaking and he sounded like he had laryngitis. "I'm too old, and I need to figure out how to get over this somehow, else I'm not gonna make it too long after today."

Tess was wiping her eyes at the other end of the table. "Oh dear Lord in heaven," she said, making the sign of the cross, "please be with us in this time of great need." Then despite the fact that her tears kept flowing, she stood up, stuffed a handful of shredded tissue into the ample depths of her cleavage, and used her apron again to mop her face. "How about more coffee? I also have an apple pie that I just baked this morning."

"Got any ice cream to put on that?" Zeke mumbled.

*****

Zeke's comment about the possibility of his not surviving this trauma had been sobering for every person around that table and resulted in a collective effort to establish a more conciliatory mood. But as everyone worked to find a graceful exit from the gathering, there was an obvious, unspoken understanding that the gaping wounds gouged open that day were going to take a long time to heal. Still, they all agreed to remain in town until after Abby's funeral, although Zoie, Zeke, and Rosa backed out of attending the second viewing that afternoon.

"I think Dad's had enough for the day—the understatement of the month," Zoie said to Isaiah. "And I think I've reached my limit for the time being too. But I was wondering if you and I could spend a little time together this evening? Maybe we could go through that folder? I'm going to need some help coming to terms with the fact that you're my brother. *Wow!*" she added after a pause. "That's as hard to say as it is to believe, now that I hear those words coming out of my mouth!"

"You're right," he said, putting his arm around her. "I think we all might be a little numb. And I'm going to need your help too. Maybe I should make a trip out to North Carolina. What do you think? Would that be useful?"

Zeke perked up at this suggestion from the stretched-out position he'd taken on the recliner after finishing his apple pie and ice cream. "I been dreaming 'bout seeing you and your sister on the farm together where you was born. That would sure be something 'fore I die."

"Well, we'll have to work on making that happen," Isaiah said. "And then," he added, gathering Rosa into his other arm, "maybe Zoie and I could come to San Francisco, or we could all get together in Seattle."

"Or maybe that could happen in North Carolina too," Zeke threw in.

"Maybe. Let's try to stay open to the possibilities," Isaiah replied, giving both women a tender squeeze.

"But let's not rush things," Rosa said, unwinding herself from Isaiah's embrace. "I don't know about you, but I still have a lot of anger to work out that keeps bubbling up—toward lots of people. And I might not *ever* be ready to get all lovey-dovey with you guys, to be perfectly honest, just so you know." She paused for a minute. "I do have to tell you, though," she said, with an unmistakable grin breaking out, "that I thought I'd really done a screw-up job on my own life. But compared to *this* goat rodeo, my history doesn't look half bad—and that's making me feel better, in some demented sort of way."

A polite wave of laughter rolled through the room, as if no one was sure whether they should be happy for her or concerned. Then further conversation was replaced with rote movements, as everyone pitched in to clear away the mess from the living room.

When the dishes were finished, the table had been wiped clean, and all the chairs had been returned to their original places, Sarah asked Isaiah if she could speak with him privately. They stepped out on the front porch, closed the door behind them, and sat down beside each other on the swing suspended from the ceiling as a light drizzle began to fall.

"I'm sure you'll understand," she said, "but I'm not going to stay for the funeral tomorrow. I have a lot to think about, and I'm anxious to get home. So I'm going to drive back to Spokane this afternoon and take an early flight in the morning."

"Will you be all right, Mother?"

She smiled at him and reached up to touch his face. "Thank you for calling me 'Mother.'"

"Regardless of everything that's happened, I can't seem to think of you any other way."

"And I'm grateful for that blessing. I didn't realize how much I'd been worrying through the years about what you would do when you found out. Of course, I'm not sure what I would have done if I'd known about the rest of this situation. All I know for sure is that I don't think I could have survived losing you."

"Well, you can stop worrying about that now," he said with a smile, holding her hands between his. "We've hit a big bump, to be sure. But when all's said and done, I don't think I'll be going anywhere."

"Thank you, dear. Not carrying that weight of worry around with me will take some getting used to."

"Meanwhile, I'm concerned about your being alone over the next few days until I get back."

"You needn't be, Isaiah. I've been on my own for four years, you know."

"But this is different."

"Perhaps. And we'll have plenty of time to talk about everything when you get home. I'll be fine until then. By the way, I want you to know that I like your Ava very much. Are you going to bring her to Seattle with you for a visit?"

He looked away from her for a moment, wishing he had a better answer. "No. I don't think she'd be up for that. Maybe ... down the road, given some time. We'll see."

"Well, she's a good one, and I hope you don't let her slip away. You're not getting any younger, you know," she added, playfully pinching his cheek.

He laughed as they stood up and embraced, and then they walked back inside arm in arm. Sarah graciously said good-bye to each person in the odd assembly, shaking their hands and telling them how much she appreciated meeting them, even under the circumstances.

"I hope we'll all stay in touch," she said, "since Isaiah will now be a part of your lives." Then she came to Tess and pulled her into a hug. "I'm sincerely sorry about what I did, and for the way I spoke to you," she said softly. "Can you please forgive me?"

Pulling back from the hug so she could see Sarah's face, Tess said, "Forgiveness used to be part of my life's work, Mrs. Mellington, and it still comes easy. Of *course* you're forgiven. But I need to ask your forgiveness as well, for being so hateful and shouting at you. I need to take that one to confession, for sure."

"You're a good person, Tess, *and* forgiven. If you're ever going to be in Seattle, please call me and let me know you're coming so I can have you over to the house. I make a mean cup of coffee too."

After a final wave to everyone, Isaiah walked Sarah out to her rental car, holding one of Tess's large umbrellas over their heads to shelter themselves from what was now a steady downpour. They kissed each other, and then he watched her drive away. *We'll be okay*, he thought as he went back inside. *I think we're going to be okay.*

*****

Once Isaiah felt comfortable that Tess was going to be all right by herself, they all agreed to meet at ten the next morning at the mortuary for the motor procession to the church for the funeral. Then Isaiah and

Ava drove off in the Jag followed by Rosa, Zoie, and Zeke in Rosa's rental car.

"I'll stop off at the lodge," Isaiah said, glancing over at Ava, who seemed to get more beautiful the less she did to herself. "You can pick up your things from my room and get your car."

"You don't want me to go with you to the mortuary?"

He wasn't sure how to respond, having assumed that their dustup earlier meant changes to all of their plans. "Yes," he said, gingerly picking his way through the word groupings lined up in his head. "I mean, I'd love to have you with me. But I thought you didn't—"

"Isaiah," she said, cutting him off, "I've decided to be with you until you get through tomorrow. After that, we'll see where we are and how we feel about any next step. Okay?"

"Okay," he replied without any embellishment, feeling as if they'd just consummated a business arrangement.

When they reached Colville, he watched in his rearview mirror as Rosa turned into the lodge parking lot while he continued on to the mortuary. The public wake was scheduled to begin at four o'clock, and even though they were a few minutes early, Isaiah was hopeful that Mr. Arthur would let them in anyway.

Inside the lobby, Isaiah and Ava didn't see anyone, not even Mr. Arthur. So they went left and down the hallway as they'd done the day before, finding themselves alone in the viewing room. Up at the front, below the altar, Abby's casket was still open and waiting.

"Why don't you go ahead?" Ava suggested, sitting down in one of the chairs. "I'll wait here for you."

Feeling hesitant, Isaiah moved slowly toward the front of the room, the figure resting low inside the casket becoming more visible as he approached. He'd seen her so many times before, alive and animated during all the years past, and even silent and still after she died. But he'd never once looked upon her while understanding that she had given birth to him. She had tried her best to ensure a good life for both him and Zoie, and for Rosa, while following the clarion call from the Almighty, finally freeing herself to pursue her destiny. And he honestly did not believe she'd had any idea about the mess in the making as a result of her stewards' spurious behavior.

Walking around the kneeling rail, as Zeke and Zoie had done the previous day, he came right up to the side of the casket and peered down at Abigail Louise Ryan—Sister Mary Abigail—Sister Abby—his mother.

He didn't want to touch her because he knew her essence wasn't there, just her body. And he didn't want to disrupt his memories of her warmth and life.

Feeling his knees weaken a little, he steadied himself by placing his arms on the edge of the casket where he was almost certain he could feel Abby's presence. In his mind, he could hear her voice saying that she loved him, assuring him that she was holding him in a protected place in her heart. And she was content, waiting for everyone to join her someday, in the heaven she had struggled so hard to reach.

*****

Sunday, September 10, 1950

My dearest children, Isaiah and Zoe—

Mass was over about an hour ago, and I have a few minutes by myself before I go to Rosary. The two of you have been on my mind more than usual, so I want to write this while the opportunity is available.

"Isaiah" is Hebrew for "salvation of the Lord," and "Benjamin" means "Son of the Right Hand." No names on Earth could hold more power or more hope, and those names are now yours, my son. Live proudly with them.

"Zoe" means "life." (I understand that your father has changed the spelling, but I suppose I can't do anything about that.) "Evangeline" means "bringing good news." You came out first, ahead of your brother, bringing both life and good news into my world in a single instant, my precious daughter. I hope your names surround you always with their joyful meaning.

You are now four months old, and I can only imagine how beautiful you must be. Perhaps I'll be able to see you occasionally as you grow up—something else I must add to my prayer list. And I hope you'll be reunited with each other one day while I'm still alive to see that. By then, I can only pray that you'll understand why the decisions were made. If you have come to believe by then that I didn't, or don't, love you, please know that nothing could be further from the truth. Precisely because I do and always will love you, as I cherish my own soul, I have given you up rather than have you suffer throughout your lives, which you most certainly would have done, if I had continued to deny who and what I've been called to be.

Every morning when I awaken to a new day, I beseech the Lord for confirmation that I have done the right thing. At least I know that you are in the care of two good men. One, Isaiah, is a dear and loyal friend who has never ceased to be there when I needed his help. The other, Zoe, is truly the only gentle man I have ever known. The Lord let me experience him for a moment so I could come back here in peace, no longer believing that love requires pain and violence and heartbreak in order to exist. My brief time with your father was a gift that has freed me from evil memories in the past and enabled me to finally move on.

When the time is of God's choosing, I pray that the two of you will also come together with your sister Salome Rosabella ("peace" and "a fair rose"). When you do, I hope you will see yourselves in each other. Perhaps—and I say this knowing I'll need to confess the prideful indulgence—you will see a little of me in there as well. And if any of you are angry with me, I hope you'll be able to forgive me.

Always in the Lord, I am honored to be your mother.

Abby

Isaiah and Zoie sat next to one another on a sheltered bench in the dimly lit lodge courtyard. True to her established pattern, Abby had written two identical copies of the same letter, which they were holding in their hands. On their laps were several small black-and-white pictures they'd found in the infamous folder, images of the twins as newborn babies propped up side by side against pillows on what looked like a daybed. As they studied the photos and absorbed the words in Abby's letter, they remained silent, allowing the newfound details of their heritage and the peacefulness of the night to begin filling all the empty places in their hearts.

"So," Zoie said softly, smiling up at him after several minutes had passed, "I'm the oldest, huh?"

He laughed and put his arm around her, pulling her close to him. "Apparently. But don't let it go to your head."

*****

The small, newly forged group stood with a few other mourners under the porte cochère on the side of the mortuary, watching as six men in matching black suits rolled Abby's casket from the building to the waiting hearse. Then Tess and Ava climbed into a black stretch limo with Isaiah, his father, and his sisters, for the short motor procession to Immaculate Conception Church. They waited while those in the small caravan behind them parked their cars and went inside. They waited a few minutes longer while the six men in matching black suits removed the casket from the hearse and slowly carried Abby up the front steps to the church entrance. The same priest who'd presided over the short service at the mortuary was standing there.

He said a few prayers, and then those in the solemn procession—the altar servers, the lay ministers, the priest, the casket, and the little family—began moving down the center aisle. At that point, Isaiah realized that there didn't appear to be a single empty place in any of the pews. When they'd reached the altar railing, and when the opening prayers and blessings had been offered, he felt overwhelmed by the broad reach of Abby's work as he followed Tess, Zeke, Zoie, Rosa, and Ava into the front pew.

Look at the number of people whose lives would somehow be different or worse off, he thought, *if Abby hadn't listened to that unrelenting voice calling her all those years! Hundreds—probably thousands—would have missed out on the blessings of knowing her, compared to only the four of us who were left behind.*

*****

The Mass was haunting and beautiful. At designated points in the liturgy, flawless harmony from a chorus of nuns drifted out from the elevated choir loft at the back of the church. The voices rode on swells of melody surging from the massive pipe organ, filling the air above the congregation with tones that seemed empowered by a celestial hand. There were four hymns in total, and the first two were such a perfect reflection of Abby that she could have easily selected them herself.

The first began with these words:

I will come to you in the silence,
I will lift you from your fear.
You will hear my voice, I claim you as my choice.
Be still and know I am here ...

And then, a few minutes later, the second hymn rang out:

We walk by faith and not by sight;
no gracious words we hear
of him who spoke as none e'er spoke,
but we believe him near ...

The readings from the Old and New Testaments were delivered by two lay members of the congregation. Isaiah knew that the selection of those participants at a funeral Mass was generally made because of some significant association with the deceased, and he hoped he would remember to ask Tess who those people were. The responsorial psalm in between the two readings was sung by the choir. When all of that was complete, the officiating priest read the Gospel in a commanding voice. Then he delivered a homily that was short and rather generic, speaking of death, resurrection, and redemption, and mentioning Abby's name a couple of times. His remarks concluded with, "May God bless her soul *and* each and every one of you."

"With all the planning that's obviously gone into this," Ava whispered to Isaiah as the priest stepped down from the ambo and returned to his seat behind the altar, "I'm surprised that his comments weren't more personal. He doesn't seem to have known Abby at all."

As the Mass proceeded, just prior to the exchange of peace, the Lord's Prayer was sung by a soloist whose contralto voice and emotional interpretation produced goose bumps on Isaiah's arms. And after the Eucharistic Rite had concluded, when everyone who'd received Communion had returned to their places in the pews, "Ave Maria" was performed by a soprano whose soaring rendition seemed to stop all breathing inside the church, leaving few people with dry eyes. When the last resonation of her voice had quieted, Tess passed two small travel packets of Kleenex down the row. By the time they'd reached Isaiah, only a couple of tissues were left.

261

Then, as the unbroken silence persisted and the celebrant remained seated behind the altar facing the congregation, an elderly priest who'd assisted with Communion walked to the center of the sanctuary. His body appeared sort of boxy beneath his vestments, not very tall and almost as wide, and what little hair he had left around the edges of his bald head was snow white. He bowed in reverence to the altar, lifting himself up slowly, as if his back might be hurting him, before walking in a measured pace to the ambo, where he mounted the steps with obvious difficulty. At first, he was barely visible inside the ornately carved wooden enclosure, but then he rose in height as he apparently stood on some sort of stool. After pressing the long black microphone down closer to his mouth, he began speaking in a clear, deep Irish brogue.

"Good morning, everyone."

"Good morning, Father," hundreds of voices replied in unison.

"My name is Father Michael Moynihan. I first met the woman we celebrate today—Sister Mary Abigail, who came to be so fondly known as Sister Abby—when she was still Abigail Ryan, way back in 1947, in San Francisco."

Isaiah recognized his name from Abby's writing and was surprised to learn not only that was he still alive but also that he was still involved somehow with Abby.

"She stayed in touch with me as her life unfolded," Father Moynihan went on, "and she wrote to me with varying regularity after she returned to the convent. In the beginning, back in 1947, my role with her was no different from my role with any other parishioner—advisor, confessor, healer, friend in need. And those early days after I met her were not easy. I was a relatively new priest, certain that I was prepared and knowledgeable enough to correctly handle every situation the Lord might place in front of me. But I was wrong, and as the years passed, I ended up being a student of this remarkable woman. Her open and selfless sharing of her life's journey with me helped me become a better priest—and ultimately a better man.

"'The fear of the Lord is the beginning of wisdom.' Psalm 111:10," he said. "I don't think Abby ever had a problem feeling drawn to the Lord, but I do believe she had some difficulty coming to fear him. She viewed her blemishes and the mistakes she was making as reasons for *avoiding* the path she'd been chosen to take. She didn't yet understand that all of us, despite our fearfulness, need to face that fear, carrying our failings and mistakes *to* the Lord, in order for our wisdom to begin flowering. Abby's journey to that discovery was a long one as she struggled to find her way to her life's purpose. And," he said, looking directly at Isaiah and the others in the front pew, "she was blessed to live a full life in the secular world before finally letting God's word and wishes enter her heart and move her to action. Then, as *she* became wiser, so did I—something for which I'll be forever grateful.

"She was, despite her flaws, a truly holy woman," he continued, his eyes now fully fixed on those in the front row. "But her life's mission and purpose only became clear to her when she stopped trying to define and direct them herself and began, instead, to *listen*. What she eventually allowed herself to hear led her to deep sacrifice but also to peace and to the wondrous good works that touched so many in this community. This church is filled today with beneficiaries of her devotion—family and friends of hundreds of souls whose end-of-life experiences were joyful, dignified, peaceful, and loving, primarily because of her, although she would most certainly excuse herself from any credit.

"Her compassion, born of heartbreaking events in her own past," he said, lifting his focus from the front pew and directing his words to the hundreds of others who were watching him, "opened her up to the concept of hospice care long before the idea became commonplace throughout this country. In the midst of sterile, frightening hospital environments, she slowly began transforming the aesthetics surrounding terminal patients while increasing the involvement of their families and friends. She believed that the same support system and joyful experiential sharing, which is so visible around hospital nurseries on the day of a baby's birth, should also be encouraged and enabled when someone is preparing to *leave* this life. That belief evolved into a mission led by Sister Abby for thirty years, and her inspired innovation influenced hospice endeavors throughout the United States. But looking around at this standing room-only crowd, I think I can safely say that her most important and valued scope of influence was right here in this community.

"In the end," he said, his voice slipping into a conclusive tone as he looked again at Isaiah first and then down the row, "the simple lesson of Sister Abby's life is that no matter where your life has taken you or how old you've become, the time is never too late to pursue your destiny, to use your God-given gifts to achieve the purpose for which you've been placed on this earth. But first you *must* be willing to listen—to change something, to sacrifice something—and you must also learn who you *are* before you're set free to discover what you can *be*. A full and forgiving God is always speaking to us with the answers, if we will only tune ourselves in to Him.

May the Lord be with all of you always, and may His loving arms envelop our Sister Abby with peace. Amen."

As Father Moynihan turned and slowly stepped down from the ambo, Isaiah leaned across Ava and reached out for Rosa and Zoie's hands. From the other side of Zoie, Zeke extended his hand to Isaiah. And the members of this small uncommon family, loosely stitched together in a patchwork of life's fabric, did their best to feel as one in the moment, trying to accept the changes about who they were and to understand the woman whose life had made theirs possible.

CHAPTER SEVENTEEN

Sarah Mellington entered through the ornately carved front door of her Queen Anne home, wondering if the funeral was over yet. Her flight had been scheduled to leave Spokane at eight thirty that morning but had been delayed for more than two hours because of fog in Seattle. They'd finally landed at Seattle-Tacoma International Airport just before noon, and the drive home, once she'd located her car in the parking lot, had taken almost another hour. And all the while, she hadn't been able to get her mind off what was going on in Kettle Falls. But now she was home. Now she'd be able to rest.

Entering the small vestibule, everything seemed normal. On the walls to her left and right were the same brass coat and hat hooks that had been there for fifty years. Below the array of hooks were the wooden boot benches topped with the needlepoint cushions she'd had someone make for her when Isaiah started elementary school. After she deactivated the security control behind the front door, just as she did every day, she slipped out of her raincoat, looping the fabric hanger inside the collar over one of the hooks, in a habitual movement. Then she removed her high-heeled designer rain boots and pushed her feet into the same furry black mule slippers that were always parked and waiting for her beneath one of the benches. Normal. Everything was normal.

But when she walked through the next doorway, which was made of the opaque beveled glass that she had never ceased to admire and appreciate, the realization that *nothing* about her life would ever be the same again came crashing in around her.

Pulling her carry-on bag behind her, she came to a stop in the core of the Mellington home. There in the circular foyer darkened by the effects of low-hanging fog that had descended outside again, she could see all of her furniture in place and the four days of mail brought in by Edna stacked neatly on the round mahogany table. But the memories of Sinclair's fragrances that used to comfort her when she walked into their home were no longer welcome. The echoes of his voice that she used to call upon for consolation had been forever silenced. The longing for his touch was now as dead as he was.

All the tenderness and trust she'd associated with this house had been constructed on top of a lie. The husband she'd adored for all those wonderful years had never been able to stop loving another woman. And that love had turned not only him into a fraud but Sarah into one as well. Leaning against the mahogany table, she lowered her head and closed her eyes. Her privileged life, financial security, and enviable home were not offering her even a shred of protection against the torment of her shattered heart, the jagged edges of which were mutilating the very foundation of her being. There she stood, unmoving in the silence for several minutes, with only the foggy light seeping through the windows.

Exhausted but not feeling a hint of any tears left unspent, she began considering her options. Keeping her body and mind fit enough to sustain an active, independent lifestyle required more time, struggle, and money every day. What would be the point of moving forward with all those routines now? At best, she only had a few years left to go. Certainly not long enough for a second run at anything authentic. And staying here— trying to pick up the ugly pieces inside this house—was clearly not going to be possible anymore.

But what about Isaiah? Just the thought of his name caused her throat to tighten up. And without warning, she began to weep, the escalating pitch of emotion rising from a reservoir that she couldn't believe had anything left to drain after the last few days.

"Oh Isaiah!" she cried out loud, her voice a loan moan and her body shaking as despair and fear intermingled in that lonely spot.

Then, gradually, the strength that had enabled Sarah Mellington to survive to the age of eighty-one with good health and meaningful days began to override the despondency pressing down on her. No matter what else had happened, her belief that she would continue to at least have Isaiah as part of her world began edging up over her distress. And around the single blessing of still being loved by the man she'd raised as her son, she thought she'd be able to build whatever might be necessary to get her through her remaining years.

"I guess I might have to start letting someone help me," she said to herself as she shuffled in her slippers down the darkened hallway without turning on a single light. "Do you think *you* might be available?" she asked, looking upward and holding out her hands with her palms open.

She did finally switch on a small lamp on the kitchen counter as she began rummaging around in what she called her "miscellaneous drawer." A few moments later, from beneath a disorderly pile of matchbooks, pushpin boxes, rubber bands, packets of fresh-cut flower food, scissors, and spare tools, she pulled out a small white envelope with the words "Isaiah's extra key" written across the front in her handwriting.

Then she closed the drawer, switched off the lamp, and walked back out to the foyer. When she'd shoved all of the mail into her travel tote, she grabbed the handle of her carry-on bag and went through the beveled glass door out into the vestibule. After exchanging her slippers for her rain boots, she slipped on her coat, activated the security alarm, and left the house, locking the door and as much of the pain as she could escape inside and behind her.

*****

Following the procession to the cemetery and the short service at the grave site, Tess left with the other congregants so she could preside over the repast—the reception being held in a banquet room at one of Colville's large restaurants. Isaiah and the rest of his group opted out, preferring to remain with Abby for just a little while longer. The casket was poised over the open pit that had been prepared, but the actual lowering into the ground wouldn't take place until everyone was gone. So Abby's three children, along with Ava and Zeke, remained seated under the canopy facing the grave. They were sheltered from the heavy mist that had been falling all day, although a damp breeze added a chill as they huddled close to one another.

"The casket looks so beautiful now," Zoie said softly, referring to the rainbow of roses covering every inch on the top of the coffin. Each flower had been placed there one at a time by those in attendance at the cemetery service as they were leaving. "She must be very pleased with the way this whole day has been handled."

"I still can't get over how many people were in that church," Rosa added.

"I know," Zeke said. "If all funerals was like this one, I'd prob'ly go to more of 'em."

There was a nominal pause before the laughter.

"Are you sure you guys don't want to stop by the restaurant?" Isaiah asked. "Tess told me there's supposed to be a huge buffet."

"Is that the only place in town selling food today?" Zeke's question was barely audible beneath the braying as he blew his nose into a huge white handkerchief.

Ava turned to Isaiah sitting next to her. "Do you think they might enjoy taking a ride up to Barney's?"

"Hey, Zeke," Isaiah said. "How do you feel about chicken-fried steak?"

"That come with mashed potatoes and gravy?"

"The best."

"I think I hear my name being called, Son."

Slowly and with obvious hesitation, they began leaving the grave site. Each of them touched the casket as they passed, but Zeke leaned down and softly kissed the gleaming copper.

"The last time I told her good-bye," he said, pulling the huge handkerchief out of his pocket again, "I believed I'd see her again somewhere. Not so sure 'bout that this time, though."

"Of course you'll see her again," Zoie replied, taking his hand and leading him across the grass behind the others toward the Jag and Rosa's rental car. "We'll *all* see her again."

"Yeah. Maybe. But she'll be flying all over the place, real busy, and organizing stuff."

Zoie just put her arm around his waist and hugged him without saying a word, leaving the magical imagery undisturbed and hovering over them.

*****

They returned to the lodge about three o'clock after their meal at Barney's and stood in the lobby debating whether or not to do anything on their last night together.

"Tomorrow's going to be a very long day for Dad," Zoie said. "The fact that there aren't any direct flights between here and Charlotte didn't bother us flying out. The time change got us here by early afternoon, even with the connection in Denver. But going home we *lose* those three hours.

So if we're going to do something tonight, we need to go early. Besides, we have to pack."

Isaiah had arranged for the limo to pick Zeke and Zoie up at five thirty the next morning since their flight was at nine. He'd tried to arrange for Rosa to turn in her rental car in Colville so she could ride in the limo as well, but her contract required her to turn the car in at the airport.

"I don't mind," she said. "I'll just get up early and follow the limo."

"If we have time after we get to the airport," Zoie added, lifting a stray white thread off the shoulder of Rosa's black jacket, "maybe the three of us could visit a while longer before our flights board. I've spent so many years waiting to meet you, and now I'm sort of afraid to let you go."

"Hey, I have an idea," Isaiah said. "Why don't we reconvene around five thirty or six and just go out for dessert? Then we can all talk about getting together again, because I'm like Zoie. I don't want to let *any* of you go."

They agreed to meet back in the lobby at six. When he and Ava were finally alone in his suite, they hung up their coats and sat down on the sofa.

"What a day!" Isaiah said.

"What a *week*. I'm amazed you're still standing."

"If you'll notice," he said, his legs sprawled out over the coffee table, "I'm not."

She smiled. "I'm glad you're already talking about spending time with your family. As hard as this has been, I think you're very lucky to have discovered each other while you're all still young and healthy enough to heal and build some relationships."

"All of us except Zeke. I'm not sure how much time we'll have left with him."

"I wouldn't count him out just yet, if I were you. He's a pretty tough old guy."

"Maybe. But I've been thinking that I don't want to take any chances." He sat up and took her hands in his. "Before I forget, I want to thank you for being around through everything that's happened, especially since I know you're not too sure if you like me anymore. I honestly don't think I would have survived the last couple of days without you."

"Of course you would have—but I'm glad I was able to be there."

He kissed her on the forehead, still holding her hands. "You said you have to work again tomorrow, right?"

"Right."

"What about Saturday?"

"Not until three."

"Would you mind driving me to the airport that morning?"

"No. But why? Where are you going?"

"North Carolina. Tomorrow I need to visit with Tess to make sure she's okay, and I want to stop by the cemetery again. But Saturday I'd like to go see where I was born. I don't want to wait."

"I think that's a wonderful idea, Isaiah. Have you mentioned this to Zeke and Zoie?"

"No. I'll tell them tonight."

"What about your Jag? Do you want to park it at my house?"

"You can drive me to the airport in it, and then you can use it while I'm gone."

She just looked at him for a moment. "Are you *serious?*"

"*Dead* serious. But you have to promise that you'll come back to the airport and pick me up when I come home. If you run away with my car, I won't be very happy."

"I can't believe you're trusting me with that masterpiece!"

"I can't either. But—"

Just then his cell phone started ringing. Reaching inside his jacket pocket, he looked at the caller ID. "It's my mother," he said. "I'll call her back later."

"No, I think you should answer it. She's all by herself out there."

He looked at Ava and shook his head. "Are you *always* right?" he asked as he put the phone up to his ear.

"Probably," she whispered through a smile.

"Hey, Mom. I was going to call you later. How are you doing?"

"I guess I've been better."

"I'm sorry I'm not there," he said, feeling even more guilt than when he'd moved to Bellevue. "But I'll be home soon, and then we'll figure things out together."

"Yes, dear. I do know that, and I'm very thankful. But I was wondering if I could ask you a favor in the meantime."

"Anything. Just name it."

"Well, when I got home, I ..." He could hear her voice beginning to quiver. "I just couldn't stand to be there. I guess I need some time to process what's happened and figure out what I want to do. I'm thinking that maybe the time has finally come to sell the house. I don't know. But I don't want to be there right now, and I was wondering if … if you'd mind my staying at your place for a little while."

"Of course you can, Mother," he said immediately, relieved that there wasn't anything more serious than that going on. "You know I put that third bedroom together just for you anyway."

"And I didn't realize how much I appreciated that gesture until now."

"Great. Do you still have that extra key I gave you?"

"Yes, I went right to it."

"Okay then. Drive on over there and make yourself comfortable."

"Uh … I'm sort of here already."

He grinned and looked at Ava. "Well, I'm happy to hear that, Mother. Sounds like a good first step. And I'm relieved that you're safe and feeling at home in my place. Hopefully, you can get some rest now, and we'll talk about the Queen Anne house when I get back."

"When *are* you coming back?"

"Not until next week. I'm going to North Carolina on Saturday for a few days."

There was an extended pause before Sarah said, "I see."

"It's just going to be a quick trip, but I think I need to see the place before I can move on."

"Well, I guess that's not so hard to understand, dear. Do be careful, though. And what about Ava?"

"Ava?" he repeated for Ava's benefit. "What *about* Ava?"

"Do you have any plans to bring her here for a visit sometime soon?"

"No, Mother, I don't," he said, lowering his eyes to the floor. "You asked me that before, remember? And something like that might *never* happen, you know. So don't get your hopes up."

"Oh. How disappointing. I really thought you two worked well together."

"Thanks. But we'll just have to wait and see."

When they'd said good-bye, Ava stood up and walked across the room where she slipped on her coat. "What was it that she wanted to know about me?"

"She likes you very much, and she wanted to know if I was going to bring you to Seattle for a visit any time soon."

"Ah. Well, you gave a good answer, Isaiah. No one should be getting their hopes up, and I appreciate your being truthful with her. Now I really need to get going."

His heart was briefly in his throat as he sat there watching her, with the thought of losing her flashing through his mind. Rising to his feet, he walked over and put his arms around her, holding her close, and memorizing how she felt, how she smelled—just in case this was the last time.

"I'm so sorry, Ava, about what happened yesterday. Would it be okay if I call you from North Carolina?"

"Sure," came her muffled response from inside the curve of his shoulder.

"And you do promise not to steal my car, right?"

"Of course."

"In that case, I need to tell you something."

"What?"

"If you decide you don't want to see me anymore, I'll never be able to watch *Steel Magnolias* again, and you'll have to carry that cross for the rest of your life."

He could feel her laughing as he continued to hold her. At least he thought she was laughing.

*****

Isaiah had taken the earliest possible flight out of Spokane on Saturday morning, but even so, the time difference and the fact that he had to change planes in Minneapolis meant that he wouldn't be landing in Charlotte until after five o'clock eastern time. Consequently, he'd declined Zoie's offer to pick him up at the airport and had arranged for a rental car instead.

The flight from Spokane to Minneapolis had taken three hours and was followed by a two-hour layover. By the time he was in the air again for the final two-and-a-half-hour leg, Isaiah understood what Zoie had been saying about the trip being such an unbelievably long haul.

He was looking over her written directions from the Charlotte airport to Harmony when the flight attendants stopped at his row with the beverage cart. He ordered one of the tiny airplane-sized bottles of merlot, and after the cart and attendants had moved on, he eased his chair back a fraction farther to relax into his thoughts.

Only eight days earlier he'd headed out from Bellevue to Kettle Falls, anticipating a weekend filled with nothing much of anything notable. Instead, his life had been turned inside out, like a science fiction movie where the characters tear off their faces revealing completely different people or aliens underneath. And his visit with Tess yesterday had been a world apart from the one a week ago. Not only was *he* different, but so was she. Despite her loss of Abby and the traumatic drama in her little yellow house on Wednesday, Tess seemed to have a lighter heart now. Her smile came more easily, and her movements were calmer, less flustered.

She must have been so stressed by what she knew, he thought, *and so worried about what was going to happen when everything came out.* But all of that tension was gone when she hugged him good-bye yesterday.

And then there was Ava. Eight days ago there hadn't even *been* an Ava Lindsey. *Well, she was somewhere,* he thought with a smile, *but certainly not with me. Oh, my lovely Ava. Where did you come from? And can you be slipping away just as quickly as you appeared?* Had he actually been stupid enough to screw up the predetermined alignment of stars that Tess believed had put him and Ava in Barney's the previous Saturday? Had he really managed to derail something as huge as destiny? *When I said I wanted to be successful at something,* he thought, *this isn't what I had in mind.*

Leaning his head back against his chair, he tried to escape those thoughts by closing his eyes and picturing the dark green velvet curtain he'd been taught to visualize as a kid at nap time. The next thing he knew, one of the flight attendants was touching him on his shoulder.

"Excuse me, sir. We're getting ready to make our final approach into Charlotte. So I need you to close your tray and bring your seatback forward. Are you finished with your wine?"

"Yes, thank you," he said, looking at the full glass untouched, except for that first sip, after what had to have been about a ninety-minute sleep.

Once he'd straightened his seat and latched his tray shut, he turned to look across the two passengers next to him so he could see out the window. Not much daylight lingered, but enough for him to tell that they were flying over a dense landscape, with flecks of orange and yellow fall colors spreading across the trees.

"North Carolina is one of the most beautiful places on Earth!" Zoie had said after he'd told her about his plan to visit. "And I can't wait for you to see it!"

Having lived within the splendor of Seattle all his life, he didn't think she stood a chance of being right.

*****

Charlotte was a large, well-lit city like he was used to, and I-77 heading north was a standard interstate. So Isaiah didn't understand Zoie's concern about his getting lost until he'd been driving for close to an hour. At that point, darkness was fully entrenched as he exited I-77 and took the "slight right at Turnersburg Hwy / US-21 N" indicated in Zoie's directions. By then, all street lights had virtually disappeared.

About fifteen minutes later, he came to an intersection of several roads where he struggled to see street signs that matched Zoie's handwritten "turn right at N Carolina 901 S / E Memorial Hwy." He thought he was going the right way, but he was having trouble finding the landmarks she'd emphasized by printing and underlining each description. He was supposed to be watching for a "corner post," "a large clump of trees where the road curves right," and "a long expanse of trees on the left that goes on for two and a half miles and then gives way to wire fencing."

"She can't be serious," he said, speaking in full voice to himself and turning off the radio, as if the absence of sound would help him see better. He'd never experienced the phenomenon of one mile seeming like ten when driving in the pitch black on an unfamiliar rural road. And he suddenly understood how the nearest movie theater could easily be an hour away.

Certain he'd made a wrong turn somewhere, he pulled over and came to a stop, pushing the button for his hazard lights as he did so. Then he smiled at himself for the precaution because he hadn't passed another car or even seen another headlight since the "corner post" at least five miles back.

Removing his cell phone from his inside jacket pocket, he noted the time as almost seven thirty when he dialed Zoie's number.

"I was wondering how lost you were going to be before you called," she said without even saying hello first.

"The problem is that I don't even know how to tell you where I am."

"Okay. Get out of the car for a minute and I'll help you."

"I'm not sure what good that will do. There isn't anything here."

"Just get out of the car, Isaiah. Please. And turn off your headlights."

He did as he was told, feeling extremely uneasy in the darkness, like he was the only person remaining on the planet, or like he was about to be mugged.

"Now what do you see on the right-hand side of the car?" she asked him.

"Positively nothing."

She laughed. "Where are you standing?"

"By the driver's door."

"Well, close the door so there isn't any light then walk around to the other side of the car and look again. Scan your eyes across the darkness and things will start to lighten up. I promise."

He obediently followed her instructions, keeping one hand on the car to steady his footing in his leather loafers. After a few moments, he was amazed that his eyes did start to adjust, and a few signs of civilization began to emerge through the shadows.

"Do you see anything yet?"

"Yes. As a matter of fact, I do. I see a tall, round, white or gray structure sticking up out of the ground. Maybe three or four stories high."

She laughed again. "That's called a silo. It's a place to store grain, in case you care. Is there only one of those?"

"No. Looks like there are three of them."

"And is there a two-story house a little ways off to the left?"

"Uh, I see some lights, and I think it's a house. Yes, I see two floors of lights."

"Guess what?"

"I have no clue," he said.

"You're almost here."

"Seriously?"

"Just a few minutes away. Keep driving in the same direction, and in less than a mile those thick trees on the left side of the road will end and our fencing will begin. Our driveway will be the next one on your left, and we have every light on in the house, and on the porch too. You can't miss us."

"That's what they all say," he joked, climbing back inside the car.

Shortly after the trees gave way to the fencing, he did see the house come into view in the distance, and he spotted the final landmark—a huge yellow ribbon tied around the mailbox at the foot of the driveway.

He turned left and felt the car's tires crunching over the thick layer of crushed seashells she'd told him they used on the quarter-mile long driveway. She said this was a fairly common practice on southern farms to keep the dust under control. He hadn't asked why they didn't just use asphalt, but maybe the subject would come up while he was here.

When he finally reached the house where a wide, fully lit porch extended across the front and down the sides, Zoie came running out to meet him and showed him where to park. After he switched off the ignition and opened the driver's door, she literally pulled him out of the car and into her arms.

"Oh Isaiah!" she squealed from inside their embrace. "I absolutely cannot believe you're here!" Then she stepped back and looked up at him. "You know, I never used to think there was anything missing in this place. But since we got home from Washington I've been remembering Christmases and birthdays when Dad would do or say something that made me feel like something else should be happening. Of course, now I know that it wasn't some*thing* else but some*one*."

Isaiah opened the trunk and removed his bag and then put his free arm around Zoie as they walked up the front steps into the house.

"Where *is* Zeke, by the way?" he asked.

"He's around back, waiting for you." Then she gave him a quick tour of the small house, which was basically one huge all-purpose room plus two bedrooms and a bath. "We enlarged the end with the kitchen ten years ago by knocking out a wall to what used to be a third bedroom. But the bad news, Isaiah, is that the room where you'll be staying used to be a closet in that old bedroom. It was a bigger-than-average closet, but there's no window. I hope you don't mind."

Then she opened a door to a tiny space just big enough for a twin bed covered with a blue and white quilt, and a narrow three-drawer dresser. A tall lamp shaped like a lantern was on top of the dresser, and an oval mirror was mounted on the wall near the lamp.

"This will be perfect," he said, setting his bag on the floor.

"Yesterday, while we were still in Charlotte, I bought a couple bottles of shiraz for you and me *and* a bottle of cognac for Dad, just for this occasion. Why don't you go say hi to him, and I'll bring our drinks out."

"Let me help you."

"No. I'll take care of it," she said, pointing him down the hall to a door on the back side of the house.

He followed her instructions once again. And when he stepped outside he found himself on another portion of the wide covered porch, which he realized wrapped around the entire house, not just on three sides. At the far right end, a light was turned on in a ceiling fan mounted over wicker furniture arranged in a conversation area. But what caught his attention was coming from the *other* end of the porch—the rhythmic squeaking, back and forth, *of a rocking chair*!

Turning in that direction, he noticed another ceiling fan, but that light was off, leaving just the dim illumination from one of the house windows. An old man was clearly visible, however, sitting there in the rocker and looking at Isaiah as his feet pushed against the porch floor to keep the chair in motion.

Oh my God! The dream, Isaiah thought, moving closer, although this time the air was fresh and crisp rather than the sour smoky haze of the dream's oppressive room. And the man in the rocking chair was not a cadaverous stranger with a sunken face and unfocused expression. No, this man was smiling, and his cobalt eyes continued to dance despite the tears that he didn't even try to stop. *There's no way my subconscious could have made that dream up before I even knew anything about Zeke.* Feeling a little spooked, he dared to think her name. *Abby?*

As Isaiah approached him, Zeke remained in the rocking chair with open, extended arms. "I pretended to believe," he said, his voice broken with emotion, "that this would be possible some day. But I never *really* thought I'd live long enough to see it happen. And now here it is. Here *you are.* Welcome home, my son."

Isaiah caught his breath as he fell to his knees in the place where he was born. Letting himself be surrounded by his father's arms, he felt their strength, their nurturing, and the pure joy of a parent's affection minus any expectations. For a brilliant, kaleidoscopic moment, he was a boy again. And instead of being dismantled in the dream, the puzzle was fully assembled this time, leaving no more room for blustery admonitions or scary mountains without names. Just love—undemanding, unadulterated love.

CHAPTER EIGHTEEN

Voices in the next room awakened him, but he couldn't make out what they were saying over the hum of the fan circulating the air in the former closet where he'd been sleeping. He checked his watch and saw that it was four thirty. Then he remembered that he hadn't changed the setting from Seattle time. Even when he added in the three-hour time difference, seven thirty was still a bit on the early side for him.

He'd stayed up with Zeke and Zoie until almost midnight while they toasted each other and began catching up on all their missing family years. Then he'd been unable to close his eyes while his rational mind tried to wrap around that dream. The clairvoyance of the whole thing was disturbing. He recalled Tess again and her insistence that there weren't any coincidences. So what had that dream been? Some sort of extraterrestrial DVD playing in his head? *One that just happened to match the scene on the porch last night?* He smiled in the dark, dismissing his thoughts because he was getting a headache trying to come up with a logical explanation.

After that, he'd obviously slept straight through for nearly seven hours, something that virtually never happened with him. Feeling unusually well-rested, he flipped on the lantern light on top of the dresser and watched himself in the mirror as he combed through his hair with his fingers. Then he opened the door and walked into the kitchen, wearing the navy blue striped flannel pajamas and the sheepskin slippers that Zeke had insisted he put on.

The room was warm and smelled tantalizing from something already baking in the oven and from the wood burning in the living room fireplace. Zeke was seated at the long, narrow farmhouse style dining table, drinking from a huge mug and reading a newspaper. Zoie was at the stove, layering slices of bacon in a cast-iron skillet.

"Good morning, everybody."

"Good morning to you too, Isaiah," Zeke said, leaning back in his chair and grinning.

Zoie turned around and wiped her hands on her apron and then raised herself on her tiptoes to kiss him on the cheek. "I can't tell you how amazing it was," she said, "to wake up this morning knowing that my *brother* was in this house."

"You're not tired of me yet?" he asked, giving her a hug and then heading for the coffee pot and mug rack on the counter.

"Not yet. But ask me again after breakfast."

When he'd fixed his coffee, he sat down at the table across from Zeke. "Is that today's paper?"

"Yeah. Why?"

"Well, I think it's pretty impressive that someone delivers the newspaper so early way out here, especially on a Sunday morning."

"Folks 'round here have to get up earlier 'n *this*, boy, every day a the week. Gotta feed chickens, milk cows, chop wood. Somebody might as well deliver papers too."

"*Dad*," Zoie said. "Don't be mean."

"Oh, all right. You're no fun at all, girl. Truth is, Son, I took the truck to the BP station 'bout half an hour ago and *bought* the paper."

"I see. And what about feeding the chickens, milking the cows, and chopping the wood?"

"I'm sure somebody's doing all that somewhere close by. Here," Zeke said, pushing the paper into the center of the table. "What section you want?"

*****

After breakfast, when they'd each taken turns showering in the small bathroom, Zoie filled two travel mugs with fresh coffee as she prepared to take Isaiah on a walk around the property.

"When you get back," Zeke said, "I got something I wanna talk about."

Zoie looked concerned. "What is it, Dad? We can go later."

"Like I said, it's something I wanna talk about *when you get back*. Honest to Betsey, girl! I swear you're gonna worry yourself into old age

279

one a these days." Then he shuffled down the hall and out the door to the back porch.

"He's probably right," Zoie said when the door had closed. "I do worry about him."

"I know, and he obviously loves you for it. But he's a tough old guy, Zoie, with a lot of life still in him."

"I hope so. I know the day will come eventually, but I can't imagine him not being here."

"So don't think about it. Come on. I thought you wanted to take me on a tour."

They left the house by the front steps and followed a stone walkway around to the side where he'd parked his rental car and where Zeke waved to them from his rocker on the back porch. A few yards later, the stone walkway dissolved into a well-worn footpath that meandered along the edge of the farm's sweet potato acreage.

"The old guesthouse used to be over there," Zoie said, pointing to a spot down the path and to the left that was now tilled ground.

"What happened to it?"

"Dad knocked it down after Abby left. I didn't even know there'd *been* a guesthouse until I was about ten, when some neighbors who were over mentioned it."

"Why do you think he knocked it down?"

"He told me he couldn't bear the memories of her that ran over him every time he looked at that little house."

"Boy. That was some kind of love."

She just nodded and moved off the subject by switching her remarks to the history around the tobacco and cotton crops that used to be the farm's business. She directed Isaiah's focus to land in the distance that had once been part of the farm.

"We held onto these last fifty acres after we sold that section," she said. "But we lease almost everything, except the forested area over there and two acres that include the house. Our tenant farmers grow these sweet potatoes, corn, and a few other crops. They give us a small percentage of what they make, and Dad still likes to help them out with the planting and harvesting as much as he can."

"At the risk of getting too personal, Zoie, are you guys doing okay?"

"If you mean financially, we're holding on. Some years are easier than others, but we've paid off the mortgage on the farm, and we've never needed much else to keep us happy. Land is an amazing asset, Isaiah. It not only feeds your body but your soul as well."

"I think I'm beginning to understand that," he said. "But now that we're all in the same family, I want you to know that I'm in a position to help out. In fact, I *want* to help out, if there's anything I can do to make your lives easier."

"Thank you." She linked her arm in his and looked up at him as they continued to walk. "I do appreciate that, but we're fine. Really." He studied her face, trying to read between her words. "I promise to call you, though," she added, "should there ever be a need."

He patted her hand as they reached the base of a large hill that seemed oddly out of place in the middle of all the flat land.

"This is Haven Hill," Zoie said as if reading his mind again. "Dad built this, with the help of his friends, when I was in elementary school. Dirt and rocks were hauled in and packed down for months until the size and shape of the hill were perfect, and then everything in the mound was allowed to settle. More was added gradually for another year to make sure the thing wouldn't collapse. Then Dad and his little crew put in those brick steps up the side, installed the irrigation system, and planted the grass. All of that took *another* year or more. But he wanted a place high up where he could see all of his land, where he could watch the sunrises and sunsets and the weather approaching over the trees, or where he could just sit."

"This is really incredible," Isaiah said as they were climbing the steps. "Where did he learn how to do something like this?"

"Oh, he had lots of help. Not all of Dad's contemporaries stayed in farming, you know. Several brothers and a couple of sisters of friends he grew up with went on to study geology, architecture, landscape engineering, and various other sciences that came in handy when word of Dad's plan started spreading. Some general contractors in the area even got wind of the idea and called us themselves, offering their assistance. *Everyone* wanted to help," she said as she and Isaiah neared the top of the steps. "And the project sort of became a community-wide challenge—and a mutually shared accomplishment when finished. After we built the gazebo, right before I turned thirteen, people started asking us if they could get *married* up here," Zoie added when they reached the hill's crest and the large white screened in gazebo came fully into view.

"You're kidding!"

"No, I'm not. Our little farm has hosted *dozens* of weddings now. Folks don't usually want much in the way of decorations because of the steps, but a few flowers and ribbons are all that's needed anyway to transform the place, once you add in the bridal party. I'll show you the scrapbook later, if you'd like to see it."

"I would. Very much."

As the two of them stood on top of Haven Hill, Zoie introduced him to all 360 degrees of the farm—the boundaries, the history, and the neighbors, all of which had been linked together since before the Civil War. Isaiah was struck by the difference in perspective from such a height, being able to see everything so clearly for miles in every direction. The stopovers on Snoqualmie Pass with Sinclair came to mind as a comparison. But he preferred today's sense of peace and empowerment to those feelings of intimidation he'd ended up experiencing as a kid. He wasn't sure how much genetics had to do with the difference, but he suspected a good bit.

"Your father is one extraordinary guy," he said. "And I'm sort of bowled over by his vision and the courage he must have needed when he first started talking about building a hill like this in the middle of his farm."

"He is definitely a character. But folks around here have always looked up to him, trusting in his ideas, no matter how crazy they might sound at first. And, by the way, he's *your*—"

"I know. He's my father too. Hope you can understand that those words don't automatically roll off my tongue yet."

"Yes, I do understand, Isaiah."

She led him inside the gazebo, where there were two white wrought iron chaise lounges side by side, each with blue and white striped seat covers. Next to the lounges was a matching wrought iron table with two chairs.

"Please sit down," she said, taking one of the chairs at the table herself. "I have a confession to make to you." He sat down with a surge of uneasiness, not at all certain that he was ready to assimilate anything else that would qualify as a confession. "I just need to get this off my chest," she went on, "to both explain and to prevent any misunderstandings."

"I certainly don't want to interrupt you," he said, "but I'm perfectly comfortable with who we are and how this is progressing. There *aren't* any problems or misunderstandings, as far as I'm concerned."

"I know. But this is more for me, so *I* can fully move on—and that requires my telling you something."

"Okay. I'm all yours."

"Thanks," she said, looking down at her fidgeting fingers in her lap. "When Dad showed me the letter from Sinclair ten years ago and told me the story about Abby, he also explained that Sinclair was a close friend who'd been very helpful to Abby throughout the years. So I started doing a little research on the Seattle Mellington family." Isaiah cocked his head and raised his eyebrows. "You're right," she said. "I should probably be ashamed of myself for the espionage. But Dad and I were really into computers by then, and there was this new thing called Google that gave people access to all sorts of information online, including information about other people. And through my searches, I found out about *you*."

"*Me*? What could possibly be in there about me? I've never *done* anything."

"Ah, but that's not true. When we get back to the house, I'll Google your name and show you. You've been in the newspaper a lot with all of your charity activities, and I even saw your engagement announcement. What ever happened with that, by the way?"

"Divine intervention," he said, taken off guard by how comfortable that phrase felt.

"Oh," she said with a wry smile. "Well *anyway*, in addition to your charity work, I discovered that several of the articles you've written have been picked up by various publications over the years."

"Yeah, but I was never paid more than one hundred dollars for anything—and no one ever read them."

"Oh, Isaiah, you *so* underestimate yourself. I *love* your writing. And if you had a Web site where people could communicate with you, you'd be surprised at how many other people love it too—and you'd probably be a very famous guy right now. Your ideas and political commentary have really been quite fascinating and provocative."

He laughed, shook his head, and gave her a bow while still seated. "Well, I thank you very much, my sweet and only fan, even though you are clearly delusional," he said, using Ava's favorite word and hearing her voice as he did.

"Isaiah, I know I'm stumbling around with this, but I'm really trying to tell you something."

"Sorry."

"Whoo boy," she said. "This is harder than I thought. What I'm trying to say is that I studied you for so many years because I knew I was going to meet you one day. And I created a little fantasy in my mind that kept me happy, one in which I thought you were going to be the … well … the man I'd been waiting to find."

Isaiah sat there looking at her lovely, ageless face, with her words tumbling around in his head until they came to rest, in order, in an uncomfortably recognizable sentence.

"Oh," he said. "Uh-oh."

"Right. Uh-oh. When I first saw you the day Dad and I arrived in that limo, I was meeting a man I'd been following forever, it seemed. I was so certain that I knew where things were going. And then, of course, I met Ava. And then, of course, I found out you were my twin brother, for God's sake. Imagine my surprise. So things have been sort of muddled for me, and I wanted you to know why I might have been a bit short, or crisp, or rude during our first couple of days in Kettle Falls. I need to apologize to Ava too, and I plan to write her a letter. But I wanted to get this conversation over with first. And now I feel pretty foolish. Dad doesn't know anything about this, and I'd rather he didn't, if that's okay."

Isaiah stood up and then lifted her to her feet, wrapping his arms around her.

"Dear, dear Zoie," he said, resting the side of his face on top of her head. "You have nothing to apologize for. I think it's very sweet—and I'm very flattered—that you had me in mind that way. And I never even noticed any crisp or rude behavior from you. You know, under the circumstances, I think we should both give ourselves a break. We have a lot to get used to here, and a lot of years that need to be merged together. And," he said, stepping back from her, cupping her face in his hands and using his thumbs to stem the soft flow of tears down her cheeks, "I'm overwhelmed that you actually read and even liked my articles. No one's ever told me that before."

"Well, they should have," she replied, taking a tissue from her jacket pocket and blowing her nose. Then they each put an arm around the other's back and left the gazebo, standing out in the open once again on Haven Hill, overlooking the land that was in their blood. "And if you don't start writing again," she said, "I'm going to beat you up. After all, I *am* the oldest, you know."

*****

Zeke was sitting on the hearth, putting more logs in the fireplace, when Zoie and Isaiah returned to the house.

"What do you think a my hill, Son?" he asked, looking up right away.

"I *think* it's an engineering wonder, and I really can't believe what you did out there."

"Me either. Must a been out a my damn fool head. Never mind about that, though. I made a new pot a coffee, so you two just go sit down at the table. I'll be right there."

Without any resistance, Zoie and Isaiah rinsed out their travel mugs and refilled them with fresh coffee and the sweet cream that Isaiah was finding quite addicting. Then they sat down at the table across from each other and waited while Zeke went into his bedroom. He emerged holding two white letter-sized envelopes, stopped at the kitchen counter to fill his own coffee cup, and sat down at the end of the table, with Isaiah and Zoie on either side of him. When he'd taken a sip of his coffee, he slid an envelope in front of each of them.

"Don't touch those yet," he said, stopping their hands in midair. "You might a figured this out already, Isaiah, from all that stuff Tess gave you. But then, maybe not either. So here's what it is. Quick and short."

"That's the same thing, Dad," Zoie said.

"What is?"

"Quick and short. Those two words mean the same thing."

"Oh for Pete's sake, girl. They do not. One means fast, and one means small. You wouldn't say the fox ran *short* 'cross the road, would you?"

"He has a point, Zoie," Isaiah said.

"But—"

Zeke held up his hands, a palm facing each of his children. "Stop. I'm here to talk 'bout those envelopes. Simple. How's *that*, girl? One word. *Simple*."

Zoie sat with her hands folded on top of the table. She was obviously trying not to laugh as she looked at her father, but she didn't say anything.

There's nothing simple about any of this, Isaiah thought, eyeing the envelopes with trepidation, *or quick or short either. But what could there possibly be that he hasn't told us already?*

"When Abby left San Francisco," Zeke proceeded, as if he'd been inside Isaiah's head, "the Whitmores gave her a lot a money to get out a town and go as far away as possible."

"She wrote about that in her journals and letters," Isaiah said. "But she never said how *much* money."

"Enough to take care a her for the rest a her life, if she'd stayed in a regular life. A real fortune in 1948."

"Dad," Zoie said, leaning in over the table, "how *much* money?"

"Twenty thousand, that's how much—in 1948 dollars."

Zoie was transfixed as she looked across at Isaiah. "I can't even imagine how wealthy the Whitmores must have been to have an extra twenty thousand dollars lying around in 1948 to give to Abby."

"To *bribe* her, you mean," Zeke said, his face beginning to flush. "They scared her to death and bought her baby."

"So, what *did* she do with the twenty thousand dollars?" Isaiah asked, trying to shift Zeke's focus off the Whitmores, whose very name still inflamed the old man after six decades.

"At first it went in the bank in DC. She took out a few hundred when she came down to Charlotte. A few hundred went a long way in those days, you know. Then, after we learned how they'd tricked her, we drove up to DC together and got the rest a the money out. We put it in another savings account in a bank in Charlotte. Later, when we found out you kids was coming, she insisted on changing the account into my name. Before she left, she told me she wanted me to use the money to take care a *you*, girl," he said, looking at Zoie. "But I didn't wanna touch it. So it just sat there. One bank bought that one, and then another bank bought that one, and another bought that one, and on and on. But I kept getting reports on the money, so I just kept leaving it there."

"And *then*," Zoie said softly, her eyes widening as she seemed to be remembering something, "you insisted that we go into Charlotte early on the day we left for Kettle Falls. You told me you wanted to be there when the bank opened so you could have them working on part of the farm refinancing while we were gone."

"Well, that was true—kinda. At least, that's what I been hoping," Zeke said. "They know me real well there at that bank after all this time, and after you told me about Isaiah's call that Saturday morning, I called 'em. They said they'd have everything ready for me that Monday morning, so that's why we stopped by on the way to the airport."

"Wait a minute!" Isaiah said, directing his attention to Zoie. "*What* farm refinancing? You just told me an hour ago that everything was fine with you guys."

Zeke held up his hands again. "Hush. Both of you. Just open your envelopes now and be quiet."

Zoie was anxious but meticulous as she opened hers, while Isaiah's was completely mangled within seconds. But the contents of the envelopes were identical—checks for $109,000, their equal halves of the $218,000 that Abby's original deposit had become over sixty years.

"You can use yours for anything you want, Son. And you can too, girl. But I was hoping you might want to use a little bit for the things we been talking 'bout doing 'round here."

Now that Zeke was finally ready for their commentary, both Zoie and Isaiah were speechless.

*****

Within the confines of his small sleeping room, at five thirty on Monday morning, Isaiah was reflecting on the way time moved with a difference cadence on a farm. The open spaces and clean air injected an energy that was vital for the long days. And the nights, which were so unbelievably free of all sound except an occasional late-season cricket or the wind rushing through the trees, induced a sleep unlike any he'd ever experienced.

After shedding his flannel pajamas and dressing in his jeans and sweater, he pushed his feet into his loaner sheepskin slippers and then quietly made his way to the restroom, hoping he wouldn't awaken Zeke and Zoie. He washed his face and brushed his teeth then managed to make a pot of coffee without banging anything. When he'd poured one of the clean travel mugs halfway up with coffee, he filled the rest with sweet cream from the refrigerator and snapped on the mug's cap. Then he replaced his slippers with the socks and sneakers borrowed from Zeke that were beside the front door, slipped on his bomber jacket, and took his coffee out into the misty charm of an early morning on a farm.

As he walked around the house and onto the path toward Haven Hill, the sun was up just enough over the trees for him to see where he was going but not enough to intrude upon the peacefulness. He wondered how different his life would have been if this was where he'd grown up—if he'd awakened every morning to absorb the energy of land that belonged to his family for as far as he could see in every direction. And he wondered how different things would have been if he'd shared that little house with Zeke, along with his resilient, insightful twin sister.

There must be something incredibly powerful about sharing a womb and a birth canal, he thought, because he and Zoie were already connecting in eerie sorts of ways. Their unspoken sensitivities toward each other seemed almost paranormal, such as his suspicions the previous morning that she and Zeke were having some sort of problem that he might help resolve. That suspicion had escalated when she'd mentioned their plan to refinance the farm. Further discussion, once the shock of Abby's money had worn off, had revealed that the planned refinancing had not been due to any financial problem but rather for an addition to the house. They wanted to put in a second bath and renovate the kitchen and existing bath.

Since the estimates they'd been collecting were less than half of Zoie's share of Abby's money, any refinancing was no longer going to be necessary. *No wonder they're both sleeping in so soundly.* And the remainder, if invested soundly, would provide a cushion against unpredictable seasonal downturns—a security they'd never had before. Consequently, Isaiah's offer to turn his half of the money over to them had been graciously declined.

After meandering down the path for about twenty minutes, slowly sipping his coffee, he reached the base of Haven Hill and then climbed the steps at a measured pace. If he'd been mesmerized by the view the day before in the full light of day, he was spellbound by the scene at sunrise. Trails of white smoke slithered skyward in the still air from Zeke and Zoie's white chimney and the red brick of their neighbor's on the adjacent farm. Awakening congregations of birds were warbling and twittering in competing choruses from branches and bushes, and the yellow and pink hues from the breaking sun sprayed across the brightening sky over square, tilled patches of farm land below.

Sitting down on the grass in front of the gazebo, he rested his arms on bent knees and surveyed the landscape, beginning to understand what he'd missed and feeling determined not to miss anymore. He would need to come here often from now on, maybe once a month, as part of a new routine. He wanted to play some sort of role in the new construction and renovations, providing whatever assistance he could, or just being around to talk things over. The existing house had not been part of his life, but the new version could be, if he made the effort. And he wanted to be with Zeke as much as possible, recognizing the precious quality, and most likely the limited quantity, of that remaining time. Then, of course, there was his part of Abby's money. *What am I going to do with it? I certainly don't need it. What would Abby do with it?* And as he thought back on everything he'd learned about her over the past week, the seed of an idea began to germinate.

He also thought about Rosa. Somehow he needed to find a way to include her in his life as well, assuring her that both he and Zoie sincerely wanted to build a sibling relationship with her, if she was willing to let them in. *Maybe she could fly out to North Carolina when the new addition is finished. Perhaps everyone could come to Seattle, but that would mean two more long connecting flight days for Zeke. Maybe it would be easier to get from Charlotte to San Francisco—probably connecting in Atlanta, which is only a short hop from Charlotte. How about Thanksgiving or Christmas in San Francisco? That might be a good place to start, for all of us. Mother too.*

Finishing off the last swallow of his coffee, he got up and took one more look around the farm from this literal bird's-eye view, noting that the sun was already up far enough to have chased all the lingering shadows away. Then he began descending the stairs down the side of Haven Hill, hanging on to the railing, which felt a little wobbly. *Hey! This is something I could pay to have fixed*, he thought, already starting a mental list of how he could help. *Maybe I could even learn how to fix it myself.*

By the time he got back to the house, Zoie and Zeke were up and in the same places they'd been the previous morning—Zeke at the table reading the newspaper and Zoie at the stove, this time making pancakes.

"Hi!" she said, turning around and greeting him with open arms as usual, spatula in hand.

"Nice walk?" Zeke asked, not looking up from the paper.

"Hi," Isaiah said, kissing Zoie on the forehead. "And yes, the walk was great. This place is really spectacular, especially early like this. I've never been a fan of mornings before eight o'clock. But I think that could change around here."

"Would *have* to, Son, if you wanna stay very long."

As Isaiah began walking over to the counter to refill his coffee, his eye was drawn to a framed painting on the living room wall. Moving closer, the pastel oil of a field, with a hill in the middle and a white gazebo on top, became clear.

"This is a beautiful piece of artwork," he said. "Did you have this done after you finished building everything?"

"Nope," Zeke said. "You got it backward. Christmas 1948, when Abby was staying with us, and Andy was still alive, and life 'round here hadn't turned to crap yet, she gave me that as a gift. Said she found it in a shop by her hotel in Charlotte. I'd already told her 'bout my dream of that hill, and she somehow came up with that painting. When we finally started building the thing, that's what we used as our model. Came pretty damn close, didn't we?"

As Isaiah gently let his fingers touch the brushstrokes, he was deeply moved by the connection of past to present and the ease with which Abby's essence had been sustained in this house.

"It's amazing," he said, "how something simple like this painting can keep stories and memories alive forever."

"That's why it's hanging there, boy. Wouldn't make much sense otherwise, would it, since I got the real hill outside?"

Isaiah smiled and sat down beside Zeke, patting the old man on his shoulder. "You know, speaking of that hill, I was thinking about lots of things up there in the peace and quiet, and I'd like to run some ideas by both of you."

"Later, boy," Zeke said, turning his head and fixing his kind blue eyes on his son. "We don't talk 'bout nothing 'cept breakfast before breakfast in this house. Here," he added, pushing the paper in front of Isaiah. "What section you want?"

*****

By the end of the day, both Zeke and Zoie were making lists of things they'd been putting off doing around the farm, exclusive of the renovations and the new addition, for which Isaiah could be responsible. They'd also decided that Thanksgiving would be better as a first gathering for the whole crazy-quilt family than Christmas.

"I think we should ease into this," Zoie said, "and Christmas might require a little more time for Rosa. If *you'd* like to fly out here for the holidays by yourself, though, we'd love it."

Holding that as a possibility, they'd called Rosa about the idea of having Thanksgiving in San Francisco. After hearing an unexpectedly positive reaction from her and enjoying a warm conversation, Zoie began shopping online for the least complicated flight arrangements while Isaiah reached his mother on his cell phone. She sounded a little forlorn, but Isaiah was comforted by the fact that she was at his house and by the song in her voice when he told her he'd be home Wednesday night.

"And will Ava be with you?" she'd asked.

"Mother, that's the third time you've asked me—and the answer is still no. So stop pushing."

"Okay, dear. But I'm going to keep my fingers crossed, no matter what you say."

After he'd finished speaking with Sarah, his next call was to Tess.

"Hey, there! This is Isaiah."

"Oh my goodness. What a surprise! I'm so happy to hear from you, dear. Where are you?"

"I'm still in North Carolina. But I'll be flying back in a couple of days."

"Will you be coming to Kettle Falls?"

"Only long enough to get my car. But I'll be back next month for sure, and there's something I want to talk to you about." After hearing a heavy sigh on the other end of the line, he added, "This is a *good* thing, Tess, and something I'd like you to help me with, if you want to."

"Oh. Okay," she said, her voice uplifted again. "What is it?"

"Well, it turns out that I've come into a little bit of extra money, and I'd like to use it to start a foundation in Abby's name."

"Really? What sort of foundation?"

"I was thinking of something related to her hospice work. A facility. Something we could build."

"Seriously? A whole building?"

"It would take time and a lot of fundraising, and the ideas are just beginning to formulate in my head. But I've had a lot of experience with that sort of thing, and I was hoping you might be interested in helping me get things started."

"Oh my yes, Isaiah! I would *love* to help you. And I know plenty of other people who would too."

"Terrific. I'll call you when I get home, and we'll set up a time in early December for me to come to Kettle Falls for our first planning session. Meanwhile, start jotting down ideas, and I'll do the same."

"Okay. My mind is spinning already. You *really* want to try to build a whole building for hospice care?"

"Yeah, I do. Maybe a place for people who can't afford to pay for that kind of care on their own. A really nice place that feels like a home."

"Ah," she said. "What a lovely thought. Perhaps there could even be a little library in there somewhere. I've been so worried about what to do with all these *Life* magazines. I just can't bring myself to throw them away."

"Well, I'm sure we can figure something out, and that's exactly the sort of detail I'd like you to work on. Start making a list of what you think Abby would want in a place that she would build herself, if she were still here with us." He could hear her sniffling on the other end of the line. "Are you all right, Tess?"

"Yes, Isaiah," she said, blowing her nose. "Better than I've been in weeks. Thank you."

He'd spent the next several hours with Zeke and Zoie, talking, laughing, and taking a walk over to the forested section of the farm. But now they were both napping after a big lunch, and Isaiah had one more phone call to make. So he went out on the front porch and sat down in the cushioned wood swing suspended by heavy chains from the porch ceiling. A few moments of swaying back and forth didn't make him feel any less anxious, so he just took a deep breath and dialed Ava's cell number.

"Hi there," she said after three rings.

"Hi." The sound of her voice was like a back rub. "What have you been up to?" he asked.

"Well, I'm at work right now, which is pretty much where I've been since you left."

"Should I call back later?"

"No, this is fine. Things are slow at the moment. So how's the visit going?"

"Unbelievable. More than I ever expected, and I can't wait to tell you all about it."

"That'll be nice."

"I'd like to fly back on Wednesday," he said, trying to ignore the notable absence of enthusiasm in her voice, "but I thought I'd better check your schedule before making any reservations."

There was a pause before she responded. "Thank you, Isaiah. I appreciate that. On Wednesday, though, I'm supposed to work the three-to-midnight shift."

"Um ... not good," he said, thumbing through all of the itinerary options he'd printed out using Zoie's computer. "Looks like I can't get to Spokane before one thirty whether I connect in Minneapolis or Denver, and that assumes there won't be any delays. This is going to be a problem for you."

There was another pause. "I'll work it out, Isaiah. Don't worry. Just let me know when you're coming in, and I'll be there to pick you up."

"I can take a limo."

"No. I promised I'd pick you up, and that's what I'm going to do."

He didn't know which way to lean. Should he push harder to take a limo so she wouldn't have to rearrange her work schedule for him again?

Or should he be thankful about her picking him up, even though her being late for work would most likely cause problems for her and raise an issue between them? Either way, *her work* was central to the discourse, which answered the main question on his mind. *She isn't thrilled about this relationship going any further.*

"Fine," he said, doing his best not to sound disappointed or upset with her. "I'll call you with my flight number and arrival time as soon as I make the reservation."

"Okay. Enjoy the rest of your visit."

"Thanks, Ava. So … how's my Jag doing?"

There was another pause. "I think it misses you."

*****

That evening, after devouring Zoie's mouthwatering beef stew and cornbread, he sat with her and Zeke on the front porch and was gratified to observe that they were talking more about the future than the past. They were making plans, trying to imagine what Thanksgiving would be like in San Francisco, and batting around ideas for the addition to the house. Certainly there would be more conversations about the past and lingering issues yet to be settled, but those conversations would now be part of their future together. And as they said an early goodnight to each other shortly after nine o'clock, Isaiah felt a hopeful sense of normalcy begin to settle in around them.

They would have one more day together, and then he would leave on Wednesday. But this time they all knew that he'd be back soon. And they had occasions to anticipate where they would be together, which surrounded them with a protective buffer of comfort and peace. There might be brief periods of time from now on when they would be away from one another, but they would never really be separated emotionally again.

Lying on his bed after he heard them close their bedroom doors and switch off their lights, Isaiah's thoughts turned to Ava. *She's decided to move on. She's decided to move on.* The words kept playing over and over in his head like a recorded chant on repeat. To turn them off, he began focusing on his next trip to Kettle Falls in a month, for his meeting with Tess. But Ava immediately crept back in.

She will have had more time to think by then, which might be a good thing—or maybe not. If they were really meant to be together, though—if they were going to find in each other the partner that had been so elusive in both of their lives—he would need to let events unfold in their own time, without pushing her. *This isn't over. It just can't be. Have a little faith!* The unfamiliar phrase caused him to sit up in bed. *Where did that come from?*

"Probably the same place as the damn dream," he whispered in the darkness. But then he began reflecting one more time on all that had happened during the last week. And given the upheaval, he wasn't surprised that his mind was an amalgamation of novel thoughts and images.

Closing his eyes, he tried to visualize Abby walking the grounds of the farm, just as he'd done earlier that day. He imagined what the little guesthouse must have looked like, especially at night, with a light shining through the window as she sat inside writing. He also thought about her internal struggles—how fierce the battle must have been to overcome the awful things that had happened to her. But then she'd also faced the dilemma of deciding between a quiet, peaceful life with a good and gentle man like Zeke versus the life defined by powerful voices exhorting her to follow her "calling." And no matter how many mistakes she'd made, how far off the path she'd veered, or how appealing an alternate choice might have been, she'd never allowed those unrelenting voices to be marginalized or mitigated. She'd continued to let them speak to her, however deep in the background she might have pushed them at times, until, at last, they were the only things she'd allowed herself to hear.

"What was it that Father Moynihan said at the funeral?" he asked, still whispering to himself.

> *Her life's mission and purpose only became clear to her when she stopped trying to define and direct them herself and began, instead, to listen ... In the end, the simple lesson of Sister Abby's life is that no matter where your life has taken you or how old you've become, the time is never too late to pursue your destiny, to use your God-given gifts to achieve the purpose for which you've been placed on this earth. But first you must be willing to listen ...*

Then he remembered Zoie urging him to start writing again. He'd only been thinking about that suggestion in terms of his novel, but now he was acquiring a different view. Throwing off his covers, he pushed his bare feet into Zeke's slippers, closed the door to his closet room, and turned on the dresser lamp. Then he took his laptop out of his bag and powered on, hoping that transferring the jumble of words from his head into notes in his computer would be enough to let him fall asleep. In a new, unnamed Word document, he began typing.

Despite my Catholic education from kindergarten through high school, I've been adrift from the church for many years. And from my lengthy, lapsed perspective, the concepts of destiny, a "calling," a "life's purpose" are new to me and need to be researched and studied. They also need to be explored in the context of the past ten days, which have virtually upended everything and everyone I've ever known.

How could something as theoretically significant as destiny, or "a purpose," be real, if someone is able to reach middle age without ever running into either one? Or is there another element at work here? Is this a question of the cart before the horse? Is there something being overlooked that needs to come *first*? Could that "something" be *faith*? And does that faith need to be in place before a destiny, or a calling, or a life's purpose can get through? Is that what I'm supposed to be learning from this? Is that what I'm being asked to believe?

And what is the difference between faith and belief anyway? Is faith something you *have*, and belief something you *do*? First you have faith. Then you believe in possibilities. Then life's purpose is revealed.

Of course, there's always the chance that I'm overthinking everything. Maybe this isn't complex at all but is rather about faith alone. Faith. Do we view that word as disconnected, as separate and set apart, something we call upon to operate independently from the tangible realities of our lives? We have faith in Column A, but we live in Column B when, in fact, Column A must *overlay* Column B in order for our lives to have any meaning. Is that the formula?

Ten days ago there was not a shred of purpose or direction in my life, which is seventy-five percent over, by the way, assuming the best. But then came Abby and her story, which is now part of *my* story. And if Abby's life isn't a lesson in faith, I don't know what is. So I'm trying to let what's happened speak to me. Still, I'm a long way from believing anything, but I am finally feeling like some things might be possible.

Yes, my perspective on absolutely everything is changing, and I am going to start listening. Perhaps faith won't be far behind.

He sat for a moment, reading what he'd written, and he felt that at least the first wave had been captured. No other words seemed to be hammering to get out of his head yet—a perfect opportunity to try sleep again. So he clicked on "File" and then on "Save As." He paused briefly before naming the document "Faith.A Separation.Draft."

*****

On Wednesday morning, Isaiah, Zoie, and Zeke were all up by three thirty since Isaiah's flight was leaving at six forty-five. Zoie prepared a large travel mug—half coffee and half sweet cream—for his drive to the airport. "And you can just bring the mug back," she said, "on your next visit."

That sense of continuity, along with all the plans they had in place, strengthened them for the moment of Isaiah's departure. As he stood beside his rental car, however, holding on to each of them individually at first and then both of them together, small cracks appeared in their collective composure. But they never stopped smiling as they went through one more round of cheek kisses before he slid behind the wheel and closed the door.

Through the open window, he held their hands, promised to call them as soon as he arrived home, and then said good-bye. While steering the car down the seashell driveway, he watched them in the rearview mirror, standing arm in arm and waving to him. A swell of emotion caught in his throat as he felt the pull of family and home being left behind. *But it's only for a little while this time,* he thought. *Just a little while.*

On the way out of Harmony, he couldn't help but notice that Zoie's original reference points, such as the "corner post" and the various "clumps of trees," were, even in the early morning darkness, so easily identifiable that he wondered how he could have ever missed them in the first place. And the drive to the airport seemed to be shorter too, everything made easier and less complicated by the fact that he now knew where he was going.

*****

Isaiah's flight landed in Spokane shortly before two o'clock on Wednesday afternoon. By the time he'd made his way to the departure level, which was generally less congested than arrivals and where he'd agreed to meet Ava, another half hour had passed. Standing on the curb outside the terminal, he didn't see the Jag, so he called Ava's cell.

"Are you here?" she asked, answering on the first ring.

"I am. How about you?"

"The police made me circle around again, but I'll be right there. Just watch for a silver Jaguar."

"Right. Thanks for the heads-up."

Moments after he slipped his phone back in his pocket, he saw her heading in his direction, trying to navigate around other cars that had stopped to let people off. So he walked down to meet her, waving his arm over his head to make sure she saw him. After easing out of the moving traffic behind her, she pulled as close to the curb as she could get, turned off the engine, and virtually threw the driver's door open to run to him.

He dropped his bag to the ground, surprised to see her so excited, and watched her blonde pouf of curls bouncing as she raced toward him. And when she entered his arms, wrapping her obvious joy around him, he pressed her close to him, inhaling her fragrance and not wanting to let go of her, ever. But a police whistle broke the spell, and when they stepped apart from each other and saw that they were both crying, they started laughing.

"We must look ridiculous," she said.

"Speak for yourself, woman," he replied, putting one arm around her shoulders while taking the keys from her and popping the trunk open with his other hand. "I'm completely comfortable and fully in touch with my emotions."

"Yeah, right," she said as he picked up his bag and then came to a stop, staring inside the trunk.

"What are *those*?" he asked.

"Looks like a couple of suitcases to me," she said.

"Yours?"

"No, the mayor's. Of *course* they're mine."

"But I thought you decided you didn't want to see me anymore."

"Maybe you're not as in touch as you think you are, Isaiah Benjamin Mellington."

The police whistle blew again. "C'mon folks!" he shouted, seemingly at everyone. "Get moving."

"What happened?" he asked once they were inside the car. "Why did you change your mind?"

"How do you know I changed my mind?"

"Well, I just—"

"I took a leave of absence," she interrupted. "Tess came over to my house yesterday for a glass of wine and told me about your idea for a hospice center in Abby's name, which I think is amazing. And she said you'd be coming back to Kettle Falls in a month to start planning things. So I figured I'd have a ride home at that point, in case we can't stand each other by then." After several moments of silence, she asked, "Is this too scary for you?"

"I don't know what to say," he replied, trying to split his attention between Ava and weaving his way out of the airport traffic mess. "You really caught me off guard."

"Good," she said, grinning broadly.

"Where are we going?" he asked, glancing over at her as he slowed down to avoid a merging car.

"Well, I recommend I-90, unless you know a better way to get to Seattle."

"Honest to God, Ava, I guess I'm a little shell-shocked. I *really* didn't expect this."

"But are you *happy*? That's the question."

"You'd better believe I am!" he said, reaching across the console and taking her hand. "I can't even tell you how much!"

"Me too. Now, how many hours will this drive take us?"

"About seven. We could stay over in Spokane and start early in the morning, if you'd prefer."

"No, I say we keep going. We should be there by about ten tonight, right?"

"Right. And we need to call my mother to let her know. You're not going to believe how happy this is going to make *her*."

"And then you can tell me all about North Carolina. I can't wait to hear every single detail about the farm and all the other things you learned while you were there."

"It's an extraordinary place, Ava," he said. "More than fifty acres of peace that you wouldn't believe. And forty-five years ago, Zeke and a bunch of his farmer buddies built a huge hill about thirty feet high right in the middle. Steps go up the side, and there's a beautiful gazebo on top where the view is 360 degrees of spectacular. And Zoie said that people have *weddings* up there."

"You're kidding."

"No I'm not. And they're also planning an addition to the house. Oh, and we've made some plans for Thanksgiving, and—"

Ava put her hand on his shoulder and pressed the first program button on the CD player. "Isaiah, we have seven hours for you to tell me everything. So slow down a little and start from the beginning."

"*Which* beginning?"

"From when you landed at the airport on Saturday. Was it a long drive to the farm?"

With Rod Stewart singing softly in the background, they talked and listened and laughed, answering each other's questions and telling each other stories. The seven hours began to melt away, and as Isaiah steered the Jag west on I-90, the driving seemed effortless, as if the tires were skimming along a stream of air rather than spinning hot against pavement. There were even moments when he thought he could let go of the wheel and the car would still keep flying forward, safely and in a straight line, as though a powerful protective spirit and unseen nurturing hands were at the controls.